# THE BLUE FAIRY AND THE PYROMANCER

## BOOK ONE

# ZEISS SCHREIBER

*To K, Kolson and Rory*
*Without whom the blue fairy wouldn't be*

# ACKNOWLEDGEMENTS

I almost never read acknowledgements. Unlike the opening credits of a movie or TV show, there is no music or imagery to accompany them, and they always mention people we know nothing about. Maybe I'll read them when I go take a break in the bathroom, but that's about it. And yet, the people who worked on this book deserve to be recognized for their efforts—I couldn't have done it without them.

So here are the people who helped make *The Blue Fairy and the Pyromancer* a reality:

Sérgio Alves, my 3D animator. His contribution was invaluable, and I will always be grateful for him going above and beyond what I would ask of him.

Kelly Sweet, my copy editor. She not only tidied up and polished my manuscript, but she also taught me valuable lessons that have made me a better writer.

David Aretha, my proofreader. He found and destroyed the last few typos that remained. In the unlikely event that some managed to escape his attention, just tell me and I'll make sure to crush them.

Jeff Brown, my cover designer and illustrator. The most professional individual I've had the pleasure to work with. He brought my vision to life after I had abandoned the hope anyone could.

My family, who always encouraged me and never made fun of my hobby, even though they don't read fantasy novels.

And my friends, who are also my first readers and collaborators. Thank you for your help.

Now, let us return to what's really important here: the story.

# CONTENTS

# PROLOGUE

AMBER WONDERED HOW long it had been since she last
saw sunlight.

At first, she'd tried to measure time by listening to
her own heartbeat, but she lost track once she fell asleep and
woke up in the pitch darkness of her cell. She then attempted
to rely on the periodic visits from the guard who came to bring
her food and empty her bucket, but when her hunger became
painful, she started to suspect that he sometimes deliberately
skipped a visit. Desperate, she decided to risk a beating and ask
him how many days it had been since her arrest, but he refused
to answer. He'd probably been ordered not to speak to her. Or
maybe he was just afraid.

Would Kieran be afraid?

No. No, he wouldn't. Not her son. He'd always trusted her,
even during the worst times.

She brought her legs up against her abdomen and wrapped
her arms around her knees. Her chains clanked as she moved,
but she welcomed the noise—it reminded her that she was still
alive. What she'd rather forget was the unpleasant smell of the
bucket they'd left for her. And the silence. The unbearable silence
pressing against her skull.

So she closed her eyes.

She imagined the warm touch of the sun against her skin while she walked with Kieran to the marketplace. Imagined him marveling at all those sweet apples, juicy grapes, and ripe tomatoes that the merchants had so perfectly lined up to tantalize potential buyers, until his eyes stopped on his favorite: strawberries. She'd buy him the ripest ones so they could share them together later. He would smile at her, and they'd walk back home, hand in hand.

The sound of approaching footsteps put an end to her reverie.

Were the footsteps real? Or was she dreaming? The footsteps didn't sound like those of her jailer. In fact, they sounded like multiple people. Amber held her breath for a moment and stopped moving, petrified by an idea she had pushed to the back of her mind up until now—that they were done with her.

The footsteps stopped in front of her cell.

Amber heard the tinkling of keys followed by a loud *click*, and the door opened. Bright light invaded the room, blinding her, and she recoiled back into a corner to escape its radiance. When her eyes grew accustomed to it, she saw two prison guards beyond the doorway of her cell, torches in their hands. A third person stood behind them, one who Amber hadn't seen in what felt like weeks: Inquisitor Karolina Dow, the woman who'd arrested her.

Even now, Amber couldn't help but notice how beautiful she was. Inquisitor Dow wasn't much older than her, maybe thirty years old, and her long raven hair contrasted starkly with the immaculate white of her cassock. What identified her as an inquisitor and not a regular Azarian priestess was the cincture she wore around her waist: crimson red instead of the common white.

"Amber Fowler," the inquisitor said. "Stand up."

Amber kept her head down and slowly rose up to her feet, her legs shaking. She knew what the inquisitor was going to say next, but she wasn't ready to hear it. Right at this moment, she would have preferred the silence of her cell to Karolina Dow's next words.

"After extensive deliberations, the jury has found you guilty of infanticide, witchcraft, heresy, and apostasy. Your execution will take place today in Saint Periphanes's Square, where I will escort you and pronounce your judgment. Do you wish to receive the last rites?"

Amber gawked at Inquisitor Dow, stunned. She repeated in her mind what the inquisitor had just said but couldn't come up with an appropriate response. Was that how they would announce her death to Kieran? So crudely and heartlessly? She felt a burning sensation grow in the pit of her stomach, and for a moment, she thought she was going to vomit. Tears welled up in her eyes and threatened to spill out, but she held them back. She couldn't let it end like this.

"What about Kieran?" she asked, her lips quivering. "I-I'm the only one he has."

The inquisitor frowned. "He will be entrusted to one of our orphanages, where he will be raised by Azarian priestesses until the day he turns sixteen."

Her throat began to hurt. "No," she said. "Please, no. He needs me."

"You should have thought of that before you joined that vile witch. If it were up to me, you would never see him again."

This gave Amber pause, and with a cracking voice, she asked, "W-what do you mean?"

Inquisitor Dow sighed and reluctantly replied, "The Great Mother has judged it merciful to let you see him one last time."

Amber blinked in disbelief. After a moment of hesitation, she wiped away her tears and lowered her head. "Thank you," she said. "Thank you so much."

The inquisitor stared at her and didn't bother to answer, but that didn't matter to Amber; she was going to talk to Kieran again, and she needed to thank someone for it.

"Do you want me to perform the last rites?" the inquisitor inquired.

"No," Amber said.

This seemed to disconcert the priestess. "I urge you," she insisted. "Your soul is at stake. Confess your sins, and God *will* show you mercy."

There was nothing more important right now than her son. "Please, take me to Kieran."

The inquisitor clenched her teeth. "Very well then," she relented. She turned and gestured at one of the two guards. "Reed, put the cuffs on Ms. Fowler and then remove the chains."

The younger of the two men stepped forward and inserted his torch into the sconce next to the door. He couldn't have been more than twenty years old, and by the way his hands fidgeted, Amber deduced he hadn't been doing this for long. She couldn't clearly see it, but she knew that the emblem on his red tunic was that of the Periphanesian Order. He approached Amber and pulled out a set of keys, only for Karolina to immediately reprimand him: "What are you doing?"

"I'm, uh—" Reed stumbled over his own words and instinctively looked at his partner for help, but the older guard just shook his head. "I'm removing the chains?"

"You do that *after* you've put the handcuffs on her. These restraints have been consecrated so that she can't use her sorcery on you. Do you understand?" Inquisitor Dow glared at the young man, who promptly nodded.

"Yes, ma'am," he said. "It won't happen again."

He then took the handcuffs that dangled on his belt—right next to his brand-new wooden baton—and put them on Amber's wrists. They exchanged a short glance, one that should have meant nothing, but it lasted long enough for her to realize that he didn't want to do this. She didn't have time to think about it, however, as Reed finished removing her chains and pushed her toward the door. He kept his hand on her arm and nudged her down the dark corridor, the inquisitor and the other guard close behind them.

Amber couldn't hear anything except for the crackling of the torches and the scraping of her captors' boots against the floor. They had confiscated her shoes many days ago, so she had to endure the cold touch of the stones under her bare feet, though she knew it wouldn't last much longer.

Reed told her to take a left, but her movements were so sluggish that he had to help her walk through the dark corridors of the dungeon. It didn't take long before they arrived at a set of stairs that led up.

She climbed one step at a time, wishing that it didn't hurt so much when the handcuffs chafed her wrists. Little by little, they left the darkness of the dungeon behind and stepped into multicolored light. Amber covered her eyes with her hands and squinted at the first stained-glass window she could find. They didn't stop to let her admire the daylight, and after her escorts deposited the torches into empty sconces, she was led down a hallway. A guard she had never seen before came out of a room, saluted the inquisitor, and went on his way.

This place wasn't just a prison, she realized; it was the garrison of the Order of Saint Periphanes.

Amber's heart skipped a beat. She frantically looked for a clear glass window, and when Reed finally passed by one, she peered through it. Just outside the building was a large plaza where a crowd of hundreds, maybe thousands, had already gathered. And although she only caught a glimpse of it, she knew that what she saw on the other side of this mass of people was a scaffold, one that had been built just for her.

For an instant, she stopped breathing. She had been one of these people once, a young and stupid woman who was curious to see what a human looked like when they died. She remembered the uneasiness she'd felt when the convict—a man young enough to be her brother—finally stopped moving, and now she wondered if anyone in this crowd would feel the same way about her.

Reed opened a door and guided Amber into a small bedroom.

Sitting on the bed was Kieran, her little boy. He looked at her and nervously said, "Mom?"

"Kieran." The lump in her throat made it difficult to talk. "Hey, sweetie."

When Reed let go of her arm, she rushed to her son, dropped to her knees, and squeezed him tight against her chest. Neither of them said anything for a long while. His lack of reaction began to worry her, and she wondered if the inquisitor had managed to turn him against her. But then he wrapped his arms around her shoulders and buried his head into her neck, and her lips curled into a smile at the realization that despite everything that had happened, he still trusted her.

She opened her eyes, glanced at the only window in the room, and let out a sigh of relief when she realized that it was impossible to see the scaffold from here.

"Mom? They said you're a bad person."

Amber slowly backed away and met her son's gaze. Now that they were face-to-face, she didn't know what to say to him. She thought about explaining to Kieran what the Inquisition really was, but one glance at Karolina Dow's grim expression was enough to confirm that if she did, she'd be separated from him immediately. And she couldn't let that happen.

She gently ruffled Kieran's brown hair and forced herself to smile. "Kieran, listen to me," she said. "It's very important."

"Okay…"

Amber took a deep breath and tried to stop herself from shaking, to no avail. "We're not going to see each other again, sweetie. You're going to be living with other kids from now on. You understand?"

He didn't say anything at first, but his eyes told her that he understood. "Is it because you're bad?" he asked in a small voice.

"Oh, Kieran." She took his face in her hands and spoke to him more softly. Tears welled up in her eyes again, and she couldn't hold them back this time. "I love you very, very much. You know that, right?"

His voice cracked, but he answered, "Yes."

"And do you love me too?"

He sobbed and said, "Yes. I love you, Mom."

Amber hugged him again, as hard as she could, and he melted in her arms. She did her best to cherish this feeling and wished it would never end. If only she'd taken him to the market to buy him strawberries one more time. Maybe then it wouldn't be so hard to let him go.

The touch of Reed's hand on her shoulder reminded her that reality cared not for one's wishes.

With great difficulty, she slowly broke the embrace, stood up, and looked at her son's red eyes. Tears were streaming down his face, and she used her thumbs to wipe them away. "Kieran," she said in a trembling voice. "You have to promise me something."

He met her gaze; he tried to speak but was unable to do so without sobbing, so he nodded.

"Promise me to be a good boy. Okay?"

Kieran nodded more confidently this time. "Okay," he cried. "I promise."

Amber kissed him on the forehead and embraced him one last time. She could barely see through her tears.

"Ms. Fowler," Reed said. "It's time."

For a moment, her arms refused to move. She didn't want to leave, but she knew that if she refused, they'd drag her away by force. And Kieran shouldn't have to see that.

So she let him go.

Reed helped her stand up and quietly took her outside the room. She looked at her son for as long as she could, and just before he disappeared out of her sight, she told him, "I love you!"

He didn't get a chance to reply. The other guard closed the door to the bedroom, and they marched down the hallway. Kieran was gone, and very soon, the only thing he'd have left of her would be memories. Lost in a haze, Amber was barely aware of her surroundings and automatically followed Reed's lead. When she felt the wind blow on her moist cheeks, she lifted her head and saw what she had dreaded: Saint Periphanes's Square.

The crowd had grown since she last saw them, and new people were streaming in from the streets, adding to their numbers. Every stratum of Holiburg's population had gathered here under the scorching heat of the afternoon sun to witness the execution of what they feared the most—a witch.

Amber peered at the mass of people and spotted the scaffold on the opposite side of the square. Laetor's Temple stood behind it, its massive frame of marble and limestone dwarfing the small wooden structure. The site of her execution. There was only one way to reach it, and it was by walking through this crowd.

She shuddered at the thought. She knew what would happen once they surrounded her.

"Don't let any of them approach the heretic," Karolina Dow commanded.

Amber looked behind her and saw that a dozen Periphanesian guards had exited the building, all armed with wooden batons. Now that she was outside and in the sunlight, she could discern clearly the emblem of the order sewn into the deep red of their tunics: a black tree enclosed within a white shield.

The guards walked forward and surrounded her, the inquisitor, and their two comrades in a compact formation that shielded them from all sides. Reed tightened his grip on Amber's arm and nervously grabbed his own baton. She stared at him, perplexed by his anxious state. He looked back at her and opened his mouth, ostensibly to say something, but then decided against it and shifted his gaze forward instead.

"Advance," the inquisitor ordered.

The procession began marching to the scaffold—and the crowd. Amber wiped away her tears and tilted her head down. She could already hear the chatter quiet down at her approach, and a moment later, she saw the first of them out of the corner of her eye.

She kept her head down and focused her attention on her naked feet. She couldn't hear anything except for the clank of her escorts' armor and their footsteps. The citizens of Holiburg had fallen into an almost solemn silence. They shuffled out of the procession's way and then merged back together, like water swerving around the dorsal fin of a shark.

"Sinner!" someone yelled.

Amber stiffened, and so did Reed.

"Whore!" another shouted, this person much closer than the previous one.

"Devil's pawn!"

"Go back to hell!"

The voices grew louder until they turned into a clamor that overwhelmed every other sound except for her own breathing. The guards slowed down and raised their batons at those who took too long to move out of the way. One man lunged forward and tried to grab Amber's hair, only for his arm to be smacked away and his face smashed in. Amber recoiled and lost her balance, and just when she thought she'd hit the ground, Reed caught her in his arms. He helped her stand up, and before she could understand what had happened, they were walking again.

She had almost reached the scaffold. A dozen more guards surrounded the wooden platform, waiting for the convict to arrive. Amber tried to avoid their gaze, knowing that she'd find neither kindness nor pity in their eyes. The moment she finished this thought, something round and squishy hit her in the face.

"Take that, witch!" a man shouted.

Amber fell on her knees, stunned. The foul odor of rotten fruit overwhelmed her sense of smell, and she felt the urge to vomit. She couldn't suppress her sobs anymore. She frantically tried to wipe away fruit juice from her face while her tears rolled down her cheeks.

"Reed!" the inquisitor shouted. "Get her back on her feet!"

The young man obeyed. He kneeled down next to Amber and whispered in her ear, "Come on. I'll help you."

At first, she wondered whether or not she'd heard him right. Maybe the clamor from the crowd had distorted his words into something she wanted to hear. But sure enough, Reed gently lifted her by the arm and helped her stand up again.

And so they walked together. It wasn't far now, only five meters away. Amber approached the small set of stairs and slowly climbed them. When she looked down at the steps, she noticed many nail holes at both ends of the wood planks. This scaffold must have been assembled and disassembled multiple times in the past. Were they using the same one she first saw years ago?

The nudge Reed gave her reminded her that the time for questions was over. He guided her to the center of the scaffold where she saw a large iron shackle fixed into the floorboard. She remembered the next part: the convict would kneel down and wait for the Periphanesian guard to attach the shackle to the handcuffs. And this was exactly what Reed did, albeit with shaky hands. His movements were well practiced, but she could tell that this was the first time he'd ever done this. Once he finished tethering Amber to the floorboard, he looked up and gazed at her. She saw hesitation in his eyes, something she didn't expect.

He then pulled a handkerchief out of his pocket and delicately wiped the last of the juice from her face.

Amber's whole body relaxed. She gazed at Reed's gloomy expression and whispered a hoarse "Thank you" to him. He froze for an instant, caught off guard by her words, and no one but Amber noticed the imperceptible nod he gave her. Once he finished cleaning her face, he put his handkerchief back in his pocket, stood up, and walked away.

She now had a full view of the crowd that had gathered on Saint Periphanes's Square, and she realized that not all of them were shouting at her: a few stayed silent, while a handful had turned away and were leaving this place. The guards positioned around the scaffold kept the most hot-blooded of them at bay—not to protect Amber, but to preserve the sanctity of her execution.

The inquisitor stepped onto the platform.

Her gait exuded unshakable confidence, the sort that intimidated even the most boisterous of men. The crowd gradually began to quiet down, and just by raising her hand in the air, she silenced the rest of them. A lull descended upon the plaza, and even though everybody's attention was on her, she waited. Seconds at first, and then a full minute. She was staring down at the whole crowd with fury in her eyes.

"Citizens of Holiburg," she finally said. "I am Inquisitor Karolina Dow, a humble servant of the Azarian Church."

Using her power, she sent her voice booming across the plaza, allowing everyone, even those at the far back of the congregation, to hear her speech. This display of divine power had astonished Amber in the past when she was a young girl, but not anymore.

"Today is a cruel reminder of our own weaknesses. At every moment of our lives, we are besieged by wicked desires and heinous temptations. But even in these instances, we must remember not to abase ourselves to the level of those who willingly sin against the holy memory of our Lady. And when we are confronted by a sinner like the one here today, we must remember to show them pity, *not* hate."

Amber listened, stunned by what the inquisitor had just said. She peered at the crowd and saw a similar reaction.

*"For if we scorn the damned, we harm the purity of our souls.* This lesson has been taught to us throughout the ages, ever since the Fall of the Aurelian Empire. Amber Fowler has sinned against the Word of God, and she will now answer for these crimes. Learn from her mistakes. Learn from your own. May the Kind Mother watch over us all."

"May the Kind Mother watch over us all," the people chanted.

Karolina Dow turned away from them and walked up to Amber. This was it. This was the end.

"Amber Fowler," the inquisitor said, now in a normal voice. "Please, let me perform the last rites. This is your last chance."

Amber stared at her, feeling completely drained after crying so much. She didn't believe that confessing her sins would save her soul, not after all she had experienced. She shook her head.

"Very well," Karolina said.

The inquisitor walked to Amber's left side and faced the crowd again. "Amber Fowler. The Inquisition has found you guilty of infanticide, witchcraft, heresy, and apostasy. By God's will, you are hereby sentenced to death. Do you have any last words?"

This was the second time Amber had heard someone ask this question. She couldn't hear the convict's answer then, but other people had relayed it to her. It had taken her years to understand the meaning behind those words, and now that she was here on what might have been the same scaffold, they were the only ones that seemed appropriate.

"May God have mercy on your soul, Inquisitor."

Karolina Dow narrowed her eyes. She stayed silent for a long moment and then placed her hand on Amber's neck. Only a few more seconds and she'd start the final prayer.

Amber clenched her teeth and braced herself for the pain. She didn't want it to hurt. She didn't want any of this.

*"O Lady in White, I beseech you."*

She regretted not telling Kieran how happy he'd made her feel the day he came into this world. How alone she'd felt beforehand.

*"Bestow upon me your power."*

She hoped he'd become a good man. She wanted him to grow old, have a family, and tell them about her.

*"For we must shatter this tower."*

She wanted someone—anyone—to remember her. To miss her.

*"And one day, build it—"*

*Please, don't make it end. Not like this. It's too much—*

*"—anew."*

Pain.

Her chest burned, but there was no fire. She gasped for air, to no avail, and an acute pressure spread to her left arm, and gradually to her whole body. She fell forward, clutching at her chest, but no one helped. Not even Reed.

Her strength was quickly leaving her, and before it abandoned her completely, she forced herself to fall on her back; she didn't want this scaffold to be the last thing that she would see. Although her vision was blurred with tears, she turned her gaze upward.

Blue. There was so much blue. She wanted to fall in it—drown in it—so that it could quench the flames raging in her chest. She remembered the times when Kieran would look at the sky and tell her about all the animals he saw swimming up there. She hadn't listened to him then. How she wished he could tell her about them now.

Tiny black dots started to pierce through the ocean of blue. There were hundreds of them, emerging from the edges of her vision, and before long, new ones rose from the center. Little by little, they swallowed all of the color, taking the pain with them until only one black void remained behind.

Amber gazed at it for a very, very long time until finally, the void swallowed her whole.

# CHAPTER 1

*Twenty years later*

**B**REEZE WATCHED THE squirrel sneak toward the strawberry plants.

Damn thief. How dare he steal her strawberries? She had worked so hard to protect them from all sorts of swarming bugs and ravenous birds, and this newcomer thought he could stride into this forest and eat the first comestible thing he saw? No, mister, not on her watch! She'd even used twigs and dandelion stems to build a fence around the thing. The message was clear: "This is a fairy garden, so paws off!" You can't just ignore a clear warning like that. Except he could, apparently.

Very well then. He wanted to intrude on fairy property? Go ahead. She was going to show him how things were done—wait. Was this squirrel a boy or a girl? She couldn't tell from here. Maybe if she got closer—*no*! What was she thinking? She had other things to worry about. Whichever gender that rodent was, she'd make sure that he or she would leave her garden for good.

Breeze hid in a small bush and waited for the animal to make its move. It slowly climbed down a tree and examined its surroundings, no doubt afraid of becoming someone's dinner. Lucky for it, the fairies of this forest had decreed that squirrels were far too cute to be hunted down for food. However, there was no law against scaring them half to death.

It creeped down onto the ground and approached the one carrot-and-a-half-tall fence that Breeze had set up around the strawberry patch. After one last look around, it got even closer and then did the unthinkable: it put its paws on the fence and intentionally knocked it down! This act of vandalism was enough to rouse Breeze, and she rushed out of her bush and zoomed through the air, ready to fight herself some rude thief.

What the squirrel saw emerge from the shrubs was a tiny human-looking adolescent the size of two apples stacked on top of each other. Her short hair was the same color as the sky above them, as were the butterfly wings on her back, and her piercing green eyes, now fixed on the intruder who'd dared undo many hours of her work, metaphorically burned with the fury of a thousand bees. What most terrified the rodent wasn't her angry scowl, however, nor the fact that her shirt and trousers were made of tanned animal skin—that alone should have been terrifying enough—but by how vicious she sounded as she started screaming at it.

"GET OUT, GET OUT, *GET OUT!*"

The squirrel squeaked in terror and dashed to the top of the nearest tree, the fairy right on its heels.

"That's right!" Breeze shouted. "You better find your own strawberries!"

With her fists on her hips and a frown on her face, she watched it jump from tree to tree. No way was it going to come back, and if it did, she'd give it more of the same!

Nodding in satisfaction, the blue-haired fairy turned to inspect the fence; fortunately, it hadn't suffered too much damage. She only needed to tighten a few stems—which served as ropes in these parts—and drive the twigs back into the ground again.

"Don't you worry," she said to the plants. "I'll fix it right away."

It took her a few minutes to put everything back in its place. Once she was done, she admired her work with a smile. It was perfect. "See?" she said. "It's as good as new! Now, let's take a closer look at you…"

The fairy flapped her wings, flew over the fence, and walked under the leaves of one of the plants to check on their fruits. The sweet aroma of strawberries whetted her appetite. "Ooh!" she exclaimed. "They're all red! Well, most of them are. I'll pick the good ones and leave the others for another day, okay?"

She flinched when she heard a familiar voice call out, "Breeze! Where are you?"

Hiding would just cause him to worry more about her, so she decided to step out of the plants' shadow and fly high in the air, just below the first branches of the nearest tree. She looked around and searched for the source of the voice but saw no one except a bird who was happily chirping at the wind.

"I'm here!" Breeze said. "Follow my voice!"

A few seconds later, she saw a raven-haired fairy fly by a large oak tree.

"Right here!" she shouted.

He turned in his sister's direction—causing his red butterfly wings to briefly reflect the sunlight—and flew toward her with narrowed eyes. Even though they were the same age, he always had been more serious than her.

"What's up, Bubble?" she tentatively asked.

"You know *what's up*," he answered. "You're too close to human territory!"

"What? Noooo… Really?"

"Oh, don't you play dumb with me. Look at that!"

Bubble pointed past the tree line to the overgrown meadow beyond it. Located only a few leaps away from Breeze's garden—a leap being the distance a fairy can glide after one jump, or approximately six carrots long—this grassy field was home to numerous cicadas that enjoyed singing during these summer days. Breeze often sat under a large tree and listened to them while enjoying the touch of soft earth between her toes. It was so relaxing.

"Are you listening to me?" Bubble asked, annoyed. "Stop daydreaming for a second."

"Oh, come on," Breeze retorted. "The humans haven't touched this field since last year. It's perfectly safe."

"No, it's not. One of them could come check on their land at any time. What will you do then?"

"I'd hide, obviously."

"It's still a risk."

"I'm so sneaky, humans would never see me," she reassured him with a bright smile. "Besides, you're the one shouting my name. What if they heard that?"

"Uh, well, yeah, but—wait, you were also shouting!"

"Because there are no humans here!"

"Argh!" Bubble groaned before shaking a finger at his sister. "Just promise me you won't come back here again."

She crossed her arms and turned away from him. "Don't want to."

"Breeze…"

"Nope."

"I'm warning you."

She covered her ears with her hands. "Can't hear you!"

"You really want me to tell the others? Because I will."

Breeze resisted for a few more seconds before she finally sighed and muttered under her breath, "Fine… I promise not to come here anymore."

Her brother smiled and nodded, satisfied to have put this matter to rest. "Glad to hear it," he said.

"Starting the day after tomorrow," she added, and turned away from him.

Bubble glared at his sister's back, silently boiling in anger until he finally exploded. "You dullhead! Why are you being so stubborn?"

She faced him again and calmly replied, "Because I have to dig these out of the ground and bring them back to the village." She pointed down at the plants she had protected from the ferocious squirrel only a few minutes ago.

Bubble examined the fence she had built around her small garden, squinted at the plants, and then asked, "Wait, are those strawberries?" His eyes shone at the ripeness of the red fruits.

Breeze smiled. "Yes, they are. I was planning to bring back a batch of them to the village today."

"Hmm... Well, you still shouldn't have ventured this far out."

"Oh, come on, Bubble." She put an arm around his shoulders and slowly hovered toward the ground. "We've been looking for strawberries ever since Nana told us about them. And now, we'll be able to grow hundreds of them!"

"How do they taste?"

"I haven't tried them yet. I was waiting to share one with you."

"What, really?"

"Of course!"

They landed inside the fence, and Breeze picked the ripest strawberry of the bunch. "Yikes," she exclaimed. "This thing is heavier than I thought it would be!"

"Why don't we just bring the whole plant with us?" Bubble suggested.

"We can't do that! We'll exhaust the poor guys if we take their fruits and move them somewhere else on the same day."

"I don't think that's how it works."

"Come on! It's snacky time."

Bubble sighed and didn't bother to correct his sister's grammar. Breeze presented one side of the strawberry to him, and they each took a bite out of it—so juicy and sweet! It had to be the best thing she'd ever eaten up until now. Disobeying the rules had been worth it, and even though her brother would never admit it, she knew by looking at his elated expression that he thought the same thing. She swallowed her bite, then took a seed out of her mouth and studied it for an instant before putting it in her pocket. Fairies never wasted anything that could be used later.

"I wish we could eat it with Nana," Breeze mused. "Where do you think she is now?"

"Somewhere east," Bubble said. "That's where she said she was going to awaken more fairies, no?"

She remembered the day Nana left, how sad she'd felt when she and her siblings all said goodbye to her. Breeze didn't want to think about this, so she shook her head and said, "Okay, let's put this strawberry in my basket, pick a few more, and go home."

"Your basket?" Bubble looked around to find it. "Good idea. It'll be a lot easier this way. But where did you put it?"

"It's back here, right behind that bush. I hid it because of that squirrel who was trying to steal from us."

"What do you mean 'steal'?"

While the two fairies used their magic to levitate the rush basket toward the garden, Breeze recounted how she had vanquished the greedy rodent who intruded on their property. Bubble retorted that animals didn't understand the concept of "fences," but she disagreed. How could they not? This squirrel seemed to understand well enough once she got the drop on it.

For the next couple of minutes, they picked a few dozen strawberries—only the ripe ones—and placed them in the basket. Once they were finished, Breeze put her fists on her hips and marveled at their loot. "Look at that," she said. "Just one harvest and there's enough for all of our brothers and sisters!"

"We still have to bring the basket back home," Bubble interjected. "I'll carry the left side and you handle the right, okay?"

"Got it!"

They focused their magic on the basket and lifted it in the air like Nana had taught them: just off the ground at first, so they could determine how much power they should exert to achieve the right balance, and then a few leaps higher in the air.

"I'm ready," Breeze said.

"Let's go then," Bubble replied.

The two fairies traveled deeper into the forest, far away from human lands. Far away from everything, really. In these woods, Breeze could only talk to her siblings and the wildlife, and no one else. Had Nana been here, things might be different, but she'd left five years ago and hadn't come back since. Not even to visit them.

"What's wrong?" Bubble asked.

"Nothing," Breeze said. "Why?"

"I thought you looked down, that's all."

"Nope, I'm fine!" She put on a smile and pointed ahead. "Look, we're home!"

Dreamland, their village.

Located far off the ground, Dreamland's multiple small houses were built around the trunks of twenty or so trees and joined together by suspended bridges. This was a paradise by fairy standards; when they wanted to play board games or hold a special event, they gathered on one of the four terraces, two of which were covered by a roof. If one was hungry, they went to the refectory, a common area spread on twelve levels and accessible by ten entrances. It was separate from the dinner hall, of course, which was located at the bottom of a tree and used exclusively for supper. And if someone needed to store the food they had hunted or picked during the day—such as Breeze and Bubble—they went to the pantry, a large elm tree that had been hollowed out for this purpose. There were other pantries, of course, but this was the biggest one.

On their way there, they saw many of their siblings walking on the bridges or flying between the trees. A few of them waved at Breeze and Bubble and greeted them with a jolly "Welcome back!"

All of the fairies in Dreamland were adolescents. And while the majority of them resembled humans—or so Nana had said—a few, like Breeze, had unusual hair color: purple, green, silver, and even pink. Breeze, however, was the only one who had blue hair. This difference had bothered her at first, but not anymore. This color was awesome, and it matched perfectly with her wings.

"Bubble! Breeze!"

Breeze searched for the source of this voice and found Dewdrop, one of her sisters, hollering at them from the platform next to the pantry. Dewdrop was one of the three fairies in the village who had silver hair, and unlike Breeze, she liked to try different hairstyles with it, such as the chignon, bun, bangs, ponytail, fishtail, pigtails, half-up half-down, half-up topknot, braided, braided crown, and today, a reversed braid. When a fairy needed a haircut, they went to Dewdrop.

"Hi, Dewdrop," Bubble said. "Look what we've brought."

"Oh, what is it?" Dewdrop hovered toward the basket to examine its contents. "Wait…it can't be!"

"Oh, it can," Breeze confirmed. "The best strawberries in the land are now ours!"

The sight of these legendary fruits rendered Dewdrop speechless. Breeze and Bubble landed on the platform with the basket and watched their sister gawk at their loot. "They look amazing," she whispered. "Where did you find them? I thought there were no strawberries in these woods."

"Oh, you know," Breeze said, fidgeting. "It was a lucky find, really."

"But we explored every inch of this forest. Our team couldn't have missed it."

"Well, uh…"

Bubble came to the rescue. "Unless the strawberries weren't out yet," he said. "What's the first area you surveyed at the beginning of spring?"

"The Sparrow's Field, just south of here," Dewdrop replied. "Ooh! Is that where you found them?!"

"That's where Breeze found them, yeah."

"Good job, Breeze!" Dewdrop patted her sister's back.

"Thanks," she replied. "Just doing my best for Dreamland, you know?"

"You certainly did! I never thought we'd be able to grow our own strawberries. I'll send a team there tomorrow morning to dig the plants out of the ground and move them to our garden."

"You don't need to!" Breeze almost shouted. "I-I mean, me and Bubble were already planning to do that tomorrow morning. Right, Bubble?"

"Yes, we were."

"See? We'll take care of it."

"Wow, thanks, Breeze," Dewdrop said, impressed. "You sure you don't need any help?"

"Nah, we'll be fine. But thanks!"

"Great! Let's get these darlings into the pantry then. You two wanna give me a hand?"

"Sure!" they both said.

Breeze followed her sister and mouthed "Thank you" to Bubble, to which he answered with a discreet nod. Without him, she'd be in the deepest of all trouble right now. Who knew what kind of punishment her siblings would have exacted on her for disobeying the rules? No desserts for a week? Two weeks? A *month*? That'd just be horrible.

The three fairies each picked up a strawberry from the basket and entered the pantry. When Breeze passed through the large set of wooden doors that led into the hollowed tree, she took a deep breath and savored the various odors of dried meat, fruits, vegetables, maple syrup, honey, and old wood that all mixed together into a gentle aroma.

Dewdrop flapped her wings a few times, and they began to shine with sparkling pink light that cut through the darkness of the tree hollow. Bubble and Breeze did the same with their red and blue wings, and between the three of them, it was enough to illuminate this whole level of the pantry. Bubble looked around and asked, "Where do you need them?"

"Put them right next to the beans," Dewdrop replied. "I don't think they'll stay fresh for long, so we'll eat them for dessert later tonight."

"Wow, the tree is almost full," Breeze remarked.

"Yeah, we're only putting fresh crops in it right now. You'll have to use the second pantry starting tomorrow. You sure you don't want to join my team for a few weeks? I could teach you how to work the inventory."

"I would love to, but I know I'd be hungry all day if I did that."

"Well, if you change your mind, just let me know."

For the next couple of minutes, they carried the strawberries one by one into the tree. They didn't have to do it by hand, but Nana had been very clear on that: "Use magic only when necessary." Besides, there was nothing better than taking a bath after a hard day of work. The thought of diving into cool water spurred Breeze to work even harder, and she began running between the basket and the pantry.

"Come on, slowpokes!" she exclaimed. "After this, it's fun time!"

"Goodness, Breeze," Bubble muttered under his breath.

Dewdrop chuckled and let her sister sprint across the platform. Before long, they were finished.

"We've won!" Breeze shouted while fist-bumping the sky.

"And what exactly did we win?" her brother asked.

"A bath! It's like the best moment in the day after dinner and stargazing."

"Well, I won't say no to that."

"Let's go together then," Dewdrop suggested. "Just let me close the doors first."

"I'll help you! You too, Bubble!"

The three fairies pushed on the large doors and latched them shut with a drawbar. Then they heard one of their brothers hail them from above. "Hey, guys!"

It was Cosmo, one of the hunters. He landed on the platform and greeted his siblings with a smile. "How's it going?" he asked.

"Super great!" Breeze said. "Just you wait until dinner. We've got a big surprise for everyone."

"Really? What is it?"

"The bestest of all surprises!" she exclaimed while spreading her arms wide.

"Aw! Can I get a hint at least?"

"No chance! You'll have to suffer like everyone else."

"Dewdrop?"

"If Breeze doesn't want to say it, I won't," Dewdrop said, smirking.

"How about you?" Bubble asked. "Did you catch anything?"

"Oh, we did," Cosmo replied. "Two turkeys, enough to feed all of us. That's why I'm here actually. I'm supposed to gather everyone."

"To the usual place?"

"Yeah. I'll do one last flyby and see you there."

"Okay. Later, Cosmo!" Breeze said.

"Later."

The three fairies watched their brother fly into the air and holler at the others in the village. All of them immediately stopped what they were doing and flew to the center of the settlement. "Let's go," Dewdrop said.

They followed their siblings to the meeting place, a small patch of beaten earth located at the foot of a large oak tree. A few hundred fairies were already on the ground, quietly talking to each other while waiting for everyone to arrive. Breeze landed on the thickest root and focused her mind on her back, right at the spot her butterfly wings emerged from. They slowly began to shrink into her skin, and after a few seconds, they were gone.

Bubble and Dewdrop landed next to her and did the same.

The fairies of Dreamland had gathered around the bodies of the turkeys Cosmo and the other hunters had brought. The poor animals had each been hit by an arrow and were now lying on the ground, their lifeless eyes open. Breeze stared at them in silence, hoping they hadn't suffered too much.

It wasn't long before Cosmo arrived with the last of the fairies behind him. The chatter in the clearing began to quiet down when the latecomers joined the crowd and then fully subsided when Cosmo hovered to the speaker's spot near the oak tree and crossed his arms.

By then, only the rustling of the leaves and the chirping of birds remained.

"Hello, everyone," he said, projecting his voice with magic so it would reach all ears.

Some of the villagers greeted him with a "Hello" of their own or by waving their hand at him.

"You know why we're here," he continued. "We've hunted down these turkeys, and they'll be tonight's dinner. So, let's pay our respects to them."

Breeze lowered her head and closed her eyes, as did the two hundred and ninety-nine other fairies present here. She thought about the poor families these turkeys had left behind, and how sorry she felt for all of those who would miss them. The only thing she and her siblings could do now was eat the meat and build tools from the remains. Everything else would be used as fertilizer for the garden. Fairies never wasted anything.

A full minute passed, and everyone raised their heads. Cosmo nodded, satisfied by how smoothly the ceremony had gone, and then called his siblings to attention.

"Okay, Team Apple is in charge of plucking the turkeys today," he said. "Team Raccoon is in the kitchen, and Team Squirrel serves the food. Everyone else can go take a bath. See you all at dinner!"

The fairies cheered and began to disperse everywhere. The majority of them deployed their wings and flew together in the air, forming a flock that flickered with multicolored light. The fairies from Team Apple—twenty-five of them—stayed behind and used their magic to move the turkeys to the skinning area. Those who remained gathered in small groups at the foot of the oak to chat about the tribulations of the day.

.    Breeze's group was one of the latter. She drooped her shoulders and let out a sigh of dejection.

"What's the matter?" Dewdrop asked.

"I'm on Team Squirrel," Breeze answered.

"Let me guess," Bubble said. "You forgot you were on service duty today, right?"

"Yes."

"That happens at least once a month," Bubble said to Dewdrop. "She's just sad her bath will have to wait."

"What, that's all?" Dewdrop said. "I can cover for you if you want, Breeze."

The blue-haired girl perked up at this offer. She turned to her sister with wide eyes and asked, "Really? You mean it?"

"Of course! We wouldn't be having strawberries for dessert today if not for you."

"Thank you! Oh, thank you, thank you!" Breeze lunged at

Dewdrop and gave her the biggest hug she had, one that she reserved for special occasions. "I won't forget it!" she said.

"She probably will," Bubble retorted. "Come on, Breeze, you should let her go before the rest of your team starts looking for you."

"Oh, right." She released her sister and told her, "In return, I'll work your shift tomorrow. You're on Team Blueberry, right?"

"Uh, yes, but you don't need to," Dewdrop replied. "Like I said—"

"No buts! The decision has already been made. Come on, Bubble, let's go."

Breeze grew her wings back to their full extent and stepped off the tree root. She hovered in the air, waved at her sister, and shouted, "See you at dinner!" Before Dewdrop even got the chance to respond, Breeze flew at full speed toward the treetops. It was generous of her sister to work the tables this evening, but there was no way she wouldn't repay her kindness by doing the same. Besides, she had kind of lied about the origin of the strawberries… It wouldn't be fair to take advantage of her.

Just as she passed by the kitchens, Breeze saw Team Raccoon carry a big carrot into the cutting room. Bubble appeared right next to her. "So," he began with a grin, "you didn't tell her where we found the plants?"

Breeze glanced at her brother and nervously asked him, "Will you?"

"Not as long as you don't forget your promise."

"I won't."

"Good. Let's go take a bath then."

Breeze fell silent and mulled over her brother's words. She had promised that after tomorrow, she would never ever go to the edge of the forest again. Nana's last command had been very clear: "Never venture beyond the borders I have set. The outside world is too dangerous for you."

And yet, Breeze had disobeyed her. She'd done something she never thought herself capable of, and Nana hadn't been able to stop her.

Why would Nana impose a rule she couldn't enforce?

# CHAPTER 2

"CAN I GET everyone's attention please?"

Cosmo's voice, amplified by magic, resonated throughout the dining hall, and the fairies seated at the long tables quieted down to listen to him.

Shaped into a half dome and made of curved planks of wood, the huge room had been erected at the base of a sycamore tree, far below the kitchens. A vertical hallway built around the trunk connected the two areas, making the whole building look like an elongated hourglass when viewed from the outside, with the bottom part being five times larger than the top. The other half of the dome, accessible by several doors through the middle wall, served as an auditorium for certain events and was closed for now.

The fairies on duty for serving food used the vertical hallway to transport the plates from the kitchens at the top of the tree to the dozens of tables at the bottom. If they weren't careful, they risked crashing into each other in mid-flight, which could cause them to lose control over their magic and drop the levitating plates of food onto their siblings down below.

Breeze had been on the receiving end of such an accident once, and even though they ended up laughing about it, she wasn't eager to relive it again. Which was why it was so unexpected to see Cosmo hover above the rest of them, even though he wasn't on service duty today—only the servers were allowed to fly inside the dining hall when it was dinnertime. "Please, everyone!" he commanded while projecting his voice.

The rest of the gathered fairies turned to listen to their brother. Breeze looked at those sitting at her table, wondering if any of them knew what was happening, and noticed a glimmer in Bubble's eyes. "What's going on?" she asked him.

"Shh. Just listen."

Breeze raised her eyebrows at his response but did as he asked. Cosmo spoke again. "Hi, everyone! How was the food?"

The fairies replied with shouts of approval, some even holding up their empty plates of food as evidence of their full bellies. This wasn't surprising: turkey with a side of carrots and potatoes was one of their favorite dishes, after all.

"Good!" Cosmo continued. "Because Team Squirrel has a special announcement for us. Dewdrop?"

The silver-haired fairy rose above the crowd and joined Cosmo's side. One fairy immediately exclaimed, "Hey, you're not on Team Squirrel!"

"You're right," Dewdrop replied. "I'm filling in for Breeze because today is a special day." Just as the fairies began to murmur among themselves, Breeze realized what her sister was going to say next. "I'm happy to announce that today's dessert will be strawberries! And it's all thanks to Breeze! She's the one who found them. A round of applause for our blue fairy, please!"

Right on cue, the whole room started to clap and cheer for the woman of the hour.

"What, really? That's awesome!"

"You're the best, Breeze!"

"Wait, we're really going to eat strawberries?"

"Didn't you listen?"

"Strawberries are the best!"

"Shouldn't you wait to eat one before you say that?"

"Wait, where's Breeze?"

"She's right at our table!"

Bubble smiled at his sister and gestured for her to stand up. She blankly stared at him, wondering if he was serious, but before she could say anything, another one of her siblings took her by the hand and made her stand on the bench.

This was so embarrassing! Nobody had warned her about this!

The clamor grew even louder when the rest of her family finally saw her. It was too late now; she had to do *something*. She hesitantly raised her hand and waved at her brothers and sisters, who were more than happy to wave back at her.

"Hey, it's Breeze!"

"Thanks, sis!"

"We owe you one!"

Breeze couldn't help but smile, and she began to scratch the back of her head. What should she do now? Give a speech? No, that was a bad idea; she'd just end up stumbling over her own words and make a fool of herself. Luckily for her, Bubble took her arm and sat her down on the bench.

"Now let's eat some strawberries!" Dewdrop said. "Eat earthy, everyone!"

"Eat earthy!" said the assembled fairies.

A second round of applause roared through the dining hall, and the fairies on Team Squirrel descended from the vertical hallway with the promised dessert. The strawberries had been cut into small portions and served in wooden bowls that were now floating in the air. The servers set them down on the tables one by one, and when it was Breeze's turn to receive hers, one of her sisters also put a pitcher full of maple syrup right next to it and said, "Enjoy!"

Breeze could barely contain her giggle. This was awesome! She poured syrup on her portion of strawberry, picked up her wooden fork, and ate one mouthful of this unique dessert.

"How is it?" Bubble asked her.

"It's so yummy!" she said, savoring the taste.

Apparently, everyone at her table shared the same opinion. Comet and Violet squealed each time they took a bite and very loudly told everyone this was the best thing they'd ever had in their life. In contrast, Nimbus hadn't even touched his bowl yet, wanting to admire his pile of neatly cut strawberry for a while longer. Ash had already emptied her bowl and was now begging Badger to share some of his with her—with no success. As for Moonbeam, he couldn't decide how he preferred it: with maple syrup or with honey?

Breeze could see similar reactions throughout the dining hall. They were all happy. They all expressed it in different ways, but it was unmistakable. This day would be fondly remembered for years to come...and yet something felt off. It was if a cold blanket had enveloped her and dulled her senses. Breeze tried to shake it off by focusing on her dessert and the happy banter of her siblings, but despite her best efforts, the strange feeling didn't go away. She needed to talk to Bubble about it.

For a moment she sat still, debating whether or not she should bring up the subject, but the more she thought about it, the more certain she became aware of the necessity of it—until finally, she put down her fork and turned to face her brother, determined to see this through.

He caught her off guard by speaking to her first. "I wish every day was like today," he said, a content expression on his face as he watched their siblings enjoy their dessert.

Breeze gazed silently at him, unable to form an immediate response. Then, she leaned toward him and said, "It could be."

He raised his eyebrows at her. "What do you mean?"

"I just..." Breeze looked around, uneasy about what she was about to suggest. She leaned toward her brother and spoke in a whisper. "We could keep exploring the outside world."

Bubble immediately frowned. "That's forbidden," he said.

"I know! But we've got strawberries now. Think about all the other stuff we could find and bring back here. Like beans, or peaches, or even new sorts of fish."

"Breeze, no," he murmured. "Nana warned us—humans are dangerous."

"She also said some of them were good."

"We can't take the risk."

"But—"

"No! You *promised*."

Bubble glared at her, making it clear he didn't want to listen to more of her nonsense. Breeze glared back at him and clenched her jaw. Why was he so adamant about following this rule? Nana was gone, and he didn't want to even *consider* the idea of leaving the forest. Maybe she should talk to the others, tell them where the strawberries really came from. That could change things.

"Whatcha talking about?" a new voice asked.

It was Dewdrop. She and the rest of the fairies on Team Squirrel had just finished serving the desserts and were now joining their siblings at the tables. "Is everything all right?" Dewdrop asked.

Bubble maintained Breeze's gaze and said, "It's nothing." He then turned away and resumed eating. Breeze hesitated for a moment, contemplating her previous idea of telling everyone about the strawberries, until she realized that all of the fairies in their vicinity were staring at the two of them with looks of concern. Feeling sudden remorse for interrupting this happy moment, Breeze restrained herself from uttering anything she might later regret. Instead, she lowered her head and said, "Yeah, it's nothing."

She then stood up and walked away, leaving her dessert half-finished.

A few fairies watched her briskly walk down the aisle,

wondering where she was going. She didn't know herself. The only thing she knew for sure was that she needed a breath of fresh air. Maybe that would clear her head. Bubble certainly didn't help her with that, not one bit. So, without paying any mind to the joyous chatter of the hundreds of her siblings, Breeze left the dining hall and stepped outside.

Twilight had engulfed the forest. There was half an hour of daylight left, maybe less. The serenade of crickets had now replaced the chirping of birds and was accompanied tonight by the gentle rustling of the leaves in the trees. Just like the fairies of Dreamland, the forest adhered to a routine that she was well accustomed to.

Breeze closed her eyes and focused on her back. One second later, her blue wings emerged from her shoulder blades, ready to take her away from here. She immediately lifted herself off the ground and flew toward the canopy, shielding her eyes from the wind by using her magic to push against it—a basic technique Nana had taught them long ago.

Less than a minute later, she arrived at her destination: the top branch of a tall red ash tree, located just past the edge of the village. It was a secluded spot she had discovered a few months ago, right when the snows had begun to melt, and since then, she often came here to admire the sunset and watch it turn the blue sky into a palette of bright colors. Not today, though.

After retracting her wings, she sat down on the branch, leaving her legs to dangle in the air, and watched the sun slowly sink below the horizon. How had it come to this? She and Bubble had never talked this way to each other before. Maybe she shouldn't have been so insistent, but he shouldn't be so stubborn either. How could he just ignore *everything* outside of the forest? The world was so vast, and they were stuck here! And what about Nana? She'd left five years ago, so why not them? Humans were supposed to be dangerous, but Nana had never explained why exactly. There was so much Breeze didn't understand, and now her best friend was angry at her.

Breeze shook her head in an attempt to clear her mind of these nasty thoughts. There was no use getting so worked up about this. Without Nana here, the only way her siblings would change the rules about venturing outside the forest was if Breeze convinced them to. But why would they? Even without the strawberries, she could see how happy they were to live here. They woke up each morning, content with their lives.

Unlike her.

Breeze heaved a sigh and stared off into the distance, feeling strangely tired by the events of the day. Hopefully, tomorrow would be better. She had to believe it would be.

Kieran gazed upon the overgrown meadow he'd found.

The farmers who lived on the other side of the hill probably used it for grazing. He wasn't sure why they didn't let their cattle feed on it, but that didn't matter to him. This place was secluded, far away from the roads, and it was unlikely anyone would come here: the perfect place to camp for the night. He need only wait for the sun to go down before lighting a fire; he couldn't risk one of the farmers seeing a trail of smoke rising from their own land. If they did and came here to confront him about it, he'd have no choice but to defend himself.

A large forest marked the boundaries of the peasants' land. The trees were old, untouched. Give it a few more decades, he thought, and the king of Kantner would cut them down for his fleets and armies. Maybe even build a palace or two.

Kieran approached the tree line and set his bag, bow, and quiver full of arrows next to a large, leafy tree. He then sat down and rested his back against the trunk, his eyes fixed on the setting sun. Gone were the familiar odors of the cities; here in the countryside, he smelled the fragrance of wildflowers, the moisture of humid mornings, and the occasional whiff of a cow fart.

It was far from ideal, but at least he wouldn't have to worry about inquisitors ambushing him in the middle of the night.

# CHAPTER 3

"COME ON, YOU can't stay in bed all day."

Even half-asleep, Breeze could recognize the voice of her brother. She didn't want to get up just yet, though, and she hid her head under her pillow and enjoyed the softness of her feather bed. This was so much better than working...

"I already let you sleep longer than usual," Bubble continued, shaking her shoulder. "We still have to move your plants to the village."

Oh, right. The strawberries. She'd brought some back to Dreamland yesterday and the whole village celebrated the occasion by eating them for dessert. And then—

Breeze opened her eyes, now fully awake. She turned in her bed and searched the room for her brother. He was sitting at the table—a piece of bark propped up by twigs, just like the chairs—looking outside an open window. He was eating blueberry toast as he watched their siblings leave their homes and fly off to work.

Everything indicated that today would be a good day: the sun shone brightly, the birds sang away, and the wind gently carried the fairies through the air. And yet she couldn't shake this feeling in her chest that made it hard for her to look at Bubble. So, she sat there, wondering what she should do.

Bubble turned away from the window to talk to her again, but he paused when he saw her sitting in bed. "Oh, you're up," he said. "I thought I would have to take the blanket off of you again. How are you feeling?"

"I'm good," she answered. "Uh, what about you?"

"I'm fine. You should eat before we leave. You want some toast?"

"Yeah, sure," Breeze stood up and cautiously joined him at the table while many questions raced through her mind: Was he still mad about yesterday? Did he tell anyone else about their conversation? And why did she feel so awkward right now? She wasn't sure what to even say in this situation.

"One or two?" Bubble asked.

"One or two what?" she replied.

"Slices. How many do you want?"

"Oh, just one please."

A few slices of bread remained on the table. He took one of them with his right hand, put his left index finger under it, and focused on the magic that surrounded him. Breeze felt the invisible energy swirl around his index finger, and one second later, a small flame ignited at the tip of it and began to toast the bread.

Breeze watched him, thinking of what to say to lighten the atmosphere, until an idea popped into her head. "I can do it," she said.

Bubble raised an eyebrow at her and extinguished the flame. "Are you sure?" he asked. "Last time you tried, you—"

"I know, I know, but I've practiced since then! Let me show you."

"Sure." He handed the slice of bread to her and sat back in his chair. "Just don't burn yourself."

"I won't."

With her eyes set on the would-be toast, Breeze raised her finger and opened her mind to the magic around her. It felt like jumping into the cold water of a gigantic lake, one without a shore. Waves and waves of magic cradled her mind and slowly threatened to seep into her body. She fought against it, brought it under her control, and took only what she needed—a single drop. She then reshaped it into a spark and very carefully began to fan it.

Until a flame appeared at the tip of her finger.

Breeze smiled, amazed that she'd succeeded. She had finally done it! She was grilling her toast without burning her own finger! "Look! I told you I could do it!"

"That's good," Bubble said. "Very good. Now, don't use too much magic or you'll lose control of the fire."

"So I just stay like this?"

"Yeah, don't change anything."

Breeze looked away from her hand for just a moment and asked, "How long do you think I should—"

"Stay focused!"

But it was too late. The flame was already growing out of control and engulfing the slice of bread in fire. Instinctively, she jumped up, dropped the burning toast, and flapped the hand that had conjured the fire, hoping it would go away. "Whoa, whoa, whoa!"

"Put it out!"

"I'm trying!" Breeze continued to flap her hand while her brother tried to suffocate the burning toast with a ball of cotton. Luckily for both of them, they managed to put out the fire and prevent a disaster. Even though the incident didn't last more than ten seconds, she felt her heart beating loudly in her chest.

She and Bubble both plopped down in their chairs. A burnt smell permeated the air around them, and black marks now spotted the previously white cotton ball.

"I think you should practice a little more," Bubble said.

Breeze couldn't help but laugh a little. "Yeah, I guess I should."

"I'm serious."

"I know, I know. I'll do it outside the house too." She kept smiling at him, happy that they were back to their usual banter.

He gazed at her for a moment, clearly repressing a grin, and picked up a new slice of bread. "Here," he said. "*I'll* toast it this time. Then we can go get these plants of yours."

"Thanks! Can you put some jam on it too?"

"Sure."

And with the greatest of ease, he conjured fire from his hand.

The forest basked in the summer sunshine, rays of light piercing through the canopy. Of course, Breeze made a game out of it; she flew around in zigzags, doing her best to avoid all the light beams that dropped in front of her.

"What are you doing?" Bubble asked.

"I'm playing dodge-a-ray!" she answered.

"I mean, *why* are you doing this now? Help me carry this basket."

The basket in question levitated behind Bubble, following the two fairies to their destination.

"But it's still empty," she pleaded. "And it's a perfect day to play."

Bubble sighed. "Fine. But you carry it once we're halfway there. I'll need to rest."

"Yippee!" The blue-haired girl smiled and resumed her game, laughing when she narrowly dodged direct contact with the sunlight and playing dead when she didn't. She could tell that her brother thought this was silly, but it was so much fun! If only he were a smidge less serious, they could play so many more games together. Alas...

"It's time to switch," he told her.

"Aw, already?" Time passed way too quickly when she was having fun. Nevertheless, she flapped her wings toward her brother and resigned herself to taking over for him. With a flick of her mind, she nonchalantly imposed her will over the magic surrounding the pannier and held it in the air. She then went inside of it, grabbed the rim with her hands, and shrank her wings. "Come on, Bubble! Get in! I'll take us there."

"Wait, what? Why not fly instead?"

"Because it's way more fun this way!"

"Of course it is. Are you sure you won't get too tired?"

"I'm sure!"

He hesitated for a moment and tested the balance of the floating container with a tap of his foot. Unwavering in her confidence, Breeze smiled at him and waited until, finally, Bubble relented and joined her at the edge of the basket. She watched him shrink his wings and get into position, but before he could fully prepare himself for what was about to happen, she shouted at the top of her lungs, "Now hold on!"

"Wait, wha—"

The wind almost pushed him off the pannier. He tightened his grip on the handle and looked at his sister, who was propelling the basket forward with her mind, and grimaced as she nearly reached the maximum speed fairies could attain.

"Woo hoo!" she shouted.

"Couldn't you slow down a bit?!"

"Yes, I could!"

Overjoyed, she maintained the same speed. Trees passed by them in a blur and the wind whistled in their ears; it wouldn't be long before they'd arrive at their destination. She might as well take a detour with the time they had left, she thought.

She steered the basket above the canopy to bathe in the sunlight, then down to the ground to see the roots and leaves disappear under her. Bubble screamed whenever she took sharp turns, but that didn't stop her. Animals stayed out of their way, too scared to approach this strange flying object. Breeze waved at them, giggling at the thought that one might wave back at her one day. Until finally, the tree line appeared in her sight and she started to slow down.

To Bubble's visible relief, they landed next to the strawberry plants, and he couldn't have disembarked from the pannier faster than he did. "I am *so* going to get you back for this," he said, leaning against the basket.

She laughed. "Looking forward to it!"

"Are you not even a little tired?"

"Nope!"

"Ah, figures." Bubble dropped to the ground and gazed at the sky as if he had just experienced a difficult ordeal. Was flying without wings that scary for him? Maybe she should have been more careful. Despite his protests, he didn't seem angry, which meant he must have enjoyed the ride quite a bit. Silly Bubble.

Breeze approached the garden and examined the state of her fence. Lo and behold, it was still standing! That damn squirrel had learned its lesson. The only thing left to do was dig the plants out of the ground, place them in the basket, and—

Wait a second.

"Bubble! The strawberries are gone!"

Her brother raised his head in surprise and said, "What, all of them?"

"Yeah! Well, all of them except the green ones. There were a few left, I swear."

He rose from the ground, dusted off the dirt from his clothes, and looked under the plant's leaves. "Oh, you're right," he said. "Hmm, nothing we can do about it."

"Huh? You don't think it's strange?"

"How so?"

"The fence is still standing!"

Bubble sighed. "Like I said, animals don't understand what a fence is for. They'll just take the food if they're hungry."

"No, what I mean is…" Breeze searched for her words. "If an animal ate *all* of the good strawberries, it would have knocked down the fence, right?"

"Hmm, maybe?"

Breeze smiled at his response. She straightened her shoulders, placed her closed fists on her hips, and happily declared, "We should totally investigate this!"

"What? Oh, no, no, no. We definitely *should not*."

"But it's a mystery!"

"Yeah, well, we can…add it to the pile, I guess. Come on, enough talking. We should start digging."

"But—"

"But nothing." Without wasting any time, Bubble pointed at the soil and started to shovel it away with his magic, one handful at a time. Breeze crossed her arms and pouted at him.

"So, are you gonna help?" Bubble asked. "It'll go faster if you do."

"Yeah," she said. "I'll dig on the other side."

Breeze took a deep breath, grew her wings to full size, and jumped over the fence. She couldn't get angry at her brother again. Last time she did, she almost felt sick because of it. Better to just finish what they came here for, go back to Dreamland, and find another way to—

Wait, what was that?

There was a large depression in the ground, right next to the plant, as if something big had landed and flattened the earth. She couldn't get a good view of it from the ground, but if she went higher…

Breeze spread her wings and flew upward, causing Bubble to raise his head and ask, "Hey, what are you doing? You better not be leaving me with all the work!"

"I just saw something!" she said. "It's like a dent in the ground."

"A 'dent'? What kind of dent?"

"Uh, I'm not sure. It almost looks like a—"

She fell silent as her eyes widened in disbelief; it wasn't a dent at all but a footprint! A *gigantic* footprint. It was at least three apples long! Just *huge*! And the indentations, arranged in specific patterns over the whole length of the footprint, were even stranger, hinting at some unknown purpose. What kind of boot could do that? Fairies sewed their moccasins with an almost flat underside. Why would anyone want to add small knobs to it?

"Well, what do you see?"

When Breeze didn't answer, Bubble joined his sister and followed her gaze; there was not one footprint but many, all coming from beyond the tree line. For a few seconds, he stared at them with his mouth agape, until he finally said, "We have to leave."

Breeze didn't respond. She simply continued to gaze at the new discovery, astonished by its implication.

"Breeze, come on!" Bubble shook his sister's shoulder. "We have to go! There's—"

*Thunk!*

Both fairies froze and looked in the direction where the sound had come from. Whoever had made these footprints was close; in fact, if Breeze flew toward the tree line, she'd be able to see them.

*Thunk!*

Bubble grabbed her hand and pulled her toward the basket, but before she could even think about it, she shook him off and advanced in the direction of the sound. Her brother gazed at her with his mouth agape, and she realized what she had just done. For a brief moment, she considered apologizing to him and going back the way they'd come, but then she heard that sound again.

*Thunk!*

Breeze looked at the meadow and saw the long blades of grass swaying in the wind. After a short moment of reflection, she nodded to herself and made her decision. "I'll be right back."

"Breeze, wait!"

The blue-haired fairy spread her wings and flew out of the forest, leaving Bubble behind.

# CHAPTER 4

**B**REEZE HID BEHIND a lavender flower while she planned her next move.

Given that she was surrounded by the grassy field on all sides, it was unlikely that anyone could see her in here. Even if they did, they'd probably mistake her for a butterfly. All she needed to do now was get closer…

*Thunk!*

Breeze took a left and followed the tree line. She glided between blades of grass and flowers while doing her best not to bother the bees, who were collecting their nectar. A few more leaps and then she'd take a peek above the grass, after which she would—

*Woosh!*

Something whizzed through the air two or three leaps ahead of her before it hit the trunk of a tree not far away on her left!

*THUNK!*

Breeze immediately recognized it: an arrow. A dangerous and useful tool that Cosmo and the other hunters used to hunt food. At first glance, there was nothing particularly special about the ones sticking out of the tree, but a quick examination of their black fletching and longer shafts revealed that they hadn't been crafted by fairy hands.

Breeze realized that she had been holding her breath and needed to inhale again, or it wasn't just her hair and wings that would be blue. Then, she heard something on her right move through the grass. It was quite a ways away, but it was getting closer—she was sure of it. Maybe she should go back to the forest? As long as she stayed low and followed the same path that she'd taken to get here, no one would be able to see her. She'd meet up with Bubble again and—

Wait, no!

She wasn't going to chicken out, not after all of this! It's like what Nana had always said about important stuff: "Always finish what you've started." And *this* was important. So, no going back to the forest. Instead, she closed her fists, slowly poked her head above the grass, and looked to her right.

Breeze caught her breath when she saw the colossal silhouette approach the tree line—it was big. *Really* big. Like, bigger than a stag, probably! And it hadn't even reached her yet!

It was a human.

The urge to run away grabbed her again. It was stronger than before, but strangely, it was easier to brush off. She had already made her decision. So instead of imagining the worst that could happen, she focused on the approaching silhouette and studied it.

His appearance surprised her. Except for his gigantism and the absence of wings, he resembled her brothers in a lot of ways. He wore a long-sleeved tunic, frayed at the edges and green like a fir tree. His gray pants, patched at the knee with a darker piece of material, reached down into a pair of soft leather boots. It looked as if he hadn't combed his short brown hair for days, and he had some hair around his mouth and jaw. Was this what Nana had once called a "beard"?

But what really got Breeze's attention was the curved stick

in his right hand. Nana had called it a "bow": a tool humans used to shoot arrows without having to rely on magic. If Breeze remembered correctly, the best way to use one was by holding the arrow in one's hand while pulling on the string with the other, then to let go when the target was in sight. Humans apparently needed a lot of training before they could shoot accurately.

Was that what he was doing? Training?

She didn't have time to think about it; he had almost reached her position. Knowing she couldn't risk being seen, she ducked back into the grass and waited for him to pass.

He walked through the field without care for the insects or flowers he might crush underneath his feet, and his piercing gaze—accented by furrowed eyebrows and hazel eyes—could have intimidated even Cosmo, the best hunter in Dreamland. His sunken cheeks, partially hidden in stubble, indicated that he might not be eating enough, and the way his lips were pressed tightly together made it hard for her to imagine him with a smile.

Breeze held her breath and waited for him to pass by her.

He approached the tree he was using as target practice, carefully pried the arrows stuck in its trunk, and returned them to the worn leather quiver he wore on his right hip. He accidentally broke one of the arrows and then muttered a curse under his breath, one she'd never heard before. "Almazar."

Once he had gathered all of the arrows, he picked up his bow and turned around.

Breeze waited until a few leaps separated the two of them and carefully trailed behind him, her eyes glued to his back. Concealed by the long grass, she levitated from one hiding place to the other, slowly moving farther from the forest she had called home all her life.

Breeze's thoughts were cut short when the human stopped walking. She barely had time to take cover behind a cluster of grass before he turned around to face the tree line again. In one swift movement, he raised his bow, nocked an arrow, and aimed at the tree.

*Woosh!*

The arrow whizzed toward its target at a curved angle, and—

*Thunk!*

—hit it dead center.

Breeze gaped at the human's skill. How far was that shot? Fifty leaps? No, sixty at least. He must have practiced a lot to shoot with such accuracy. And he did it while aiming at his target for barely a second! The hunters of Dreamland couldn't do that, not even with magic.

*Thunk!*

This impromptu expedition outside the forest had turned out better than she could have ever hoped for. Not only had she seen how gigantic humans were, but she'd also caught one of them in the middle of training! Oh, how she wished she could talk to him and learn about the outside world! But no, she had to stay hidden in this stupid grass and not make a peep. Shucks.

All of a sudden, Breeze felt a pull on her mind.

It was a delicate, almost imperceptible feeling. This wasn't the first time she had experienced it. In fact, she felt it every day: when her siblings would bring the carcass of a dead animal to the kitchens, when Dewdrop put heavy provisions into the pantry, when Bubble lit a fire with his hand, and when she herself grew wings from her back. Every time someone drew from the ambient well of magic, she felt it.

At first, she thought that Bubble had followed her into the field. Who else could it be? Maybe he was trying to catch her attention. But when she focused on the origin of this magical buzz, her gaze fell on the human. One of the arrows in his quiver began to levitate and moved right next to his head. At the same time, he raised his bow, drew back the arrow on the bowstring, aimed at his target, and—

*Woosh!*

—let both arrows loose.

*Thunk! Thunk!*

They did not hit the same tree; one of them buried itself into the smaller oak on the right. Seemingly indifferent to this outcome, the man repeated the process, nocking one arrow with his right hand and levitating another with his mind just like a fairy would.

Breeze continued to stare, her eyes sparkling with happiness. Nana had once spoken of humans who were capable of drawing on the well of magic—she called them "mages." They were supposed to be super rare, even more so than strawberries! Breeze couldn't believe just how lucky she was to see one. What else could he do with magic? How powerful was he? Who taught him the basics? She had so many questions and no way to ask him directly. If only she could get a little closer...

She heard something rustle beneath her feet.

Wondering what it was, she calmly looked down and saw a most unexpected creature: a squirrel. The rodent's eyes fixed on the fairy, and it took only a second for the two of them to recognize each other. They had met already. Unlike yesterday, however, the squirrel wasn't going to skedaddle. Oh no.

It all happened in an instant. The animal flexed its hind legs, bared its long teeth, and jumped in the air. Breeze barely had time to flutter her wings and fly away before her archnemesis reached her.

"WHOA! Whatcha doing?!" she yelled at it.

Knowing that it had missed its chance, the squirrel made a tactical retreat and disappeared into the grass.

"Yeah, you better run! Jerk!"

The sound of its footsteps quickly faded into the distance. Breeze would usually celebrate such a victory, but a sudden realization came over her: she was hovering almost a leap above the grass. Not only that, but she had also yelled her indignation for everyone to hear. Including the human standing a few leaps behind her.

Breeze broke out in a cold sweat, and she noticed that the sound of arrows whistling through the air had stopped. This was bad, *really* bad. And worst of all, she didn't know what to do next. There was only one rule regarding humans, and she had broken it already! Sun curse her wings, she had really botched the stew on that one. And yet the silence dragged on. For some reason, the human didn't say or do anything, even though she felt his gaze on her back. And so, with her heart beating so fast it made her dizzy, she very slowly turned around while hoping nothing bad would happen.

The human stood only four leaps away from her, the bow still in his hand. However, he had lowered his weapon at some point and was now gawking at her, his mouth so wide she could fit her whole head in it. The two arrows in his right hand dropped to the ground at the sight of her, and just when she thought this might not be a complete disaster, the human spoke.

"What the fu—"

Before he could finish his sentence, Breeze immediately yelped and hid in the grass again—his voice was so loud! The only times she'd heard someone speak this loudly was when one of the fairies used magic to address the whole community of Dreamland.

She needed somewhere to hide, and quick! This tall grass wouldn't be enough, nor would the small rocks scattered here and there. She needed something big and colorful, something like—like this bloom of dandelions! If she stood in the middle of it, he might lose track of her and go somewhere else! Yes, this was a good plan.

Suddenly, she heard him walk in her direction, his long shadow already enveloping the area around her. She wasted no time and ran into the bloom of yellow flowers. The only thing left to do was to wait for him to pass, after which she'd fly back to the forest and—

*Crack!*

His enormous boot landed not far from her. Breeze froze, tightly clutching the stem of one of the flowers.

"I can see your wings," the man said.

She blinked multiple times and then looked at her sides; the human was right. She had forgotten to retract her wings.

"You can come out," he said. "I'm not going to hurt you."

The fairy hesitated and wondered if she should flee into the grass like the squirrel had. He probably wouldn't be able to catch her if she flew at full speed through the field. However...the man had lowered his voice and spoken to her in an almost soft tone. Maybe he was trying to befriend her? He was so much louder than a fairy that it was difficult to tell. She had to know for sure.

She carefully peeked at him through the petals of the dandelion. "Do you mean it?" she asked.

She recognized the expression on his face; it was the same one she'd had when she first discovered the strawberry plant. The man carefully put his bow on the ground and kneeled down in front of her. "I can't hear you," he said. "Can you repeat that?"

Breeze didn't understand what was happening. She had spoken with her normal voice, like she did everyday with her siblings. Except, today wasn't a normal day. The human was so big, her question probably sounded like a quiet whisper to him. No wonder he couldn't hear her. Luckily for both of them, fairies knew how to project their voice. She only had to draw from the well of magic and—

"GET AWAY FROM HER!"

Bubble's voice blasted across the meadow like thunder in a storm. Both Breeze and the human spun to look in the direction of the booming sound. Breeze couldn't see anything from here, so she flapped her wings to fly above the grass and searched for her brother with her eyes. She felt his presence before she saw him—he was drawing an enormous amount of magic while charging at the human. The mysterious stranger probably felt it too because he hurriedly picked up his bow again and drew on the surrounding magic.

"Wait, no, Bubble!" she yelled, projecting her voice with magic. "He's not dangerous!"

Her brother had dashed through the field and was now fifteen leaps away from them, fireballs blazing at his side. The stranger backed away while nocking an arrow and levitating two others in the air. She had to stop them from coming to blows, and fast!

She stepped between the two of them and raised her hands. "STOP! No fighting!"

Bubble came to a halt right next to her, confused by what she'd just said. But the two apple-sized fireballs continued to crackle and churn, ready to charge at their enemy if given the order. "What are you doing!" her brother asked.

"The human isn't dangerous. We were just talking!"

"He's got his arrows pointed at us!"

The archer had lowered his bow but still had two floating arrows aimed at Bubble. "Only at you," he said to Bubble. "You're the one who came at me."

"How about you lower them if you're so nice, huh?"

"Will you do the same?"

Breeze looked back and forth between her brother and the stranger, hoping they'd stand down. They stared at each other for a long moment until finally the fireballs began to dwindle and diminish in size. In response, the arrows slowly retreated to their quiver and stopped moving.

"Just don't hurt my sister. Or you'll regret it."

The human stared back at her brother. "I wasn't going to," he replied.

Breeze breathed a sigh of relief. She had successfully prevented a fight from breaking out. She hadn't considered the possibility that Bubble would come to her rescue if anything happened. Even though the fireballs had now vanished, she could see in his eyes that he was ready to summon them again if the archer threatened her in any way.

An awkward silence settled in. Unwilling to speak first, Bubble folded his arms and glared at the stranger. The man, however, showed no sign of backing down and met his gaze head on while he studied the two fairies. She noticed his expression soften when he glanced at her.

"What's your name?" she asked tentatively. "Mine is Breeze."

"Breeze?" the human repeated, sounding baffled. "Like, a breeze in the wind?"

"Uh, yeah! What's yours?"

"Kieran. Kieran Fowler."

Breeze beamed from ear to ear and eagerly asked, "You have two names? How does that work?"

"Um…" The question had caught him by surprise. "Well, there's my name, like yours, and my family name."

"Really? Human families have names of their own?"

"Yeah. That's how it works."

Bubble, who hadn't stopped frowning during this whole exchange, decided to interject. "That's enough," he said. "Breeze, we have to leave. We're not supposed to talk to humans."

"But—"

"No. You know the rules, and you broke them. We're leaving."

Breeze put a hand on her brother's shoulder and told Kieran, "We'll just be a minute," before pulling Bubble away.

"What are you doing?" he asked her.

Once they were out of earshot, she leaned toward him and whispered, "I'm trying to make friends with him."

"What do you want to do that for? You've got us in deep enough trouble already. What if he tells other humans about us, huh? What do we do then?"

She looked down at the ground and slumped her shoulders. "I'm sorry about that. I really am."

Bubble pursed his lips and looked back at Kieran; the human was staring at the both of them, his bow still in hand. "It doesn't matter now," he said. "We have to go."

"No, we can't," Breeze replied, meeting his gaze again. "We need to talk to him."

"What?! Why?"

"Because we have to convince him not to tell anyone else about us. He's already seen us, so we might as well try, right?"

Her brother was about to protest the idea but stopped himself when he realized the wisdom of her words. It truly would be the best way to protect all of their siblings back home—*if* they managed to convince him.

"And how are we supposed to do that?" he asked.

"By making friends with him," she answered, a faint smile on her face. "He's not attacking us, is he? Look, I think he's even curious about us. Let's just go talk with him and see where that gets us."

Bubble hesitated for a few more seconds before he finally sighed and said, "Fine. But if he does anything threatening, I won't hesitate to blast him to bits."

"I'm sure he won't," she told him.

They returned to Kieran and stopped a leap away from him, just so Bubble would be more comfortable in his presence. The human hadn't taken his eyes off the fairies since the moment they'd first appeared and was now studying them the same way Breeze had examined the strawberry plants when she first discovered them—with amazement and awe.

"Sorry about that," she told him. "Bubble here was just a little worried that you might tell other humans about us."

Her brother's eyebrow twitched when she revealed the truth to Kieran. Would he have preferred that she didn't?

"I didn't plan to," Kieran said.

"Great!" Breeze exclaimed. "That's a weight off our minds. You see, we're not really supposed to be out here."

"Then why are you?" he asked, cocking his head to the side. "I heard you screaming at someone back there."

"Oh, that? That was Mr. Squirrel. He's a meanie who knocks down fences and steals strawberries, and he tried to attack me! Can you believe it?"

"I'm...not sure I can."

"Oh, but I swear that's what happened! We can even go look for Mr. Squirrel if you want. Then you'll see for yourself."

"No, that's fine. I believe you."

"Really? Great!"

Kieran just stood there for a second, seeming unsure how to respond to that, before his gaze shifted to the tree line. "So, you're the one who put the fence around that patch of strawberries over there?"

"Yes, I am! Wait..." She gasped and pointed an accusing finger at him. "That means you're the one who ate the rest of the strawberries!"

Kieran shifted uncomfortably. "Uh, sorry? I thought one of the local kids had made that fence just for fun."

"You're not entirely wrong," Bubble commented.

"Hey! I'll have you know it's a really nice fence," Breeze retorted.

Her brother ignored her and focused his attention on the human. "We're here to take the strawberry plants back with us," he explained. "What about you? Why are *you* here?"

Bubble narrowed his eyes as he waited for the answer, but Kieran didn't flinch under his piercing gaze. "I only came to craft new arrows before I went on my way," he said. "Never thought I'd meet fairies here." He shook his head in disbelief.

"And you're really not going to tell anyone about us?" Bubble continued.

"Of course not," said Kieran. "We're the same, after all."

The two fairies shared a brief look of bewilderment. "What do you mean, we're the same?" Breeze asked.

The archer glanced between the two of them, his eyebrows squished together in uncertainty, before he presented his left hand to the fairies and gathered magic from his surroundings. Bubble immediately tensed up and prepared to summon his fireballs again, only for Breeze to stop him by grabbing his arm. They both watched as they sensed the energy swirl in Kieran's hand and transform into something new—a thin flame.

"There you go," Kieran said, as if that explained everything.

Bubble frowned. "So, you made fire. That just means you're a mage."

Kieran gave Bubble an incredulous look before he snuffed the flame out. "Yes, I'm a mage," he said. "Isn't that enough for you?"

"How could it be?"

Her brother looked more annoyed than before, which seemed to confuse Kieran even further. "Have you never heard of the Inquisition before?" he asked. "Even in passing?"

Breeze perked up at this new word. "No," she answered. "What is it? Some sort of club for mages?"

Kieran blinked at her. "No, they're not mages. They *hunt* mages. Anyone who can use magic."

Breeze gasped and covered her mouth with both hands. "They eat mages?" she exclaimed. "That's horrible!"

Kieran stared at the blue-haired fairy before he put his palm to his face. She must have said something very wrong for him to react this way, but what was it? Her brother seemed as confused as she was, so it had to be something only a human would understand.

"What do they do with mages?" Bubble asked.

Kieran met the fairies' gazes again and paused. Even though

the expression on his face betrayed nothing, Breeze could tell it was no laughing matter for him.

"Nothing good," he said. He seemed about to elaborate on his answer, but then a shadow passed over his face and he fell silent. It was obvious that something weighed on his mind, but Breeze had no idea what it was or what she could do about it. That didn't mean she didn't want to help, however.

"How about we sit down?" she suggested. "The middle of a field isn't really the place to have this kind of conversation, right?"

Kieran eyed her for a long moment before he nodded toward Bubble and asked, "Is that going to be okay with him?"

Her brother still had his arms crossed and his brow furrowed, and for an instant she worried that he would oppose the idea of sitting down with a human, but he surprised her when he nodded and said, "I want to learn more about this Inquisition."

The archer pointed at the tree line behind him. "I've set up camp right over there," he said. "Follow me?"

Breeze's mouth broke into a smile. "We're right behind you," she said.

# CHAPTER 5

**B**REEZE BOUNCED AROUND the campfire as she marveled at its size.

Big rocks sat in a circle around a pile of ashes. No fire was burning at the moment, but judging by the absence of embers, it must have gone out sometime during the night. Kieran was sitting less than two leaps away, right under the shade of a big oak tree. He was rummaging through his haversack—a weathered leather bag on a strap—until he pulled some sort of hard, circular flatbread out of it.

"What's that?" Breeze asked.

"Hmm? That's crispbread," Kieran answered. "You want some?"

She nodded rapidly multiple times. The human smirked and broke off a small piece with an audible snap, causing many crumbs to fall into his lap. She stared agape at him when he casually brushed them off and they dropped to the ground. How could he waste so much food? Fairies could get a whole meal out of some of these crumbs! Was it because they were too small for him? Before she could question him about it, he handed her a piece of bread big enough to last her for a whole day. She hovered next to Kieran to examine it, curious about its texture, before she took it and weighed it in her hands.

"Wow, I've never smelled anything like it. Bubble, come have some crispybread!"

Her brother was standing on one of the rocks bordering the campfire, directly opposite Kieran. He didn't join her side immediately; he seemed to be pondering whether or not he should get closer to the human, until he relented and flew to her side.

"He called it *crisp*bread," her brother said. "Not crispy."

"But it sounds so much better my way!"

Bubble didn't get any time to retort because his sister shoved the large breadcrumb in his face. He reluctantly took a bite, chewed on it for a few seconds, and then carefully swallowed it. Breeze was much keener to try it out, and as soon as she finished her first bite, she took another and exclaimed, "Itsh sho good! Can I keep the rhest?"

"Sure," Kieran said. "I didn't think you'd like it."

"I don't," Bubble said.

"I don't either."

"Weally?" Breeze asked, looking at both of them. "You shouln't eat shtuf you don' like den."

She flew down to one of the large roots jutting from the ground and sat down on it. After placing the breadcrumb next to her, she waved at her brother to join her, which he did, but not without letting out a sigh. Kieran openly stared at the two fairies, and his eyes widened when their wings retracted and disappeared into their back.

"You can grow your wings?" he asked.

"Sure we can!" Breeze responded. "It'd be hard to sleep with our wings out all the time."

"What about your clothes? Do your wings go through them?"

"We've made holes in our shirts for that. Looky here!"

She turned around and showed Kieran her back. The poor human had to get closer and squint to spot the slits Breeze had cut for her wings. "Right, I see them," he said before leaning back against the tree.

"Cool, huh? Sometimes our wings get stuck if we grow them too fast, and we have to shake our shirt until they get out."

Bubble interjected into the conversation. "Can we go back to the Inquisition?" he asked impatiently. "What is it exactly?"

"Oh, right," Breeze said, smiling sheepishly. "I almost forgot."

So had Kieran apparently, because his facial expression hardened at the simple mention of it. From what little he'd said about the Inquisition, it sounded like they hated magic. But why? Magic was so useful! She couldn't imagine what her life would be without it. Was that why Nana had told the fairies to never leave Dreamland? Hoping that Kieran would explain it all to her, she leaned forward and waited for him to speak.

The archer stared at the two fairies for some time before he seemed to realize he hadn't eaten any of his crispbread. After a moment, he wrapped it in a small white cloth, put it back into his haversack, and asked, "Do you know what God is?"

Both Breeze and Bubble shook their heads.

"I'll keep it simple then: God is the creator of everything that exists. The earth, water, air…whatever you can think of. She is everywhere and can see everything. And because of that, we're supposed to worship her and do what she tells us to do."

"Worship her? What does that mean?" Bubble asked.

"It means to pray to her. To pay our respects."

"Why would anyone do that?"

"Because if you don't, you go to hell when you die."

"Is that a bad place?"

"A very bad one."

"I'm not sure I want to worship someone like that."

"Me neither."

"What about the man?" Breeze asked, hanging on Kieran's every word.

"What man?" Kieran repeated.

"The man-god. What does he do?"

"There isn't one. That's just how people talk about God. She gave birth to the world, so she has to be a woman. That's what the Church says anyway."

"What's the Church?"

"It's a group of women—human women—who've decided to dedicate their lives to God. In exchange, God shares her power with them."

"Wow. And what do they do with it?"

"They perform miracles, help other people, and try to convince them to pray to God."

"And what about the Inquisition?" Bubble asked. "Are they part of the Church?"

The archer nodded. "The inquisitors are not that different from the priestesses of the Church, but they're also trained to fight. Their job is to find and capture sorcerers and witches like me, and then kill them."

Breeze gasped in horror. "Why would they do that?!"

Kieran frowned until wrinkles appeared on his forehead. He looked at the blue-haired fairy and said in a bitter tone, "Because they believe that anyone who uses magic is evil."

Both Breeze and Bubble fell silent at these words. That couldn't be right. Why would any human think that? The fairies of Dreamland did use magic to hunt animals, but they always paid their respects afterward, just like Nana had taught them to.

"Would the Church call us evil then?" Bubble asked.

Kieran's expression briefly softened, and he let out a long sigh. "I don't know," he said. "I didn't think fairies existed until today. Some people might call you demons, but I'm not sure."

"Demons?"

"A really evil spirit from hell," he explained.

"So...you're the first human to meet one of us?" Breeze asked.

Kieran raised his eyebrows in surprise. "You're asking *me*? I'm the one who's stepped into a fairy tale. If anyone should know, it's you."

"A fairy tale?" she repeated, her ears perking up. "What's that?"

The man stared at Breeze, his mouth agape. "Almazar," he swore. "You...you don't even know what a fairy tale is?"

"Um, no. What about you, Bubble?"

"I've never heard of it. What is it?"

Breeze thought the question was simple enough, and yet Kieran struggled to come up with an answer. He massaged his forehead for a while before he launched into an explanation. "It's a story that could never happen in real life. Like finding a pot full of gold at the end of a rainbow—it just doesn't happen. That's why it's called a *fairy* tale. They don't exist."

"But we do!" Breeze said. "You can tell, right?"

"Yes, *I* can. But if I ever told anyone else about you, they'd call me a lunatic and stay the hell away from me."

"But...we're real," she retorted, with less energy. When she looked into Kieran's eyes, however, she knew this statement alone wouldn't change anything. Did all humans really think that fairies didn't exist? Why would Nana keep quiet about this?

"Kieran," Bubble began with a worried tone, "what would happen if an inquisitor learned about us?"

"I'm not sure," he answered. "I guess that she would tell the rest of the Inquisition first. Then they'd probably mount a search to capture you and confirm that you really exist. After which... they'd tell the Great Mother."

"The Great Mother?" Bubble repeated.

"She's the leader of the Church. An old woman who gives orders to the others."

"And what would she say?"

"I imagine she'd tell the Inquisition to kill you, just like they would any other mage."

When Breeze heard these words, she felt all of the muscles in her body tense up. Her heartbeat quickened and a fire lit up in the pit of her stomach. Words then came to her mouth, ready to explode with full force, and before she could even think them through, she shouted them at the top of her lungs: "THAT'S NOT FAIR!"

Magic swirled around her, carrying her voice farther than any normal human scream would, and both Kieran and Bubble instinctively covered their ears with their hands, shocked by what had just happened.

Breeze was now standing on top of the root with her hands closed in tight fists. She could feel her arms shaking, but she didn't care. She had to say something! "Why would they do that to us?!" she yelled. "My brothers and sisters are good fairies! We take good care of our plants, we're nice to the animals, and we don't hurt anyone!"

Bubble still looked shaken from his sister's outburst, but he tried to calm her down. "Breeze," he began hesitantly, "we already knew that humans were dangerous. Kieran only confirmed it."

"Nana didn't tell us about this Inquisition!" she said. "She knew about them, what they did to mages, what they could do to us, and she said nothing!"

"She was only trying to protect us. She—"

"Then she should have told us the truth! Because that's what good fairies do!" Breeze yelled. Her throat began to hurt, making it harder to speak. "That's how you protect someone! If it's something really, really important, you don't lie. Ever!"

"I-I'm sure she had a good reason. She didn't tell us everything, but—"

"She lied to us, Bubble!"

This snapped his mouth shut. Bubble stared at his sister, incapable of saying anything.

Her eyes welled up, and a heavy weight settled in her chest.

"Nana lied to us..." Tears began to flow down her cheeks. Breeze tried to wipe them off with her sleeve, but they kept coming. Bubble attempted to comfort her by wrapping his arm around her shoulders, but it did nothing to remove the weight that had settled in her chest, which only became heavier, like a sponge soaking up water in the rain. Breeze then remembered that Kieran was sitting right there, watching all of this. What a bad impression she was making on him. "I'm sorry," she said.

"Um, no, it's all right," he said, sitting in a rigid posture. It was clear he didn't know what to do with himself. When she looked at him through her blurred vision, he avoided her gaze. His eyes darted between her and the ground for a few seconds, until he quietly said, "I shouldn't have been so blunt."

Breeze blinked at the human, uncertain as to whether or not she'd heard him correctly, and wiped away the tears. Kieran was being kind to her, just like Bubble. Maybe humans weren't that different from fairies after all. He was big and hairy, yes, but he wasn't mean like the ones Nana had warned them about.

"Thank you," she said.

Her brother continued to hold her while she regained her composure. He then asked Kieran, "When were you planning to leave?"

"Tomorrow morning," he said. "Is that going to be a problem?"

"No. Can you just promise that you won't tell anyone about us?"

Kieran sighed. "Like I said, I wasn't planning to—"

"I want your word." Bubble spoke with a tone that indicated he wouldn't accept anything less than that.

For a moment, Kieran didn't seem sure of how to respond. Before Breeze could intervene and help him, her new human friend slowly nodded and said, "I promise on my mother's grave."

"Thank you." Bubble turned to Breeze again. "Come on, let's go. Dewdrop will send for us if we take too long."

Breeze nodded. She picked up her piece of breadcrumb, spread her blue butterfly wings, and followed her brother into the air. Bubble was right. Dewdrop was expecting them to return any minute now with the strawberry plants. If they didn't, she'd send fairies to the Sparrow's Field, where they wouldn't find Breeze or Bubble. There was just one thing she needed to do before leaving.

With puffy red eyes, Breeze hovered in front of the archer, gave him a shaky smile, and said, "Goodbye, Kieran. It was nice meeting you."

"Likewise, Breeze," he said with the smallest hint of a smile on his face. He then fell silent for a bit, as if contemplating something. "We're not going to see each other again, are we?"

She hung her head. "Probably not, no."

"Well…take care then. You too, Bubble."

The red-winged fairy nodded at the human and flew back to the forest, where he'd hidden the basket before he came to his sister's rescue. Breeze followed him without protest, but not without turning one last time to wave goodbye to Kieran.

There were so many other questions she had wanted to ask him. How many humans are there? How big are their cities? What kinds of food do they eat? Kieran had the answers to all of them. Well, maybe not all of them, but he knew a whole lot more than she did. At this moment, though, her thoughts were focused on one person: Nana.

The old fairy had left Dreamland five years ago on a quest to awaken more of their brethren. She must have faced many dangers since then, maybe even the Inquisitors themselves. That meant she knew how to avoid them, maybe even fight them off, but she hadn't taught the fairies of Dreamland how to do the same.

Breeze didn't realize they had reached the strawberry patch until Bubble spoke to her and proposed that he dig up the plants alone. Not being one to shy away from a bit of work, even when she didn't feel up to it, Breeze shook her head and landed on the ground, ready to help him with the task. They dug into the earth with their magic, moved it away from their prize, and then placed the plants into their rush basket, all the while thinking about what she should do with the knowledge she'd just obtained.

After a few minutes of work, they were done. "We're good to go," Bubble said. "Let's hurry back home."

"Yeah, let's," Breeze replied.

She glanced one last time at the tree line and wondered if Kieran had ever faced an inquisitor. Even if he hadn't, he could at the very least teach her siblings how to avoid them. But no, she knew her brothers and sisters too well. They wouldn't accept a human's help, not so soon. She had to think of another way.

"Breeze, come on, help me carry this. It's heavy."

"Oh, sorry," she said. "Here, I'll take the left."

They lifted the basket and flew back to Dreamland.

# CHAPTER 6

F AITH FIDGETED IN her seat, wondering how much longer she would have to wait for Inquisitor Harlow to return.

It had been five minutes since her mentor had left her here, and she could already feel her stomach churning. If she failed the trial... No, she couldn't let that happen. She had studied twelve years for this, trained harder than any other novitiate in her class, and knew every single verse in the Scriptures by heart. She *couldn't* fail.

Faith closed her eyes and inhaled the soothing fragrance of incense that permeated the air. She reminded herself of everything she had accomplished so far: healing her first patient at fourteen years old, growing back the limbs of war amputees at seventeen, and becoming one of the youngest priestesses in the history of the Church at nineteen. If she could do all of that, then she could pass the trial to become an inquisitor. And yet, despite these achievements, she couldn't stop her hands from shaking.

She opened her eyes again and looked around the room.

The inner chapel of the Inquisitorial abbey was devoid of people save for Faith herself. She was sitting in the right pew of the first row, next to the center aisle. Numerous candles placed on racks in front of the chancel cast a dim light in the chapel, which was outshone by the sunlight beaming through the three stained-glass windows built into the eastern wall and giving life to the scenes depicted on them: the birth of Alma Azaria in the Dark Forest of Ermanloth, where her mother and father brought Alma into the world; the first time Alma healed the wounded with God's power, a feat that terrified the Aurelian sorcerers who had come to arrest her; and her death at the hand of Acklea, who became an assassin to save his children from the Aurelian Magistracy.

After looking at these scenes, Faith noticed that her hands had stopped shaking. She shifted her gaze to the symbol placed at the top of the altar—a seven-pointed star enclosed by a circle. Her insides were still quivering at the idea of failing the trial, but she knew that God was guiding her every step of the way. As long as she kept following the path laid out for her, she was bound to prevail.

"Thank you, Kind Mother," she whispered, joining her hands together in prayer.

The double doors of the chapel opened behind her, followed by the sound of footsteps moving up the center aisle. She recognized the soft and unwavering gait of Inquisitor Harlow by the way her sandals tapped against the marble floor. When the footsteps stopped next to her, Faith rose from the pew and turned to face her mentor.

"They're ready for you," Harlow said.

The old woman wore a white cassock, the standard attire for all members of the Church. What identified her as an inquisitor was the band cincture that ran around her waist and hung down in the front; instead of white, it was a crimson red. Faith wore the same type of outfit, but in gray, which signified her rank as an inquisitorial novitiate. She hoped to receive the white cassock later today.

"Did you make sure to not wear your underwear?" the inquisitor asked with a raised eyebrow.

The question snapped Faith out of her reverie. She gawked at her mentor, unsure whether or not she'd heard her correctly. What was the old woman thinking? Speaking this sort of language in a place of worship! There were other, subtler ways to ask her this question.

"Oh, don't give me that look," Harlow continued. "Did you or did you not?"

Faith's cheeks flushed, and it was with great difficulty that she formulated an answer. "I-I did, ma'am."

"Good. Trust me, it'll feel a lot less awkward when it's time for you to undress. You really don't want to get your feet stuck in your panties when you take them off. You'll just end up falling to the ground and mooning the inquisitors."

"Ma'am!"

"Oh, shush! You're lucky I'm here to mention the little details to you." Harlow started to smooth out Faith's cassock and straighten her hair. "Do you have any idea how embarrassing it is to fall down in front of the Council during your ordination as Inquisitor? I swear, I can remember the cold touch of the floor on my breasts to this day. Petrifying."

Faith did her best to keep a straight face while the inquisitor finished this last-minute inspection, but she could already feel a flush creep across her cheeks. At first glance, Inquisitor Harlow fit the stereotypical image of an old Azarian priestess: long white hair braided in a bun, a narrow face strewn with wrinkles, and bright blue eyes that could pierce into the thickest of skulls. If one took the time to know her—or spent years under her tutelage, like Faith had—they'd realize very quickly that she was also quite candid.

"There, you're all good now," Harlow said, keeping her hands on the young woman's shoulders. "How are you feeling?"

*Far from good*, Faith thought, but that wasn't an answer she could give. "I'm a little nervous," she said. "I-I've never learned how to swim."

"You won't need to, Faith. But if that's what worries you…" Harlow gazed into her student's eyes and gave her a comforting smile. "Your name is the solution to all the problems you'll face in your life. It's no mistake that your mother chose it for you. She knew you were destined for great things. And whatever happens today, I know you'll be made stronger by it come tomorrow."

Faith didn't know how to respond to these words. The idea that failing the trial wasn't necessarily a disaster hadn't even crossed her mind. However, Inquisitor Harlow spoke with such sincerity that Faith couldn't suppress a smile. "Thank you, ma'am."

"I'm only speaking the truth, dear," Harlow replied. "But enough talking. We'd better be on our way."

The knot in Faith's stomach tightened, but it wasn't enough to deter her, not after what Harlow had told her. Before the two of them left the chapel, however, there was one thing she wanted to ask. "Um, Inquisitor Harlow?"

"Yes?"

"Is my mother present?"

"Of course. She'll be the one to officiate the trial."

"I see." Faith bit the inside of her cheek and admonished herself for asking this question. Of course Mother would be there. Hoping otherwise was quite naive of her, silly even. It was best to just move along. "Let us go then."

The old woman peered at her student, no doubt suspecting the thoughts going through her mind, and Faith did her best to remain poised in the face of such scrutiny. Looking satisfied, the inquisitor then walked down the aisle and left the chapel. In accordance with protocol, Faith followed her two steps behind and closed the double doors behind them.

They arrived in the western hallway of the main cloister. Through the colonnade, she could see the right side of Saint Lucretia's statue standing in the center of the inner courtyard. Dressed in a stola and armed with a long staff, the saint had her weapon raised against an invisible enemy while she kept her other hand on her heart, using her faith to shield herself from all attacks.

Faith continued down the hallway and glanced at the many flowers planted in the courtyard: tulips, daffodils, and daisies, all arranged in colorful clusters and rows that appealed to the eyes. The fragrance emanating from them competed with the mouth-watering odors wafting from the kitchen. But Faith had no time to appreciate any of it; she had almost arrived at her destination.

The Well House.

The large double doors leading to it were located on the northern side of the inner courtyard, and the only people allowed to walk through them were full-fledged inquisitors and the novitiates ready to undertake the trial.

"Here it is," Harlow said. "Are you ready? I can give you a minute if you need to prepare."

Faith shook her head. "No, I'm fine. I'm as ready as I'll ever be."

"Yes, you are." The inquisitor nodded, turned to face the large wooden doors, and slowly pushed them forward. Faith clenched her hands into fists and waited with bated breath for the doors to open.

The first face she saw was that of her mother, Grand Inquisitor Karolina Dow.

She stood in the middle of the room, flanked by two high inquisitors: Saskia Kapsner and Iris Devlin. All three of them wore not only the white cassocks and red cinctures of the order but also ceremonial silk capes of different colors: dark blue for Saskia and Iris, light purple for Karolina.

Faith almost recoiled when their gazes met her own. Especially her mother's. Her first instinct was to turn away and leave, but she quickly suppressed the feeling and took her first step forward.

The novitiates had speculated for years on what was inside the Well House. They knew that it was the same size as the chapel and that no windows had been built into it, but not much else. The only source of light here was a small ball of white light that floated near the ceiling above them. There were no carpets on the cold floor, no torches on the stone brick walls, and no furniture in any corner of the room.

There was only the well.

She shivered when she looked at the hole, two meters wide, at the very center of the room. The surface of the water was almost flush with the floor, and the slightest disturbance would most assuredly spill water onto the floor.

Faith stopped in front of the well and shifted her gaze toward her mother, who was standing on the other side of it. The resemblance between the two of them was undeniable: the same square-shaped face, straight nose, thin lips, and green eyes. They even had the same raven hair, which they let flow freely down their backs. Faith had once thought about cutting hers to differentiate herself from her mother, but after careful consideration, she decided against it. It would only have fueled even more gossip from the other novitiates.

Then she heard Harlow close the doors behind her. She looked over her shoulder and saw the sunlight gradually vanish while the ball of light near the ceiling also diminished. Finally, only darkness remained.

For a long moment, the only sounds were the scraping of her mentor's footsteps on the floor and the thumping of her own heartbeat. Would there really be no light for the ceremony? She assumed they'd have a few torches or candles at the very least, but there was nothing else here.

Then, out of nowhere, Faith heard the sound of grinding stone. She raised her head and saw a circular skylight slide open, allowing sunlight to beam into the room, blinding her. Once her eyes adjusted to it, she realized that the skylight's dimensions matched the well perfectly, and the column of light descended directly upon the water.

"Novitiate Faith Dow," Grand Inquisitor Dow said, "it has been only two years since you arrived at the abbey, and yet you've told the Council that you are ready to undertake the Trial of Faith."

Faith wet her lips before she responded. "Yes, ma'am."

"Then you understand that, should you fail today, there will be no second chance. You will have to leave the abbey and find another way to serve the Kind Mother."

"I understand, ma'am."

"And you still wish to undertake the trial?"

Faith glanced at Saskia and Iris and wondered whether they thought she was trying too hard. The other novitiates certainly did, and they often talked about it behind her back, but she knew the truth better than anyone.

"I am ready," she said. "May God be my witness."

The grand inquisitor exchanged a look with her two subordinates, who both responded with a silent nod. She then turned to face her daughter again. "Undress yourself."

Faith froze for a second.

Even though she had prepared for this moment and imagined the many ways it could play out, she still felt her cheeks flush red with embarrassment. It was one thing to bathe in a public bath where everyone was naked, but another to undress in front of fully clothed inquisitors. Still, there could be no hesitation. She unbuttoned her cassock and let it fall to the ground. The cool air immediately brushed against her skin and sent shivers down her spine. How much colder would the well be?

"Inquisitor Harlow, please proceed."

The old woman stood a few steps behind her student; in her hands was a ball and chain, so heavy that she strained to carry it to the well. Faith's first instinct was to help her teacher, but she stopped herself at the last second and instead watched her drop the shackles at Faith's feet. A heavy thump followed by the clanking of chains resonated in the empty room.

"Novitiate Faith Dow," Saskia said in a low and solemn voice, "the life of an inquisitor is rife with mortal dangers, and many heretics seek to destroy the peace we have established. Our most valuable weapon against them is and always has been our faith in the Kind Mother. Today, you shall prove you possess the resolve necessary to brave these dangers. If God deems you worthy, she will grant you the power you need to escape the well."

While Inquisitor Kapsner spoke, Harlow kneeled next to Faith and secured the manacle around her leg, just above the ankle. The weight of the metal almost immediately began chafing at her skin, and she knew with absolute certainty that she could not remove it by any normal means.

"Do not fear for your life," Inquisitor Devlin said in a neutral tone. "If you drown, we will immediately bring you back and reanimate you."

This did little to reassure Faith. She tried to slow down her breathing and focus on something else, but she couldn't take her eyes off the well. It was more than just a hole filled with dark water: it was the mouth of a large monster, ready to swallow her whole. And if she failed, it'd spit her back out into the world, powerless and without purpose, the victim of her own hubris. The other novitiates would certainly remember her as a cautionary tale, and her mother would...what? Berate her? No, she would do far worse: she'd ignore her own daughter.

Faith closed her eyes and chased the thoughts away. It was unfair to blame her mother and classmates. They were searching for their place in life, just like her. What really mattered at this moment weren't her small problems but her sacred allegiance to God. Today was the most important day of her life.

"Inquisitor Harlow," her mother said, "please help the novitiate."

Harlow put a hand on Faith's shoulder and spoke softly into her ear. "Sit down at the edge of the well and put your feet inside."

Faith did as she was told and gasped when she felt the chilly water engulf her lower legs. Even more peculiar was the unexpected contrast between the cold touch of the stone floor on her bottom and the warm caress of the sunlight on her thighs. The iron ball had been placed right next to the well and its chain was now extended to its limit. Harlow held on to it firmly, making sure her student wouldn't be dragged into the well until it was the right time.

"Listen carefully," her mentor said. "You will dive into the water exactly when I tell you to. If you don't, the ball could break your ankle. Understood?"

Faith nodded.

"Then be ready. And don't worry about the water. It's not cold enough to send you into shock. Just make sure to take a deep breath."

"Inquisitor Harlow," Grand Inquisitor Dow said with a disapproving frown, "begin the trial."

"Yes, ma'am." Harlow put a comforting hand on Faith's shoulder and whispered, "On my count."

She then lifted the iron ball with her two hands and prepared to throw it into the well. It was all happening so fast that Faith almost forgot that she needed to hold her breath.

"Three."

Just like Harlow had taught her, she inhaled deeply and then exhaled all the air in her lungs.

"Two."

She leaned forward and put her hands on the edge of the well.

"One."

She took one last deep breath—

"Now!"

—and dove forward. The chilly water enveloped her whole body and almost made her gasp for air, but like Harlow had said, it wasn't cold enough to send her into shock. What really frightened her was the sudden sharp pain that shot through her right leg.

It was the ball and chain. The metal was digging into her skin and pulling on her ankle as if trying to break it. She tried to ignore it, but to no avail. How could it hurt so much? Cold, creeping fear threatened to overwhelm her, and there was nothing she could do to stop it except wait until she reached the bottom of the well.

She opened her eyes and saw a swirling mass of darkness on all sides, with one faint source of light far above her head. She needed to think about her escape, and fast. She had already lost too many precious seconds focusing on the pain. If she could just empty her mind and pray for help, renew her link with God, she'd—

*Thump.*

Faith suddenly stopped falling. The water wasn't flowing around her anymore, and the chain had loosened its grip on her ankle; she had finally reached the bottom. The pressure on her ears was unlike anything she'd ever experienced, muddying her thoughts into an incoherent mess. She had a minute at most to get out of here and make her way back to the surface.

*Remember the plan*, she thought. *Break the chain and you'll be fine.*

Faith closed her eyes and joined her hands together. She did her best to ignore the growing need for air and imagined herself back in the chapel, sitting in that pew. She pictured the flames of the candles slowly burning the wax and releasing an herbal fragrance unlike any other, specks of dust dancing in the light that gleamed from the stained-glass windows, and walls of stone that muffled the chaotic sounds of the outside world. A safe place where she could almost feel the soft caress of the Kind Mother on her cheek. As long as this memory never left her, she'd always find her way back home.

Even though her eyes were still closed, she could now see the shackle fastened around her leg. The metal was thick—too thick. Knowing she could never break it in time, she searched for the weakest link in the chain instead. None of them appeared more fragile than the others, so she settled on the third one from her leg and began to exert a sliver of divine power on it. She sensed its internal composition—sturdy and dense iron that had been forged not too long ago—and selected one section of it while ignoring the burning pressure growing in her lungs. With practiced meticulousness, she then twisted the metal and altered its very structure.

The metal turned into water in all but an instant.

Faith wasn't yet free, however. Her concentration now broken, she leaned down and attempted to unhook the link from the rest of the chain. Pain spread throughout her chest as she floundered in the dark. Where was the damn link? She didn't have much time left! Was it this one? No, not that one. Wait, she remembered— third one starting from the shackle. She felt for the chain with her hands and started counting. An instant later, she found the fractured link and unhooked it from the others.

Free at last.

She immediately pushed against the bottom of the well with her legs and propelled herself upward. The pain in her chest was getting worse by the second, and she had to clench her mouth shut so water wouldn't fill her lungs. She needed air! She kept moving toward the light, flailing in the water like a clumsy newborn fish, but fatigue was wearing her down. She was so close. Just a little more, and she'd finally reach the surface of the water...

A veil of darkness appeared at the edge of her vision. It would drag her back to the bottom of this hole and leave her to be rescued by the inquisitors.

Faith redoubled her efforts and pressed onward; she didn't care if she hurt herself in the process! She'd heal herself if need be! She just had to keep swimming and not stop, not until she emerged into the light. She began to feel the familiar warmth of the sun caressing her skin. Just a little more and—

Air. Sweet, delicious air.

Never before in her life had she so dearly appreciated the sensation of air filling her lungs, and a wave of elation washed over her. It was cut short when she reached for the edge of the well with her hands and found...nothing. Her head sank below the surface of the water again, and pain suddenly shot into her chest when she breathed some of it.

Faith flailed around, trying to grab hold of something, anything, but all she could see was a blur: the skylight, water bubbles, and her own wavy hair. Why wasn't anyone helping her? She had reached the surface! They had to help her! They had to!

And just when Faith thought she would drown here, her head hit the hard stone of the curved wall. She turned around and grabbed the edge of the well, her hands searching for a firm grip on the floor tiles, and once her head emerged from the water, she coughed so hard that she barely had time to breathe in before the next coughing fit started. The only clear thought in her mind was that she needed to get out of this well.

With great difficulty, she climbed onto the floor and crawled away from the water, only to be blocked by someone's legs. She had no idea who it was until they kneeled down next to her and wrapped a blanket around her shoulders; it was Harlow. Faith raised her head and saw the hint of a smile on the old woman's face.

"Inquisitor Devlin," her mother said. "Please help her up."

The high inquisitor grabbed her left arm and lifted her to her feet while Harlow began drying her body with the blanket. The trial was over, Faith realized. It was over, and she had passed.

"Can you stand on your own?" Harlow asked.

"Yes," she answered, still a little shaken.

"Then please raise your arms behind you," Iris said.

Faith didn't understand the purpose behind that request until she saw her mother circle around the well with Saskia in tow, the white cassock of the order in her hands.

Without a word, the grand inquisitor approached her daughter and helped her put on the cassock while Saskia moved Faith's wet hair out of the way. The light, breathable wool rubbed against her skin just like the previous cassock she'd worn, and even though there was nothing different about it aside from the color, the sensation still warmed her heart.

Saskia fastened the buttons for her before she joined the grand inquisitor's side. Faith knew the next step of the ceremony, and although her foot still hurt, she kneeled in front of the inquisitors and joined her hands together.

"Novitiate Faith Dow," her mother began, "by God's grace, you have proven yourself worthy of speaking in the name of the Kind Mother. Now, repeat after us: I, Faith Dow—"

"I, Faith Dow—"

"—do solemnly swear to dedicate my life to the protection of God's children."

Faith repeated the words.

"To cure the ill and teach the sinners, to confront the face of evil and tear down its disguises."

"To steel my heart," Iris continued, "and shield the innocent."

"To raise my arm," Saskia said, "against the malevolent."

"And to surrender my life to the Kind Mother," the grand inquisitor concluded. Once her daughter had repeated the words, she nodded and said, "You have made the vow. Now arise, Inquisitor Dow."

A shiver ran down Faith's spine when she heard that. She repressed a smile and rose to her feet, only to be greeted by the happy expressions of Saskia and Iris. Her mother displayed no smile, but Faith could have sworn that her frown was less pronounced than usual. It was difficult to tell in this dim light.

"Inquisitor Harlow, please bring the young inquisitor to my office so I can brief her on her first task."

"Yes, ma'am."

And just like that, the grand and high inquisitors shuffled away toward the exit. Iris opened the doors, flooding the Well House with sunlight again, and followed her comrades outside the room. Faith brought a shaky hand to her chest to feel the fabric of the cassock while she watched the inquisitors go through the doors. She replayed her mother's last words in her mind, and the corners of her lips curled upward.

"Congratulations," Harlow said as she put a hand on her shoulder. "You've just become the youngest inquisitor in the history of the Inquisition. An impressive feat."

"I-I'll do my best not to disappoint you," Faith stammered.

"No need to be so modest, Faith. Not with me."

Faith hesitated for an instant and peered into the old woman's eyes. What she saw was unconcealed and genuine pride in her student. The kind of pride that made her cheeks flush red and her chest tighten with emotion.

"Thank you," Faith said. "For your kind words, and for teaching me."

"It was my honor," Harlow replied. "Now, let's get you changed. You can't very well attend your first mission briefing in this outfit only."

"Right."

The old inquisitor walked up to the left corner of the room and searched for a hole in the wall with her hand. Faith couldn't see what she was doing, but she soon heard the clanking of chains, followed by the sound of grinding stone. The skylight in the ceiling slowly slid shut, obscuring the sun like the moon during a solar eclipse. Once it was done, Harlow grabbed the gray cassock Faith had previously worn and led her outside of the Well House. "Maybe one day, you'll be the one to ordain a new inquisitor," Harlow said.

As her mentor pulled on the handles of the doors to close them, Faith looked one last time at the well and pondered the possibility. Would that be her new goal? To become grand inquisitor? She had been so focused on passing the Trial of Faith that she had never given serious thought to what she would do afterward. It was quite disconcerting. But as long as she followed the Kind Mother's will, everything would be fine. Of that Faith was certain.

# CHAPTER 7

THE GRAND INQUISITOR'S office was everything Faith had expected it to be.

Bookshelves packed full of theological memoirs, epistemological essays, and medical treatises lined the walls on her left and right. She recognized many of the titles from her training and briefly wondered how many of them were first editions—enough to make this one of the most valuable collections in the Azarian State at the very least.

Faith turned away from the books and parchments and examined the large wooden desk her mother used for work. Nothing cluttered its smooth surface, not even dust, and she spotted only a few faint stains of ink. As for the chair, it was well crafted but unadorned, just like the one Faith was sitting in.

The only thing she liked about this room was the view. Built into the wall on the other side of the desk were two windows that offered a view of Saint Lucretia's Park, a vast grass lawn where priestesses and inquisitors could stroll during their free time. Faith herself often sat in the shadow of one of the cherry trees and studied there instead of in the library. It was the best way, she had found, to avoid the acerbic gazes of her classmates.

She sighed to herself and began fiddling with her fingers;

it had been nearly ten minutes and Mother hadn't arrived yet. Something was holding her up, and if Faith had to guess what exactly, it was probably the "task" her mother alluded to earlier. Newly ordained inquisitors needed to gain experience before they could work on their own, so she fully expected to be assigned to one of the Inquisition's outposts across Kantner. If she was lucky, she would work in one of the major cities where heretics and Ophician spies were most likely to hide.

Just as Faith began to imagine herself chasing a shifty-looking man down a dark alleyway, the door opened and her mother entered the office. Gone was the light purple cape she'd worn during the trial, and her expression was as stern as ever.

Faith stood up from her chair and welcomed her superior with a slight bow. Karolina Dow ignored the salute and walked across the room, the sound of her shoes against the white marble floor the only thing to break the silence. Her presence had always been suffocating, and the wrinkles on her face and the few streaks of gray in her hair had only added to it over the years. Her mother circled around the desk, sat in her chair, and finally met her daughter's gaze.

"You can sit down," she said.

Faith cautiously lowered herself into her seat and put her hands on the armrests. For a moment, no one said anything, and the young inquisitor began to feel her stomach quiver.

"First," her mother continued, "I should congratulate you on your success. You are now an inquisitor."

Faith waited to see if she would say something else, but when she realized that wouldn't be the case, she nodded and replied, "Thank you, ma'am."

Another uncomfortable silence settled in. The grand inquisitor stared at her daughter and furrowed her brows, but only for a moment before she caught herself and relaxed her countenance. She momentarily cast her eyes downward and shifted her posture in her chair, and after a moment of consideration, she added, "Your father would be proud of you."

Faith almost jolted in her seat when she heard that. Her father wasn't a subject either of them often brought up. In fact, they never had, not since he died six years ago. But looking into her mother's soft gaze after hearing these words…she felt warmth radiate through her chest. Faith never realized just how much she'd wanted her mother to speak to her like this, not until now.

"Thank you, Mother," she said, her voice trembling with emotion. "I-I'm glad you think so."

The grand inquisitor continued to stare at Faith with a seemingly impassive expression on her face, and then, just for a fraction of a second, the corners of her mouth twitched into a small smile. If Faith hadn't seen it so clearly, she might have thought it was her imagination playing tricks on her. But it really happened. She suddenly felt the urge to hold her mother close in her arms, like she never had before.

Instead, she cleared her throat and chased the silly thought out of her mind. Childish fantasies would only distract her from responsibilities. Luckily for her, her mother changed the subject.

"I apologize for making you wait," she said. "I was seeing to the last arrangements I made for your mission."

"My…mission?" Faith repeated. "I don't understand."

"You are to find and apprehend a known sorcerer. Once you've captured him, you will bring him back to Holiburg so he can face the charges he's accused of."

Faith stared at the grand inquisitor with wide eyes. This had to be a mistake. "Mother…" she began hesitantly, "I-I can't do that. It's my first assignment."

"Yes. And were the circumstances any different, we'd instead assign you to a more experienced inquisitor. However…a new situation has arisen, one that demands unorthodox solutions."

"What do you mean?"

Karolina Dow sighed and leaned back in her chair. Whatever she was talking about, it was alarming enough to worry even her. "Scouts report that the Ophicians are mobilizing their forces," she continued. "By our last count, they have 120,000 men, two thousand golems, and five hundred sorcerers and witches, all marching on Faxe. If their invasion is successful, they will undoubtedly advance on the other realms."

Faith sat very still in her chair, her hands tightly gripped around the armrests. "And the other realms' response?" she asked. "Kantner, Lospes—"

"The Great Mother has already called for their aid," Karolina said. "And if their kings are true Azarians, they will answer the call—as we have."

"You're sending inquisitors to the front lines?"

"Of course. Without them to counter the foul sorcery of the Ophicians, we stand no chance."

Faith briefly held her breath. She knew what question she wanted to ask next, but she was afraid of the answer she would receive. Nevertheless, she had to ask. "Are you going too, Mother?"

The response came faster than Faith had anticipated. "No," Karolina said, matter-of-factly. "The Inquisition will need me here, more than ever. With so many of our inquisitors in Faxe, we'll be stretched thin everywhere else. Which is why we need *you* to track down this heretic."

This didn't reassure Faith in the least. "I don't know if I can face down a sorcerer. I—"

The grand inquisitor raised her hand to interrupt her daughter. "The Council and I wouldn't send you if we didn't believe you were ready for it. Besides, all the evidence indicates that the heretic in question has not received any sort of formal training. He's young and wild, which will make him all that much easier to capture."

"Wait—we already know his identity?"

Her mother nodded. "He now calls himself Kasper Acworth, but his real name is Kieran Fowler. Also known as the Pyromancer."

"I thought we purposefully avoided giving heretics monikers?"

"We do. It's the City Watch who started calling him that when he burned down the Lunaris orphanage."

Faith's mouth fell open at this revelation. Although she was but a child when it happened, she still remembered the long trail of black smoke rising above the city and the turmoil that followed when people learned that a teenage sorcerer was responsible for it. For the next few days, you couldn't go anywhere without seeing an inquisitor on a street corner, questioning and searching all who fit the description of the heretic who'd burned down the Lunaris orphanage. How he'd managed to escape the Inquisition's watchful eye remained a mystery.

"How can we be sure it's the same person?" she asked.

"We have a witness who confirmed his identity," the grand inquisitor said. She opened one of her drawers, pulled a leather folder out of it, and slid it across the desk. "Here's all the information we have about him. Use it well."

Faith peered at the file with hesitation. She knew there was no getting out of it, not after learning about the situation up north. All she could do was accept the mission and trust that God's plan would soon reveal itself to her. And yet...

"What about my knight?" she asked. "I haven't even had time to choose one yet."

"Don't worry," her mother said. "I've already handled that part."

Faith immediately stiffened. "What do you mean?"

"Because we don't have time to let you pick your own knight, I did it for you. It's only temporary, of course. You two will work together until you've brought Fowler back here, after which you'll decide whether or not you want to keep him as your partner. He's waiting for you just outside my office."

Faith gritted her teeth and began squeezing her knees hard—she should have seen this coming. The worst of it was that she knew that no matter what she said, her mother wouldn't listen to any of it. This was happening, one way or the other. "And who did you choose?" Faith asked with a measured tone.

A pregnant pause passed between them before the grand inquisitor answered. "Sir Aiden Hawkon, knight of the Purple Order and King Rowan's third son."

Faith scoffed despite herself. "Really, Mother? Kantner's royal family?"

"His heritage had no impact on my decision, Faith. Sir Aiden is a good man, and an even more capable knight. He's—"

"I'm not going to keep him as my knight."

Karolina frowned at the interruption. "That is your prerogative," she said. "But until then, you two will travel together."

Faith clenched her fists and bit the inside of her cheek to stop herself from saying something she might come to regret later. God knew she already would have had she been a few years younger. Instead, she fumed in silence and waited for her mother to speak again.

"I realize you do not approve of this decision," her mother continued. "But you will need a skilled knight to protect you on this mission, one who has fought a sorcerer before. And Sir Aiden is more than qualified for this task."

"Yes, I'm sure he is," Faith retorted. "But that's not the only reason you picked him, right?"

Karolina held her daughter's gaze, knowing exactly what she meant by that. "Correct," she admitted. "I also thought you might fancy him."

Yes, of course she did. Why else would the third prince of Kantner be paired with the grand inquisitor's only daughter? Faith could already imagine the amount of gossip it would generate at the royal court. Even with the threat of war looming, it would certainly become one of the nobles' main topics of conversation.

"I do not need your help looking for a husband."

"Duly noted," Karolina replied. "There is a stagecoach in front of the building ready to take you and Sir Aiden to Waterlone, the town where Fowler was last seen."

She didn't need to say anything else to let her daughter know that she was dismissed. For an instant, Faith considered ignoring her mother's command and telling her exactly what she thought about her "help," but one look at Karolina's green, piercing eyes dissuaded her. Instead, she stood up from her chair, picked up the leather folder from the desk, and walked to the door. Just before she put her hand on the doorknob, her mother stopped her. "Faith."

It would have been so easy to ignore her and just walk out. Maybe that would even make Karolina feel guilty. But no, Faith wasn't a child anymore, and she knew that if she did it, she'd be the one beating herself up over it. No inquisitor should ever act this way. So she did the only thing she could do: she took a deep breath and turned to face her mother again.

The grand inquisitor was now standing with a stern expression on her face. Only one word came out of her mouth. "Godspeed."

For the next few seconds, Faith simply stared at her mother, having no idea how to respond to that. She was leaving on a mission to find and capture a heretic while a war was brewing up north. To reply with a quick "thank you" seemed awfully inappropriate. And yet, these were the only words that came to her mind.

"Thank you, Mother," she said.

Her mother nodded. Faith opened the door and left to meet the knight.

The chamber outside the grand inquisitor's office was small and sparingly furnished. There were no paintings or decorations, only two windows that offered another view of Saint Lucretia's Park, and one low table with six chairs arranged around it. Sitting in one of the chairs was Sir Aiden Hawkon, the third prince of Kantner. As soon as Faith entered the room, he stood up, placed his right hand on his heart, and respectfully bowed to her. "Inquisitor Dow," he said. "It's a pleasure to meet you."

He raised his head, and his eyes widened in surprise when he saw Faith; she quickly understood why when his gaze lingered on her curves. Although she hadn't met many men these last few years, she knew the effect she had on them—and to her shame, she used to enjoy that kind of attention. Even now, she couldn't help but feel a certain warmth spread through her face. And then, she remembered the reason why her mother had chosen this man as her knight. One of the reasons, anyway. With that in mind, she furrowed her brows and stepped forward to greet the new knight.

He was a tall and broad-shouldered man who had physically trained his body for combat. The Inquisition demanded the same of its novitiates, but a woman's body had its limits—hence why each inquisitor paired herself with a knight. And looking at Sir Aiden and how muscular he was, she knew he would at the very least protect her adequately. He also wore the uniform that identified him as one of the witch hunters of the Purple Order: a long-sleeved white shirt worn under brown leather armor with shoulder pads; bracers and gloves of the same color on his wrists and hands; dark gray trousers that disappeared into thigh-high leather boots; and on the left side of his chest, a circular silver pin embossed with the Order's emblem—the iris flower.

At first glance, one would assume that this uniform didn't offer as much protection as full plate armor, but each piece of clothing worn by a Purple Order knight had been consecrated by Azarian Keepers, the guardians of the Church's most precious relics. Any man of God wearing them would receive additional protection, not only from physical attacks but also from magical ones. To complement it all was a sheathed longsword that Sir Hawkon carried on his belt, one that could cut through even the most powerful of spells, according to Faith's teachers. An indispensable weapon for a witch hunter like him.

"Sir Hawkon," she said. "Have you been waiting for long?"

"Not at all," he answered. "I arrived at the same time as the grand inquisitor."

"Good." Faith had no idea how to talk to him, or what about. It was not something her teachers had ever taught her, not even Harlow. It didn't help that he was also a handsome man; his square jaw, straight nose, and high cheekbones fit the idealized image most people had of knights. He also kept his black hair short and his face clean shaven, a habit the Order had surely instilled in him over the course of his apprenticeship. His round, amber eyes, however, were soft, warm even, and seemed more appropriate for a lad who hadn't seen much of the world than a hardened combatant.

"I hear congratulations are in order," he said. "From what I was told, you've been ordained quite recently."

"Today, actually," Faith answered, thankful that Sir Aiden had brought up a new subject of conversation. "Actually…that was only an hour ago."

His mouth fell open at this revelation. "Really?" he said. "I mean—my captain told me this assignment had been decided at the last minute, but I didn't realize how literal that was."

"You've just learned about this?"

"Yes. I've actually been on standby since last night, but my captain briefed me less than an hour ago."

"I see."

So, her mother had been planning this for less than a day. She'd probably contacted the Purple Order as soon as she received information about the heretic. Which also meant she had most likely expected Faith to pass the trial…

"Is something wrong?" Sir Aiden asked.

"No. No," the inquisitor answered. "I was just thinking about something else. We should get moving. My mother—I mean, Grand Inquisitor Dow—arranged a carriage for us. It's waiting outside."

The knight straightened his shoulders, put a hand on the hilt of his sword, and said, "Ready when you are, ma'am."

Faith glanced at him and already felt uneasy at the prospect of having him follow her everywhere she went. Just how long would they be traveling together? Weeks? Months? It all depended on where Kieran Fowler was at this moment and how much of a trail he'd left behind.

Faith clenched the leather folder against her chest and moved to leave with Sir Aiden in tow.

# CHAPTER 8

THE RAYS OF morning sunshine rose from below the horizon and immediately warmed Kieran's cheeks.

For the last half hour, he had been sitting against the trunk of the tree he had used as target practice yesterday. He had damaged quite a few arrows then and was now mending the last of them by replacing their feathering or reattaching the arrowheads with materials he had gathered from the forest. He'd done it so many times over the years that he didn't even need to pay attention to the movement of his hands, which was perfect because the only thing on his mind right now were the fairies he'd met yesterday.

All of his life, he had heard rumors and tales of fantastical creatures living in faraway lands, such as aefterfylgans, the elusive guardians of the forest, or gimlets, little monsters who creeped into the homes of peasants who had inadvertently disturbed their nests. Only a handful of those, like the golems from the Ophician Confederation or the bitrogs from the Strandkeit Kingdom, were proven to be real; everything else was fiction. Or so he thought.

How come no one ever found them? The one called Bubble said his brethren had rules, and avoiding humans was apparently one of them, but that didn't explain how they could have kept their existence a secret for so long. They should have attracted *someone's* attention at some point. Unless all the humans who did meet the fairies and told others about it were then severely punished by the Church. That might explain it. Otherwise, it meant that Kieran was the first human in history to meet a fairy, and that idea was simply ridiculous.

And then there was the one called "Nana."

The way Breeze talked about her, it sounded like she was a mother figure of sorts, a leader of the fairy community living in the forest—and she definitely knew more about the human world than she let on. He had no idea as to why she wouldn't tell the fairies about it, but whatever the reason, it was deliberate. Maybe she'd predicted fairies like Breeze would get upset over it. Maybe even planned on it.

Kieran lowered the broken arrow in his hands and looked back at the forest. Should he go and try to find Breeze? It wasn't like he was pressed for time, and he was curious to see how she was doing. The truth about the Church and the Inquisition seemed to have upset her quite a bit, and it didn't feel right leaving without at least checking up on her. Besides, talking to her helped him forget less pleasant things, such as what he planned to do once he arrived in Holiburg, an idea that had been hounding him for the last few months.

Remembering his goal, Kieran immediately turned away from the woods and returned his attention to the feathering of his arrow. How foolish of him—he had almost let himself daydream again. Getting involved in other people's business could only bring trouble. Even the fairies knew that. He should try to forget about them instead.

And yet, he couldn't help but recall her gleeful smile. Like a happy kid who'd discovered a new friend to play with. He'd rarely seen it before, and never directed at him. He'd been avoiding people for a long time now and spoke only when necessary. Maybe that's why Breeze's naive joviality felt so...refreshing.

Kieran looked back at the forest again. Was he overthinking this? Although he hadn't talked with the fairies for long, he doubted they would do anything to antagonize him. If he really wanted to meet them again, he only had to stand up, grab his gear, and walk into the woods.

There was one small problem: the other fairies. They weren't allowed to speak to humans, and he doubted Breeze and Bubble had informed them about his presence. Seeing a random human stroll onto their land would certainly cause a commotion, and he wasn't eager to find out how they would react. Especially since they were magically talented.

If the majority of them were like Breeze, they'd throw acorns and cones at him until he left. If they were more like Bubble: fireballs. Either way, they'd chase him out of the forest.

Just as Kieran tried to come up with an excuse to linger here for one more day, he caught something out of the corner of his eye. When he looked to his left, he saw three men marching toward him. He narrowed his eyes and saw farming tools in their hands. Judging by their drab woolen clothing and the way they glared at him, these were the farmers who owned this field.

He glanced at his bow, which he had placed against the trunk of another tree, four meters away. He still had time to pick it up if he wanted to, but it would only escalate the situation, and he'd rather avoid coming to blows over this. Instead, he put the broken arrow back into his quiver, stood up, and waited for the three farmers to arrive.

The one in the middle had streaks of gray in his hair. He was holding an old axe, which he probably used to remove stumps from his fields and chop down wood for the winter. The two young men at his sides had a clear resemblance with him—his sons, undoubtedly—and they carried pitchforks dirty with traces of manure. They all seemed eager to use their improvised weapons on him.

Kieran took a deep breath and braced himself for what was coming. He had to be very careful with what he'd say next, or this would take a turn for the worse.

"You enjoying your time here?" the father barked, his right hand so tightly gripped on the handle of his axe that his knuckles turned white. "You need anything else? Breakfast maybe?"

He stopped one meter away from Kieran while his sons moved forward to surround him. The one on the left, a dark-haired boy of no more than sixteen years, noticed the bow leaning against the tree. He frowned at the sight of it and, after stepping between the weapon and Kieran, said to his father, "He's a poacher. Come to steal the king's game."

"I'm no poacher," Kieran retorted. "I've got a permit for that bow. To defend myself from bandits."

"There are no bandits here," the older man said. "And I certainly don't remember giving *you* a permit to bivouac on my land. 'Cause that's where you were sleeping, right? Or were you dumb enough to enter the king's reserve too?"

"The reserve?" Kieran repeated.

"The forest, half-wit."

Kieran followed the man's gaze and looked at the forest behind him. So, this land belonged to the king of Kantner. Not a bad place for fairies to hide. The locals would never dare enter these woods, or God forbid, hunt the animals that dwelled in it. If they did, they'd run the risk of being thrown into a dungeon. Maybe worse.

Which meant Kieran couldn't tell these peasants about the materials he had gathered there to repair his arrows.

"No, I didn't," he answered confidently.

"Good. Then we can settle this between ourselves."

The other son, a broad-shouldered fellow with red hair who appeared to be a few years older than his brother, spit a huge wad of phlegm at Kieran's feet. Kieran ignored it and glanced at his quiver. He could easily scare them away without hurting any of them, but the risk of being discovered by the Inquisition was too high. He had to resolve this dispute without relying on his magic.

"Look, you're right," he told the farmers. "I shouldn't be here. I'll grab my stuff and leave immediately, okay?"

"Now hold on a minute." The father took one step forward and slightly raised his axe. "You come onto my land, stay here for God knows how long, and now you think you can just leave without paying reparations? No. I don't think so."

"Damn right," the redhead said.

Kieran looked between the three men, acutely aware of how precarious his situation was. They weren't killers, but they'd beat him half to death if he gave them a reason to. "I don't have much money," he said.

"No shit," the father scoffed. "As if I hadn't figured that already. But that's all right. We'll just keep that bow of yours."

He took another step forward and closed the remaining distance between himself and Kieran. The next time he spoke, the unpleasant hotness of his breath—mixed with the earthy, coarse smell of a farm—invaded Kieran's nostrils.

"Here's what you're going to do," the uncouth man said. "You're gonna leave and get your ass back to the road. 'Cause if you don't, me and the boys are gonna make damn sure that you do."

The sons moved closer together, ready to carry out their father's threat at a moment's notice. None of them seemed to realize that at this range, they wouldn't be able to use their weapons effectively; pitchforks were like spears, and they were standing right next to Kieran. They would never have the time to step back and strike him if he decided to attack first.

Kieran clenched his hands into fists and glared back at the farmer. It'd be so easy to kill him and both his sons if he wanted to. He only needed to lift a few arrows from his quiver and aim at their throats, and it'd all be over.

Instead, he tried to talk to them again.

"I need that bow," he said. "I've got a permit for it. It's in my—"

"Do you take me for a fool?" the farmer retorted. "There's no fucking way this permit is real, not when you lurk about my land! I'll tell you exactly what you are: a good-for-nothing thief who gets his hands on everything that's not tied down. I swear to God, if you don't scamper away right now, I'll knock some sense into you until you do!"

Kieran's hands began to shake uncontrollably, and for just an instant, he seriously considered punching the man in the face. "I can't," he said while gritting his teeth. "That bow was expensive, and—"

Before he could finish his sentence, the farmer pulled back his axe and hit him right in the stomach with the handle's end. Kieran fell to his knees, the pain radiating through his belly. He retched and heaved with each breath, his saliva trickling down his chin and landing somewhere on the ground below him.

*How stupid of me.* He should have expected this kind of attack. He'd tried to resolve this peacefully, but this stubborn, arrogant, righteous old fool just had to have it go his way.

"Now look at you," the farmer said. "You'll stay down if you know what's good for you. Derek? Go check his bag. I'm sure he has some contraband in there."

"On it, Pop," the younger son answered.

Kieran raised his head and watched the lad open his haversack and rummage through it before his gaze shifted to his quiver, which was still in the same spot as before. If everything else failed, he'd have no choice but to use his arrows.

"There's an old cloak under it," the teenage boy remarked. "There's not much inside the bag, though."

"What's in it?" his father asked.

"Some crispbread, a flask of water, a knife, a shirt, a scroll... There's also a figurine of some kind and—oh, here's the coins."

Kieran did his best to ignore the farmers and the dull pain in his stomach. He slowed down his breath and reached outward with his mind. He immediately felt the heavy but soothing presence of the magic all around him, blowing through his thoughts like the soft wind of spring. Taking care not to lose himself in its current, he stretched his will and amassed a gust of raw, unbridled power. It swelled within him at a rapid rate, threatening to rush outward and escape his grasp. He wrestled with the wild fragment of magic until he had exerted complete control over it.

"That scroll must be the permit he was talking about," the redhead said. "Should we show it to the alderman?"

"There's no need," the father replied. "I'm sure our freeloader has learned his lesson. Haven't you?"

Kieran nodded weakly while his mind stayed focused on the magic he had gathered. He compressed it on a single point, like he had done so many times before, and stopped only when it was ready to burst. The only thing left to do was to unleash it.

"Good," the man continued. "Derek, grab his bow and arrows. And give him back his bag."

"Yes, Pop."

After planting his pitchfork in a patch of dandelions, the youngest son did as he was told and walked toward Kieran with his belongings in hand. The boy had no idea what was about to happen. None of them did. Kieran slowly rose to his feet while holding his stomach and keeping his head down. The lad approached him without suspecting anything and tossed the haversack next to him.

"Take it and go," his father said.

"No," Kieran replied, raising his head to meet the man's gaze. "I'm not leaving without my bow."

The man frowned and prepared to strike him again; he briefly hesitated when he looked into Kieran's eyes, seeing something there. Something dangerous. And then an invisible, silent blast punched him in the face, and the farmer fell onto his back.

It all happened so fast, his sons couldn't understand what they had just witnessed. All they could do was watch their father collapse on the ground with blood gushing from his nose.

Kieran drew another gust of magic from the aether and set his eyes on the redhead. As expected, the oldest son turned to face him with fear in his eyes. He couldn't explain what had happened, but he instinctively knew where the attack had come from. He grabbed his pitchfork with both hands, intending to aim the pointy end of it at Kieran. At the same time, his brother cried out for their father. "Dad!"

Kieran unleashed another blast.

The redhead dropped the pitchfork and collapsed like his father, moaning in pain as he curled up on the ground and held a hand to his bloody face. He tried to hold on to his pitchfork, but Kieran kicked it away before he got another brilliant idea. The youngest son dropped the bow and quiver and yelped, too terrified to help. Kieran didn't pay attention to him; instead, he focused his attention on the father, who had recovered enough to raise himself onto his knees and elbows.

Kieran had no intention of letting him stand up.

He ran up to the man and kicked him in the gut, eliciting a cry of pain. Then he kicked him again. And again. And *again*. Wishing that with the next hit, he'd just stop squirming altogether.

"Stop! Please!"

Kieran whirled his head toward the source of that plea— the younger son. This pathetic excuse of a man was shaking in his boots. "We'll leave you alone!" he cried out. "Please! Don't hurt them!"

Kieran glared at the lad and, without even thinking, stomped toward him. The boy flinched and moved to flee in the opposite direction, but his foot tangled in the bowstring and he tumbled headfirst into the grass. He tried to crawl away on all fours, only to be grabbed by the collar and shoved onto his back. His lips trembled and tears were welling up in his eyes. Unable to defend himself, he whimpered like a child as Kieran put a foot against his throat and slowly began pressing on it.

"Not my boys!" Despite his injuries and the blood smeared on his face, the middle-aged man was attempting to stand up, only to fall to his knees in a pitiful manner. "Not them!" he croaked, clutching at his broken ribs with his right hand. "Take me instead! I'm the one you want!"

This gave Kieran pause; he suspected a trap of some kind. But then he looked at the result of what he had done: the redhead lying incapacitated on the ground, blood still gushing from his nose, while his brother continued to sob under Kieran's foot, a stain of piss growling larger on his trousers by the second.

They were beaten. Helpless.

"Take me," the father repeated. "Just…just let my boys go."

When Kieran heard that, he felt the sudden urge to crush the kid's throat right in front of his father—this man had tried to steal Kieran's bow with the help of his own sons. And now that the sons were suffering the consequences of his mistakes, he was begging him to spare them? *This fucking bastard.* If he really cared about keeping them out of harm's way, he shouldn't have brought them to a shakedown!

Kieran felt the lad wriggle under his foot. He looked down and saw the boy choking, his face turning beet red. He immediately got off the kid's throat and watched him struggle to catch his breath. The father let out an audible sigh of relief and would have probably run to his son's side had he been able to.

Looking at the sorry state of the three farmers, Kieran decided it was enough. For better or worse, they knew what he was capable of now, and from that point on, they'd do everything in their power to avoid him. The real problem was whether or not they'd report this incident to the Church. Sooner or later, they would surely be tempted to do so.

Kieran looked at his bow and pulled at it with his mind. To the father's astonishment, it rose up in the air and landed right into the sorcerer's hand. The same happened to the quiver, which he fastened to his belt. In one swift movement, he nocked an arrow and magically lifted two others in the air, aiming all three at the man who had attacked him.

The color drained from the farmer's face. Maybe he had hoped to receive only a beating for his mistakes. Or maybe he had already accepted his own death and was simply scared of facing it. Kieran didn't care either way.

"Take your stuff and go," he told the farmer. "And never tell anyone else about this."

The father hesitated for a moment. But when he saw the archer lower his bow and recall the floating arrows to his quiver, he knew that as long as he didn't push his luck, he would be safe. He slowly rose to his feet and stepped over to his younger son, who hadn't moved or said anything since Kieran let go of him.

"Derek? Are you all right?"

The boy simply whimpered.

"Come on, help me carry your brother."

"And don't forget your weapons," Kieran said.

The father didn't need to be told twice, and in a matter of seconds, they were all standing on their feet, fleeing back the way they'd come while glancing fearfully at the sorcerer who had so easily beaten them.

Kieran watched them go, his hands ready to nock another arrow if they attempted anything suspicious. Slowly but surely, the farmers shrank into the distance until they disappeared beyond a small hillock. Kieran looked down at his hands and noticed that they were trembling. In fact, his whole body was tense. Why?

After everything he had experienced in his life, everything he'd done, why couldn't he just shake this off? How pathetic.

Kieran walked back to the tree line, threw his bow and quiver to the ground, and plopped down at his previous spot. He held his head in hands, cursed under his breath, and sighed.

What a mess he had gotten himself into—again. He'd have to leave this place before the farmers informed their neighbors about him. Or even worse, the Church. For years, he had skirted the reach of the Inquisition, but always with someone's help. Now that he was alone, he had to be more careful than ever. Otherwise, the Inquisition would catch up to him before he even reached Holiburg.

Having regained a semblance of composure, Kieran let go of his head and looked at his bow. It would all be over soon. In a few more days, he'd arrive in Holiburg, find Karolina Dow, and then…the end. Maybe for her—if he didn't miss his shot—but definitely the end for him. He'd be surprised if the guards would even bother to take him alive. If that happened, the Inquisition would undoubtedly execute him in the same manner they did his mother. Maybe they'd use the same scaffold.

And yet, something else nagged at his mind. For months, he had imagined countless scenarios for how he would meet his end. That's where his thoughts always went to when he had a moment to himself. Only now, he thought of Breeze instead. Of the way she smiled at him when he'd asked her about her wings. Of how gracefully she fluttered through the air when something caught her attention.

Of how horrified she would have been, had she witnessed this scene.

Kieran shook his head and looked over his shoulder and into the woods. He would have liked to see her and her brother again. And maybe, with some convincing, they would have agreed to introduce him to the rest of their brethren. Sadly, he couldn't risk the Inquisition following his trail into the forest. His presence would only endanger the fairies.

He had to leave. Today.

# CHAPTER 9

BREEZE STOOD NEXT to Bubble's bed, watching him sleep with his favorite blanket tightly wrapped around him. He had such a peaceful expression on his face, one she rarely saw. Normally it would be him rousing her from sleep, not the other way around. But knowing they wouldn't see each other again for a few weeks, possibly months, she wanted to commit this image to memory.

The first rays of sunlight beamed through the window, announcing that a new day had come. The birds were already chirping their hearts out, a sign that the rest of the fairies would soon head to work. She didn't have much time left.

"Bubble? Wake up," she said, gently shaking his shoulder. "I need to talk to you."

Her brother groaned and hid his face under his blanket, unwilling to leave the comfort of his bed. Breeze shook his shoulder again. "Bubble!"

"What?" he grumbled. "It's my day off."

"I need to talk to you."

"Now? Can't we do this later?"

"I can't. It has to be now."

He sighed and rolled onto his back. "I wanna sleep."

"Please… I really need to talk to you."

Bubble turned his head toward her, clearly disconcerted by the tone of her voice. He lowered his blanket to peek at his sister and saw her wearing not only the usual fairy attire—a tunic and a pair of trousers made of animal skin—but also a shoulder bag stuffed with supplies.

The raven-haired fairy slowly rose from under the blanket and sat at the edge of his bed, now completely awake. Silence hung in the air for a long moment as Bubble examined his sister's gear with an incredulous expression. "What's this?" he asked.

"This is my travel bag," Breeze answered, avoiding her brother's gaze. This was turning out to be even harder than she'd thought it would be, but she had to tell him the truth, and she had to do it while looking him in the eyes; he deserved that much. After some more hesitation, she raised her head to meet his gaze again and finally said the words. "I'm leaving Dreamland."

Bubble stared at her with an expression of complete disbelief. She knew why: No fairy here had ever contemplated doing such a thing, let alone act on it. No one except Breeze. Her brother stood up from his bed and said, "What? What do you mean you're leaving?"

"I'm going to find Nana," she explained. "She said she was going somewhere east, so that's where I'll be going."

"East? Breeze, the—the world is *huge*. We don't know where she could have gone. It could take *years*."

"I know, Bubble, but I have to. Nana… Nana lied to us. She knew about the Inquisition, about how dangerous they were, and she didn't teach us how to protect ourselves from them. And we need to know why." She looked down at her feet as she felt her chest tighten and wondered: Did Nana feel the same way when she left Dreamland?

"Breeze, you can't," Bubble retorted. "There are too many humans outside the forest. What if they capture you?"

"I'll ask for Kieran's help," she answered. "He knows which humans to avoid and how to do it. If I ask him nicely—"

"No," her brother declared. "Go put your bag away. You're not leaving with him."

Breeze jerked back, caught off guard by the sudden change in attitude. Her brother went from worried to irritated in all but an instant, and the simple mention of Kieran's name appeared to be the sole reason for it.

"What? No," she protested. "I know Kieran will agree to help me. He's a good human. And if I'm careful—"

"I said NO!" Bubble almost shouted. "He's human, and you're not leaving with him! End of story!"

Breeze gaped at her brother and stood there motionless. He had never raised his voice like that before, and certainly not against her. She lowered her head and looked away for a second while a painful tightness crept up her throat, but then she remembered what Kieran had told them about the Church and the Inquisition, and what they might do to the fairies if they ever discovered them. And so she raised her head to confront Bubble again.

"No," she replied. "I'm leaving to find Nana."

Her brother glared at her. "No, you're not," he said. "There's no way you can convince me to let you go, so forget it. Take your bag and—"

"I'm not asking for your permission!"

Bubble blinked at his sister; he seemed stunned that she would yell back. He opened his mouth to say something, but nothing came out. Breeze noticed that her fists were shaking slightly, but she ignored it and stood her ground. Then finally, her brother spoke again. "Even if you leave, you're never going to find her."

"You don't know that," she said.

"Yes, I do. And you do too! What if she already moved on to somewhere else? What are you going to do then?!"

"I-I'll find her. I'll ask around and see if—"

"That's crazy, Breeze! You can't just randomly fly east and hope that you'll pick up her trail! The world is too big and we're too small!"

"That doesn't mean we shouldn't try! What if a human wanders into the forest?! What if they tell the Inquisition about us? We need to learn more about the outside world! We need to learn how to defend ourselves!"

"She's *gone*! Nana is gone! Forever!" Bubble's chest heaved with effort, his voice strained because of all the yelling. "The sooner you get it through your thick skull, the better it'll be. Now stop this nonsense and put that bag away!"

Breeze ground her teeth while looking directly into her brother's eyes. He didn't understand. He wasn't even trying to. He simply assumed that she hadn't thought about any of this, but she had. In fact, it was the only thing she'd had on her mind since yesterday. She wouldn't back down so easily.

"I'm leaving," she said with some difficulty, the lump in her throat more painful than before. "I'd like us to say goodbye before I do."

Bubble's mouth fell open, these words having dazed him as sure as a blow to the head would have. For a moment it seemed like he was going to resign himself and accept her decision. But instead, he closed his hands into fists and said, "Go ahead then. Leave. Go risk your life over nothing."

"Bubble, I—"

"I said GO!"

Breeze jolted when he yelled at her. She searched for his gaze, hoping that he actually didn't mean that, but he turned away from her and crossed his arms, hiding his face from her. Tears stung her eyes as a heavy weight settled in her chest. What had she done wrong? She thought that if she were honest, he would understand the importance of her mission. Or at the very least, that they'd hug each other one last time before she set out on this journey. But now he didn't even want to look at her.

Then her expression hardened and she felt the weight in her chest transform into a red-hot ball of anger. Before she realized what she was doing, she opened her mouth and let everything she had suppressed over the last few years come out all at once.

"FINE!" she yelled. "I'm not scared of the outside world like everyone else here! I'll go and find Nana, and when I'm back, you'll see that I was right!"

Bubble turned to look at her again, his face clenched into an expression of fury. "You stubborn—"

But he didn't get to finish his sentence. Breeze spun on her heels and stomped out of their house, slamming the door on her way out. She walked to the edge of the platform while wiping away a tear that had rolled down her cheek, immediately regretting what she'd said, but without slowing down.

There was no turning back. She spread her wings and jumped into the air without so much as a glance at the house where she and Bubble had lived together for years.

It was time she left Dreamland.

Back in the meadow, Kieran was shaving the last of his beard with his pocket knife, using a small mirror that he'd bought in Firstkin several years ago to peek around corners. He would have altered his appearance further by trimming his hair, but he didn't have the time, nor a good pair of scissors, to do it correctly. This would have to do for now.

Once he finished shaving, he put his knife in his pocket and ran his hand over the newfound smoothness of his skin; it would make it harder for the inquisitors to recognize him, but not by much. After all, not many young men traveled alone with a bow slung across their backs. On the other hand, no inquisitor would expect a sorcerer to walk *toward* Holiburg, the holiest of Azarian cities. As long as he was cautious, he should arrive there by the end of the week.

Kieran leaned his back against the trunk of the tree and watched the wind blow gently through the wildflowers of the meadow. This was a nice spot. He would have liked to stay a little longer here and relax, but the farmers might have already told the Church about their violent encounter with him. He had no choice but to depart immediately.

He stood up and secured the straps of his quiver to his waist while making sure he'd have easy access to the arrows on his hip, placed his haversack so it would hang on his left side, and then slung his bow across his back. Once he was ready, he peered at the forest one final time.

There were no fairies in sight. He waited there for a bit while scanning the undergrowth, searching for the colorful flutter of blue and red butterfly wings. After a minute, he started to feel like an idiot and shook his head; they were not coming back. It should have been obvious from the way they spoke about humans yesterday. Even if they did come to say goodbye, he couldn't wait for them all day. For all he knew, the local priestess had already spoken to the farmers and was now writing a letter to the nearest inquisitorial outpost.

Kieran turned away from the forest and walked eastward along the tree line, the opposite direction the father and his two sons came from. If he wasn't mistaken, there should be another country road on the other side of this field. He only needed to follow it and he'd eventually rejoin the main road, which would take him to Holiburg. Hopefully, the rest of his journey would be less eventful than this morning had been.

Two minutes later, just when he passed by a squirrel who scampered off into a tree at the sight of him, he heard someone call out.

"Kieran!"

Her voice was so faint, he would have assumed it was his imagination playing tricks on him had he not met her the day before. Kieran stopped and looked around, attempting without success to locate the blue-haired fairy. Only when she shouted his name again did he manage to spot her.

"Kieran! Wait!"

Breeze was zooming through the air at an impressive speed, having followed the path he had taken to get here. As she closed the distance, Kieran began to fear she would soon collide with his face, which while comical would most likely also be quite painful. Luckily for the both of them, she slowed down and came to a halt before him, a little out of breath.

"You all right?" Kieran asked.

"Yeah…" she answered, panting. "Just a little winded. Also, your beard is gone!"

"That's because I shaved it. Where's your brother? Is he coming too?" Kieran looked behind her to see if the red-winged fairy was on his way. When he realized that Bubble wasn't, his gaze returned to Breeze; she had fallen silent at the mention of her brother. Her eyes were also a little red. Had she been crying?

"He's not coming," she answered, her head hanging low. "Actually, he didn't want me to come at all."

"Why not?" he asked.

"Because… I've decided to leave Dreamland, our village. I want to learn how to defend it. I want to find our Nana. She's the one who woke us up thirteen years ago. I don't know where she is exactly, except that she went somewhere east."

Kieran gaped at the small teenage fairy, unsure how to respond. She had briefly mentioned this "Nana" during her outburst yesterday, but he'd assumed that Nana was still living with the rest of the fairies deep in the forest. To think she was somewhere out there… "Why did she leave?" he asked.

"She said she was going to wake up more fairies and that we might never see each other again."

"'Wake up'? What does that mean?"

"You know, to wake up someone who's sleeping— Wait, do humans not sleep at all?"

"No, no, we do. It's just, you make it sound like you weren't alive before that."

"Oh no, we weren't. Not like we are today anyway. Nana told us that before she woke us up, we were sleeping in magic and that she had to work really, *really* hard to bring us out of it."

Kieran narrowed his eyes at this revelation. From what he was hearing, the process of "waking up" fairies was a lot more complicated than what Nana had initially let on, and Breeze didn't seem to realize it. "It sounds a lot like she gave birth to you," he pointed out.

"Hmm?" Breeze cocked her head to the side and placed a finger on her lips. "Yeah, I guess you're right. I should ask her about it when I find her."

"Is that why you're here? To ask for my help?"

Her hands fell to her sides and she nodded. "Yes. I don't know anything about the human world or where to start searching for Nana, but you know a lot of things, right? Like where human cities are, and how to avoid the Inquisition?"

"I know a little, yes—"

"Great! So, will you help me? I won't be a bother, I promise! I can even hide in one of your pockets if need be."

Breeze looked at him with big, round eyes, hopeful that he would say yes. He had to tell her that the situation wasn't as simple as she believed.

"Look, Breeze," he said, "I want to help, but I can't have you tag along with me. Some farmers found me here less than an hour ago, and I had to chase them away with my magic. They know I'm a mage, and if they tell the Church about me, you'll be in danger too."

"Will they search the forest?" she asked.

"No, I don't think so. They'd search the roads for me."

"You think they're going to find you?"

"No, I don't, but—"

"Then it's fine! You've been avoiding the Inquisition people for a while now, right? If I stick with you, I can learn to do the same."

The fairy spoke with such optimism, it was difficult to tell her no. And in all honesty, he didn't want to. Maybe that was misguided of him, but it was the truth.

Kieran sighed and scratched the back of his head. "Look," he said, "I'm first going to a small town called Ballybridge, just north of here. You can travel with me until we get there, and then... we'll see how it goes. Sounds good?"

A wide smile spread on the fairy's face, and she immediately lunged at him with open arms to hug his neck. "Oh, thank you, thank you, thank you, thank you! You won't regret it! I promise!"

Kieran stiffened at her touch, suddenly feeling very uncomfortable, and stood still for several long seconds before he cleared his throat and said, "Yeah, yeah, don't worry about it. Just...stay out of sight, and we should be fine."

"Will do!" She let go of him and floated away to give him some space. "So, are we leaving right away?"

"Yeah, we should. Did you say goodbye to your...'friends'? I can wait a bit if you'd prefer."

She stared down at her moccasins and pondered the question for a while, until finally she shook her head. "No, there's no need to," she said. "It'd take too long to explain to them why I have to leave, and you can't stay long either, right?"

He briefly hesitated before giving his answer. "No, I can't. The Inquisition might already be on my trail."

"Then we leave."

Kieran considered inquiring more about what had happened

between her and Bubble, but from the way she dropped her chin to her chest, he knew it wasn't anything good. Best leave it be for now.

"All right. Do you have everything you need in there?" he asked, pointing at her shoulder bag.

"Yes," she said. "I also brought my winter clothes too, just in case."

"Good. Let's go then." He turned around and resumed walking alongside the tree line, only to realize after a few steps that Breeze wasn't following him but looking at the forest, a wistful expression on her face. Kieran stood still for an instant and then shuffled back to her side, mindful not to say anything that would disrupt this moment for her.

Finally, Breeze let out a sigh, turned to him, and said, "I'm ready."

"Are you sure?" he asked. "You can always go back."

"No, I can't," she said with the utmost certainty. "Not without talking to Nana first. She needs to explain herself."

Breeze's furrowed brow and resolute gaze left no room for doubt. Kieran readjusted the bow on his back and started walking again.

"Come on, then."

Without hesitation, she hovered next to him and landed on his right shoulder, holding on to his earlobe to keep her balance. He immediately stiffened at her touch but then relaxed when he reasoned that she was completely harmless. Breeze must have felt his discomfort because she leaned forward to look him in the eye and said, "I'm sorry, I should have asked. Is it okay if I stand here? At least until we've left the forest behind?"

Kieran noticed that her voice was much quieter than it was before. The only reason he could hear her now was because she was standing right next to his ear. How curious. Before, the only people he'd heard amplify their voice were Azarian priestesses.

It appeared that fairies possessed the magical equivalent of that power, which would explain why her scream had been so loud yesterday.

"Yeah," he replied. "You can even sit down if you want to."

"Thanks!" She took him up on his offer and made herself comfortable while still clinging to his earlobe. The small fairy then asked in a melodious tone, "So how long before we arrive in Ballybridge?"

Having already done a quick calculation of the distance that remained between Waterlone—the last major city he'd passed through—and Holiburg, Kieran gave an answer immediately. "By the end of the day if we keep a good pace."

"Really? Then let's hurry! I've always wanted to see a human city!" She flapped her legs up and down as if to make him go faster.

"Whoa, calm down. Just sit back and—I don't know—enjoy the scenery?"

"Oh, that's a good idea." She leaned forward and peered intently at the landscape of green hills and patches of forest surrounding them.

"With less intensity," he suggested.

"Hmm. I don't wanna miss anything, but I'll try."

Kieran grinned at the silliness of her comment and fixed his gaze on the horizon. Whatever the future held for the both of them, he had a feeling it would be quite memorable.

# CHAPTER 10

F AITH EXITED HER bedroom and closed the door behind her. After a full day of travel by coach, she and Aiden had stopped for the night at The Warm Pillow, one of the main inns on the road that connected Holiburg and Waterlone. The inn was also near the border that separated the Azarian State from the kingdom of Kantner, which meant that by the time the sun reached its zenith, she would have left the safety of her homeland and stepped into new territory.

She walked down the hallway and headed to the stairs while thinking about the journey ahead. In two more days, she and Aiden should arrive in Waterlone, the city where Kieran Fowler was last seen. From this point onward, the plan was simple: interrogate all the people Fowler had spoken to and investigate the places he'd frequented. With that information, she should be able to ascertain possible locations where he might be hiding and, if he had left the city already, where he might have gone.

As Faith reached the top of the stairs, she smelled a waft of freshly baked bread, cooked meat, and rich oatmeal coming from the first floor. Oh, how she longed to sit in the hall and enjoy a hearty breakfast like everyone else. However, time was short, and she had to depart immediately. No rest for the wicked, as her mother would say.

Faith was halfway down the stairs when she heard the approaching sound of laughter; it was two men talking about their business and all the profits they were going to make selling their products in Holiburg. They were so engrossed in their conversation that they didn't notice Faith until they were about to climb up the stairs.

When they did, they stopped dead in their tracks and looked at the red cincture wrapped around her waist. Keenly aware of what that color meant, they suddenly changed their demeanor, replaced their smiles and cheery laughs with the silent reverential expression one would usually wear in a church, and stepped away from the stairs and bowed their heads as she passed by them. They even went so far as to press themselves against the wall so she would have enough space to walk, unconcerned by the dust that might adhere to their fine clothes.

Unsure of how an inquisitor should conduct herself in the presence of merchants—her training covered the etiquettes of the nobility and the clergy only—Faith settled for a respectful nod and quickened her step toward the exit while doing her best to avoid their gazes.

*How did Mother ever get used to this kind of reverence?*

Once Faith was outside the inn, she searched the courtyard for the stagecoach that had brought her here yesterday. There were many other travelers spread across the courtyard and preparing for their own journeys. A few of them were workers of the merchant caravan that had stopped here yesterday and who were now taking inventory of their employers' goods; others were farmers on their way to the markets of Holiburg, where they periodically went to sell what they cultivated on their land; and then there were those who followed the capricious winds of opportunity, wherever it might take them: wanderers, immigrants, and mercenaries.

All went about their lives, unaware of the Ophician threat massing on Faxe's borders. Some of them might die in the upcoming conflict, she realized, and she felt a pang of sadness at the mere idea of these men never seeing their loved ones again.

As tragic as their fates might be, however, there was nothing she could do about it. For now, the best way to make a difference in this world was for her to accomplish the mission she had been entrusted with. God willing, it might give another the opportunity to do the same.

Faith refocused her attention on the present and searched for her transport. When she saw no sign of it, she walked across the beaten earth of the courtyard to check on the other side of the stable, where there were fewer people.

Many of the workers and travelers in the courtyard stopped what they were doing to gawk at her. No doubt most of them had never seen an inquisitor before, especially one as young and comely as she. Faith did her best to ignore their gazes and rounded the corner of the stable.

Finlay Pyresky, the attendant who had been assigned to drive Faith wherever her mission took her, was hitching the horses to the coach with Aiden's help. When she had met the gaunt, balding man yesterday, he hadn't left much of an impression on her. It was only after traveling the whole day with him that she started to suspect it might have been on purpose. An experienced assistant with an unassuming appearance like his wouldn't arouse suspicion on their journey, which was ideal for the mission they were on.

The driver cast her a glance when she approached the front of the coach but continued with his work. "Good morning, Inquisitor."

"Good morning, Mr. Pyresky," she replied before looking over at Aiden, who was hitching the two horses on the right side, opposite her and Finlay. "Good morning, Sir Hawkon."

"Good morning to you, ma'am," he answered with a nod.

"How soon before we are ready to leave?"

"We're almost finished here," Finlay said as he made one last inspection of the harnesses. "Was there any place you wanted to stop at on our way to Ballybridge, Inquisitor?"

"No," she answered. "Just take us there as fast as possible."

"As you wish. Sir Hawkon?"

"I'm all done."

"Then let us go." Without further ado, Finlay climbed up onto the driver's seat while Aiden approached from the other side to do the same. Faith was about to turn away and enter the coach, but she stopped herself at the last second when she remembered something she had been deliberating over since yesterday. Before Aiden could sit down next to Finlay, she peeked around the coach's body and said to him, "You may sit in the back with me if you prefer."

He looked at her with surprise and probably would have said something if she hadn't immediately opened the door and entered the coach. Hopefully, he wouldn't misinterpret this invitation as romantic interest on her part. He was smart enough to have figured out by now that she hadn't picked him as her knight, but that didn't mean there needed to be any kind of animosity between the two of them. She might as well try to befriend him. Besides, she could do worse for a traveling companion than a handsome knight who, up until now, had been the very model of a gentleman.

When she realized her thoughts were beginning to wander toward fantasies of him holding her in his strong arms, she shook her head and tried to think of something else. She couldn't let herself be distracted by impure thoughts.

Aiden opened the door and followed her into the stagecoach while holding the scabbard of his sword in his left hand. Once he was seated across Faith, he placed his weapon on the floor behind his feet and tried to make himself comfortable. If the frown on his face was any indication, he didn't sit in leather seats very often. Nor did she, but after spending a whole day in this box, she knew he would easily get used to it.

"Are we ready?" Finlay asked.

"Yes," she answered.

"Then here we go. Yah!"

Finlay spurred the horses forward and the whole carriage soon began to shake, gently at first, and then a little more vigorously when the horses gained speed. Faith looked out the window and watched the travelers and workers in the courtyard go about their business, right until they disappeared from view when her driver turned to the left and took the highway, leaving the inn behind. Now, all she saw were numerous grape fields that stretched across rolling hills, and far into the distance, low mountains covered with vast hardwood forests.

Faith marveled at this enchanting landscape, one she hadn't had the chance to see yet because of how late they'd arrived at the inn last night. Beyond these mountains lay Kantner. There, she would prove herself worthy of her new title by capturing Kieran Fowler, the man who'd burned down the orphanage that took him in.

"Is this your first time outside of Holiburg, ma'am?" Aiden asked.

The question interrupted Faith's thoughts, and she looked away from the window to meet the knight's gaze. "No, it's not," she answered. "Our instructors would sometimes take us to the countryside for field training, but...never outside the Azarian State."

"You've lived all of your life in the Holy Land then?"

"Yes. Born and raised here."

"I see." An uncomfortable silence settled between the two of them, and Faith began to fiddle with the cuff of her sleeve. Should she ask a question? It felt like Aiden was going to follow up with something else, but maybe he was just as clueless as she was when it came to making small talk. Luckily for her, Aiden did ask another question. "You're twenty-one years old, correct?"

Faith raised her eyebrows in surprise, hesitant to answer. "Yes?"

The young prince seemed to realize what he'd just asked and quickly replied, "I apologize, I didn't mean to be indiscreet. It's just… Well, we've heard rumors about you. About how young you were."

"Ah. So even the knights of your order know about that." She crossed her arms and legs, leaned back against her seat, and looked out the window again.

"Some of us, yes," Aiden said. "It is quite an achievement to become an inquisitor at such a young age. Your mother must be proud."

Faith watched the stone-paved road go by while she recalled yesterday's conversation with the grand inquisitor. "What about your mother?" she asked. "Is she proud of you for becoming a knight?"

Aiden's face twitched a little. "Queen Isobel isn't very… maternal with her children," he told her. "Nevertheless, she and King Rowan have approved my decision to join the Purple Order."

"I wasn't aware princes had a choice in the matter."

"You do, if you're third in line to the throne. The choices are limited, of course, but as long as I continue to honor the family name while staying away from the royal court, I am free to decide how I live. And since there's no greater purpose in life than to serve God and the Church, the choice was obvious."

He spoke about this so matter-of-factly that Faith couldn't help but wonder whether or not he had ever wavered in his belief. "Your piety does you great credit, Sir Hawkon."

"You're too kind, ma'am, but I don't hold a candle to you."

"I'm not so sure about that."

"I assure you it's true. I've heard about the trial of Elsa Yarwood and your involvement in it—you were only sixteen years old back then, and yet you helped bring this murderer to justice. *That* is true piety."

Faith clenched her jaw and clutched her arms when she heard that name. Elsa Yarwood. A rush of memories flooded into her mind, and she did her best to push back against them. She didn't want to remember the late-night conversations she'd had with Elsa in the dorms of the seminary, nor the many nicknames they came up with for the historical figures they read about in *Saints and Martyrs of the Azarian Church*. And most of all, she didn't want to remember the tears in Elsa's eyes when Inquisitor Karolina Dow pronounced her sentence.

Aiden must have noticed the shift in attitude because he straightened his posture and hastily said, "I apologize, ma'am. I shouldn't have brought it up."

"No, it's...fine," she replied. "And please, stop calling me 'ma'am.' At least when we're alone."

He paused to consider the request. "What should I call you?"

"Faith. Just Faith."

"As you wish, Faith. Please call me Aiden. May I ask you something else concerning our mission?"

"Go ahead," she said, welcoming the change of subject.

"Who is our target?" he asked. "I'd like to know more about them before we arrive in Waterlone."

"I thought you had already been briefed?"

"No, ma'am—uh, Faith. My captain only told me that I was to be assigned to an inquisitor by order of your mother, Grand Inquisitor Dow. She informed me of the nature of your mission but gave no specifics about it."

"Oh, I see." She uncrossed her legs and began searching the cabin for her bag. "Let me just grab the file. We'll go over the details and...ugh, where is it?"

"I put your bag in the compartment under your seat."

"Ah, thank you. Sorry, I can't believe I didn't even think to ask what you knew of the mission."

"It's my fault. I should have been clearer about it."

Faith placed the haversack on the empty seat next to her and pulled a leather folder out of it. She flipped it open, revealing a neat stack of sheets of paper that smelled like peppermint oil and charcoal, and started to read from it.

"The name of our target is Kieran Fowler, also known as the Pyromancer."

Aiden frowned when she said that nickname, as if already familiar with it. Faith glanced at him, expecting him to say something, but she continued on with her briefing when he didn't. "He was born in 1447 in the slums of Lower Gleapok, Holiburg. His father, Wyatt Fowler, was a mercenary who died the previous year fighting Valadorian raiders off the coast of Laastehalt. His mother, Amber Fowler, had no close family to speak of. She raised her son alone and earned a living by selling sexual favors at one of the Kusanoha's brothels."

"The Kusanoha?" Aiden repeated. "I wasn't aware the thin-eyes hired local whores."

Faith froze when she heard him use the racial slur, and she was somewhat startled by the harshness of his opinion. It was true that easterners who came to live in Holiburg often joined a criminal gang known as the Kusanoha, but it was only a handful of them. And to call Amber Fowler a whore, no matter how accurate the statement was, felt inappropriate for some reason. Not wanting to broach this subject, she fixed her gaze on the dossier and continued to read from it.

"She worked as a prostitute for four years, up until she became the apprentice of an old witch named Astaril. Together, they distributed contraceptive herbs to young women in Holiburg, performed abortions of unwanted pregnancies, and healed many patients with the power of blood magic. All done for the prospect of monetary gain."

Aiden wrinkled his nose in a look of disgust but said nothing to interrupt her. She kept on reading.

"In 1454, after an investigation that lasted seven months, Amber Fowler was arrested and subsequently found guilty of the crimes of witchcraft, heresy, apostasy, and infanticide. She was executed on the fourteenth of Solis on Saint Periphanes's Square by Inquisitor Karolina Dow."

Aiden stared incredulously at Faith when she revealed this fact. "Did your mother also lead the investigation?" he asked.

"Yes," she answered, remembering the many late nights her mother had spent away from home to work on this case. "She was made a judge soon after that."

"What about the other witch? Astaril?"

"Killed during her attempted arrest."

"So, Kieran Fowler's mother is the one who corrupted him with dark magic?"

"No. My mother examined the child and concluded that he had been spared this fate. Since he had no relatives to speak of, he was sent to the Lunaris orphanage to be raised by priestesses. But there were some…complications."

"Of what kind?"

Faith pressed her lips together, looked down at the file, and read one passage verbatim.

"'Despite the measures taken by the Inquisition to hide the child's parentage, the identity of his mother was revealed to the other orphans soon after his arrival. The children ostracized and persecuted Kieran Fowler over many years, hampering the priestesses' efforts to raise him into a faithful Azarian. In 1462, this culminated in an altercation between Fowler and six other orphans—Quintin Shields,

*Reuben Poole, Erich Weninger, Henry Webb, Kyle Munoz,
and Gwyndaf Purcell—who cornered him in the basement
to assault him. Fowler could not escape his assailants and
received a severe beating from them, which is when he made
a pact with a demon and gained the power to summon
hellish fire on his enemies. He retaliated by burning Quintin
Shields, the leader of the group, who stumbled across the
room in a panic and set the rest of the orphanage ablaze. The
other orphans fled the basement and warned the priestesses
of Fowler's deed, but by the time they had evacuated the
building, the sorcerer had already escaped.'"*

Faith's eyes lingered on the word *escaped* while she imagined
Kieran running away from the orphanage, trying to find a safe
place to hide. If only he had gone directly to the Church, maybe
he could have been spared this fate.

"The Inquisition never found him?" Aiden asked, a pensive
expression on his face.

"No, they didn't," she answered while flipping to another page.
"The Inquisition launched a manhunt for him that lasted three
weeks and spanned three realms, but all they learned was that he
was last seen on Ivy Lane, heading east. The inquisitors came to the
conclusion that by the time the City Watch and the Inquisition had
fully mobilized their forces, Fowler had already left Holiburg. The
only other explanation for his disappearance is that he had help
from somebody who hid him somewhere in the city."

"Help from who?"

"This report suggests it could have been an Ophician agent.
The Ophicians have apparently been stepping up their foreign
activities in the last twenty years."

"The Ophicians." The knight's gaze grew sharper at the
mention of these heathens. "I assume you've heard the news
about them?"

"Yes. They're marching on Faxe."

"Then Kieran Fowler could be one of their agents, sent to spy on the movements of enemy forces, maybe even sabotage the defenses of Azarian cities."

"That's possible but unlikely," Faith said while lowering the folder. "Aren't you familiar with the methods of infiltration the Ophicians use? My mother said you had faced other sorcerers and witches before."

"I never took part in the investigations myself," Aiden replied, "only the arrests."

"Ah. Well, there are two types of Ophician agents: those who settle in one place and go undercover using one alias, and those who travel between cities and use a multitude of them. Kieran Fowler is a wanderer who uses the same alias wherever he goes—Kasper Acworth."

"And I assume this name first popped up after the fire at Lunaris?"

"Yes. Three years later." Faith raised the folder again. "Sometimes in 1465 or 1466, Kasper Acworth started working as an enforcer and hired killer for the Kusanoha in Holiburg. A year later, he moved eastward into Kantner and hired himself out to whoever needed his services." Faith flipped to another page. "The Knives in Firstkin, the Black Wolves in Mistyhill, the Iversen Brothers in Redfield…the list goes on. The timeline we have for this period of his life is spotty at best. The inquisitor who investigated him had to rely on, and I quote, 'the poor memory of information brokers and the dubious honesty of the criminals who collaborated with the sorcerer.'"

"This doesn't inspire much confidence. How can we be sure this Acworth truly is Kieran Fowler?"

"Because someone identified him. Six days ago, a crime lord in Waterlone hired him to 'repossess' the goods of a local merchant who failed to pay back a debt. One of this merchant's employees was Henry Webb."

"Henry Webb?" Aiden repeated in disbelief. "The same Webb who bullied him back at the orphanage?"

"Yes. He has been living in Waterlone since 1466 and began working for the merchant in 1470. Even though they hadn't seen each other for years at this point, Webb recognized Fowler almost immediately. When Fowler realized his cover was blown, he left the shop and disappeared into the crowd. Here's the description we have of him."

She handed Aiden a sheet of paper so he could read the description for himself.

"He has a bow," he pointed out. "In Kantner, you need a permit signed by the local Hunt Master to carry one."

"The authorities in Waterlone already checked for a permit filed under the name Kasper Acworth," she revealed. "They found nothing. If Fowler has one, either it's a forgery, or it was filed under another name."

"I thought you said he only used one alias?"

"When dealing with his contacts, yes."

"Mm-hmm. I assume the constabularies of the cities and villages around Waterlone have already been warned about Fowler?"

"Yes. As well as all the priestesses and inquisitors posted in Kantner."

Aiden sighed and handed the sheet of paper back to Faith. "Do we have any idea where he might be?"

"No," she answered, shaking her head. "The Inquisition believes he has left Waterlone and is now lying low somewhere else. It's our job to track him down, capture him, and bring him back to Holiburg."

"Very well then. What is the plan?"

Faith had pondered the same question all day yesterday, wondering where to start first. Although the numerous lessons she had received at the abbey prescribed one particular course of action for this situation, Harlow had also taught her that theory was sometimes insufficient when dealing with the unpredictability of reality. One mistake and Fowler could disappear again, free to roam the land and hurt any poor soul unlucky enough to stand in his way.

She closed the folder and placed it in her bag again.

"First, we question every person in Waterlone who spoke to Fowler, starting with Henry Webb. We find out how long he stayed in the city, what he did while he was there, and where he was planning to go next. We'll need to identify his friends and allies too, if he has any. One of them might have helped him leave the city."

"Who would be foolish enough to help a sorcerer?"

"Someone who didn't know who he was or didn't care. In any case, once we have a lead, we'll pursue it until we find Fowler, wherever he is. That is our plan."

"Understood, ma'am." She gave him a pointed look and he quickly added, "Um, Faith. I meant Faith."

The corner of her mouth curled up into a smile, which she hid from him by looking outside the window, fixing her gaze on the mountains protruding into the horizon. It would certainly take some time before he'd get used to her name.

She then remembered one question she'd meant to ask Aiden yesterday. It concerned one of his most crucial tasks as her knight, a tradition as old as the Inquisition itself. "Before I forget again," she said, "do you have the handcuffs with you?"

"Ah, yes," he answered. "I've left them in their box since I received them."

"Where are they?"

"Right under my seat."

"Please take them out. From now on, you'll be carrying them on you at all times."

"Understood." The wooden box he brought out of the compartment was small enough to fit in a bag, and to the untrained eye, resembled a casket used to hold jewelry. The symbol of Alma Azaria—a seven-pointed star enclosed by a circle—had been engraved on the top of it. Aiden opened the box and pulled out two pairs of iron handcuffs. "There are also two keys that come with it," he told her.

"Do they work for both pairs?"

"They do. I tested them yesterday."

Faith took one of the keys and placed it in the inner pocket of her cassock, the one above her left breast. Then the coach unexpectedly began to slow down.

"Whoa!" Finlay exclaimed as he reined in the horses. The landscape outside the window abruptly came to a halt, and the sound of the wheels turning on the stone-paved road was now replaced by the cry of cicadas and, surprisingly enough, the bleating of sheep.

"There must be a flock crossing the road," Aiden said as he attached the handcuffs to his belt.

Faith leaned against the window and caught a glimpse of said flock. They didn't appear to be moving.

"Is something wrong?" Finlay shouted, most likely addressing the shepherd leading these sheep. A short response, which she couldn't hear, followed his question.

"What did they say?" Aiden asked.

"One of their sheep is hurt," the driver answered.

She and Aiden exchanged a glance, puzzled by how this had happened, and the prince stepped out of the coach to see the injured animal for himself. "I'll take care of it," he said.

Faith watched him close the door behind him and walk to the front of the coach. She pondered for a moment whether or not she should follow him, right until she remembered what Finlay had said about the sheep. If anyone could do something about it, it was her.

She opened the door and followed Aiden.

A cool breeze was blowing through the fields of grass flanking the highway, heralding the end of summer. Up ahead, she could see the sheep, at least a hundred of them, bleating and shuffling about. The shepherd was standing in the middle of the flock and telling his son, a young man of maybe fourteen years, to herd them into the field and away from the road.

At the urging of the lad and his sheepdog, the sheep scurried away and revealed the reason for this unexpected stop: a lamb who had broken its leg and was now lying down on the stone pavement.

The shepherd kneeled down next to it and placed a comforting hand on its neck in an effort to calm it down. He looked up at Aiden to say something to him when he noticed Faith and the red cincture around her waist, and he openly stared at her, clearly at a loss for how to act in her presence. Aiden followed his gaze and raised his eyebrows in surprise when he realized that Faith had decided to accompany him, but he quickly shifted his attention back to the shepherd and asked him the obvious question.

"What happened?"

The man jerked his head back toward the knight and glanced a few more times at the approaching inquisitor before saying, "The sheep's leg got stuck between two stones, milord."

Faith winced when she got a better look at the blood. The poor creature was hurting so much, it didn't even try to stand up on its other legs. All it could do was stay on the pavement and whimper in pain. An older sheep, probably its mother, was standing by its side, licking its face to calm it down.

"When did it happen?" she asked.

The man jolted at the sound of her voice, which was not quite the reaction she was hoping for. The role of the Inquisition was to protect humanity from the evil forces of this world, not punish them for every little sin they committed. This man had clearly never met an inquisitor before or he would have known there was no reason to fear her questions.

"Answer the inquisitor," Aiden demanded in a firm tone.

*Up until now*, she thought.

The shepherd licked his lips and said, "Just before you arrived, ma'am. I-I think another sheep pushed it from behind while its leg was stuck."

"So it's only been a few minutes," she muttered to herself. She stared at the whimpering lamb for a moment and mulled over the various difficulties of healing an animal. Its anatomy was completely different from a human's, but the basics should still be the same. The very least she could do was try.

Faith kneeled down next to the whimpering sheep, garnering curious glances from both the shepherd and her knight. She did her best to ignore them and focused her attention on the broken leg. Joining her hands together, she placed them right above the fractured bone while she recalled the first verse of the Prayer of Healing.

And then, she spoke the words.

"O Kind Mother, shine your divine light through me, for your children plead for your mercy."

Faith felt a familiar presence emerge at the edge of her consciousness, a soothing wave of clarity that washed over her and revealed what her eyes couldn't see: the anatomy of the animal lying before her. She could picture in her mind every muscle, blood vessel, and tendon that surrounded the broken bone and formed the sheep's leg.

With practiced ease, she summoned the divine energy granted to her by the Kind Mother and directed it into the broken limb, which numbed the pain and provided some respite to the creature.

"Let the harmony of the heavens heal the wounds of this earth," she continued, "and guide the souls of the lost back to the embrace of rebirth."

Faith focused the invisible energy into the broken bone and mended it back to its original shape. Then, she accelerated the healing process of the lamb's body and restored every artery, vein, and tendon that had been damaged by the fall. It was slow and tedious work that required great concentration to perform, which was exactly what she had trained for over the last six years.

While she finished mending the broken leg, she uttered the last verse of the prayer. "For in death we remember your words, and in life we bow to your grandeur."

The faint but familiar presence lingering at the back of her mind withdrew. The lamb raised its head and tentatively moved its leg, realizing that the pain was now completely gone. It slowly stood up and then bleated happily at her, even rubbing its head against her chest to thank her for the relief she'd given.

Faith smiled and petted the young animal between the ears, its mother nestling against it.

"Thank you," the shepherd said, bowing his head very low. "Thank you so much! I will never forget what you've done. I don't know how I can repay you."

"Thank the Kind Mother," she replied. "It's by her grace that I could help you."

"Of course, yes, I will, but…you still stopped to help us, right?"

Faith hesitated for a second before she nodded. "That's correct."

"Then I still should thank you, Inquisitor…?"

"Dow. Faith Dow."

"Thank you very much, Inquisitor Dow. I will pray for you. You can be sure of it."

He placed his hands on the ground and bowed his head low to her, making her feel very uncomfortable. Ever though she had healed her first patient many years ago, she never got used to the gratitude of the people and how they expressed it to her, and although she had learned to accept it in the name of the Kind Mother, she hadn't been able to shake off the feeling it was undeserved.

She gently grabbed his arm and helped him to his feet. "Please," she said. "There's no need for that."

The shepherd looked up at her with wide eyes, as if amazed that an inquisitor would deign to touch him. He obediently stood up and waited for her to speak, too dumbstruck to do anything else. Luckily for him, Faith knew exactly what to say in these types of situations.

"What's your name?" she asked.

"It's, um, Lucas. Lucas Reid."

"What about your son? That is your son over there, right?"

"Yes," he answered, a little more relaxed. "His name is Ethan."

"Ethan," she repeated, sounding out the word. "That's a good name." She watched the young man and his dog patrol the perimeter around the flock of sheep. Their gazes met for a second, and he quickly averted his eyes, surely intimidated by the fact that she was an inquisitor—or maybe that she was a young woman.

She turned to face the shepherd again. "It's nice to meet you, Lucas. I would like to look after your lamb a little while longer, but my knight and I must take our leave now. We have urgent matters to attend to."

"Oh, of course! I'm sorry for the delay, Inquisitor. I'll get right out of your way." The man nudged the lamb and its mother toward the other sheep and hastily got off the road to join his son.

Faith turned to face Aiden, who for the last few minutes had stood immobile behind her with a hand resting on the hilt of his sword, ready to defend her if the need arose. He was looking at her bright-eyed, his lips parted in amazement. "I didn't know it was possible to heal animals," he said. "The Scriptures mentioned nothing of the sort."

Faith pressed her lips together and pondered how best to answer that question. He was right about the Scriptures making no mention of it, and yet it was an undeniable truth that God had allowed her to heal this lamb just like she would a human. She had already been aware of this discrepancy in the Church's dogma but never experienced it herself. And now, she had to explain it to someone older and more experienced than her.

"It's something I've learned from one of my teachers," she told him. "I researched the subject and learned of various instances where priestesses would successfully heal various kinds of animals—horses who got injured in battle, or cattle that got sick on a farm."

"Really? But... I've heard nothing of the sort before."

"Probably because unlike our prophet, Alma Azaria, there is a finite number of miracles we priestesses and inquisitors can perform before we need to rest. We *have* to focus on healing people, not animals. If we didn't, innocents might die."

"I see." He stared at her with a pensive expression on his face. "Thank you for explaining this to me. It was very enlightening."

Aiden's quick acceptance of her explanation caught her off guard. When she'd asked the same thing of Harlow a year ago, she had found this answer both unsatisfying and insufficient, but like her old mentor often told her, God worked in mysterious ways.

"We should go," she said to the knight.

"Right behind you, ma'am," he replied.

They returned to the carriage and Finlay spurred the horses forward, resuming their journey to Waterlone. Faith looked outside the window again and watched the flock of sheep shrink into the distance. She thought about the lamb walking among them, free of all pain, and the corners of her lips curled into a small smile.

# CHAPTER 11

KIERAN LOOKED UP to the sky and noticed that the sun had already begun its descent toward the horizon. He studied the length of his own shadow and estimated that he had three or four hours of daylight left, which meant he must have been walking for almost…eight hours now? Yes, eight hours of answering the questions of an overly enthusiastic fairy who wanted to know everything about humans and their society, and no matter how many questions she asked, she always managed to come up with a new one.

"So, humans use different types of streets?" she asked.

Breeze was hovering right beside him, seemingly unbothered by the soft wind blowing through the vale. The idyllic scenery they were passing through would have been ideal for a landscape painting: a narrow river wounding at the bottom of a verdant valley, flanked on both sides by farmhouses and barns, with a stone-paved road older than Kantner itself running alongside its right bank. Good thing there was no one else on the road, or Breeze would have had to hide in his hood again and ask her questions from there, and that just felt awkward.

"Yes," Kieran answered. "First, there are the back alleys,

which are narrow, shady-looking streets. Try to avoid those, if possible. You never know what kind of people are lurking there."

"Like bad people?" Breeze asked.

"Sometimes, yes."

"I will avoid all shady-looking streets!"

"Good. Then there are the highways, like the one we're walking on right now—well, I'm the one walking on it. I guess it's not really a street either. More like a road."

"And they're all made with blocks of stones?"

"*Slabs* of stones. And yes, highways usually are. That's how the Aurelians built them, anyway."

"Aurelians? What are those?"

"They're people. They lived in the Aurelian Empire a long time ago."

"What's an empire?"

"An empire is like…a *really* big country. Many realms that exist today—like Kantner—were once part of it."

"Wow! Really?"

"Yes."

"But that'd make it super *huge*… Even for humans!"

"You're right. That's why the empire was divided between four God Emperors—very powerful mages who were in charge of everything. There was Kristel Sirel, the Empress of Sight; Adelheid Welf, the Empress of Creation; Waldemar Serafim, the Emperor of Control; and Victorius Polus, the Emperor of Destruction."

"You remember all of their names?"

"Yeah. The man who took me in taught me all about them." As he said it, Kieran realized it had been years since he last saw this man, which was probably for the best.

"Besides," he remarked, "didn't you say you lived with three hundred other fairies in the forest? You remember all of their names, no?"

"Two hundred and ninety-nine! And yes, I do, but they're my

brothers and sisters, so it's different. You can't forget the names of your own siblings."

"Wait—they're your brothers and sisters? *All* of them?"

"Yes, of course! Nana woke us up all at the same time, after all."

Kieran stopped dead in his tracks and gawked at his small companion while new questions popped into his mind: What kind of creature was she exactly? How did she and her siblings come into being? And who exactly was this Nana she kept talking about? The more he learned about Breeze and her people, the more confused he became.

"Are you all right?" the blue fairy asked, her head tilted to the side.

"Yeah," he answered. "It's just… Breeze, can you tell me something? About Nana?"

"Sure I can! What do you wanna know?"

"Well, first of all, is she a fairy too?"

"A fairy? Of course she is. Only fairies are allowed in Dreamland. And owls, and crows, and squirrels, and deer…"

"But not humans."

"Nope! But maybe you could come visit one day."

"And how old is your Nana?"

"Hmm…" Breeze placed a finger on her lips and pondered the question for a moment. "I remember her saying that she was the oldest of all fairies," she said. "Does that help?"

"I'm not sure." Kieran started walking again and Breeze followed him closely. "It could mean a lot of things, but from what I gathered, Nana visited the human world before, right?"

"Yes, she did. She didn't tell us much about it, though, except that humans were dangerous and that it's often hard to tell who the good ones are."

Kieran suddenly felt exposed when Breeze said that, and he

did his best to keep a straight face while he changed the subject. "All you know is that she went somewhere east, correct?"

"Yes."

"That doesn't exactly narrow it down, but I might have an idea on how to find her."

"Really?"

"Yeah, but I'll need some more time to think about it. And if I'm right, that means we would have to head east and go to Firstkin once we're done in Ballybridge."

"What's Firstkin?"

"Kantner's capital city. That's where the king lives."

Breeze passed by Kieran and stopped right in front of him, her eyes full of hope. "Does that mean you'll help me find my Nana?" she asked, her hands clasped together.

The sorcerer gazed at her and bit the inside of his cheek. He *had* implied this morning that he would consider joining her on this quest of hers, but he hadn't thought he'd have to make his decision before reaching Ballybridge. And did she have to make those puppy eyes at him? After spending a whole day with her, he strongly doubted she had an iota of slyness in her, but after years of working for the ill reputed of this world, he couldn't help but wonder.

Kieran hung his head and sighed. No, she was nothing like all those people he'd dealt with before. In fact, she had proven herself to be the most honest and spirited person he had met in his entire life.

"Yeah, sure," he finally said, defeated. "I'll help you find her."

"Yippee!" Breeze threw her fists in the air and twirled around like a spinning top. When she stopped, she swirled back toward him with a smile on her face. "Oh, thank you, thank you, thank you!" she said. "I knew traveling with you was the right decision. I just knew it!"

"That makes one of us. Are you sure you want my help,

though? If the Inquisition ever learns where I am, they'll send someone after me, and you might get into trouble too."

"Yes, I'm sure. It's because you're a mage that I wanted to travel with you. You know how to avoid the Inquisition and stuff, and you already taught me so much about the human world! You're the best companion I could have asked for."

Kieran, unused to compliments, winced and cleared his throat. "Well, I'm glad to hear that. But if it's advice about the Inquisition that you want, then there's something you should know."

Breeze leaned forward and listened attentively to what he was going to say next.

"Don't tell anyone about Dreamland or where to find it. Even those who are nice to you. Understood?"

"Huh? But what if they promise they'll never tell anyone else about it? Wouldn't it be fine then?"

"No, it wouldn't. Listen, Breeze, your Nana might have not told you everything, but she was definitely right about humans being dangerous. I've seen some people tell bold-faced lies to their friends with a smile on their face. You can't trust anyone with your secret, and even if you could, someone else might try to make them talk."

"'Make them talk'?" she repeated.

"Hurt them. *Torture* them. That sort of stuff happens out there in the human world, Breeze, and there are people who wouldn't hesitate to do it if it meant they could learn more about you and where you come from."

The fairy's mouth fell open and she stared at him with wide eyes, unable to say anything. It was obvious she had never conceptualized the cold, harsh reality of human cruelty before, but from now on, she would have to, or this world would swallow her whole and spit her back out like she was nothing.

"Do you understand?" he asked.

"Y-yeah," she answered. "I understand."

"Good. Now let's keep walking—we're losing daylight."

"Okay…but what about you, Kieran? Are you going to be all right?"

"What do you mean?"

His companion clasped her hands together in worry. "You said some humans might do bad things to learn more about me and Dreamland, so…what if they try to hurt you? Are you in danger now because of me?"

It was true that traveling with a fairy would put an even bigger target on his back if the Inquisition ever discovered her existence. However…

"I'm already living a dangerous life, Breeze," he told her in a well-rehearsed, matter-of-fact tone. "I'm a sorcerer. If the Inquisition ever captures me, I'm dead, no question about it. So don't get your knickers in a twist. I'm not in any more danger traveling with you than I am alone."

He was lying about that last part, but she didn't need to know that. He only wanted to reassure her, and judging by the sigh of relief she let out, she believed him. But then her shoulders drooped and she looked down at the slabs of stone passing by under her.

"That's…sad," she said somberly. "I'm sorry. I didn't realize how hard your life was."

"Don't be. You didn't know."

"Maybe, but after everything you told me, I should have guessed. I just can't understand why humans hate magic so much."

Kieran fell silent and recalled everything he had been taught about sorcerers and witches, not only from the priestesses at the Lunaris orphanage but also from the man who took him in after his awakening. Breeze needed to know about it, or she would never understand why so many humans viewed magic this way.

"Remember what I told you about the four God Emperors?" he asked her.

"Um, yeah? I don't remember their names, but..."

"Their names aren't all that important. What's important is what they did—they used their magic to become immortal, and they conquered a large chunk of the continent. They created the Aurelian Empire. If you were a mage like me, you could either work for them or flee somewhere else. If you weren't a mage, well...I guess you would get the same choice, but your life would be even harder."

Breeze tilted her head to the side. "Sounds like they were bad people," she said.

"Maybe. It was a long time ago, so we don't really know. The Church says they were false gods, humans who had been possessed by 'evil demons intent on enslaving us all'—even though we still use their damn roads." He gestured at the stone-paved highway. "Their mages came up with the aqueducts, the public baths, the sewers, even the calendar we use. Hell, the Scriptures were first written in the Aurelian language."

"Were they good people then?" the fairy asked, confused.

Kieran sighed. "No, Breeze. They were a mix of good and bad. We usually are more of one than the other, but rarely just one thing. Not like you."

She lowered her head, and her wings flapped a little slower than before. "I do bad things sometimes too."

"I'm sure you do, but I doubt it's anywhere as bad as what the God Emperors did."

"What did they do?"

"They—" Kieran stopped to try and find the words. He'd never had the chance to retell these events before, and he didn't want to screw it up. Not to her. "They destroyed a whole city," he finally said. "And when I say 'destroy,' I mean completely. When they were finished, there was only a crater left behind and nothing else."

"A city?" Breeze repeated. "What happened to the people?"

"They all died. Thousands of them."

The fairy cupped her hands over her mouth and gasped. "That's horrible! Why would they do that?"

"Because they were at war," he explained. "And to win the war, they destroyed the place where their enemies lived."

"But...but that's *horrible*."

"Yes, and that's not all."

Breeze lowered her hands and braced herself for what he would tell her next.

"There must have been some kind of disagreement about the destruction of the city, because a few days later, the God Emperors returned home and fought each other in the skies above Aurelia, the Empire's capital. Their spells rebounded against each other and landed on the city, killing thousands of their own people this time. When the battle finally stopped, the God Emperors were gone and the Aurelian mages started to fight among themselves to decide who would replace them. The Empire collapsed quickly after that."

"So that's why humans hate magic so much."

"One of the reasons, anyway."

"But there's something I don't understand. You called them 'God Emperors' even though they were humans?"

"Yes."

"Then what's the difference with that other god? The one the Church likes?"

This question stumped Kieran, and his immediate reaction was to stare at the fairy, unable to respond. The difference between the two had always seemed so obvious to him, but he had never articulated the idea before. How exactly was he supposed to do that now?

He took a few seconds to reflect on this problem, remembering everything he had been taught about God and the Aurelian Emperors, and then gave a tentative answer. "Well, like I said," he began, "the Emperors were humans, while God isn't."

"Then why would they be called gods?"

"Because they were powerful. So powerful they even discovered the secret to immortality—that's the story people like to tell anyway. Maybe they only discovered the secret to a very long life and they killed each other before we could find out how long that really was. Point is, God, the Church's God, isn't human—"

"—she's everywhere and she sees everything?"

"Something like that, yeah."

"Hmm. Then how do we know she exists?"

*What a great question*, Kieran thought, a grin forming on his face. An overzealous priestess might even call it blasphemous. Unfortunately for him, the existence of God was an irrefutable fact that could not be denied. "Remember when I said God shared her power with the priestesses of the Church?" he asked the fairy.

"I think so?" Breeze said uncertainly.

"That's how we know. Without God, the priestesses wouldn't be able to perform miracles...or catch people like me."

"What? But you're not a bad person!" Breeze protested. "You helped me out so much!"

"It's like I told you," he said, meeting her gaze. "We're a mix of good and bad."

"Hmph!" She scowled and turned away to look at the road. "Then the Church is wrong. I know you're a good person, even if they don't, and if they try to catch you or something, I'll give them a piece of my own mind! Like this: Yah! Ah ah! Foosh!"

She started to attack an invisible enemy in the air, striking them with the edge of her hands. It looked more adorable than menacing really, and it made him chuckle a little. "I appreciate the thought," he said with a grin. "You should stick with your magic, though. Hitting them like that will only tickle them."

"I'll show them 'tickle'! Yah! Boom boom, pah!"

"All right, all right, enough with the punching. We're almost there."

"Almost where?"

"Ballybridge."

A few kilometers before them, the valley opened onto a large plain of gentle rolling hills. The river they had been following for the last two hours continued into yellow fields of wheat that stretched over the horizon, and built on the edge of the water, surrounded by high walls of weathered gray stone, stood the gateway town of Ballybridge.

"Wow," Breeze murmured. "It's so much bigger than I had imagined. Does that wall surround the whole town?"

"Yes," Kieran answered. "That's how they protect themselves from invading armies. And bandits."

"Awesome. And that house over there? Why is it alone?" She pointed at the only building built on the western side of the river, next to the stone bridge.

"That's a tollhouse," Kieran said. "Travelers need to pay a fee if they want to use the bridge and enter the town. That's where they do it."

"Ooh. That's weird."

"All right, it's time for you to hide. We can't let anyone see you out in the open."

"Oh, right."

Just like they'd discussed earlier, Kieran pulled up the hood of his green cloak, and Breeze went inside of it. Her wings were broad enough that one of them brushed against his cheek, but she retracted them and placed herself behind his left shoulder. From this position, she could pull herself up and stick her head above his shoulder if she wanted to look outside, allowing her to observe the human world while concealing her presence.

"You comfortable?" he asked.

"Yup! It smells kind of old in here, though."

"That's the cloak. I've had it for a few years now."

"Are you sure it's not you? 'Cause I don't mind if it's you."

"What? No, it's not me. I washed myself in a river three days ago."

"Three days? You haven't taken a bath in three days?!"

Kieran winced when she raised her voice. "No need to yell," he said. "You're right next to my ear."

"Oh, sorry. But still, three days… Don't you feel itchy right now? I always do when I haven't taken a bath for too long."

"Nope."

"You're so lucky."

The sorcerer continued onward with his new companion clinging to his shoulder. For the next thirty minutes or so, Breeze didn't say much; she seemed enthralled by the sight of the town slowly growing into her field of vision. It was only when she saw two men guarding the south gate that she spoke again.

"Look, look!" she exclaimed, pointing at the guards. "Humans with pointy sticks in their hands!"

"They're called spears," Kieran explained. "They're weapons that allow you to strike from a distance."

"And what are they doing just outside the town?"

"They're guarding the entrance, making sure everyone who comes inside isn't a troublemaker. They also inspect the goods of merchants looking to trade at the market."

"Don't they get bored standing there all day?"

"I guess they do. But guards usually have four-hour shifts before they switch with someone else."

"Oh, that's smart."

Suddenly, Breeze went quiet and Kieran felt her body shift nervously on his shoulder. "What is it?" he asked her.

"Nothing," she said hesitantly. "Well, it's not exactly nothing, but…are you sure they won't find me?"

"Who? The guards?"

"Yeah."

"No, they won't. And even if they ask me to take my hood off, you can just stay inside it and hide there."

"Are you sure?"

"Yes. Trust me, you'll be fine."

"All right. I do trust you."

A hundred meters away from the entrance to the town, Kieran noticed two other sentinels standing on the fortification, ready to warn the rest of their cohort in the barracks of any potential trouble appearing at the gate. Hopefully, the only notable facts they would later remember about him were that a man carrying a bow on his back asked which inn offered the cheapest rooms.

The slabs of stone under Kieran's feet changed as he approached the town; instead of the squarish contours he had walked on all day, these stones were rounder, indicating a recent renovation of this part of the road. The river on his left disappeared behind the fortifications, and the fields of wheat he'd passed by had now been replaced by grassland. He turned his gaze forward and walked up to the two guards, who must have spotted him around twenty minutes ago. When he reached the gate, he raised his hand in greeting and nonchalantly said, "Hello there."

The two men wore blue gambesons, clearly visible at the arms beneath the yellow surcoats of the local constabulary, and were armed with not only spears but also wooden truncheons that dangled on their belts. Nothing Kieran couldn't handle, even without magic.

The guard on the right, a middle-aged man with a graying beard and scarred skin, placed his weight on his right leg, ready to strike with his spear at a moment's notice. His younger cohort did the same but positioned himself to Kieran's left, keeping a distance of at least two meters between the two of them so that they could flank him.

"That's close enough," the older guard said. "Hands where we can see them."

Kieran glanced at the guard on his left, feigning perplexity at what was happening. "Uh, sure," he replied. "Is something wrong?"

*Something is definitely wrong*, he thought. Watchmen would never be this cautious unless they had a good reason to suspect him of wrongdoing. What gave him away? The farmers? No, that couldn't be it; had they talked to the constabulary about him, there would have been at least six more guards surrounding him right now, and the two men standing behind the battlements would be aiming their crossbows at him. No, it was something else.

Was it…Waterlone?

The middle-aged guard didn't bother to answer his question and instead asked one of his own. "What's your name and destination?"

Kieran knew there was only one way he could answer this question. He met the man's gaze, gave him a shaky smile, and nervously said, "My name is Asher. Asher Brooks. I'm, um, looking for a job. I've heard the White Legion was hiring in Holiburg, so that's where I'm going."

The man narrowed his eyes and loosened his grip on his spear when he heard the name of the holy city. "Hmm. Holiburg, you say?"

"Yes," Kieran confirmed.

"I see… And do you have a permit for that bow?"

"Yes, right here in my bag. Can I take it out?"

"You can, but no sudden movements."

"Of course." Kieran reached into the bag hanging on his side and pulled out a scroll of parchment. He handed it to the watchman, who carefully unrolled it and held it up in such a way that he could read from it while keeping an eye on Kieran. For a long moment, all Kieran could hear was the distant rippling of the river flowing downstream and the rustle of the guards' gambesons every time they moved.

Finally, the guard nodded, rolled up the scroll, and gave it back to Kieran. "Everything seems in order," he said. "You may enter town."

He gestured to his cohort to stand down, and the younger man obeyed the command, albeit reluctantly. "Are you sure about this, Lieutenant?"

"Yes. He's not the man we're looking for."

"Really? How can you be sure?"

"Look at his necklace."

"His necklace?" The lad squinted at the chain, which was barely visible from under Kieran's shirt. "What about it?"

The first man sighed in exasperation and pointed at it. "Every eighth link is made of silver instead of copper. It's a star necklace. He's Azarian."

"Oh. I, uh, I didn't notice."

"Obviously."

Kieran looked down at his chest and touched the seven-pointed star pendant through his tunic, acting confused. Presenting himself as a devoted Azarian was the best way to avert suspicion in these lands, but he couldn't be too overt about it, or else he'd draw more attention. If he could keep up the pretense for a little longer, he would soon enter the town as a free man.

"Uh, I'm not sure I understand what's happening," he told the two guards. "Were you looking for someone in particular?"

"Yes," the lieutenant answered. "The Inquisition sent word to look out for a sorcerer named Kieran Fowler, although he might be calling himself Kasper Acworth. He carries a bow on his back, same as you."

"And you thought I might be him."

"Evidently, we were wrong. It's not that surprising, however— what kind of heathen would walk *toward* Holiburg instead of away from it?"

"One who has a death wish," his cohort remarked.

Kieran glanced at him for just a second before he fixed his gaze back on the lieutenant. "Well, I hope they catch him, and soon. I'd rather avoid having to explain myself to an inquisitor. I hear they can be quite, um…intense?"

"That's one way to put it," the lad chuckled. "My cousin talked to one of them once. I swear, I've never seen him so rattled before. Like a kid who almost got caught plundering the pantry."

"That's enough," the lieutenant interrupted, looking askance at his cohort. "We're here to keep the peace, not make small talk."

"Uh, yes, sir. Sorry, sir."

The man kept his gaze on the younger guard for several more seconds before he returned his attention back to Kieran. "I apologize for my companion here. He means well."

"It's no problem," Kieran replied.

"Nevertheless, we wish you safe travels on your way to Holiburg, Mr. Woods. May the Kind Mother watch over you."

The middle-aged man let his spear rest against his chest and extended his right hand to Kieran, offering him a handshake. Kieran accepted the gesture and said, "Uh, the name is Brooks, actually. Thank you, Lieutenant."

For just a moment, it was as if time slowed down and the rest of the world fell out of focus—all except for the lieutenant's piercing eyes. They stopped shaking hands, but the man didn't let go. They stood very still, gazing at each other in silence. When Kieran noticed that the man had reached for his truncheon with his other hand, he did his best not to let his face betray his real feelings and instead showed the guard a mask of unease and perplexity. It took all of his willpower to fight the urge to lift an arrow and shoot it into the man's neck before running the hell away from here.

Until at last, the lieutenant released Kieran's hand and let go of his truncheon. "But of course," he said innocently. "My apologies, Mr. Brooks."

"Um, don't worry about it," the sorcerer replied, pretending to be more anxious than he actually was. "I'll, uh, take my leave now, if that's all right with you."

"Of course. Enjoy your stay in Ballybridge."

Kieran nodded and turned away from the two sentinels. Just when he was about to cross the threshold of the town, he stopped, faced the lieutenant again, and with his lips pressed together in a slight grimace asked, "Excuse me, but…do you know where I could find the cheapest inn in town?"

The lieutenant pointed northwest and said, "Follow the wall on your left until you arrive at the third street. Then take a right and it'll be straight ahead of you."

"It's called The Jolly Stew," his cohort added. "You can't miss it."

"Thank you," Kieran said before he started walking again.

The southern entrance to Ballybridge led to a wide street paved with the same rounded stones as those outside the walls. The first floor of most of the buildings on this street were occupied by shopkeepers, artisans, and scholars, all of whom worked their trade during the day before they retired to their homes for the night. For many of them, their home was located on the second floor of these same buildings, right above their shop.

There were only three people out on the street: an elderly woman dressed in a beige kirtle who was strolling northward, her wistful eyes lingering over the stony facades of the shops she walked by, and two young girls playing hopscotch on a colorful court that they had drawn on the pavement with chalk. None of them had noticed him yet.

Kieran felt Breeze reposition herself on his shoulder, surely to get a better look at what she was missing, and then heard her exclaim, "Wow, it's so big!"

He immediately shushed her and whispered, "Not so loud."

"Oh! Sorry."

The fairy made sure that only her head stuck out above his shoulder and continued to observe her new surroundings while he got off the main street and followed the fortification, heading west. The backstreets were narrow and the buildings cramped together, but to Breeze, this must have looked like a realm of giants, a magical world where she was the one of normal size while everyone else towered over her.

"This is awesome!" she said, unable to contain her excitement.

"Shh!"

"But there's no one here," she whispered to his ear. "Shouldn't it be safe?"

"No, it's not. It's almost suppertime, so people are probably inside preparing their food."

"Ooh! Got it. I'll be super quiet."

Kieran turned around a corner and arrived on the street the lieutenant had spoken of. The Jolly Stew stood thirty meters ahead of him on his left. A sign hanging above the entrance depicted a bowl of stew on which someone had comically drawn a smile and a pair of eyes. The intended effect was simple but also effective, judging by the way Breeze chuckled.

Kieran smiled and asked her, "You ready to go inside?"

"Oh yes!" she answered.

"Let's go then."

He then stepped forward and entered The Jolly Stew.

# CHAPTER 12

THE NOVELTY OF traveling over long distances and discovering unknown landscapes quickly wore off after spending a whole day sitting in a small, bumpy box. According to Finlay, they had crossed the Kantnerian border half an hour ago and would soon arrive at Ballybridge. *Not a moment too soon*, Faith thought. All she could see outside her window were rows upon rows of leafy trees that were going by so fast, she was unable to identify which species they belonged to—except for the occasional birch trees, easily recognizable by their white bark.

She was mind-numbingly bored.

One would think that having someone to talk to would help in this sort of situation, but Aiden had hardly said anything since she healed the lamb. They exchanged a few banalities about the sunny weather and the journey ahead, but nothing like the conversation they'd had this morning. In fact, thinking back to it, most of that discussion was about their target, Kieran Fowler, and not themselves. Shouldn't an inquisitor and her knight—even a temporary one—know each other better than they currently did? Or was she simply overthinking this?

Tired of looking out the window, she glanced at Aiden and caught him doing the same to her. She stopped breathing for a second and promptly averted her eyes as a chill ran down her spine. Were her cheeks turning red too? God, she hoped not. It would be so awkward if he noticed it. She felt like a teenager again, deriving pleasure from letting a man's gaze linger on her curves. She had to remind herself of the reason Aiden was here, lest her imagination run away from her.

Her mother had chosen him. Not Faith.

Remembering that, she quickly sobered up and resolved not to let anything distract her from her task, not while her life was at stake. Kieran Fowler may not have received the training that made the sorcerers from the Ophician city-states such fearsome foes, but the dark power he wielded still made him a threat to himself and everyone else around him. If things went badly, no teacher or novitiates would be there to help her correct her mistake. The only one she could rely on was Aiden, and to become romantically involved with him while they were in pursuit of a dangerous man like Fowler—even for one night only—could have unpredictable consequences for the both of them. It was best to keep him at a distance.

"There's something I've been meaning to ask," he said tentatively, interrupting her thoughts. "If you'll allow it, of course."

The request caught her off guard, but she welcomed the distraction. Anything to pass the time until they arrived in Ballybridge. "Go ahead."

"It's about the Trial of Faith," the prince continued. "I don't know how much you're allowed to talk about it, but we've heard rumors. That you're chained to a ball of iron and dropped into a well." He paused. "Is that true?"

She raised her eyebrows at him. "Yes, it is. I didn't think anyone outside the order knew about this."

"One of the other squires I trained with bribed another Kantnerian noble to get the information."

"That doesn't seem worth a bribe."

"He was a pompous fool who liked to waste his father's money. The point is, we could never confirm whether or not he was telling the truth."

"I find it hard to imagine that someone would pay for that kind of information."

"I wouldn't have, but the Inquisition is so secretive that many can't help being curious. We hardly knew anything about you and your rituals before we arrived at the Order, and even then, we were taught only what we needed to know—such as the limits of the power God has granted to you."

"Hmm. Well, in this case, your companion told you the truth. The Trial of Faith is how we prove our faith to God and become inquisitors. Only true believers will successfully remove their chains and swim back to the surface."

"And those who can't?"

"They drown. When that happens, the inquisitors bring the novitiate back to the surface and reanimate her by expelling the water from her lungs. The novitiate is then discharged by the Inquisition and sent back to the Church to become a priestess."

"I see." Aiden's expression remained impassive, but he leaned forward to listen more closely. "Then," he continued, "the only one who can deem you ready for the responsibilities of your title is the Kind Mother herself."

"Yes. It's an old ritual that dates back to the establishment of the Inquisition. Although back then, they used it on inquisitors who were suspected of faithlessness. This is how they prove their innocence, even today."

The knight widened his eyes in understanding. "That's why there are no trials for inquisitors. The Trial of Faith is all you need."

"Yes. This is a lifelong commitment with God that we've made. And like you said, she's the only one who can deem us worthy of our power."

"And you can feel her presence? Even now?"

"When I call upon her, yes, but only then."

Aiden looked her right in the eyes. "How does it feel?" he asked.

It was a simple question, but one she'd never had to answer before. At first, she thought it would be easy to describe it to him, until she opened her mouth and found herself unable to find the right words. Nevertheless, Aiden waited patiently for the answer until finally, after much mulling over, she figured out an adequate analogy.

"It's a warm feeling," she told him. "Comforting but distant at the same time. Like a mother watching over you, ready to help you up whenever you fall. But when she doesn't, she'll just…stand by and watch while you solve the problem by yourself. Does that make sense?"

"Yes, it does," the prince said, a solemn expression on his face. "Thank you for sharing this with me. You didn't have to."

"It was nothing." Silence settled between the two of them again, but for the first time since yesterday, Faith didn't mind it. When she looked out the window, the restlessness that had been gnawing at her was gone. She felt content, at peace. Ready.

And then, the forest disappeared, now replaced by a more bucolic landscape.

Farmhouses and barns dotted a plain of gentle rolling hills where farmers grew fields of beans, peas, wheat, and barley. No one worked the fields at the moment, for today was Requisday, the holy day of rest. The farmers and their families had surely gone to the church that morning to listen to the priestess deliver her sermon, after which they would gather outside and mingle with their neighbors and friends. Most of them had probably returned home by now and begun to prepare supper for the rest of their family. Faith had often wondered how different their evening meals were from the ones she would have with her mother. Less drab, she imagined.

Finlay Pyresky opened the front window and told them, "Ballybridge in sight, ma'am. Shall I take you to the church?"

"Yes, please. The sooner, the better."

"Understood." He closed the window and the coach continued onward to its last stop for the day. She looked forward to stretching her legs and walking around town a little. Before she did that, she needed to introduce herself to the local priestess and ask for her hospitality. Hopefully, no one would recognize her as the daughter of the grand inquisitor—she could do without that particular headache.

"May I also suggest we introduce ourselves to the count of Ballybridge?" Aiden proposed. "Lord Harrowmont is notorious for taking offence at the littlest things—you not announcing your presence would be one of them."

Faith frowned and crossed her arms. "Is that so? Perhaps I *should* ignore him. He might learn something from it."

"While I agree with the sentiment, I would advise you not to act on it. Lord Harrowmont is an old dog who cannot be taught new tricks."

"Then why bother meeting with him? We'll be there only for a day."

"Because we may need his help one day. And when we do, it will be a lot easier to convince him to cooperate if he is predisposed to listen to you. Furthermore, he doesn't know about our mission or where it's taking us. Once he learns of our arrival, he might deduce that we're here to investigate one of his subjects, which would needlessly put him on edge. Informing him that he has nothing to worry about from us would go a long way to get on his good side."

"Fine, we'll go introduce ourselves, but only after we've met with the local priestess."

"Understood."

Faith didn't like this one bit, but she knew he was right. There was no reason to antagonize the lord of this land, not when she could avoid it. Hopefully, she wouldn't need to talk to him for long; from the way Aiden described him, he was an unpleasant man to interact with.

Her gaze wandered to the window and she watched her own reflection in the pane of glass. Best that she forget about Lord Harrowmont for now. There were other, more important matters that deserved her attention. The one at the forefront of her mind was Kieran Fowler, the man who'd burned down the Lunaris orphanage.

For more than ten years he had successfully evaded the watchful eye of the Inquisition, until as if by a twist of fate someone exposed his identity and forced him to go into hiding. And now she, the daughter of the inquisitor who had arrested and executed his mother, had been tasked to do the same to him. The Valadorian Seeresses from the south would probably call it destiny.

Faith would call it what it really was—a tragedy.

Kieran stared at his reflection in the window and examined his clean-shaved face from different angles. He never liked having a beard, but it provided a quick and easy way to alter his appearance if he suddenly needed to lie low for a while, which was why he'd let it grow. He doubted it would be very helpful, however; his bow was the real giveaway. Unless he disposed of it, sooner or later the Inquisition would find him and put him in chains.

He couldn't let that happen, not after promising to Breeze that he would help her find her Nana.

He looked past his reflection and down at the alley below. The innkeeper had given him a small bedroom on the second floor of the establishment, which offered a view of a back alley that people used to pile up their garbage. Luckily for him, they placed their trash in old barrels, which spared him the atrocious smell of rotten food and shit. As long as he kept his window closed, his nose should be fine.

The room itself was sparingly furnished with a newly made single bed, an empty wardrobe, and an old wooden chair. Nothing out of the ordinary, except for the little fairy running on the covers of his bed, aiming for the pillow with her head. She hit it with full force, bouncing off of it like a ball and landing on her butt. Kieran stared at her in disbelief as she blinked at the pillow—as if surprised by the result of her action—and laughed at her own silliness.

"What are you doing?" Kieran asked.

"Testing the softness of the giant pillow!" Breeze exclaimed, rising to her feet. "It looked so fluffy, I just had to try it."

"With your head?"

"Of course!" She walked to the pillow and began to climb it, one centimeter at a time. "It's more fun that way."

"Is that also why you're climbing instead of flying?"

"Exactly!" She reached the top of the pillow, turned around, and stood with her arms akimbo, looking down at the bed like she had just conquered a mountain. "A little exercise is also the best way to stay in shape!"

"I'm not sure what you did qualifies as exercise. Maybe if you did it a hundred more times."

"Hmm, that'd be boring, though. What if I climbed you instead?"

"Me?"

"Yeah! You just have to sit down."

"Can't say that's how I imagined my day going when I woke up this morning." He approached the foot of the bed and sat on it. "How's this?"

"Perfect!" The blue-haired fairy slid down the pillow and

enthusiastically ran up to him, scaling his knee first. "There. We. Go! Phew. Now to get on your shoulder…"

"You have a weird way of having fun," Kieran said, the corner of his mouth threatening to curl into a lopsided smile.

"Is it? You would totally do the same if you were my size." She walked up his left thigh and began clambering up his tunic.

"I'd be too afraid of getting eaten by a bird to even risk going outside."

"Oh, you get used to it," she said, having reached his chest. "And when something big does show up"—she stopped and took a moment to breathe—"you only need to use your magic to defend yourself, and they'll leave you alone."

"Wait—a bird tried to eat you?"

By now, Breeze had reached the top of his shoulder. She balanced herself by holding on to his left ear and leaned forward to look him in the eye. "Not me," she answered, "but Cosmo, one of my brothers. We were playing hide-and-seek in the trees when a falcon swooped down from the sky and almost gobbled him up for dinner! But fairies aren't easily defeated. Cosmo avoided the attack at the last second and shot fire at its ugly beak! Oh, I wish I was half as good with shaping fire as he is. The falcon flew away like a coward, and we never saw its feathery wings in Dreamland ever again!" The fairy smiled proudly at the memory of this glorious battle.

"Fire, huh? Too bad I couldn't meet the rest of your siblings."

"Oh, I'm sure they would have liked to meet you too—after they, you know, came around to the idea of talking to a human."

"Are you sure they wouldn't just set me on fire instead, like your brother did to that falcon?"

"Oh no, they wouldn't! We only use our magic to defend ourselves or help with work. Maybe play some games too, but never to attack!"

"Is that one of Nana's rules again?"

"It is." She nodded emphatically.

"And she's the one who taught you how to use magic?"

"Yep! Me and every other fairy in Dreamland. Although she didn't teach us everything she knew. She said it would be best if we learned the rest by ourselves."

"Really?" Kieran knit his brow and carefully considered the possible implications behind this statement. "Did she explain why exactly?"

"Hmm." She scratched the back of her head. "I don't think so. Maybe she told one of my other siblings, but I'd have to ask them. What about you? Who taught you how to use magic?"

Kieran had not expected her to question him about his past. It must have shown on his face because she tilted her head to the side and looked at him with an interrogative finger on her chin. "Something wrong?" she asked.

"No. Everything is fine," he replied. "It's just...I've never told anyone else about it."

"Huh? Why not?"

"Because of the Inquisition. Remember? Couldn't risk anyone learning about it."

"Oh, right. Sorry." She lowered her head and meekly added, "You don't have to talk about it if you don't want to."

"No, it's all right. There's not much to tell anyway. The Inquisition almost caught me once when I first got my power, but a man found me and helped me when no one else would. He put a roof over my head and food in my belly, and gave me a bed to sleep in. I'd probably be dead today if it wasn't for him."

"Wow. He sounds like a great person."

"Yeah, I thought so too. He taught me how to control my magic, blend into a crowd, even speak and write different languages. It took me a few years before I realized he was training me to become a spy. I left before he could use me for his plans."

"Oh. I'm sorry."

"Don't worry about it."

"I'll try. But there's something I don't understand. What's a spy?"

Of course she didn't know what a spy was. How could she? She'd lived all of her life in a forest, isolated from the rest of the world. How many other human concepts would he need to define for her before she'd be familiar enough with the outside world to navigate it alone?

"It's, uh, it's someone who gathers secret information about other people or countries," he explained to her. "They then give that information to their employer, which is usually the country they were born in."

"So, they're…scouts?"

"They're *professional* scouts."

Breeze stared at him, slack-jawed. She didn't say anything for a while until finally she deployed her wings and flew onto the bed. "I guess there's just one last thing I don't understand," she said, turning to face him again. "Why did you lie about your name when speaking to that man at the gate?"

"Why do you think?"

"To protect yourself?"

"Correct."

"But how does lying about that help you?"

"Because the Inquisition knows who I am. They've been hunting me for years now, Breeze. If I used my real name, they would track me down and find me really quickly. Nowadays, I'm known as Kasper Acworth—although that name doesn't appear to be safe anymore either."

"So you'll have to change your name again?"

"Yes. Obviously, the Inquisition informed the guards in town about me and my false identity. We'll have to lie low for a while."

"How did they learn about it? Is it because of the farmers you met this morning? You said you had to scare them away."

Kieran winced at the memory of the father and his two sons. He didn't want to talk about them—not with her—so he changed the subject. "No, I didn't tell them either of my names. The only person who could have told the Inquisition about me was someone I met last week. I think his name was Henry."

"Who is that?" Breeze asked.

"He used to bully me back when I was a kid. I gave back as good as I got, though. Problem is, he recognized me. I was hoping he would keep silent about it, but..." He shook his head. "Nothing I can do about it now."

"So that's why the mister outside the gate was looking for you."

"Yes."

"But he let you go."

"Because he had enough reason to believe I wasn't the man he was looking for. The description he received of me didn't match my appearance, except for my bow. And I was wearing a star necklace, something many people believe impossible for a sorcerer to wear."

"Impossible? Why?"

"Because sorcerers are evil and the necklaces are good."

"I'm not sure I understand."

"It's just nonsense that some people believe in. Don't try to make sense of it."

"Then what about that other name he called you? Mr. Woods, I think?"

"A test. Had I not corrected him on it, he probably would have tried to knock me out. I've been trained to handle this sort of trickery, though, so it didn't really surprise me."

"And you told him where you were going to spend the night to gain his trust?"

"You're catching on fast. Yes, that's why I said that—and because I really needed some directions."

Breeze contemplated this new information for a while before she spoke again. "That's a lot of lying. Is this really the kind of stuff I'm gonna have to learn to do if I want to explore the human world?"

Kieran paused to carefully consider his answer. The little fairy appeared so fragile, so innocent, he had a hard time imagining her telling a bold-faced lie to someone else. "Maybe," he said. "At the very least, you'll need to learn how to recognize when other people are lying to you."

"I see. Can we start now?"

"Start? Start what?"

"The training, of course!" With a determined gaze, Breeze balled her tiny hands into fists and awaited his response. The resolve she displayed contrasted heavily with her usual cheerfulness, so much so that it momentarily left him speechless. Maybe she wasn't as naive as he'd first thought her to be.

"Sure," he told her with a grin. "I'll teach you what I know."

The fairy's face lit up. "Great! So where do we start?"

"The same lesson I first received when I was your age. The difference between lying and deceiving."

"Ooh!"

"But first, I'm hungry. Let's go eat."

"Hey! You cannot tease me like that and then leave me hanging without an answer!"

"Sure, I can." Kieran stood up from the bed and walked over to the chair, where he had placed his belongings. After picking up his shoulder bag and putting his cloak back on, he grabbed his bow and quiver and walked to the door. Breeze didn't waste any time and hopped back on his shoulder before hiding in his hood.

"You're not leaving your bow here?" she asked.

"No. Someone could come in and steal it, and I need to sell it soon."

"Sell it? What for?"

"To keep a low profile. The Inquisition is aware that I have it, so I have to get rid of it, or they might find us."

"Oh, I see."

He had other reasons for bringing his weapon with him, but she didn't need to know that. Not yet. Kieran exited his room, closed the door behind him, and headed for the stairs.

# CHAPTER 13

FAITH DISEMBARKED FROM the stagecoach and looked around to get her bearings. Finlay had stopped the horses in a small public square, right in front of the church. An old fountain sat in the middle of the square, its pipes lazily spurting water into the reservoir below. Many stalls were lined up along the other sides of the plaza, all of them empty in observance of Requisday. Except for the three children hiding in the shadow of one of the colonnades, looking at her, there was no one else there.

Aiden stepped out of the coach, holding Faith's bag in his left hand. She could hear the distinctive clinking of the handcuffs on his belt as he walked up behind her and joined her side. The moment his amber eyes fell upon the three children, they scampered off and disappeared around a corner.

"You scared them away," she said.

"It's you who they ought to be scared of," he replied. "I'm only your bodyguard."

"I'm not sure they even know what an inquisitor is."

Aiden turned to Finlay, who was sitting in the driver's seat of the stagecoach, and asked him, "Are the stables far from here?"

"No, they're just down that street," the bald man answered, pointing south. "I'll look after the horses and meet you in front of the presbytery tomorrow morning. Unless you would prefer someplace else, ma'am?"

"The presbytery is fine," Faith said, "but where are you going to spend the night?"

"The Jolly Stew. It's an inn close to the southern gate, down that way. You'll be able to find me there if you need me."

"You won't stay with us? I'm sure the local priestess would welcome you into one of her guest rooms if you asked for it."

"Thank you, ma'am, but I'd like to have a good night's sleep before we set off again tomorrow, and it's more likely to happen if we don't all sleep under the same roof."

"I'm not sure I understand."

"Let's just say it's not the first time I've traveled with inquisitors and their knights. Thank you for your concern, however, and good night."

Surprised by the sudden farewell, Faith barely had time to say good night before Finlay spurred the horses forward and drove the carriage out of the plaza and down the street. The sound of wheels rattling against stone pavement diminished in intensity until it became nothing more than a distant background noise, like the gentle wind blowing through the empty streets of Ballybridge.

Faith looked away from the shrinking stagecoach, still confused about what he'd said. Then she remembered the circumstances that led to her birth, and it dawned on her why Finlay preferred to stay at an inn instead of the presbytery. She glanced at Aiden, but his stoic expression and demeanor remained inscrutable. Any thoughts he had about the subject, he kept to himself.

Thank God for that.

Not wanting to linger in this uncomfortable silence any longer, she cleared her throat and said, "We should go see the priestess."

"As you wish, ma'am," the knight answered.

She was about to correct him on calling her by that term when she remembered that while they may be alone, they were still out in public. Best to keep it professional whenever that was the case.

The two of them set off toward the church, Faith leading while Aiden followed her from two steps behind on her right.

While the church of Ballybridge was not as grandiose or large as the cathedral in Holiburg, Faith could tell at a glance that it could seat at least a thousand Azarians. Its two facade towers loomed over the rest of the town like silent guardians, signaling to devout travelers that they would always find refuge here.

While walking up to the main doors, Faith peered at the stained-glass windows located just below the arch and recognized a common depiction of The Funeral, the moment when Alma's seven apostles gathered around her body to mourn her death while the rest of her disciples looked on from a distance, stricken with grief. Ever since she was a child, she found this scene disturbing, for she always imagined her mother being the one laid down on a stone slab, having fallen to the viciousness of one of the many sorcerers and witches who still roamed this world. And she, as a little girl, would be forced to stare at the lifeless shell that once had been her mother.

The inquisitor diverted her gaze from the window and instead continued to the main doors of the church. She entered the building and arrived inside the narthex—the lobby area—and was immediately greeted by the distinctive, comforting smell of incense, mixed with a faint odor of mustiness. It instantly reminded her of the inner chapel of the inquisitorial abbey.

She and Aiden traversed the narthex and moved into the nave, where rows and rows of empty pews rested on the stone floor. The high-vaulted ceiling was impressive to look at, but not as much as the five stained-glass windows built into the eastern wall of the chancel where the altar was located. Each window depicted a well-known moment of Alma Azaria's life. Three of them were identical to the ones at the inner chapel of the inquisitorial abbey—Alma's birth in the Forest of Ermanloth, the first miracle of healing she performed, and her death at the hand of Acklea—but there were two more.

The first one depicted the death of her husband, Lydus Audaios, who after attempting to protect a young slave from the undeserved wrath of their master, was knocked on the head for daring to shelter someone else's property. Heartbroken, Alma could only cradle the body of her husband as he slowly died in her arms. The second window showed the moment God talked to Alma on the sea cliff near Gemma, the town where Alma was born. God manifested herself by a melodious voice carried by the salty winds of the Ariolic Ocean, entrusting her prophet with the difficult task of guiding humanity on a path of peace.

These five scenes were arranged in chronological order from left to right, starting with Alma's birth, followed by the death of her husband, the encounter with God on the cliff, the first miracle she performed, and her death at Acklea's hand.

Faith stopped a few meters away from the altar. The silence that reigned in the church was almost palpable, and she did her best not to make any unnecessary noise. Instead, she took the time to admire the stained-glass windows while remembering the many lessons her teachers had taught her during her years as a novitiate. Then her mind wandered to a vivid memory of her childhood, when her mother would tuck her in and read her the Scriptures under the yellow light of a candle, telling her of Alma Azaria and the tragedy of her life.

The voice of a young woman suddenly called out to her, interrupting her daydreaming. "Hello? Can I help you?"

A maiden with blond hair had come out of the door on the left side of the chancel and was now appraising the two visitors standing before her. She was only fourteen, maybe fifteen years old, but she was already taller than Faith and at least fifty pounds heavier. She possessed the kind of stout physique that would have been very useful on a farm had she decided to live the life of a peasant, and she wore the white cassock characteristic of Azarian priestesses, with one small difference: instead of the usual ribbonlike belt, she wore a white rope cincture around her waist, identifying her as a novitiate of the Church. Surely one of the local priestess's pupils.

The lass continued to stare incredulously at Faith and the knight until her eyes fell on the red band of cloth around the inquisitor's waist. Sensing that the young woman was about to utter numerous apologies, Faith introduced herself. "My name is Inquisitor Faith Dow, and this is Sir Aiden Hawkon. We are on a mission for the Inquisition and would like to rest here for the night." She punctuated this request with a polite bow, which Aiden imitated.

The novitiate gaped at the inquisitor and stammered what she certainly hoped to be an appropriate response. "You're, um, welcome to stay the night, of course. And you too, my lord. I mean, you'll have to ask Mother Maeve, but I'm sure she'll accept!"

"I'm glad to hear it. Can I meet her, or is she busy at the moment?"

"She's in the healing room with a few farmers from Toring's Hold. I can take you to them if you'd like."

"Toring's Hold?" Aiden repeated. "Isn't that almost twenty kilometers away from here?"

"Uh, yes, it is."

"Then why come here for healing? From what I remember, there should be a priestess living in that village."

"Oh, Mother Bethany you mean." Her face clouded over. "She unfortunately passed away two days ago—old age. Her novitiate looks after the village for now, but one of the farmers' injuries was too severe for her to handle alone. She came here with them to ask for Mother Maeve's help."

"How serious are their injuries?" Faith asked.

"Oh, um, three broken ribs, several fractured bones in the hands, and multiple bruises across the body. Mother Maeve thinks he's going to be fine, although…"

"Yes?"

"I don't know why, but they refused to talk about who was responsible for their injuries. Only said that they got into a fight with someone else."

"There could be many reasons for that," Aiden said. "Some of which might be illegal."

"Maybe. They didn't strike me as the type, though." The novitiate pondered the possibility for a moment and then said, "Oh, I'm sorry! You asked me to take you to Mother Maeve. Please, follow me."

The novitiate motioned toward the door she'd just come out of and went back through it. Faith and Aiden followed her into a narrow corridor that abruptly curved to the left and led to a spiral stairway that descended into darkness. The lass removed a torch from a sconce in the wall, the only source of light present in the stairway, and descended the flight of stairs, followed by the inquisitor and her knight.

"What is your name?" Faith asked.

"Oh my, did I also forget to introduce myself? My apologies, Inquisitor. My name is Bianca Moss."

"It's nice to meet you, Bianca. I assume you're Mother Maeve's novitiate?"

"Yes. Have been for the past four years, though I'm not the only one. There's also Renee and Penelope, who've been with us for two years now. They're with Mother Maeve, learning how to mend broken bones. You'll also see Elsie, Mother Bethany's novitiate."

"What about the farmers? What are their names?"

"The father is called Arthur, and his two sons are Derek and Reuben. Arthur is the one being treated right now."

Bianca arrived at the bottom of the stairs and continued into a long hallway. The cool temperature of the basement made Faith shiver, and she wondered how cold it would get during the winter. Walls and floors of stone weren't effective at containing heat, and she could already imagine the novitiates grumbling about having to gather whatever supplies Mother Maeve wanted from here. God knew she'd once done the same thing.

"We're almost there," Bianca said, pointing to an open double door on the right wall from which warm, yellow light was emanating. The novitiate stopped next to it and let them in first.

When Faith entered the room, the first things that caught her attention were the numerous pillars of stone disposed in perfectly straight lines that intersected with each other. The pillars themselves gradually expanded toward the top, merging with the vaulted ceiling and creating multiple groin vaults across the room. Only a handful of torches had been lit: two on both sides of the entrance, and four others on pillars located at what she assumed was the center of the room.

There she saw Mother Maeve, the novitiates, and the three farmers.

All of them except for the priestess were now looking at Faith and Aiden, clearly surprised to see that an inquisitor had come to Ballybridge. Bianca reappeared from behind them and lit the way forward through the darkness, walking the twenty meters or so that separated them from Mother Maeve and the locals.

A middle-aged man sat on a table of stone, one of many in the room, while the priestess stood in front of him, holding his hands. With her back turned to Faith, she said, "I'll just be a minute, Inquisitor."

The farmers glanced silently at each other, apparently

wondering how the priestess could have known who had entered the healing room without so much as looking at them. Meanwhile, the two youngest novitiates, skinny girls of around twelve years whom Faith surmised to be Renee and Penelope, began taking guesses in hushed whispers. The third novitiate—a maiden of the same age as Bianca and whose fiery red hair framed a beautiful face, strewn with just the right number of freckles—ogled Aiden openly without even realizing it. The moment Faith met her gaze, she instantly looked away and stared at the ground instead. That must be Elsie.

A moment later, Mother Maeve, a matronly woman with sharp features and long brown hair, let go of the man's hands and said, "It's done. I've mended all of your bones and taken care of the biggest bruises. Your body will take care of the rest."

"Thank you, Mother," Arthur replied, glancing nervously at Faith.

"You're welcome, my son, but I was only acting according to God's will."

"Wait, you're not gonna heal the rest of his injuries?" Derek asked.

The father gave his youngest son a stern glare, quietly admonishing him for his impertinence. Mother Maeve didn't seem to mind the question and answered him without missing a beat. "I could," she said, "but I won't. I must save my energy for anyone else that might need healing. Unlike Alma Azaria, there is a limit to the number of miracles each of us can perform before demons threaten to overwhelm our minds. Do you know what happens when a demon manages to possess a priestess?"

"Not exactly," Derek answered. "They start hurting other people?"

"Correct. The demon burrows deep into the priestess's soul and perverts her every thought and desire. It can take only a few seconds before it becomes an indistinguishable part of her.

Then, it takes control of the priestess's body and lashes out at anyone in the vicinity, using foul energies to protect itself and hurt others. Which is why"—she looked pointedly at her two gossiping pupils—"novitiates must learn what their limits are and work toward expanding them."

Renee and Penelope visibly flinched when their mentor's attention turned to them, and they immediately stopped gossiping, straightened out their posture, and joined their hands together in an effort to appear like unobtrusive, attentive students. Their teacher's gaze lingered on them for a few more seconds until finally she shifted her gaze to the inquisitor and the knight.

"My apologies, Inquisitor. I had hoped that my students would have known by now how to behave in the presence of an eminent guest such as yourself, but clearly they need to hear the lesson again. Allow me to introduce myself: Maeve Wright, head priestess of Ballybridge."

She greeted them with a bow, which Bianca and Elsie promptly imitated while the two younger ones fumbled to do the same. As for the three men, they had no idea how to act in this situation and only managed to bow their heads before the moment passed and the conversation resumed. They seemed somewhat jumpy.

"Greetings, Mother Maeve. I am Inquisitor Faith Dow, and this is my knight, Sir Aiden Hawkon."

Aiden saluted her with a bow of his own. "A pleasure to meet you, Mother."

"Likewise," the priestess said.

The knight's name provoked a reaction from the other people in the room: Bianca, Elsie, Arthur, and Reuben gaped at the prince, while Renee, Penelope, and Derek looked around in confusion, unsure about the man's identity. They might not have known how far up the line of succession to the throne Aiden was—few commoners would have heard the name of the third prince of Kantner—but from his last name, everyone knew he had royal blood.

Mother Maeve didn't betray any such inkling and continued the conversation as if nothing had happened. "How may I help you, Inquisitor?"

"I am here to ask for your hospitality," Faith began. "I am on a mission of the utmost importance for the Inquisition and need to rest before I continue on my journey."

"I see. You're welcome to stay the night of course, and I hope you'll join us for dinner too. Bianca has prepared her famous stew, and it would be a shame if you weren't there to taste it."

The stout lass blushed furiously under the compliment.

"We would be happy to," Faith answered with a smile. "Unfortunately, we must introduce ourselves to Lord Harrowmont first. I'm not sure how long that will take, so please don't wait for us."

"Nonsense. We would be remiss if we dined without our own guests at our table. Bianca? Go prepare their rooms, please."

"At once, Mother." The blond novitiate turned around and went back the way she'd come, torch in hand.

"Girls, go help Bianca with the chores."

"Yes, Mother," Renee and Penelope said in unison before slipping away through the door.

"Thank you," Faith said. "And I'm sorry for interrupting you while you were healing these men."

"Think nothing of it. Interruptions like these don't break my concentration anymore. Besides, I knew you were coming the instant you entered the church."

The inquisitor raised her eyebrows at that. "You did? How?"

"I sensed your presence. More specifically, the sword and armor of your knight. They've been consecrated by Guardians of the Church to protect him from black magic. Adding the fact that Sir Hawkon was following you from two steps behind, and I deduced that you were an inquisitor."

"You could tell all of that from here?" Faith asked, astonished.

"It's an ability I've honed over many years. I see by your face that the bishop has never bothered to inform the Inquisition about it, even though I told her to. We may talk more about it over dinner, if you wish."

"Yes, I would. Especially about this bishop of yours."

The corner of Mother Maeve's mouth twitched in amusement. "Of course," she said. She then turned to the remaining novitiate and told her, "Elsie? You're welcome to stay the night too if you want."

"Thank you, Mother," the redhead replied, "but I should get back to Toring's Hold. The villagers might need me there."

"Are you sure? It'll be nighttime soon."

"Please don't worry," Arthur said as he stood up from the table, the glow of the torch behind him outlining his strong silhouette. "Me and my boys will bring her back safe and sound."

Reuben stepped forward and thrust his chest out, confirming what his father had just said. His younger brother, Derek, hesitated for only a second before he walked up next to him and did the same.

*Like father, like sons*, Faith thought to herself.

"Hmm. Then please do be careful on your way home," Mother Maeve said to them. "The roads are usually safe around here, but you never know."

"We will," Arthur answered, a little less nervous than before. "And thank you for your help."

"Yes, thank you," Reuben added.

The priestess dismissed them with a wave of the hand. "If you want to express your gratitude, live your lives following Alma Azaria's example."

"Oh. Yes, yes, of course," Arthur said, his head low. He then faced Faith and bowed to her, soon followed by his two sons. "And may God protect you on your journey, Inquisitor."

"And she on yours," she answered with a smile. Faith knew that commoners found it difficult to relate to members of the Inquisition, so she thought that a lighthearted comment might help with that. "Don't let any sorcerer catch you on your way home."

It had the total opposite effect.

The man turned white, his eyes widened like saucers, and his whole body seemed to stiffen at the word "sorcerer." At first, she thought she had unknowingly dug up a bad memory and reminded him of a loved one he had lost to a heretic. But she saw similar reactions from his two sons. Derek in particular was visibly trembling.

The three men looked like children who had been caught in the middle of committing a reprehensible act and now anticipated the punishment for it. All she could hear was the almost imperceptible sound of people breathing, the crackling of the torches burning on the pillars, and the creaking noise of Aiden's leather armor. Without even looking at him, she knew he had placed his left hand on the hilt of his sword.

Both Elsie and Mother Maeve sensed that something was very wrong. The young novitiate kept throwing nervous glances at both Faith and Aiden while the priestess, ostensibly unmoved by the farmers' anxiousness, nevertheless kept her eyes on the three men.

Everyone waited for Faith to speak again.

When she did, the amicability she'd previously demonstrated was replaced by the rigorous and stern demeanor one would typically expect from one of her station. She uttered two words, and two words only, but with a severity that made Derek gulp.

"What happened?"

# CHAPTER 14

ONE QUICK LOOK at the barroom of The Jolly Stew was enough to confirm that this was indeed the cheapest inn in Ballybridge: the wooden floor was marked by years of wear and tear, the tables and chairs weren't all of the same make, one section of the bar had been renovated with wood of a different color, and none of the bottles of liquor and wine that sat on the shelves dated to more than ten years ago.

However, the inn was also very well maintained: the two windows, one on each side of the entrance, were evidently cleaned at least once a week, the tables at least twice a day, and the glasses and tankards each time a patron used them. Not only that, but as Kieran drank his beer—slick and creamy on his tongue—he also noticed it hadn't been diluted with water. What a pleasant surprise. Too bad he couldn't let Breeze have a sip.

At the moment, only one other patron sat in the room: a gruff old man with a graying beard who had taken a seat two tables away. When their eyes met, the man grunted and drunkenly took a swig from his tankard, clearly not interested in having a conversation—which was just as well, because Kieran didn't feel like talking to him either.

Out of the door leading to the kitchen came a young woman

in her early twenties with neatly combed chestnut hair that descended to her shoulders. She wore a blue kirtle over a white chemise that stretched over her swollen abdomen, revealing her late pregnancy. She carried in her hands a bowl of beef stew, still piping hot judging by the steam rising from it, as well as two fresh slices of sourdough bread that sat neatly in the middle of a wooden plate—another surprise from Ballybridge's cheapest inn. If only all the establishments he had frequented were half as pleasant as this one.

The woman approached his table and set his meal in front of him. "Here you go, mister."

"Thank you," he said.

Despite the buoyant tone of her voice, Kieran detected a smidge of unease in her. He caught her glancing at his bow—which he had propped next to him against the table—before she looked at him again, acting like normal. She probably thought he was a poacher or a troublemaker of some kind. He would have liked to put her mind at ease and end her suspicions, but Breeze was still hiding in his hood and he didn't want to inadvertently expose her existence to the world by looking at the woman in the eyes. He instead decided to take a different approach.

"Anything else I can do for you?" she asked.

"No, thank you," he said.

"Very well. Enjoy your meal."

She turned and began to walk toward the kitchen when Kieran spoke to her again. "Congratulations, by the way."

She stopped midway to the door. "Uh, pardon?"

"For the baby." He pointed at her belly with the spoon she'd given him. "Congratulations."

The server beamed at him. "Thank you," she said while she placed a protective hand on her stomach. "It's been a rough few months, but we're hanging in there."

"Worried about the baby?"

"A little."

"I'm sure it will be fine." He smiled. "You have a priestess in town, no?"

"Mother Maeve, yes."

"Then there's no reason to be worried. The Kind Mother will be there to look after the both of you."

He said this with such confidence that her whole body relaxed. "Thank you," she replied softly. "And may she watch over you too, kind sir." She then bowed to him.

The gesture took Kieran by surprise, but he quickly recovered and dipped his head in return. She smiled again and returned to the kitchen. Once she had left his sight, he shifted his attention back to his bowl of stew and examined the meat and vegetables mixed in with the thick broth—a bunch of sliced potatoes, carrots, mushrooms, and small pieces of what appeared to be pork.

Now salivating, he scooped mouthfuls of the stew into his mouth before he grabbed a slice of bread, dipped it in the broth, and ate it.

How he had missed this. It had been a few months since he'd last enjoyed a warm meal like this in peace and quiet. Taverns in big cities were always crowded no matter the time of day, and he usually avoided inns while on the road, relying instead on hardtack and fruit to sustain himself. It was nice to be able to savor a peaceful moment like this one.

Unfortunately, his meal was suddenly interrupted by the thumping of someone running on the floorboard above him, followed by the happy cry of a child. Kieran frowned; a moment later, a young boy of around four years old came barreling down the stairs, a huge grin on his face. He traversed the barroom like it was his own playground and rushed toward the kitchen with something in the palms of his hands.

Irritated by the interruption, Kieran lowered his spoon and watched the boy zip by his table. Judging by the way the other patron ignored the child and kept drinking, this was probably a common occurrence in this establishment. There was, however, one other person who shared his annoyance: the pregnant server. She came out of the kitchen with an apron on, hands on her hips and a frown on her face. Anyone with a modicum of awareness would have realized by now that she was more than a little miffed.

The child evidently didn't have any such awareness.

"Mom, Mom!" the boy exclaimed, extending his hands to her. "Look! A spider! I found a spider!"

This innocent wonderment might have placated a softer, more lenient woman. The server instead glared at her son with frightful displeasure, and the boy realized he was in trouble.

"MALCOM MARSH!" she boomed. "What do you think you're doing, running around like a dog? You know you're not supposed to do that when you're inside!"

The boy shrank back under the force of her scolding. "But… but, Mom! The spider—"

"—should be left alone!"

Kieran felt Breeze recoil in his hood and hide behind his shoulder. She'd never heard a human shout before. Just one more thing to add to her list of new experiences.

"Since you have time to disobey our rules," the woman continued, "you won't mind helping me clean the kitchen."

The boy widened his eyes and then opened his mouth to protest, only for his mother to pinch his ear and drag him into the kitchen, indifferent to his squeals of pain.

A few seconds passed before Kieran internally rejoiced at the opportunity to enjoy the rest of his meal in silence.

Well, not completely in silence. From the other side of the wall, he could sometimes hear the muffled sound of the son arguing with his mother, but it was still a noticeable improvement. If only all children could be as well behaved as Breeze.

Although now that he thought about it, she didn't look like

a child at all. She sometimes acted like one, but under the loose tunic and trousers that she wore, he had discerned the curves of a young woman. Were she human, he'd estimate her to be sixteen, maybe seventeen years old. And yet she'd told him that her Nana "woke her up" only thirteen years ago. Very curious.

Kieran made a mental note to broach the subject at a more appropriate time. In the meantime, he picked up the second slice of bread and resumed eating.

After a few spoonfuls of this delicious stew, he thought it a shame Breeze didn't get to try it for herself. Then, a new idea popped into his mind: What if he could share some of his meal without anyone noticing? He hadn't seen the owner of the inn since he'd paid for his room, and the only other patron here was a drunk who hadn't spared him a glance for the last few minutes. Surely, he could risk it.

He scooped another spoonful of stew and raised it toward his face, but then veered at the last second and held it next to his left ear, counting on his hood to provide enough cover for the fairy to taste the food without being seen. Kieran felt her move atop his shoulder and grab his ear to keep her balance, but nothing else. He waited a while longer, thinking she was probably examining the texture of the meat sitting in the spoon. After a few more seconds, he grew tired of it and prompted her to do something by shrugging his left shoulder.

Not long after, he heard some tentative chewing coming from her. She swallowed the meat and let out an "Mmm!" of contentment. Kieran smiled and withdrew the spoon to place a small piece of bread on it. He examined his surroundings to make sure no one was looking at him—the bearded man seemed more preoccupied by how much he had left in his tankard—and passed the bread into his hood like he had with the stew. After eating that, she whispered, "It's really good! I never imagined humans ate delicious food like that all the time!"

*Not all the time*, Kieran thought. There were plenty of people who'd consider such a meal a luxury, depending on their situation and where they lived. Like him and his mother, many years ago.

Kieran brushed aside these memories as soon as they bubbled up to the forefront of his mind and instead focused on finishing his meal. He didn't want to think about his childhood or the events that had led him here; he had done that enough times already. For now, he was content to eat his stew and let Breeze have a taste of its various ingredients.

Just when only a quarter of the stew remained in his bowl, the bell hanging above the entrance rang as the door creaked open and someone entered the inn. He looked up to see who it was and saw a very thin, old man with a receding hairline step through the door. Kieran immediately noticed his jacket and small backpack, clear signs that this man was a fellow traveler. However, he was also too old and too frail to be walking on the roads by himself, which meant he either possessed a means of transportation or he had paid passage to one of the merchant caravans that traveled through the countryside. If it was the latter, other travelers would soon come streaming in through that door.

The owner of The Jolly Stew, a burly man in his late twenties with short black hair and a strong jawline, came out of a door on the other side of the bar and greeted the traveler with open arms. "Mr. Pyresky!" he exclaimed with a genuine smile. "So good to see you again!"

"Hello, Mr. Marsh."

"Please, come in, make yourself comfortable. By God, how long has it been? Six months?"

"Nine," the old man answered as he set his backpack on one of the stools in front of the bar. "The last time I stayed here was just before the first snows of last year."

"Ah, yes, I remember now. Still driving that carriage?"

"For now, yes. My work has taken me elsewhere lately, which is why we haven't seen each other in so long."

Kieran made a mental note of that.

"Ah, of course," the innkeeper said. "I figured as much. We still have your room ready for you, if you want it."

"I do, yes."

"I'll get the key then." The owner returned into the back room and came back with an iron key in hand, similar to the one Kieran had received, and gave it to his new patron. "Here you go."

"Thank you. And how's the family?"

"Oh. Right. You haven't heard the news yet." The man smiled and was about to say something else when suddenly the server raised her voice.

"Don't touch that! It's dangerous."

"But, Mom! You use it every day."

"That doesn't mean you're allowed to."

The two men looked at each other, amused by the exchange between mother and son. "He's growing up fast," the traveler said.

"Too fast," the owner replied, leaning on the bar. "He's started running everywhere he goes, even inside the inn. I give it one more day before Mathilda locks him up inside his room."

"He will calm down eventually."

"Once he falls down the stairs and breaks a leg, maybe. I only hope the next kid isn't as spry as this one."

"Next kid?"

The father grinned. "Mathilda is pregnant again."

"Really? Congratulations! How far along is she?"

"Almost eight months now. It'll be a girl, according to Mother Maeve."

"A girl? Have you come up with a name yet?"

"We have a few ideas…"

Kieran wiped the last traces of stew from his bowl with what remained of his slice of bread while half listening to the conversation between the two men. He had no interest in learning which names in Ballybridge were the most popular at the moment or what the differences between raising a girl and a boy were, but he nevertheless paid enough attention to know when the subject of their discussion would change. With a bit of luck, he might hear news of what the world at large was up to without having to ask the owner about it and draw attention to himself.

Unfortunately, their conversation soon came to an end, and the old carriage driver grabbed his backpack, climbed the stairs, and went to his room. Kieran watched him go while he ate the last of his food and drank a sip of beer.

"Anything else for you two?" Mr. Marsh asked his two patrons.

The bearded drunk glared down at his tankard—only now seeming to realize that it was empty—grunted in displeasure, and stood up from his chair. "No," he answered, staggering toward the door. When he finally reached it, it took him a few tries before he managed to turn the knob and open it. He left the tavern without saying another word.

"I'm fine," Kieran said. "Thank you."

The owner gazed at him and his bow, his forehead wrinkled in worry, but opted not to say anything about it and instead replied with, "Well, in the event that you do, don't hesitate to ask."

He then returned to his back room, leaving Kieran alone. But not for long, as his wife almost immediately came out of the kitchen and walked over to him. "I see you've finished your meal," she said as she picked up the empty plate and bowl. "How was it?"

"It was very good, thank you."

"I'm glad to hear it. Would you like some dessert too? There's an apple pie in the kitchen that I haven't had the chance to serve yet. It was freshly cooked with apples gathered from the Rees' orchard. They live not far from town."

"Oh, thank you, but no. I'm—" Kieran almost said "full" when he suddenly felt Breeze squirm against his shoulder, undoubtedly alarmed by his refusal to order dessert and thus deprive her of the chance to taste another human culinary specialty. Were it not for the need to keep her existence a secret, he suspected she would have voiced her opinion very loudly.

Mrs. Marsh tilted her head to the side, most likely wondering why he'd paused in the middle of his sentence, and she waited for him to say something. "On second thought, I think I'll try it."

She beamed at him and nodded. "Right away, mister."

"Uh, how much?" he asked while reaching for his pocket.

"Oh, don't worry about it. You can pay after you've eaten."

*How trustful of her*, Kieran thought, as he watched her head to the kitchen with the empty dishware in hand. Maybe his encouragement had more of an effect on her than he first believed. Then again, people always opened themselves more to those who presented themselves as devoted followers of the Azarian faith. After all, who would be brazen enough to pretend to believe in the words of Alma Azaria and not act according to them?

Kieran waited. Patiently. He would have liked to strike a conversation with Breeze, but couldn't risk doing so in public. Even whispering might prove to be too dangerous. While he waited, he heard the footsteps of the old traveler walking down the hallway of the second floor, heading back downstairs. And then, Mrs. Marsh's voice again. "That's enough, Malcom. You can go to your room now."

"Okay, Mom."

"And don't touch that knife. I told you it's dangerous."

An instant later, she returned from the kitchen with a slice of pie and placed it in front of Kieran. At the same time, the old traveler began climbing down the stairs, one step at a time.

"There you go," she said. "Please, enjoy."

"Thank you," he replied.

What happened next went by so quick, there was nothing Kieran could have done to prevent it. He picked up the spoon and raised it above the pie just as the server left his table to return to her chores. The moment she entered the kitchen, however, her voice thundered across the inn. "MALCOM! What did I tell you!"

Something fell on the floor, and her son came running out of the kitchen while holding something shiny in his hand.

A knife.

"Malcom! Get back here!" his mother shouted as she followed him.

At the same time, the old man, who'd come back without his backpack, stepped off the stairs and turned around the corner, probably to sit at one of the tables here. The child—who was glancing back at his mother—bumped into him and lost his balance.

"*Malcom!*"

The boy attempted to recover but stumbled over his own feet. He tumbled on his right side and instinctively used his hand to stop his fall. The same hand holding the knife.

It all happened so fast, Kieran saw barely any of it, but he heard the distinctive sound of a blade stabbing into the soft flesh of a human body: a short, sickening squish, followed by a loud thump as the kid collapsed on the floor like a sack of potatoes. The child moaned weakly and tried moving, only for his whole body to go limp.

Kieran and the carriage driver stared at the scene, frozen, as the reality of the situation slowly sank in: the knife had sunk deep into the boy's right side, up to the hilt. It wouldn't be long now before he went into shock. Then, the boy's mother let out a blood-curdling, ghastly cry of terror, so chilling that Kieran felt it in his very bones. No cry of help or plead for mercy he'd heard before could compare to this.

The mother rushed to her child's side and dropped next to him, her hands already shaking. Her husband scrambled out of the back room so fast that Kieran heard him knock over a chair. His eyes immediately fell upon the inert body of his son and in all but an instant, he was on the other side of the bar and kneeling next to his wife. A small pool of blood had begun to form on the floor.

"RUPERT!" the woman cried out. "DO SOMETHING!" Tears were pouring out of her eyes as she put pressure on the wound with her hands in a vain attempt to stop the bleeding. Her husband gawked at the knife sticking out of his son's side. Kieran had never thought someone could turn white so quickly, and he couldn't blame the man for freezing like he did.

"RUPERT!"

His wife's scream snapped him out of it and he quickly rose back to his feet. "I'll-I'll go get Maeve," he stammered.

"HURRY!"

"Wait!" the old man said. "There should also be an inquisitor at the church! Bring her too! She can help!"

A cold shiver ran down Kieran's spine when he heard that. An inquisitor, here, in Ballybridge. Mere minutes away from discovering him.

"I will!" the father answered before rushing out of the tavern at full sprint. It would take only a few minutes for the priestess and the inquisitor to arrive here, which should be plenty of time for him to make his escape. He had to leave discreetly, without raising suspicions. But how?

"Let me take a look at him," the carriage driver said while kneeling down next to the boy. "We have to—oh, God."

"There's too much blood!" the woman wailed, her hands completely red. "I can't stop the bleeding!"

"We need...we need something else. A rag, or—"

"Malcom? Malcom, stay awake! Oh God, please don't let this happen. Please don't let this happen, please don't let this happen. Please, please, please..."

Tears streamed down the mother's face as she continued to put pressure on her son's wound. The boy started groaning in pain. "Mommy," he cried. "Mommy, it hurts."

"I know, baby, I know," she said, her voice cracking. "Daddy is coming back soon with Mother Maeve. She'll make everything better, okay? Okay, sweetie?"

"It…it hurts!"

"I know, I know. It'll stop soon. You just have to wait until Daddy comes back. Won't be long now."

Meanwhile, the balding man frantically looked around the room, searching for a piece of cloth that he could use to stop the bleeding. Without asking for Mathilda's permission, he grabbed the apron she was wearing and, with a knife he pulled out of his pocket, cut a large piece of it. She quickly understood his intent and waited for him to hand her the improvised bandage.

Then the boy began to close his eyes.

"No no no! Malcom! Stay awake! Please, stay awake!"

The mother desperately pressed on the wound with the piece of cloth in her hands while doing her best to avoid touching the knife. Kieran had no idea whether or not it would effectively stop the bleeding, but he had no intention of finding out. He stood up from his seat and eyed the exits, debating which one to choose, when suddenly—

"I can help!" Breeze exclaimed as she flew out of his hood, her blue butterfly wings fluttering rapidly through the air.

Both the woman and the old man turned to look at where the voice had come from and stared at something they couldn't quite wrap their heads around—a tiny human teenager with short blue hair and beautiful emerald eyes. One who wore a tunic, trousers, and a pair of odd-looking slip-on shoes made from animal skin. A fairy tale made real.

"Don't worry!" Breeze told them. "I'll take care of that."

Without waiting for a response, she landed between the

two of them and examined the child's injury with a very serious expression. All three humans gaped at her, one of them for a different reason than the others.

Kieran wasn't thinking about the child's life anymore, nor the sobbing mother or the old carriage driver. He wasn't even thinking of Breeze. No, all of his thoughts were now focused on one person, and one person only: the inquisitor. He couldn't sneak his way out of here anymore. In fact, it was going to be next to impossible to leave this town unnoticed.

Breeze had revealed herself to the world, and the world would soon be looking back at her.

Kieran felt his breath quicken. His leg muscles tightened and his eyes darted around the room, searching for the best escape route. He had to leave *now*, before every guard in Ballybridge came looking for them.

"I can heal him," Breeze suddenly declared, "but I'll need someone to pull out the knife. Can you do that?"

The mother, who up until now could only gape at the small fairy standing next to her, finally spoke. "I-I can," she said. "But the blood—"

"I can stop it," Breeze said. "I promise everything will be fine. All you have to do is remove the knife when I tell you to. Okay?"

The woman stared at the fairy with eyes wide like saucers. Her doubts were clear as day as she deliberated over whether or not she could trust this strange yet seemingly sincere creature. She glanced at the old man to see what he thought, but he appeared to be even more at a loss about what to do than she was. Then her son groaned in pain again, quieter than before, as tears began to well in his eyes. "Mommy..."

Her whole demeanor changed in all but an instant. She grabbed the hilt of the knife, made strong eye contact with the blue-haired girl, and told her, "I'm ready."

Breeze smiled and nodded thankfully at the mother. "Good. On my signal then."

Kieran watched his companion raise her minuscule hands above the wound, mesmerized despite himself by what he was seeing. Could it be...? No. Impossible. Only priestesses were capable of such a feat. But what else could she be planning to do? And how long would it take? They had been lingering here too long already!

"On three," Breeze said. "One..."

Kieran eyed the kitchen door, intent on grabbing Breeze as soon as she was done and getting the hell out of here.

"Two..."

First, he needed to grab his quiver and fasten it to his belt. He couldn't leave without his weapon. Not with an inquisitor—

"Three!"

The kid wailed in pain again as the blade effortlessly slid out of his side. His mother instantly threw it away before she grabbed her son's hand and whispered comforting words to him. "I'm sorry, sweetie! I'm so sorry... Don't worry, it's almost over."

Breeze ignored the woman's whimpers and focused all of her attention on mending the kid's injury. The boy had stopped bleeding, just like she'd promised, but her work wasn't done. With her brow furrowed and her lips tightly pressed together, she used her power to fuse the edges of the wound back together and—presumably—also repair the damage done to the internal organs.

Slowly but surely, the puncture on the kid's side gradually closed up until no traces of it remained, not even a scar. Everyone, even Kieran, waited in palpable anticipation for the fairy to say something. Finally, after a full minute, Breeze lowered her hands and took a step back, a smile on her face.

"It's done!" she proudly declared. "It was a lot harder than I thought it would be, but he'll be fine now."

"Really?" the woman asked in disbelief.

"Absolutely! Let him rest for a couple of days, and he'll be right as rain. Oh, look! He can already raise his head."

The boy looked around in confusion, unaware of what had just transpired. Although he was still pale and sluggish, he was a damn sight better now than he'd been a minute ago. With the help of the old man, he carefully sat up and gazed at his mother. "Mommy?"

"Malcom!" The woman lunged at her son and held him in a tight embrace, tears flowing down her cheeks again. "Oh my God, thank you! Thank you, thank you…"

"I'm… I'm sorry, Mommy."

"Shh, it's all right, sweetie, it's all right. You're all right now."

"I'm sorry," the boy repeated, his voice cracking. "I'm sorry…"

He continued to apologize until he broke down crying and buried his face in her neck. She placed a hand on his head and cradled him like a baby, comforting the both of them. Breeze looked at the two of them with a smile, oblivious to the consequences of her action. Even now, the carriage driver was eyeing the blue-haired fairy in both awe and fascination. Before long, others would come to take a look at her.

Kieran picked up his quiver, fastened it across his shoulder, and walked around the table, grabbing his bow as he passed by it. "Breeze," he said to her. "We're leaving. Now."

This caught the attention of the old man, who now realized where the fairy had come from. Kieran ignored him and walked toward the kitchen, where he knew he would find a back door leading to the alley he'd seen earlier from his room.

"Hey, Kieran! Wait!" Breeze exclaimed as she launched herself in the air. "Where are you going?"

Kieran clenched his jaw when he heard her use his real name, and he bit the inside of his cheek not to curse back at her. Berating her for that mistake would only cost them more time. He instead passed through the doorway leading into the kitchen and scanned the room for an exit. Breeze followed him close behind.

"Wait!" the mother called to them. "I—"

Kieran didn't let her finish. He opened the door, stepped into the alley, and broke into a run. The fairy kept up with him, flying right by his side as he rounded a corner and headed into a narrower alleyway. "Why are we leaving?" she asked.

Kieran glowered at her and curtly said, "Because the Inquisition found us!"

# CHAPTER 15

FAITH AND MOTHER Maeve ran side-by-side through the streets of Ballybridge, closely followed by Aiden and a man named Rupert, who mere minutes ago had burst into the church screaming for help. The townspeople in the streets gave them a wide berth when they recognized their priestess, and some let out audible gasps when they realized that the woman with her was an inquisitor.

Faith doubted her assistance would be required. From what she had observed, Mother Maeve could handle any serious injury, but after a short moment of consideration, she decided to come along, just in case. What really preoccupied her at the moment was the man responsible for the injuries of Arthur and his two sons.

A man who camped in the wilderness to avoid contact with normal people. A man who beat them and threatened their lives with magic. A man who carried a bow across his back.

Reason told Faith that this man couldn't possibly be Kieran Fowler, that it would be foolish for a man like him to travel toward Holiburg and not away from it. And yet she couldn't shake the feeling that it was him. There couldn't be many archers traveling the road from Waterlone to Ballybridge alone, and although the description the farmers provided of that intruder differed from the one she had of Fowler, he easily could have altered his hairstyle and shaved his beard to throw off his pursuers. In any case, she couldn't let a sorcerer roam free. She would pick up this man's trail at Toring's Hold after they healed Rupert's son.

The head priestess took a right at the next street, and they encountered a patrol walking toward the inn. The two young men wore blue gambesons under yellow surcoats, and each carried a spear in one hand and wore a truncheon at his side.

"Mother Maeve?" the raven-haired one exclaimed. "What's wrong?"

"It's Malcom!" she answered as she ran by them.

The two constables needed no further explanation; without being prompted, they hurried after her and the rest of the group. The priestess took a left and continued down another street, rapidly approaching an inn in front of which a small crowd had gathered. Faith looked at the sign hanging above the entrance and, remembering what Finlay had told her before they parted ways, knew that they had arrived at The Jolly Stew.

"Make way!" Mother Maeve shouted.

The townsfolk swiftly complied and gasped in surprise when they saw the inquisitor behind her. Faith ignored them and followed the priestess inside, preparing for the worst. After years of healing the sick and injured, she had become accustomed to the sight of blood, the expulsion of body fluids, and the cries of the survivors. It was a reality all women of God had to accept, or else their patients might die.

Nothing could have prepared her for what she saw, however: a young boy sitting in a small pool of blood, his arms tightly wrapped around the torso of his pregnant mother.

When Faith heard them crying, her first instinct was to separate them and let Mother Maeve take a look at the injuries, thinking that the woman was foolishly causing pain to the child by holding him up like that. When she got closer, she realized that these weren't tears of despair but of relief. Not only that, but the woman also didn't implore the priestess to save her child when she entered the room but merely looked at her, which only added to the incongruity of the situation.

Something was wrong.

Mother Maeve didn't wait for an explanation: she kneeled down next to the boy and carefully lifted his bloodied shirt to examine his right side, ready to heal him as soon as she determined the extent of the injury. Faith walked up behind the priestess and looked over her shoulder to do the same, only to discover no wound to heal. Nothing to explain the blood on the ground or the thin slit in the boy's tunic. Just a boy who seemed perfectly healthy, if a little pale and snotty.

Faith briefly wondered whether or not they'd gotten the wrong child but immediately discarded this ridiculous idea. The blood proved otherwise. Mother Maeve must have had similar thoughts; she asked the young mother, "What happened? Where's the wound?"

Everyone waited expectantly for the answer as the father kneeled down next to his wife and son to hold them in his arms. "You're all right," he choked up. "I can't believe it... You're all right."

His family hugged him back, deeply relieved to see him again. No one had the heart to interrupt them and demand an explanation, but luckily for Faith and Mother Maeve, someone else here knew what had happened. One single look from the inquisitor was enough to prompt Finlay Pyresky to speak. "Someone else healed the boy," he said. "And they, um...they left through the back door just a minute or two before you arrived."

"What?" Faith exclaimed, catching her breath. "Someone else healed him? Who?"

The pregnant woman answered the question before Finlay

could. "An angel," she said. "It was an angel, Inquisitor. She's the one who saved my boy."

Everyone, even her husband, stared incredulously at the woman. Unfazed by their doubtful expressions, the mother continued to stroke her son's head while they tried to make sense of her words.

"I don't know what it was," Finlay explained. "It was... I mean, it *looked* human, but..."

"Calm down," Faith told him. "Start at the beginning."

The old man sighed and rubbed the back of his head. After taking a moment to compose himself, he nodded at the inquisitor, licked his lips, and began his account of the event. "I was walking down the stairs when the boy ran into me with a knife in his hand. It happened so fast, there...there was nothing I could do. He fell and he stabbed himself through the side. Mr. Marsh went to go get help, and I stayed to help his wife, but...the bleeding. There was so much blood. We tried to stop it with a rag, and...that's when she appeared."

Everyone but the young mother hung on to Finlay's every word. Even the constables were leaning forward to hear what happened next.

"It was a small girl," he continued. "And I mean literally. She was about *that* high." His hands gestured the length of a copy of the holy book. "She had short blue hair, and wings on her back, like a butterfly. Just like—"

"A fairy?" Aiden finished. "Seriously?"

"Yes. Exactly like a fairy."

"What happened next?" Faith asked, eager to learn more.

"Well, she flew next to us and told Mrs. Marsh she could heal the boy, but that we had to remove the knife first."

"And I did," the mother confirmed.

"Yes. And then the 'fairy' healed the boy, just like I saw many priestesses do in the past. It was— I mean, maybe it was blood magic, but it didn't feel like it. Everyone else in the room was fine after it happened, so she couldn't have taken blood from us. I don't know how to explain it."

"Just tell us what happened next," Aiden said.

"She left immediately after that. A man, another patron who was sitting right over there, stood up and told her they had to leave." He pointed at a table where a piece of apple pie sat on a plate, untouched. "They knew each other, I'm sure of that. He called her 'Breeze' and left through the back door."

Faith frowned at the mention of this mysterious stranger. "Who was the man? Can you describe him?"

"Yes. He was young, in his mid-twenties maybe, clean-shaven, had short brown hair, wore a green cloak and a tunic. A bow and arrows too. The girl called him Kieran."

Faith's eyes widened and she abruptly turned to look at Aiden, who had the same wide-eyed expression on his face.

It couldn't be. The man she was sent to capture, a fugitive who had escaped the Inquisition's reach for over ten years, the one who had received the crude moniker of "Pyromancer," inexplicably turned up in Ballybridge, the first major stop in her journey?

This all had to be part of God's plan.

"'Kieran,' you said?" Rupert repeated. "He told me his name was Asher. Asher Brooks."

"Inquisitor—" Aiden began.

"I know," she said, walking back to the men who had followed Mother Maeve. "You two. I want you to run to the gates of the city and tell the rest of the constabulary to close them. No one gets in or out of Ballybridge, do you understand? *No one.* I want all of your patrols to search for the man my driver just described to you. *Do not* attempt to arrest him. Kieran Fowler is a dangerous sorcerer, and he'll kill you if you approach him. Once you find him, you send for me, and I'll capture him myself. I'll be waiting in front of the church. Now go."

The constables didn't move a muscle and instead stared at Faith with their mouths agape. The inquisitor felt a wave of heat spread through her chest until her voice exploded. "I said NOW!"

The two men scrambled through the front door, suddenly very eager to obey her command. She couldn't deny a certain satisfaction at seeing them scurry away but also made sure not to revel in it. It was that sort of attitude that had allowed the mages of the Aurelian Empire to rule for as long as they did. To act like them was a sure way of losing God's favor and the power granted to her. Once her composure returned, she turned to the innkeeper and said, "You. Did Kieran have a room here?"

"Yes," he answered, still shaken. "Room six on the second floor."

Faith turned to her driver. "Finlay?"

"Yes, ma'am?"

"Go with Rupert here and search this room top to bottom. If there are clues that can help us, find them."

"At once, ma'am."

"Sir Aiden?"

"Inquisitor."

"You're with me."

Unlike the two greenhorns who'd run out of here not a minute ago, Aiden didn't need to be told twice. Without saying a word, he positioned himself two steps behind her on her right and followed her out of the inn. They were about to walk down the street and return to the church when Mother Maeve called out to them: "Inquisitor. Wait."

Faith stopped. Eager to begin her search as soon as possible, she reluctantly faced the priestess. "What is it, Mother?"

"I'd like to assist you. If you'll allow it."

"What about the child?"

"He's fine. I examined him while your man was talking. I'm more worried about this sorcerer you mentioned. If he's somewhere in Ballybridge, he may hurt one of my flock, and I can't let that happen."

Faith considered the offer for a second. "I don't see how you could help me, Mother. I was trained to subdue sorcerers—you weren't."

"True. But I can track him down for you."

Faith lifted her eyebrows in surprise and glanced at Aiden, who again wore the same expression as her. "What do you mean?" she asked.

"Exactly what I said. I've told you earlier about my ability to sense other people's presence. I believe I can use it to help you find this man."

"Really? How exactly? He could be anywhere in town by now."

"I'll focus on that fairy your man spoke of. If she really is that small, I'll be able to tell her apart from everyone else—but I'll need time. And preferably some silence too."

"How much time?"

"It'll depend on where they are. At most, ten or fifteen minutes."

This was a lot faster than she had hoped for. It would take many more hours for the constables to finish their search of the whole town, time that Fowler could use to escape Ballybridge and disappear forever. It seemed God had once again provided her with the means to accomplish her mission.

Faith had no reason to say no. "Then please come with us," she said.

"Thank you," Mother Maeve replied.

Faith glanced at the priestess, perplexed as to the unique nature of her power, but decided to ignore it and focus on going back to the church instead. Fowler was so close now, and she wasn't going to let him endanger anyone else—ever.

Afterward, she would determine the true nature of this so-called "fairy."

Kieran ran through the back alleys of Ballybridge at full speed, slowing down to a normal pace only when he needed to cross a street where passersby were more likely to see him.

Once he had reached the western side of town and put several blocks between him and the inn, he finally stopped in a narrow alleyway and hid behind a corner, leaning against the wall to catch his breath. He had seen no patrols on his way here, but that would change very quickly—the inquisitor would see to that. She must have arrived at the inn by now and discovered the young boy already healed. The server and the old carriage driver would then explain everything to her.

How the hell was he going to get out of this one?

"Kieran?" Breeze asked meekly from the inside of his hood. "Is it safe to come out?"

Kieran sighed, irate from his companion's stupid mistakes, but he nevertheless peeked around the corner to make sure no one else was nearby.

"Yes," he answered. "You can come out."

The blue-haired fairy jumped off his shoulder, flapped her wings, and hovered in the air in front of him, avoiding his gaze by looking down at the ground instead. She now understood the gravity of their situation. "What's going to happen?" she asked.

*Good question*, Kieran thought. Unsure of how to answer it, he took a moment to think while he continued to peek around the corner, ready to flee at a moment's notice. "Once she hears about you, the inquisitor will order the guards to close the city gates. We won't be able to leave—well, *I* won't be able to, to be more exact. You can just fly out of here any time you want."

The fairy's eyes widened in dismay. "No!" she protested. "There has to be a way out of here. There has to be."

"I'm thinking about it."

"What if…what if we run to the gates before they close them? We have time, right?"

"We can't. If we leave through the gates, the inquisitor will learn about it and they'll send the guards after me. It doesn't matter if I ditch my bow now. They know who to look for."

"Oh no."

"I think there's only one way we can get out of here, but I'm not sure which side of town to take. We can't go west since there's a river running right alongside the wall, so it's either the northern or the eastern side. I may need your help to get there."

Kieran turned away from the alleyway to look at Breeze, only to see her with her head still hanging down, tears welling up in her eyes. Momentarily left speechless by this sight, he stared at the small fairy without any idea about what to say. He'd never made a girl cry before.

"I'm sorry," she said. "I…I just wanted to help."

She continued to stare down at the ground, unable to meet his gaze, and Kieran immediately regretted raising his voice against her. He shouldn't have done that; she was just a child. A fairy who, before today, had never visited a human settlement. Someone who didn't quite understand the real danger an inquisitor posed to a sorcerer like him.

*Goddammit.* Even without knowing about her ability to heal people, he should have expected a reaction from her when the child hurt himself. He could have whispered to her not to do anything, or even pretend to follow the boy's father outside to go get help. Instead, he froze and sat there like an idiot until it was too late to do anything. It was his own fucking fault he was in this mess right now. What a fucking idiot he was.

Kieran sighed again and shook his head. "What's done is done," he said. "There's nothing else we can do about it. Right now, we have to get out of here, and I'll need your help to do it."

"Really?"

"Yes, really."

"Okay," she replied, eager to prove herself and make amends. "What do you need me to do?"

The sorcerer pointed at the roofs above them. "You're going to fly above the roofs and peek down at the streets whenever I need to cross one. There's soon going to be patrols all over the town, searching for me—searching for the both of us, really. But if you're there to tell me when it's safe to cross, we should be able to avoid them and get out of here without any problem. Got it?"

"Got it! But what about the inquisitor? That man said there was one close by, right?"

"Yes. And she won't be alone either. Inquisitors always travel with a knight at their side." Breeze's confused expression prompted him to explain further. "They're a bodyguard of sort. Someone who protects the inquisitor from anyone and anything. I can't fight the both of them at once."

"Then what do we do?"

"We run before they find us, and if you see them once you're up there, you make sure to hide before they can spot you."

"Okay, but I don't know what they look like."

"Dammit. You're right. Okay, listen closely: the inquisitor will be wearing a long white robe with some kind of red belt around her waist. Don't mistake her for a priestess—their belt is white, not red. We have to avoid them too, but they aren't trained to annul magic like inquisitors are."

"Annul?" Breeze repeated. "What's that mean?"

"It means they can cancel our magic just by looking at us."

"What?! They can do that?!"

"Yes, which is why we *cannot* cross paths with her, understood? Because if we do, I'm just another guy with a bow, and her knight won't let that stop him from arresting us."

"I understand. We avoid everyone else until we're out of town."

"Exactly."

"What about her 'knight'? What does she look like?"

"It's a 'he,' not a 'she.' You'll recognize him by his leather armor and the sword he carries on his belt. Do you know what a sword is?"

"I think so. It's like a very long knife, right?"

"Right. He probably will have it sheathed into a scabbard—it's something you put the sword in so you don't cut yourself."

"Can he 'annul' our magic too?"

"No, but his sword can. His armor too."

Breeze gasped at this revelation. "I had no idea this was even possible. Are you sure we'll be able to leave town? These two Church people sound really dangerous."

"That's because they are, and yes, I think we can leave town without them noticing us, but not through the gates. We'll have to go over the walls."

"The walls? But how? I can fly over them, but you can't, right?"

"No, but I can slow down my fall if I jump down from them."

"With magic?"

"Yeah…" Except that the last time he did so, he almost broke both of his legs when landing on the ground. How he wished he had trained for that maneuver since then; the man who took him in after the incident at the orphanage had taught him how to execute it but demonstrated it only once, and Kieran absconded from his mentor's home two days after that. How ironic that the last incomplete lesson the man gave him would now help him escape from an even greater foe.

Kieran shook his head and focused on the immediate danger. The inquisitor had certainly warned the guards by now. "We need to go," he told Breeze. "Right now."

"Okay," she said, nodding confidently. "So, I go up on the roofs and tell you when the way is clear."

"Yes—but don't talk! Just wave at me or something. We don't want to risk alerting them to our presence."

"Which way do we go?"

Kieran clenched his jaw and peeked around the corner of the alleyway again. What direction indeed? He had to pick one before the patrols closed in on him. "Fuck it," he finally muttered under his breath. "Let's go north. It's closer to us than the eastern wall anyway."

"North it is! Don't worry, I'm super good at hiding. They will never find me!"

She punctuated this declaration by giving him a thumbs-up, which managed to pry a smile from him. "Do you even know where north is?" he asked.

"Of course. It's thataway!"

"Hmm. Yeah, it is. All right, go to the roof. We don't have much time."

"On it!" She started to fly upward but then stopped and immediately returned to eye level. "I just thought of something!" she exclaimed. "We can use the signals me and my family came up with!"

Kieran raised his eyebrows at this idea. "What kind of signals?"

"We'd flash our wings whenever we went out hunting," she explained. "One blink means 'stop.' Two blinks mean 'hide.' Three blinks mean 'follow.' Four blinks mean 'go!' One blink, one pause, and two long blinks mean 'regroup.' Two blinks, one pause, and one blink means—"

"Stop, stop," he said, raising his hand. "It's a good idea, but we can just keep the first four."

"Oh, okay. Do you want me to repeat?"

"No. I've got it. Now, go. We need to stay on the move."

"Going!" The fairy flapped her wings harder and flew toward the sky, disappearing over the rooftops. While he waited for her signal, Kieran watched the street down the alleyway. He trusted Breeze to guide him across town and to the wall, but feared the patrols would unintentionally box them in and force him to resort to a more…dire solution. He hoped it wouldn't come to that, especially not with a bright-eyed child like Breeze following him.

The blue fairy appeared at the edge of the rooftop, flashed her wings, and waved down at him from her spot—the way was clear. Kieran leaned back against the wall, closed his eyes, and took a deep breath. There was no turning back now.

He stepped out of the back alley and walked to the street, ready to lift arrows with his mind at the first sign of trouble.

Faith paced in front of the church, unable to stand still while the constabulary scoured the town for Fowler. She purposefully did not participate in the search, acting as the coordinator instead so that the constables would inform her of Kieran's location before anyone else. However, the wait also made her more restless with each minute that passed.

These men were risking their lives by assisting her in her pursuit of the sorcerer, and she doubted that was what they had signed up for when they put on the yellow mantle of the Ballybridge's constabulary. She felt a painful lump in her throat when thinking about how many of them would likely die by the end of the day and how many women and children they would leave behind.

Aiden, on the other hand, was the perfect image of the calm and composed knight his order was renowned for. He stood in front of the two large front doors of the church with his hands behind his back, his eyes continually scanning the whole length of the plaza, no doubt on the lookout for Fowler himself. Aiden surely knew that the sorcerer would never pass through here, but his duty demanded he be prepared for any eventuality.

Faith suddenly felt self-conscious about her pacing and stopped in front of him. She couldn't keep going like this, not when it might worsen her state of mind and affect her judgment. She recalled several meditation techniques Harlow had taught her during her two years at the abbey and chose the simplest one: she closed her eyes, breathed deeply, and concentrated on how her body moved with each inhalation and exhalation.

Once she had regained a semblance of composure, she opened her eyes again and looked at the plaza. The weight in her chest had not left her, nor had the sour taste in her mouth, but compared to the restlessness that previously gnawed at her, this was a definite improvement.

"Are you all right, ma'am?" Aiden asked.

Faith turned to face the knight, whose impassive expression betrayed nothing of his thoughts. "Yes," she said. "I'm fine now. What about you?"

"I'm ready for anything, ma'am."

"That doesn't answer my question." This response caught him off guard and he raised his eyebrows in surprise. Faith couldn't help but let out a chuckle at this unexpected reaction. "Sorry. That's what my mother used to say when I deflected a question."

"Oh." Aiden avoided her gaze for a moment while he reconsidered his answer. "I suppose you could say I'm anxious to meet our target."

"Anxious? Really?"

"Yes." He didn't appear to understand the reason behind her incredulity.

"It's just that you seem so...calm," she explained.

"Ah. Well, I assure you, it's only because I've had experience with this before. I know what to expect."

"And what's that?"

Aiden furrowed his brow and looked her straight in the eyes with an all-too-familiar severity. "I know that sorcerers and witches are prepared to do anything to escape if they don't have a family or a loved one you can use as leverage. And in Fowler's case, we have neither."

This time, he was the one to catch her off guard. The callousness of his answer, the undeniable practicality of it, sent a shiver coursing up and down her spine—because he was right. Inquisitors operated this way everywhere. By forcing sorcerers and witches to surrender willingly, they minimized casualties.

Before she could inquire further about Aiden's past experiences, she heard footsteps coming from her left. She turned and saw a raven-haired man running down a street toward her. When he stopped in front of her, she recognized him as one of the two men whom she yelled at not ten minutes ago. Evidently, he was still wary of her and didn't dare look her in the eyes. She briefly regretted treating him like that but reasoned that it had been necessary.

"Inquisitor," he began, panting. "I-I've come to report that patrols have been sent into the southern and uh…the western parts of town. Captain Duncan is the one in charge of the search, and he told me to tell you he was going to close the gates and secure the stables."

"Good," she replied. "What about the other parts of town?"

"Erik is the one who's supposed to warn the gates there."

"Who's Erik?"

"He's the other guard who was with me, back at the tavern. Um, ma'am."

"It will take longer for him to reach the gates," Aiden pointed out. "They're the farthest from the inn."

"Let's hope he's a fast runner then," Faith said. "What's your name?"

"It's Owen, ma'am."

"Owen. I want you to run back to your captain and tell him I want to be updated on his progress every fifteen minutes. If you can't handle running back and forth between him and me, switch with someone else whenever you need a rest."

"Yes, ma'am!"

"Oh, and one last thing—"

Faith was about to tell him that moving through town alone was dangerous and that there should be someone else with him at all times, but she stopped herself when she heard the footfalls of a group of people approaching from the north. They were still out of sight, but judging by the sound alone, there were at least four of them making their way toward her.

Aiden positioned his scabbard at an angle that would allow him to draw his sword without any difficulty and stepped forward to stand right by her. Faith doubted such precautions were necessary, but she couldn't fault him for fulfilling his role as her protector.

Four men in yellow surcoats, armed with swords at their sides, appeared at the edge of the public square. They were led by a fifth man who wore a white tunic under a clean-cut black waistcoat, a pair of gray breeches, and padded leather shoes. Faith surmised by his neatly combed gray hair, his clean but simple outfit, and the way he folded his hands behind his back that this old man wasn't Lord Harrowmont himself but one of his servants. He approached Faith with a humorless expression, unmoved by the sight of an inquisitor standing in front of the church, and in that instant, she knew that something was wrong.

He came to a halt two meters away from her and gave her the most courteous of bows. "Greetings, Inquisitor, and welcome to Ballybridge. My name is Lloyd Oakley, and I am the steward to Lord Ewan Barker Harrowmont, Count of Fieldagald, Baron of Ballybridge, and the Vanquisher of the Battle of the Twin Rivers. His Excellency hopes you had a pleasant journey and wishes to extend you a dinner invitation. It would be a great honor to him if you were to grace his home with your presence."

Faith frowned. It was unlikely that she would have accepted such an invitation under normal circumstances, but now she had no good reason to even consider it. How could a noble be so clueless as to think about dinner when a sorcerer was roaming free through his town?

"Thank you, Mr. Oakley," she said, a little harshly. "I appreciate the invitation, but there's a sorcerer on the loose, and we must apprehend him before he hurts anybody. I'm sure you understand."

"Ah. Yes, of course. I regrettably must inform you that Lord Harrowmont has decided to call off the search and send the constables back to their original posts. Effective immediately."

"WHAT?!"

The steward visibly flinched when she raised her voice, and he and the constables briefly lost their composure when she stomped toward Oakley, her nostrils flaring like a bull's. A heat spread through her chest like wildfire, and it took all of her willpower not to grab the old man by the collar and scream in his face. Instead, she gritted her teeth and glared at him, her arms shaking like never before.

"What do you *mean* he called off the search?" she asked, enunciating each word very clearly.

Oakley gulped and licked his lips before he answered. "Lord Harrowmont believed this to be some sort of prank," he blurted out. "After hearing young Owen's report of what happened at The Jolly Stew, he concluded that because fairies aren't real, someone was making fun of you."

"Making fun of me? I've got three farmers inside the church who've just told me they were assaulted by a sorcerer who looked *exactly* like the man at the inn!"

The steward widened his eyes at this revelation and brought

a hand to his chin as he considered what to do. "This is unexpected," he said. "Lord Harrowmont should be informed of this at once. I am certain that if you were to share the details of your investigation with him, he would rescind the order to call off the search and offer you his assistance in your endeavor. I could lead you to him, if you'd like."

"*I don't have time for that!* Kieran Fowler is going to escape the city if we don't resume the search immediately!"

"Kieran Fowler? The same one the Inquisition warned us about?"

"Yes! *Him.*"

"I see. Unfortunately, I do not have the authority to overturn one of my lord's commands. The only way I can help you is by leading you to him."

Faith refrained from screaming at the steward. This son of a bitch, piece of shit, poor excuse of a lord was endangering everyone in Ballybridge! How could such an incompetent fool be in charge of this town! How? Fowler was right here, closer than she could ever have hoped for, and this prick of a noble was going to let him escape! What a fool!

"Inquisitor, if I may."

Faith whirled to look at the person who'd spoken to her—Aiden. The knight seemingly exuded calm and focus, but the harsh glance he gave the steward and his men pointed to the contrary. At least she wasn't alone in this sentiment.

"Let me talk to Lord Harrowmont," he said. "I'll convince him to resume the search while you and Mother Maeve continue to search for the target."

She knitted her brow and considered his suggestion for an instant. "You really think you can convince him?"

"I'm certain of it."

"Go then."

"At once, ma'am. Mr. Oakley? Lead the way."

"Far be it from me to tell you what to do," Oakley said as he looked back and forth between the two of them, "but I know Lord Harrowmont well enough to tell you it is very unlikely that he will grant an audience to your knight. Your presence would also be required, Inquisitor."

"There's no need for that," Aiden retorted. "I'm sure Lord Harrowmont will agree to see me once he learns that Sir Aiden Hawkon, prince of Kantner and knight of the Purple Order, requests an audience."

The steward stared incredulously at the knight for a moment while the constables exchanged glances between themselves. He then fell on one knee and bowed his head low, as royal protocol demanded. The four men behind him quickly followed suit. "Your Highness, I-I didn't know. Please forgive my impudence."

"We're losing time, Mr. Oakley. Take me to Lord Harrowmont. Immediately."

"He's at his estate. Please follow me, my lord."

Oakley and his men rose up to their feet and hastily walked back the way they'd come. Aiden moved to follow them but stopped just long enough to put a hand on Faith's shoulder and nod at her. There was no need for words.

Two seconds later, he rejoined the escort and said, "How about we pick up the pace, Mr. Oakley?"

"As you wish, my lord." The six men began running down the street and toward the northern gate, until they disappeared around a corner.

Faith watched them go while she deliberated over her next course of action. She couldn't wait on Aiden and hope that he would successfully change Lord Harrowmont's mind before Fowler skipped town. That would be incredibly short-sighted. No, only one other path lay before her, and if it failed, she might never be able to pick up Fowler's trail again. She had to act now.

The young inquisitor strode to the church's large doors and

opened one of them. Inside, she found Mother Maeve sitting on one of the many empty pews of the nave, near the entrance. It had been nearly ten minutes since she had entered the building, and Faith had heard nothing from her since then. She could only hope the priestess had made some progress.

Faith walked down the middle aisle and hurried to the priestess's side, the sound of her footsteps echoing through the large interior of the church. When she arrived next to Mother Maeve, she saw that her eyes were closed and her hands folded in prayer. Without looking at the inquisitor, she answered Faith's question before it was even asked. "Not yet," she said. "I've only managed to comb through half of the town. I need more time."

"You'll have to hurry," Faith replied. "Lord Harrowmont has recalled the constables back to their posts."

Without opening her eyes, the priestess frowned. "I see our lord has once again proved he's unfit to rule his land," she sighed. "I can tell you they're most likely north of here."

"Most likely? Can't you be a little more precise?"

"No, I can't," she said with a pinched face. "This is the first time I've done this over such a large area, Inquisitor. I can't just 'hurry it up.'"

The snappy retort caused Faith to instantly regret her impatience. She shouldn't forget who her allies here were. "My apologies, Mother. Please, do the best you can."

The priestess nodded and returned her attention to the task at hand. There was no telling how much longer it would take for her to find Fowler and his winged friend. All Faith could do now was wait.

Faith turned around and sat in the pew on the opposite side of the aisle, cursing her own inability to locate the target herself. Instead, she had to rely on the untested talent of a priestess who had never used it this way before. Although God may have been the one to grant Mother Maeve this unusual power, success was not guaranteed. Humans were fallible, and this extended to even priestesses and inquisitors.

Faith sighed and shook her head. These thoughts only worsened her state of mind, and she needed to be focused for what would come next. She looked at the five stained-glass windows depicting the life of Alma Azaria, hoping to regain a sense of serenity from them, and she remembered the chapel at the inquisitorial abbey. There, Harlow gave her one piece of advice that she hadn't paid much attention to back then, but had since gained more significance. On the surface, this piece of advice was simple and easy to follow, but in practice, it was anything but.

*"Your name is the solution to all the problems you'll face in your life."*

The inquisitor glanced at the priestess and saw no changes in her demeanor. Faith could do nothing else but wait. How long, she wasn't sure. But she believed that soon, very soon, she would come face-to-face with the one they called the Pyromancer.

And all the magic in the world wouldn't be able to save him from the fate that awaited him back in Holiburg.

# CHAPTER 16

KIERAN COULD SEE the top of the northern wall from the alleyway where he was hiding. Only a few dozen meters, and he would finally be able to get the hell out of here. At first, he'd doubted that the fairy's eagerness to please him would translate into helpful assistance, but she quickly proved him wrong. Breeze had successfully guided him through town while avoiding the many patrols searching for them. He'd have to thank her for that later.

Kieran wiped his sweaty palms on his trousers while he waited for the fairy's signal. He let out a sigh of relief when he saw her head poke out from the edge of the rooftops and her wings blink four times. It was time. He exited the alleyway and crossed the street, walking in a way he hoped appeared casual while keeping his eyes fixed on the alley in front of him. Glancing around nervously would only tip off curious onlookers who may be watching him from inside their homes—though he hadn't seen any. Still, best to play it safe and not give them any reason to suspect him.

He entered the alleyway and motioned for Breeze to move to the last street they needed to cross. He hid behind the corner of the back alley, leaning against the wall of an old wooden house while the stench of rotten food and shit enveloped him, threatening to make him gag. He glared at the barrels from which the smell emanated and cursed whichever noble was responsible for not building a sewer system here. God, he hated that stench.

Right at that moment, Breeze unexpectedly flew down from the roof to talk to him. "Kieran!" she whispered. "There are humans coming."

"From where?" he asked.

"The—ugh! What's that smell!" The fairy covered her nose and mouth with her forearm to protect herself from the malodorous assault on her senses—it was quite ineffective.

"I'll tell you later," he said. "Where are they coming from, Breeze?"

"The next street over," she said, retching. "They're knocking at the doors and looking into the alleys. I think they'll be here soon."

"All right. We'll go back to the other alley and wait until they're finished. Let's go."

"Got it." The blue-haired girl gave a dirty look at the barrels next to Kieran before flying back to the rooftops. For the next minute or two, Kieran waited for his companion to signal him that the way was clear, during which he heard the men move closer to his location, knocking on doors and questioning the people living inside, though they were too far away for him to make out their words.

As he listened to them, a knot began to form at the pit of his stomach. He eyed the roof where Breeze had disappeared to, wondering how much longer it would take before she gave him the go-ahead, until he saw her fly off the rooftop and back toward him. He felt an ache grow at the back of his throat when he noticed her brow furrowed in worry.

"There are humans there too," she said. "They're doing the same thing as the others at the end of the street."

Kieran balled his hands into fists and looked around him; this back alley was a dead end. The only escape in sight was three doors leading into the run-down houses that surrounded him. He headed to the closest one and tried to open it, but it was locked. He tried the other two, same result.

"Goddammit," he muttered under his breath. "Fucking bullshit…"

"Kieran?" Breeze looked at him with wide eyes, just like any scared child would in this situation. "What's going to happen?"

He flexed his fingers and took a deep breath; he had nowhere to hide in this back alley, and now that the guards were almost upon him from both sides, nowhere to run either. The only solution he could think of was the arrows he carried in his quiver. What happened next would depend on how fast he could shoot down his enemies.

"Breeze," he said slowly. "Go back to the roof. Stay there until they're gone."

"What? But what about you?"

He pulled the bow from his back and nocked an arrow while lifting two more from his quiver with magic.

"What are you going to do?" Breeze asked.

"I think you already know," he answered. "Go. Now. You don't have much time."

"Wait, no! You don't have to hurt anyone. We can…we can figure something out."

"Goddammit, Breeze, you have to go! They're almost here."

He heard one of the men knock loudly on the front door of the building behind him. "Open the door, Franklin!" he heard. "I know you're in there. We're not here for you, so just come on out."

Kieran gritted his teeth and carefully looked around the corner and down the alleyway. No one else was there—yet.

"I can distract them," the fairy said. "Lead them far away from here!"

"What? No!" he objected, trying to keep his voice down. "Are you crazy? The inquisitor will chase after you if you do that!"

"But I'm faster than her!"

"Doesn't matter! You're just a kid, so go hide like I told you to."

Another voice interrupted them, and he could hear this one clearly. "Hey, Edwin! You're with me."

"We're checking out the alley?"

"Yeah."

Kieran leaned back against the wall and cursed under his breath. This was it. The moment he had been dreading.

"I'll go distract them," Breeze whispered.

"I said no! Stay here."

The fairy gazed at the alleyway, her eyes burning with determination; she had already made her decision. He couldn't talk her out of it. In order to keep her safe, he had to act first.

Just as she was about to jump in front of the two men, Kieran drew a gust of magic from the aether and used it to push Breeze away from the alley. She let out a yelp and tumbled in the air while he drew his bowstring and focused on the two arrows floating above his shoulders. He readied another magical blast, this one intended to propel the projectiles at a deadly speed.

But right before he could launch his attack, one of the men in the street called out to someone else. "Lieutenant?"

"At ease, Henry," a new voice said.

Kieran froze immediately, so startled by this sudden interruption that he almost let go of the bowstring. The two guards in the alleyway stopped moving and turned around to face the man who had just arrived. With his heart thumping hard in his chest, Kieran listened closely to their conversation.

"What's happening, Lieutenant? Did they catch the sorcerer already?"

"No, they haven't."

Kieran recognized that voice; it belonged to the same man

who'd interrogated him back when he tried to enter Ballybridge. What was he doing here?

"We're calling off the search," the lieutenant explained. "Return to your previous posts."

The guards immediately began to grumble about their new order.

"Wait, what?"

"Are you serious?"

"Almazar, tell me this wasn't just some new kind of drill."

"Lord Harrowmont wouldn't do that."

"Then why are they calling off the search, genius?"

Out of the corner of his eye, Kieran saw Breeze hover closer to him and listen to the men complain. He relaxed a little when he saw that he hadn't hurt her when he shoved her aside. He loathed having to do that, even though it was for her own safety. Unable to look her in the eye, he turned away and continued to eavesdrop on the guards.

By now, the two men in the alley had moved back to the street to join the others.

"All right, all right, simmer down!" the lieutenant said. "You've got your orders, so get moving."

The men continued to grumble until one of them said, "Come on, Adam. Can you at least tell us what's this about? We've been told there's a sorcerer on the loose."

"Yeah, I've also heard there's an inquisitor in town," another man added. "She's the one who called for the search, isn't she?"

"Has to be. I've seen her carriage pass through the north gate."

"Come on, Lieutenant. The hell is happening?"

Kieran peeked around the corner and saw the lieutenant— who was indeed the same man he'd met earlier today—heave a sigh and massage his forehead while the guards bombarded him with questions. "Fine, fine!" he relented. "Yes, there *is* an inquisitor in town, and yes, she's the one who called for the search. The sorcerer did something at Rupert's tavern, I don't know what, but that's supposedly how the inquisitor learned about him. Someone informed Lord Harrowmont, and he's decided that everyone should go back to their posts. That's it."

"Did he give a reason why?"

The lieutenant finally lost his patience. "*Did he*— are you soft in the head, you numbskull?" he shouted. "Or is asking stupid questions a hobby of yours? Maybe you'd like to ask Lord Harrowmont yourself, how about that?"

"Uh, no, Lieutenant. Sorry, Lieutenant."

"That's what I thought. Now follow your orders before Old Man Oakley shows up and docks your pay—yeah, that concerns you too, Werner! You think I care that we're the same rank? Go, before I make you." He walked away from the men and continued to talk to himself, his voice gradually receding in the distance. "'Did he give a reason why?' What a fucking moron. Gonna get himself thrown into prison, saying dumb shit like that."

The guards stood around in silence and waited for the lieutenant to be far enough away before they spoke up again. "Nice job, Alistair. You did it again."

"Shut up."

"Yeah, now he'll be cranky for the rest of the day because of you."

"You guys wanted to ask him the same question!"

"Not if it was going to piss him off."

"That's enough," the one named Werner said. "You heard the man. Go back to the barracks, on the double."

The guards followed their superior down the street while they continued to rag on each other as grown men do, unaware that the sorcerer they had been tasked to find was hiding on the other side of the house.

Once he'd made sure they were truly gone, Kieran dropped the two arrows to the ground and sagged against the wall. The sudden lightness he felt percolate in his chest almost made him thankful for the pungent smells of piss and shit assaulting his senses—almost.

Breeze hovered next to him. "Kieran? Are you okay?"

Kieran blinked at her. She should be angry with him for pushing her, but instead, she waited anxiously for his answer.

"What happened?" she asked. "Is something wrong?"

"No," he finally said. "I'm fine." He got up on his feet and magically returned the two arrows on the ground to his quiver. "I'm just a little shaken."

"Oh. Okay."

He did his best to avoid her gaze and peeked around the corner again to check the alleyway—no guards in sight. They could go.

"Are you mad at me?" Breeze asked.

He looked back at the fairy and saw her head hanging low, like a child who knew they were about to be scolded. "Why do you say that?" he asked.

"Because…you pushed me out of the way. Did I…did I do something wrong again?"

He briefly pondered the question and decided it'd be best to be straight with her. "No," he said. "You did nothing wrong."

"But…you didn't let me help."

"That's right. It was way too dangerous for you."

"But I told you, I'm fast!"

"Yeah, well, that doesn't matter. Your brother would kill me if I didn't look after you, so that's what I'm going to do." Kieran turned away from his small companion and slung the bow across his back. "Now let's go. We have to get to the wall before the guards do. You ready?"

Breeze stared at him as she contemplated what he'd told her, until strangely enough, a wide smile formed on her lips. "You need me to take a look at the street?"

"Yeah. Just in case."

"On it!" She flew high up in the air and did as he asked. It looked like that cheered her up a little. Good.

Breeze waved down at him from the rooftops while flashing her wings again before she crossed the street. Kieran took a deep breath, placed the bow across his chest in a way that wouldn't hinder his movements, and followed her at a brisk pace.

He was almost there.

Mother Maeve rose from her seat. "I found them."

Faith stood up as well, and they hurried down the center aisle, toward the church's entrance.

"They're heading north," the head priestess said. "They've just reached the wall."

"They?" Faith repeated. "You mean you found that fairy too?"

"I think so. I almost didn't notice her. The way she moves, I thought she was an insect at first. She can't be taller than a chalice."

Faith fell silent as she pondered what to do with this revelation. No matter how hard she tried, she couldn't recall a single creature from the *Bestiary of Unnatural Entities* tome whose description fit the one Finlay gave of the "fairy." Maybe it was a shapeshifter of some sort who took the form of a harmless fairy to better deceive its victims, but that didn't explain why it would save the boy when a priestess and an inquisitor were already on their way.

To uncover the truth, she would need to catch both Fowler and the creature.

She and Mother Maeve exited the church and headed north. "Can you still sense them?" Faith asked.

"Yes. I think your sorcerer might be trying to climb over the wall."

"Damn!" She couldn't let that happen. If he successfully left the town's enclosure, it would become that much harder to track him down, especially if Lord Harrowmont persisted in opposing her efforts to capture him. "We have to run! Can you keep up?"

"I can try."

They sprinted at full speed toward the north gate.

Kieran examined the surface of the wall for clefts and protrusions that would allow him to climb it, but a thorough search only confirmed his suspicions: the only way up was through the towers.

"What are you doing?" Breeze asked, landing on his shoulder.

He let his gaze linger on the battlements for a little while longer before he turned away from them and walked alongside the fortification, going west. "Nothing," he answered. "I was just thinking about climbing the wall, but I can't do it. Not without a rope."

"Then how are you going to get up there?"

"See that tower over there?" he said, pointing into the distance. "That's how."

"But I remember seeing humans on top of the wall when we entered town."

"Yes, but that was at the gate. I don't think there are guards on this section of the wall yet. Not when everybody has been alerted to our presence."

"But what if there are?"

"Then I'll deal with them."

Breeze flew in front of him and blocked his path. With her arms akimbo and a fierce scowl, she came right up to his face and said, "You shouldn't do that. That's too dangerous."

Kieran frowned and narrowed his eyes. "I know it is, but I've got no other choice."

"Yes, you do. You could just fly instead."

"Fly?" he repeated. "I can't *fly*."

"Why not? I do it all the time."

"Because I don't have *wings*, Breeze!" Kieran realized he had just raised his voice loud enough for other people to hear. He bit his lip, cursing himself for losing his temper, and glanced around at the street to make sure no one else was here. The townsfolk didn't worry him—they would have locked themselves up in their homes as soon as they'd heard about the sorcerer at large. No, it was the guards he had to keep an eye out for. Luckily for him, none were in his vicinity.

"I don't need my wings to fly," Breeze told him. "Didn't you notice?"

"Huh?" He swiveled his head back to her, staring in disbelief. "What do you mean?"

"You really didn't notice?" she asked again. "But how could you not? You're a mage, so you should have…"

"Notice *what*, Breeze?"

"It's not my wings that allow me to fly—it's my magic!"

Kieran blinked at her as if she had grown another head. Surely, he must have misunderstood her. Otherwise…

"What do you mean, exactly?" he asked.

"I just use my magic to move myself, the same way you move your arrows in the air."

"Then…what are the wings for?"

"Steering myself, of course. It'd be a lot harder to do without them. So, do you wanna try it?"

"You mean flying?"

"Yeah!"

Was it truly possible? He stared at the fairy's wings and examined them more closely than he had before. Now that he thought about it, it should have been obvious that wings such as these couldn't possibly carry Breeze. Even at her size, she would be much too heavy for them, which posed another problem…

"I can't do it, Breeze. I'm too heavy."

"That's okay. I'll help you! With the two of us, we should be able to get you up there. Here, let's get in position."

"Wait—"

She ignored him and landed on his shoulder, grabbing on to his ear so she wouldn't fall down. "Are you ready?"

"Of course not!" he retorted. "I'm not even sure what I'm supposed to do."

"I told you, it's like moving your arrows. You just have to concentrate on your whole body instead."

"That's it?"

"Yup! That's it. Think you can do it?"

Kieran looked up at the battlements and asked himself the same question. He'd heard many stories about the mages of the Aurelian Empire and how many of them were capable of flying through the air—the most famous ones being the God Emperors themselves—but he'd never imagined that they managed such a feat with telekinesis. To his knowledge, it was the simplest form of magic, and the easiest to learn. To think he could have learned to fly long before now...

"I'll try," he finally decided. "Just don't drop me."

"Of course not!" she replied. "You can trust me." She punctuated this statement with a small nod and an encouraging smile, which, to his surprise, did manage to soothe him a little. He responded with a nod of his own and set his gaze back to the battlements.

His mind expanded outward and grabbed on to the vast source of magic that surrounded him, absorbing a continuous flow of power that he redirected all around his body. Slowly but surely, he felt a wobbliness spread from his limbs to his torso, threatening to topple him like a pile of coins. Luckily for him, something caught him just as he was about to fall to the ground: another gust of magic, stronger than anything he'd ever wielded, but also less accurate. It interweaved with his own power while moving at its own pace, following an unfamiliar pattern he had never used before. And then, he began hovering in the air.

"Woah!" Kieran exclaimed. He instinctively flailed his arms around to regain his balance, to no use. "It's working!"

"Awesome, huh?" Breeze giggled. "I need your help, though. You're pretty heavy."

"Right, right." He began to exert his will on the magic that had lifted him up and gently propelled himself upward, toward the top of the fortifications. His senses had been heightened by this experience: he could see every bump and depression in the masonry wall, smell the rot and stench emanating from the back alleys, and taste the sourness of the saliva in his mouth.

He was flying. Truly flying! Maybe not at great speed or over a long distance, but flying nonetheless! Had he learned and practiced this technique sooner, maybe by now he would have been capable of dashing through the sky like the mages of old. It would have saved him so much time and—

Kieran froze. He'd made the mistake of looking down, and although he tried to not let it affect him, his ascent had already slowed to a crawl. Only a few meters separated him from the top of the fortification.

"Kieran? What's wrong?"

"Nothing," he lied. "Let's keep going."

He reached out to the wall with both of his hands and grabbed on to it to better control the rest of his ascension, arriving at the top in a matter of seconds. He didn't immediately step onto it, however. First, he peeked through one of the crenels to confirm no one else was here; it would take only one guard to raise the alarm for the inquisitor to come running, and he was already taking a huge risk flying out in the open where anyone living close to the wall could look out their window and see him. He had to hurry.

Fortunately for him, there were no guards patrolling the rampart. He climbed through the crenel and landed on the alure.

"We did it!" Breeze exclaimed. "I told you we could do it! I told you!"

"Yeah, you sure did," he said with a grin. "Now, shush. We don't want to alert anyone."

"Oh! Right." She stopped using her magic and lowered her voice to a whisper. "So, how were you planning to get down there?"

Before answering her, Kieran approached the parapet and studied the landscape. Fields of wheat covered the small hills on this side of town, although he could see other types of crops far into the distance, near a forest that stretched over the horizon. He looked at the ground and the distance separating him from it—the last obstacle standing between him and freedom.

"I was going to slow my fall with magic," he replied. "But I guess I don't need to do it alone anymore. Wanna help?"

"Of course!"

He nodded and climbed between two merlons, holding on to them to maintain his balance. Landing safely on the ground would be a lot easier with Breeze here to assist him. However, it didn't make the experience of stepping off a wall any less unnerving.

"What are you waiting for?" the fairy innocently asked.

"Just…give me a second!" Kieran bit his lower lip and took a deep breath as he gathered power from the surrounding aether. It didn't take long before his body became lighter and began to rise in the air, forcing him to grab the merlons to hold himself in place lest he drift away like a leaf in the wind. He looked down the wall once again and—before he could rethink his plan of action—pushed himself off the battlements.

His heart skipped a beat when he did.

As expected, gravity made his descent a lot faster than he would have preferred, and with a clenched jaw and tense muscles, he lowered himself to the ground. He landed amid the tall grass that grew at the base of the fortification, leaned back against the wall, and let out a sigh of relief. He was still in one piece.

"You're learning really fast," Breeze remarked. "Maybe one day we'll even be able to fly together!"

"Fly together, huh?" The idea was enough to turn his stomach. "I'll...uh, think about it." Judging by the smile she gave him, she didn't pick up on his reluctance and thought it was a great idea.

"So, what now?" she asked.

"Now, we slip away unnoticed," he answered. "You might need to get off my shoulder for that, though."

"Huh? Oh, okay." The fairy deployed her blue wings—which fluttered against his left ear for a brief moment—and then flew in a wide arc into the air. Since he didn't have to worry about her falling down his shoulder anymore, Kieran crouched into the tall grass and moved at a slow pace toward the forest north of here.

"What'cha doing?" Breeze asked.

"Slipping away unnoticed," he answered.

"Ooh, I get it. Is there anything I can do?"

"Yeah, you be the lookout."

"On it!"

Kieran nodded at his small companion and set his gaze forward. He would need to put a few hundred meters between himself and the town before he could return to the main road and resume his journey. Only then would he allow himself to feel truly safe.

At least now the worst was behind him.

Faith and Maeve rushed to the northern gate at full speed.

A small group of constables had gathered in front of it and were talking among themselves. When one of them noticed the inquisitor and the head priestess running their way, he quickly gestured at the rest of his comrades to shut up, and the constables immediately stood to attention and waited for their arrival.

Faith's first thought was to ignore them. Lord Harrowmont had proven himself useless when it came to dealing with the sorcerer, and she had a mind to keep him out of the loop for as long as possible. However, it was vital that someone inform Aiden of Fowler's movement and her intention to chase after him.

Reluctantly, she slowed down and came to a halt in front of the constables. "Who's in charge here?" Faith demanded.

"Me, Inquisitor." A black-haired man with a scruffy beard stepped forward and saluted Faith by clapping his right fist to his chest. "Lieutenant Werner Mensing, at your service."

"Lieutenant Mensing. I need you to send someone to Lord Harrowmont's estate and warn my knight, Sir Aiden Hawkon, that I've located the sorcerer and am in pursuit of him. He must join me immediately outside the wall, north of here. Understood?"

"I, uh…" The man hesitated for an instant. "I would like to, Inquisitor, but we've been ordered to return to our posts and—"

"Werner," Mother Maeve said, interrupting him while she caught her breath. "Do I need to have a talk with your mother again?"

The lieutenant stiffened at the mention of his mother and gripped his spear tighter. "No, ma'am."

"Then you will send a messenger to warn the inquisitor's knight?"

"At once, ma'am." He turned to another man. "Edwin. You heard the inquisitor. Go, now. On the double."

"Yes, Lieutenant!" The young man took off immediately and followed the wall, heading west. Faith didn't waste any time and resumed her chase, leaving the other constables behind as she passed through the open portcullis and stepped onto the road.

Mother Maeve followed close behind, although her breathing

had become a lot more labored since they left the church. Faith slowed down to let her catch up before she asked, "Are we close?"

It took a few seconds before the older woman managed a response. "We're almost there."

Faith swiveled her head and searched her surroundings for any signs of Fowler's presence, but she only saw fields of wheat for leagues around. "Where?" she asked.

Mother Maeve pointed at a spot in one of the fields on their right, maybe one hundred meters ahead of them.

"There."

"Kieran," Breeze whispered. "Someone just came out of town—wait, no. There are two of them."

The sorcerer stopped moving and pricked up his ears. Grasshoppers screamed like they were wont to do during the middle of summer, and the grass rustled gently to the rhythm of the wind, but he heard no alarm. "What are they doing?" he asked, beads of sweat gathering on his brow.

"Running on the road," she answered. "I think they're both women? It's hard to tell from here. And they have strange clothes too, ones I've never seen before. The one in the front even has a—"

The fairy froze and fell silent. Kieran looked up at her, curious to find out why. "What is it?" he asked.

"A red belt," Breeze said. "The woman has a red belt."

Kieran stopped breathing for a second and felt chills run down his spine. He couldn't see the two women while hiding in the grass but nevertheless followed the fairy's gaze to face their direction. "What about the other woman?" he asked. "What is she wearing?"

"She's wearing the same clothes, but her belt is white."

A priestess. Probably the one living in Ballybridge. But what about the knight? "Do you see anyone else?" he asked. "A man with a sword at his side?"

"A man? No. Only the two women."

"Are you sure?"

"Um. Um." She looked at them one more time, just in case she'd missed something. "Yes, I'm sure. Why? What does it mean?"

Kieran slowly removed the bow from his back so as to not alert the inquisitor. He then nocked an arrow while lifting two others with his mind.

"It means we have a fighting chance."

# CHAPTER 17

MOTHER MAEVE STOPPED running and motioned to Faith to do the same. They stood in the middle of the road, flanked on both sides by fields of wheat and grasshoppers serenading to each other. Without uttering a word, the priestess pointed at a specific spot in the field on their right.

"Right there," she whispered while catching her breath. "Maybe fifty, sixty meters off the road."

Faith followed her gaze and attempted to ignore the sour taste at the back of her throat. Although she was barely winded after sprinting over here—unlike Mother Maeve, who had never benefited from the inquisitorial training regimen—sweat nevertheless beaded her forehead and trickled down the middle of her back, causing great discomfort when it continued down the cleft of her rump.

Kieran Fowler had to be somewhere around here, lying in wait.

Although she had her back to the sun, it had only begun its descent toward the horizon and wouldn't impede Fowler's aiming if he decided to shoot at her. Her stomach churned at the simple thought of fighting him.

"Mother Maeve," she said, her hands shaking while she

tied her long hair into a ponytail. "Go back to town and bring Aiden here."

"Inquisitor… Are you sure?"

"Yes. Go, now." The priestess hesitated only for an instant before she nodded at the inquisitor and hurried back to the gate. Faith didn't spare her even a glance; she focused all of her attention on the spot where Fowler lay hidden instead, ready to protect Mother Maeve from any attack he might unleash on her.

Nothing of the sort transpired.

Faith raised one shaky arm in front of her and summoned a sliver of God's power in the palm of her hand; one second later, a filament of white light appeared in it and rapidly extended until it took the form of a staff two meters long. The divine weapon pulsed in her hand with warm energy, light made solid by the grace of the Kind Mother.

She held it upright without taking her eyes off the field and prepared herself for the worst.

"The woman with the white belt is leaving," Breeze said, hiding behind a couple of wheat spikes. "The other one is still here."

Kieran pulled on the bowstring and considered shooting the priestess before she could reach town and alert the others to his presence. Hitting her would be easy, even from this distance, but it would also be dangerous and pointless. The inquisitor somehow already knew where he was, and the guards at the gate were sure to have noticed her running out of town with their priestess in tow. There would be no putting that genie back in the bottle.

"What is she doing now?" he asked.

"She's looking straight at us," the fairy answered as she peeked between the wheat spikes. "How did she find us from so far away?"

"I have no idea. It doesn't matter now. We can't sneak away anymore."

"Then…what are we going to do?"

"You stay hidden and don't come out until I tell you it's safe."

"But—"

"No buts."

Before she could protest further, another voice interrupted the both of them.

"Kieran Fowler!" the inquisitor shouted, her voice as clear as a bell despite the distance separating them. "Surrender now, and I promise you will not be harmed. Refuse, and I'll have no choice but to take you in by force."

Kieran scoffed. "As if anything other than death was waiting for me in Holiburg," he muttered to himself. He moved the two floating arrows closer to his head and then told Breeze, "Go find somewhere to hide."

"But"—she peeked through the wheat spikes again—"she has something in her hands now. Some sort of shiny staff, I think."

"It's called an Eos. That's the only weapon inquisitors have. There's nothing you can do against her, Breeze. You gotta go, now."

The small girl looked at him with wide green eyes, paralyzed by indecision. Kieran thought about using a more forceful tone to get her moving but decided against it. Instead, he smiled at her and told her yet another lie. "Don't worry, I'll be fine. Just wait for me, okay?"

Her butterfly wings fluttered a little faster when he said that, and after some hesitation, she nodded back at him. "Okay. I'll go hide a little deeper into the field."

"Good." Kieran maintained the mask of confidence he'd put on long enough for Breeze to look at him one more time before she flew away east, away from the road and the inquisitor. He watched her disappear behind a curtain of wheat stalks, wondering if he would ever see her again. He didn't want this to be the end. He wanted to keep traveling with her and listen to her incessant stream of questions about humans and their way of life. But he knew it wasn't meant to be.

A sorcerer's life always ended at the hand of another. But that didn't mean he would lie down and resign himself to his fate. No. He would fight until his very last breath and make damn sure to take his killer down with him.

Faith didn't expect a response from Fowler and prepared herself for a surprise attack. When it didn't come, she scanned the field for any sign of movement but saw nothing. He couldn't possibly have sneaked away. Had he attempted to flee, she would certainly have noticed it.

Anxious, she grabbed the Eos with both hands and tightened her grip on it until her knuckles turned white. As an inquisitor, her abilities were mostly defensive in nature and she relied upon her knight to take the fight to the sorcerers, but Aiden wasn't here. She couldn't risk stepping into that field without seeing Fowler first.

She had to trick him into revealing himself.

"Fowler," she began, projecting her voice again so that he could hear her. "I know about your mother. I know what she did to all those babies who were yet to be born." The wheat continued to sway gently in the wind. "What if she had done the same to you?"

A sense of foreboding dread suddenly filled her, and she instinctively called upon the Kind Mother to protect her from this impending new threat. The next instant, an arrow smashed itself against the invisible surface of the shield she had surrounded herself with, snapping in two and falling to the ground. She barely had time to register what had happened before she saw a man stand up in the field and aim his bow at her.

The second arrow whirred through the air and bounced off her shield. Immediately after that, she dissolved the invisible wall and summoned another one around Fowler, imprisoning him in a cocoon of divine energy.

Kieran didn't realize what she had done until he nocked another arrow and tried to shoot her with it. When he did, it simply smashed itself against the inside of the barrier. Splinters flew at his face and he backed away, colliding with the other side of the barrier.

Faith stepped into the field and carefully approached him. "It's useless," she told him. "You cannot get out of there without my say-so."

He lowered his bow and examined his surroundings, no doubt attempting to perceive the presence of the shield with his eyes.

Only now did she get a good look at the man she had been tasked to capture: he wore a long-sleeved green tunic frayed by the passage of time, a cloak of the same color but woven with a darker material, and a pair of gray trousers. Looking at his short and uneven chestnut hair, she deduced that he had cut it himself, probably with a knife. His face was also clean-shaven, most certainly from this morning after he'd attacked and injured Arthur and his two sons.

She continued to walk toward him until less than ten meters separated them from each other. Then she stopped.

Kieran raised his left hand and tentatively touched the surface of the shield. Nothing happened to indicate that it was there, but it was obvious his hand couldn't get past a certain point. "So that's the famous Aegis," he remarked, his tone calm and rigid. "I've always wondered what it looked like. But I see nothing."

He then set his gaze upon her, piercing her with his dark hazel eyes. Although he wasn't particularly attractive, there was a certain allure to his lean face and pronounced cheekbones. The murderous intent emanating from him, however, negated what little appeal he had.

"You should have surrendered," she told him. "I could have spoken in your favor to the judge."

"Oh, really," he said, sounding unconvinced. "So I can spend the rest of my life in prison instead of on a scaffold? No, thank you."

Faith frowned and held her staff closer to her heart. Fowler was awfully calm for someone who was facing a possible death sentence. Why?

"You can find redemption in life," she pleaded. "With the right guidance, you could—"

"No." Kieran pulled a new arrow from his quiver and nocked it to his bow. "Keep your sermons. They won't help you."

She narrowed her eyes and grasped her staff tighter. "Stop this," she said. "This is pointless."

"Is it?" He glared at her and slowly raised his weapon. "How can you be so sure?"

"You know why. The Aegis cannot be broken by mere arrows."

"Yes, it can. You just have to know its weakness."

This time, it was her turn to glare at him. "Which is?"

Kieran placed his fingers around his arrow and drew on the bowstring, eliciting a distinctive creak as the cord was stretched to its limit. He stepped forward until the tip of the arrowhead touched the surface of the barrier and, without taking his eyes off of her, gave the inquisitor his answer. "It's you."

Then, she heard the sound of an arrow whirring through the air, and before she could understand what was happening, something pierced her left shoulder. She lost her breath, stumbled backward, and fell to the ground amid the wheat stalks.

Her training kicked in and she summoned another shield,

centered on her this time. It barely finished enveloping her body before a second arrow crashed against the surface of the barrier.

"Goddammit," Fowler muttered.

The pain began to spread through her left side like fire, threatening to break her concentration on the Aegis, which was the only thing standing between her and the sorcerer.

Fowler had tricked her, she realized. He'd let himself be captured so that she'd lower her guard while he aimed another arrow at her, one he'd kept hidden in the field and outside of the shield—and she had almost died because of that mistake!

"So, it's true," the sorcerer said. "You cannot annul my magic and use one of your other miracles both at the same time."

Faith groaned in pain and looked up at Fowler, who now stood right beside her with his bow aimed at her heart and two more arrows floating at his sides, three meters above the ground.

He had thought of everything.

"Here's what I'm going to do," Kieran said. "I'm going to leave, and you're not going to do a damn thing about it. If you try to cage me again, I'll shoot you with one of my birdies. If you try to annul my magic, I'll shoot you with this one instead." He motioned at the arrow nocked on his bow. "Understood?"

He didn't really expect her to answer his question, but she did surprise him by asking him one. "How?" she said, gritting her teeth. "How did you know?"

The inquisitor reached for the arrow stuck in her shoulder. He doubted she'd be able to remove it while maintaining the integrity of her Aegis, which would give him the time necessary to make his escape. He considered whether or not he should answer her question, but he was distracted when he saw the blood spread across the immaculate white of her robe.

Faith clutched her shoulder in the vain hope that it would help lessen the pain, but it only made it worse. She stifled a moan and tried to think of a way to stall Fowler. *Aiden is coming*, she reminded herself. He was coming, and Fowler needed to be here when Aiden arrived. "How?" she repeated.

Kieran met her gaze again and frowned. "Doesn't matter," he said. "Besides, I've got other places to be."

He glanced at the town and saw three figures standing in front of the gate, looking straight at him. No doubt they had seen the inquisitor fall to the ground and were now wondering whether or not she had been killed. Even if they were too afraid to send for reinforcements, her knight wouldn't share the same reluctance.

Kieran started moving away from the inquisitor, one step at a time. Only a few more meters, and he'd be out of her line of sight.

But Faith refused to let that happen.

She grabbed the arrow sticking out of her shoulder, took a deep breath, and broke it with one twist of her wrist. A new wave of agony hit her, and it took all of her willpower not to cry out in pain. With that done, she pushed herself off the ground with her right hand and slowly rose to her feet.

Kieran stopped and prepared himself for a counterattack. He eyed the staff of white light lying next to the inquisitor and wondered if she was planning to use it against him, but she didn't even bother picking it up.

"You know I can't let you get away," she declared, her blood still seeping down her shoulder. "You've hurt too many people."

"You should have stayed down," he replied, clenching his jaw. "You're going to die."

"We all are."

The two stared at each other in silence, their bodies as tense as the bowstring Kieran was pulling taut. The rest of the world faded away, along with every distraction that could endanger their lives if they paid attention to them. For each of them, all that remained was the enemy.

Kieran waited for Faith to make the first move. He couldn't do anything against her while her shield was up, and she knew it.

On the other hand, Faith also knew that she couldn't annul his magic or imprison him in her Aegis either. Just like he'd told her, attempting either option would most certainly result in her death. She could think of only one way to win this fight, but it was so unconventional, she had no idea what her chances of success would be.

Remembering her oath, she took her first step toward Kieran. He reacted like she hoped he would: by taking a step back. There could be no hesitation anymore. She had to take the offensive. With her third step, she charged forward at full speed, rapidly closing the distance between the two of them.

Kieran couldn't run backward and aim at the inquisitor at the same time. He had to stand his ground. If she truly intended to attack him, she would need to release her shield first, which would give him the perfect opportunity to shoot her.

He waited until she was right in front of him, ready to strike him with the Eos that she would undoubtedly summon at the very last second, before he released his arrow. It bounced off her shield and disappeared somewhere between the wheat stalks while she pressed on and pushed Kieran back with the Aegis.

Right when he lost his footing, Faith lowered the shield and dispelled the Eos she had left on the ground, summoning a much shorter one in her right hand instead. She aimed it at Fowler's head, but the sorcerer spun on his right leg and managed to avoid the brunt of the attack, which merely grazed his jaw.

Once he had regained his balance, he moved away and shot one of his remaining birdies at her, only to hear it break against the barrier. He realized that she was raising and lowering her shield between her attacks. And because it was invisible, he couldn't tell when.

Once that second arrow shattered, Faith pressed the advantage and swung her rod of light in an upward motion, aiming for the space between the sorcerer's sixth and seventh ribs. Disoriented, Fowler blocked her strike with the upper limb of his bow and loosed his last floating arrow at her, only to hit a wheat spike behind her as she spun away from him.

He used this opportunity to draw his knife from its sheath.

Despite the pain in her shoulder, Faith held firmly to the lower half of the Eos and pointed the other end at Fowler. Then, she called upon the Kind Mother and extended the length of her weapon until it hit him right in the chest.

It knocked the wind out of him, causing him to stagger backward and drop his knife as he gasped for air. Faith shortened the Eos to its normal length and prepared to strike him again, but she stopped when the pain almost overwhelmed her. Black dots appeared at the edges of her vision, and it was with great reluctance that she forced herself to wait before she launched her next attack, or else she might falter at a critical moment. Unfortunately for her, it also gave Fowler enough time to recover before they resumed their battle.

For several seconds, the two of them glared at each other while they planned their next move. Faith considered confining him inside her Aegis again, but before she could muster the concentration to dispel her barrier and summon another one, Fowler had successfully lifted a new arrow from his quiver and made it hover six meters away from him.

She now faced the same conundrum as before.

Kieran wasn't about to give her the opportunity to blindside him again. He knew that if he didn't end this soon, she would eventually get the better of him and put him in chains—and there was no way in hell he was going to let that happen. No fucking way.

He dropped the floating arrow to the ground, and Faith took a step back and tightened her grip on her staff. Something was coming.

Kieran roared, and a burst of flames erupted out of thin air in front of him. It rushed toward her, surrounding and enveloping her shield in a matter of seconds. The flames burned everything around her, turning the wheat stalks into flakes of ash that swirled away from the raging inferno, but that was nothing compared to the heat. Suffocating, relentless, blazing heat. The Aegis couldn't protect her against the full brunt of it, nor would it endure indefinitely. Already, she felt her concentration waning.

She did the only thing she could—she ran away. With her eyes closed and her hands covering her face to protect herself from the heat, she fled toward the town, her lungs desperate for fresh air, but the instant she stepped out of the hellfire, it doubled in size and devoured everything around her once again.

Kieran paused his attack when the fire he'd unleashed began to spread toward him. He backed away in a hurry and covered his mouth with his sleeve to keep the smoke out of his throat. The flames may have engulfed the inquisitor, but he had no doubt that she had survived and would definitely come after him if he ran away.

He had no choice but to finish her off.

He circled around the fire and kept himself at a safe distance while he nocked an arrow and lifted another in the air. He had expected to find her a few dozen meters away from the ever-growing inferno, maybe even somewhere closer to the road. But when he finally reached the other side of the fire, all he saw were more fields and a road devoid of people. No sign of the inquisitor.

Kieran swept the whole area with his eyes but found nothing. His first thought was that she was still inside the fire, waiting for the opportune moment to attack and disarm him. But no, that was impossible. Assuming her Aegis could even shield her from the heat, he knew the flames would consume all the air around her. To stay there was suicide. Which meant there was only one other place where she could be hiding.

Among the wheat stalks.

Breeze watched the battle between Kieran and the inquisitor from almost fifty leaps away. Every time she thought one of them had gained the upper hand, the other retaliated in a clever and unexpected way. The fairy almost stopped breathing, transfixed by this duel to the death.

Nana had been absolutely right when it came to humans. They were dangerous. Deadly, even. Breeze never could have imagined such a scene before today, nor did she think she could ever accurately describe it to her siblings either. It was just so overwhelming. Then, she noticed something strange about the inquisitor.

An odd feeling started nagging at Breeze the moment the inquisitor imprisoned Kieran in some kind of invisible barrier, which the fairy could feel even from this distance. It finally dawned on her what was happening when the woman created a new shiny staff in her hands.

Kieran suddenly conjured a gout of fire that lunged at the inquisitor and swallowed her whole. Not even Bubble could have summoned so many flames at once.

Breeze watched the woman in white escape the fire and stumble forward, but she lost sight of her when the woman fell to her knees in the middle of the field. Soon after that, the distinctive aura of the staff and shield vanished, making it impossible for Breeze to pinpoint the inquisitor's location anymore. Kieran circled around the fire, his bow and arrows ready to shoot, but it was already too late; the inquisitor had successfully managed to sneak away.

Or so Breeze thought. Twenty seconds later, Breeze felt it again: the peculiar aura that the staff of light emanated when its wielder summoned it. And it had appeared less than five leaps away from Kieran.

Breeze left her hiding place and rushed forward, intent on stopping the both of them.

They didn't understand what they were doing. Someone had to explain it to them before one of them ended up dead! The inquisitor stood up and charged at whom she believed was her enemy, but she was wrong! They were both wrong!

Kieran blocked the attack at the last second with his bow but dropped the arrow he had nocked. He tried to shoot the woman with the floating arrow, but he missed and fell backward when she closed the distance between them and hit him in the chest with the end of her staff. Just before she hit him again, he knocked her off balance by sweeping her legs; she fell next to him and moaned in pain because of the shock of the landing. They both had lost their weapons.

"Stop!" Breeze shouted. "You have to stop!"

They didn't listen to her. They wrestled in the field, trying to dominate each other. The inquisitor attempted to pin Kieran down by applying an ankle lock. Kieran lifted two more arrows from his quiver and aimed them at her head, but with one look from the woman, they dropped among the wheat stalks. She had annulled his magic.

"You have to stop fighting! You're—"

Kieran began screaming, like she had never heard anyone scream before. He swung his upper body forward to break free, and although the inquisitor attempted to fight it, her injury eventually got the better of her. A second later, Kieran was on top of the inquisitor, his right knee pressing against her throat while he immobilized her arms with his hands.

"Kieran! STOP!" Breeze flew to her friend's side and grabbed his arm to pull him away from the inquisitor. He didn't even budge.

"Get the hell out of here, Breeze!" he yelled as he pushed down on the woman's throat, choking her to death.

"No! You can't do that!"

"She's trying to KILL ME!"

"Don't do it! She's a mage just like you!"

"GET AWAY FROM—"

Kieran stopped. He must have misheard her. What she said didn't make sense at all. "W-what did you say?" he asked.

"She's a mage!" Breeze repeated, desperately trying to pull him away from the inquisitor. "She's using magic, just like you!"

Kieran blinked and froze at Breeze's words. That couldn't be right. She had to have made some sort of mistake. She had to. How else could any of this make sense?

"KIERAN!" Breeze shouted. "You're killing her!"

The sorcerer instinctively eased the pressure on Faith's neck to let her breathe again. The instant he did, she freed her right arm from his grip and summoned a new Eos in her hand, one much shorter than the usual length. Before he could do anything to stop her, she hit him full force on his head.

Kieran's vision turned white, and he felt all of his strength leave his body. He collapsed on his right side like a sack of potatoes and stayed there, incapable of moving any of his muscles.

"Kieran!" Breeze landed next to her friend and placed her hands on his cheek. "Kieran?"

He did not answer her. He only responded with a weak groan of pain that resonated through her arms and shook her little heart. His glassy eyes were unfocused and seemingly unaware of Breeze's presence. The blood dripping down his face alarmed her the most.

"It's okay, Kieran! You're gonna be okay!" Breeze had no idea if she was telling the truth or not, but she couldn't bring herself to consider the alternative. So much blood, all because she'd distracted him. If he continued to bleed, he would…would… No! She had to heal him! She still had time! If she healed him now, maybe they could run away before the inquisitor recovered!

Meanwhile, Faith coughed and sputtered as she tried but failed to get back on her feet. She'd somehow lost her staff during the altercation with Fowler and couldn't muster the energy to create a new one. Nor could she summon her Aegis again. If he attacked her now, she would die.

Tears streamed down her cheeks as she crawled away from the sorcerer. She didn't want to die. Not here, not like this. Not before she'd had her first kiss or held her own child in her hands. She wanted to live and leave something of herself behind. Anything for others to remember her by.

She heard a twig snap and quickly turned her head to look behind her, expecting one of Fowler's arrows to fly into her face. All she saw were wheat stalks swaying to the rhythm of the wind, and when she looked down at the broken twig under her right hand, she realized she'd been the one who'd made that sound. Fowler was nowhere in sight, nor was the fairy who'd accompanied him.

The fairy. A little girl with butterfly wings who appeared out of nowhere to stop their fight. Without her, Fowler would have delivered the killing blow and escaped, just like he had the first time he unleashed his magic. That girl saved her life—even if she had done so by spewing blasphemous nonsense.

Faith stared at the trail she'd made crawling here and bit her lower lip. She couldn't leave that girl with Fowler and let him take further advantage of her. And yet, despite her certitude that it was the right thing to do, that Alma Azaria herself would have chosen the same path, she still hesitated. She didn't want to go back there.

Kieran lay immobile in the field, his eyes fixed on the crumpled wheat stalks he and the inquisitor had trampled. The whole world was tinged in a dark shade of red where shadows creeped around every corner. Breeze was standing at his side, her hands touching his face. His mind focused on other things, such as the wind carrying the smoke toward the sky, or the crackling roar of the fire raging not far from here. It would soon consume him, one more weed into the ashes.

Then his vision slowly refocused, and the jumbled mess of his thoughts rearranged themselves into a more coherent whole. He blinked and realized there was blood in his eyes, a consequence of his fight with the inquisitor. He couldn't see her, but he knew she lurked somewhere nearby. Stalking, hunting him. Intent on punishing him for the horrible sins he had committed.

"It's okay, Breeze, you've got this. Nana showed you how to do it. Stop the bleeding first…"

Kieran watched as Breeze spoke to herself while she mended his wound with her magic, a feat impossible to accomplish except for the servants of God, or so they said. But the truth was that there was no God. No almighty creator who'd given birth to this world. Only magic and suffering, a recipe for tragedy.

"Can you hear me, Kieran? You have to stay awake, or I might not be able to save you! Please! You have to stay awake!"

Kieran blinked one more time and looked at his small companion; tears were streaming down her beautiful face, highlighting the otherworldly nature of her existence. He would have hugged her if he could, but she was so small, he'd only hurt her if he tried. This poor kid shouldn't even be here. She should have stayed in her forest, where food abounded and friends were many. If only he could have followed her there.

"It's working, Kieran! It's working!" A smile spread on her face.

The world began to shed its red skin and chase away all the shadows. Each time he blinked, he could see more colors, until finally, all of his senses exploded with clarity.

He felt a throbbing pain in his head, worse than he'd ever experienced, and this migraine signaled to him that he'd almost reached his limit on how much power he could conjure. The smell of burning wheat had also intensified, he noticed, and he deduced that they needed to leave immediately. He tried standing up, but his vision flashed white and a wave of dizziness almost overwhelmed him. He fell on his side again.

"Careful, Kieran!" Breeze exclaimed. "You'll hurt yourself!"

"We have to leave," he muttered under his breath. "It's almost here…"

The fairy looked behind her at the wall of flames devouring the sky and spouting out trails of black smoke. Only a few minutes had passed since Kieran had set the field ablaze, but the fire was already catching up to them, chasing them like prey.

"Let's go," Kieran said while he grabbed his bow and struggled to get back on his feet. Neither of them noticed the many arrows that had spilled out of his quiver and fallen onto the soft soil.

Breeze darted after him as he staggered forward, still reeling from the inquisitor's last attack. "Kieran—"

"Not now, Breeze," he said to her. "We have to keep moving."

"But you're still—"

"I know," he replied, gritting his teeth. "We'll take care of it later."

She looked behind her and saw that a crowd had gathered in front of the northern gate. Her gaze then shifted to the road leading out of town and a lone figure running toward the two of them—a man, judging by his silhouette. Before she could mention this to Kieran, her friend hit an invisible wall and cursed as he held a hand to his forehead.

"Goddammit! Fucking bitch!"

Breeze tried to approach him but sensed a barrier blocking her way.

The Aegis.

"Please, stop," Faith pleaded. "It's over."

The inquisitor, pale and shaken, appeared ten meters away from them, the Eos in her possession once again. She had followed Kieran and waited until he had put enough distance between himself and the fire before she came out of hiding and ambushed him. She'd also healed her wound.

"Like hell it is," Kieran seethed, squeezing his bow so hard, his knuckles turned white. He looked back and forth between the fairy and the inquisitor while he contemplated his next move, then noticed the man running across the field with a sword drawn. Kieran's lips pressed together into a thin line, and he relaxed his grip on his weapon. "Get out of here, Breeze."

"What? But I can help you!"

"No, you can't. That's her knight right there, coming for us."

"But—"

"Breeze, was it?" The inquisitor interrupted their conversation and earned herself a glare from Kieran, which she promptly ignored. "Don't worry, I'm one of the good people," she said with a quiver in her voice. "Whatever Fowler may have told you about me, it's not true. I'm—"

"Don't listen to her. Get out of here—I'll cover you."

"I can protect you," Faith rapidly added. "I promise. You can tru—"

"NOW!" Kieran nocked an arrow while he gathered an invisible gust of magic that he hurled at the inquisitor, only for her to dispel the barrier and summon another one around her instead. A loud *bang* resonated in Breeze's ears when his spell smashed against the inquisitor's Aegis, and her heart skipped a beat. Kieran let the arrow fly at the man heading their way, but the inquisitor intercepted it with her Aegis by stepping in front of it, and it shattered against the shield.

Only fifty leaps now separated them from the knight.

"Goddammit, Breeze!" Kieran yelled. "Get the fuck out of here!"

The sound of desperation in her friend's voice awoke her from her stupor. Thinking back to the warning he'd given her about humans, she fled north, toward the forest. She disappeared behind a curtain of black smoke blowing east and flew low among the wheat stalks so that nobody could follow her.

Faith kept her attention on Fowler. She already had her hands full blocking his line of sight with Aiden and couldn't afford to get distracted right now. Sensing the need to change tactics, the sorcerer backed a fair distance away and attempted to get a clear shot at Aiden by circling around her while he reached for his quiver.

Kieran froze for an instant when he felt only two arrows in his hand. He looked down to confirm it, then cursed himself for not checking earlier. He didn't have time to come up with another plan, so he nocked one arrow and lifted the last one with his mind, reasoning that he could at the very least stall the two Azarians for a little longer.

He aimed his bow at the inquisitor while he moved the second projectile several meters to his left. By the time Faith realized what he intended, it was already too late—Kieran shot both arrows at the same time.

The first one splintered against the Aegis while the second, aimed at a different target, whistled through the air for a fraction of a second longer. Faith whirled toward Aiden, her heart pounding hard in her chest as she expected to see him fall to the ground, a wooden shaft sticking out of his torso—but Aiden was nowhere in sight.

For an instant, she feared the worst, only to see him emerge from the field and run toward her again.

Kieran clenched the grip of his bow hard and cursed under his breath. The knight had avoided his arrow by dropping to the ground.

Aiden arrived at Faith's side and stepped in front of her.

"The Aegis is on you now," she said while transferring the shield to him.

"Keep it there," he replied. "I'm going after him."

His quiver now empty, Kieran gathered magic from the aether and unleashed another wave of fire that gave him a splitting headache. Faith backed away from the sorcerer while Aiden, seemingly fearless in the face of such power, rushed forward into the flames. Faith gasped, and were it not for her rigorous training, she would have lost control of the shield and the fire would have swallowed him whole in an instant. Instead, Aiden came out on the other side of it, unscathed and ready to fight. In vain, Kieran scrambled to block the knight's sword with the upper limb of his bow, but the blade cut through the wood like butter and, just as easily, cleaved into his left shoulder. An explosion of pain reverberated through Kieran's whole body and his legs gave out from under him.

He collapsed on his back, unable to move.

Black dots appeared at the edge of his vision and creeped toward the center, darkening the blue sky and blending into the smoke that swelled above him. Already he could feel a numbness spread throughout his body, but it paled in comparison to the pain throbbing in his torso, which suddenly flared up when the knight removed his sword.

Kieran clawed at the earth with his hands and screamed. And then, darkness.

## CHAPTER 18

"WHY DID YOU miss, Kieran?"

Ignatios stood a few meters behind the teenager with his arms crossed nonchalantly. Nothing ever seemed to get to him, especially not his protégé's mood swings.

"I don't know," Kieran replied while he grabbed another arrow from his quiver. "Because I didn't aim correctly?"

"Of course you didn't aim correctly. How else would you have missed the target?"

Kieran clenched his jaw and turned away from the tree line to look at his mentor. "Can't you just tell me? I'll get nowhere if you keep asking questions like that."

"And you'll get nowhere if you keep turning to others for answers. Now, *think*. Why did you miss your target when your posture was exactly the same as before? You didn't miss then, so why now?"

Kieran sighed and faced the tree line again. Why indeed. His shoulders, arms, and fingers were perfectly positioned, and yet the arrow had missed the trunk of the tree by at least ten centimeters. He couldn't explain it. He thought about asking Ignatios again but then realized the answer when a breeze ruffled his short hair and caressed his face. "Oh. The wind," he said.

"Exactly. You're standing sixty meters away from the tree line. Even the simplest change in direction of the wind can greatly alter your shot. You need to be more aware of the changes in your surroundings. Now try again."

Kieran nodded and raised his bow. This time, he aimed slightly to the right of the arrow-riddled tree. He drew the bowstring, held his breath, and released. The arrow whooshed through the air and hit the target exactly where he had meant it to—within the orange circle Ignatios had drawn on the trunk of the tree.

"Good," his mentor said. "Very good. I think that's enough practice for today. Tomorrow, we'll start training you for speed shooting."

"Speed shooting?"

"Yes. It's exactly what it sounds like."

"What about magic? You said you'd teach me how to shoot arrows with it."

"I will, once you've stopped missing your targets. Now go pick up your things—we're leaving."

He knew there was no use arguing with Ignatios once he put an end to the conversation, so Kieran slipped the bow on his back and walked across the field to the tree line. It took him a couple of minutes to go there, gather the arrows, and return to his mentor's side.

Ignatios passed the time by playing with a long blade of grass he'd picked, which Kieran found to be a little peculiar for a grown man like him. He had never dared to ask his mentor how old he was, but judging by his rough complexion, his mature demeanor, and the near-total absence of gray in his black hair, he couldn't be a day over forty. Old enough to pass himself off as Kieran's father, which he often did.

"Did you find them all?" Ignatios asked while keeping his gray eyes fixed on the blade of grass.

"Yeah," Kieran said. "I got them."

"How many are broken?"

"Just the one I shot into the forest. I think it hit a rock or something. I'll craft a new one when we get back home."

"Hmm. Let's go then." Ignatios threw the blade of grass aside and walked to the small path that led back into town. Kieran followed him without saying another word.

The adolescent briefly considered striking up a conversation with his mentor, but changed his mind when he concluded that it would simply turn into another lesson about survival and the practicality of skepticism. And he had heard enough about both of those subjects.

Instead, he used this opportunity to admire the quaint beauty of the clearings and meadows they passed, while also savoring the refreshing shade provided by the trees lining the dirt road. Although summer had not yet arrived, the sun beat down on him like it was the middle of Calor, and he chased the coolness of every shadow he could find. He also appreciated the fresh air of the countryside, although he wished he could avoid the stench of the cattle whenever he walked too close to a barn. That was the only thing he didn't like about living in the country—all these animals smelled like shit.

"You're quieter than usual today," Ignatios remarked without looking back at his protégé. "You're not going to ask me anything?"

"Why bother?" Kieran grumbled. "You're just gonna answer me with more questions."

"Oho! The student learns."

"Yeah, yeah." Kieran shifted his gaze back to the surrounding landscape and tried his best to ignore the sorcerer; he didn't want to play that little game anymore. Maybe instead of staying home to practice his writing, he'd sneak out into town tonight and find someone less aggravating to talk to. Even a dog would do.

The two of them walked in silence for another minute before Ignatios spoke up again. "Come on, ask me your questions."

"I'm good," Kieran replied curtly.

"No, you're not. Now ask your questions. I'll answer them this time."

Kieran looked back at Ignatios and frowned. "You will?"

"I promise."

Kieran hesitated for a moment and considered whether or not his guardian was pulling his chain. He wouldn't put it past him to do something like that. He mused on the opportunity for a little while until he concluded that the only thing he had to lose was his time, so he might as well try.

"All right then," he said. "What's the deal with the training? Why are you teaching me?"

"Hmm? I already told you. You need to know how to defend yourself if you are to survive out there."

"And that's all?"

"Did you think there might be another reason?"

"I don't know. Maybe."

"That sounded like a 'yes,' Kieran. Come on, speak plainly. What do you think I'm training you for?"

Kieran bit the inside of his cheek and wondered whether or not he should say it out loud. Depending on where this conversation went, it might change things between the two of them, and he wasn't sure he was ready for that. But he also really wanted to know the truth about Ignatios.

"Spying," he finally said. "I think you're training me to become a spy."

"Really? And why is that?"

"Your name. It's Ophician, isn't it?"

"Not all Ophicians are spies."

"But you keep using fake names whenever you talk to other people."

"Maybe the name I gave you is also a fake."

"That'd just confirm that you're a spy!"

"No, it would only add credence to the idea. Maybe I'm simply teaching you the only way I know how to survive in this world."

"So…you're not a spy?"

"Oh no, I most definitely am one."

The lad stopped dead in his tracks and stared agape at his mentor. He must have misheard. No way in hell would anyone admit so casually to that, not when the consequences could prove fatal if the wrong person heard about it.

Ignatios came to a halt and looked behind him, a sly grin on his face. "Why so surprised?" he asked.

Kieran closed his mouth and carefully considered his answer. He didn't know what to do with this information, not when he himself was a fugitive chased by the Inquisition.

"Cat got your tongue?" the spy asked again.

"N-No," Kieran replied. "It's just… I didn't think you'd admit to it."

"Why not?"

"Isn't it dangerous?"

Ignatios gestured at their surroundings and smiled. "There's no one else here, Kieran. It's just you and me. So, unless you were planning to tattle to someone else about it, I have nothing to worry about. Right?"

"Yeah. That's right."

"Good. Then we have an understanding: you protect my secret, and I'll continue to protect yours."

The sorcerer casually turned his back and resumed walking. Kieran hesitated for a second before he decided to follow. He had to know. There were so many questions he wanted to ask, but he didn't know which one to start with. After a moment of consideration, he finally settled on one. "So, how long have you been a spy?"

"Twelve years," Ignatios answered matter-of-factly. "But I've been assigned to the Southern Realms—what you call the Azarian Realms—as of four years and two months ago."

"And…what do you do exactly?"

"I gather information and identify potential threats—and eliminate them if necessary."

Kieran pressed his lips together and wondered if he should ask more about that. He could guess what his mentor meant by "eliminate," but he wasn't sure he wanted to hear the details. Besides, he had a more important question to ask. "What about me?"

"What about you?" Ignatios replied.

"The day you saved me from the Inquisition. Was that because of your job?"

"No. In fact, according to regulations, I should never have gotten myself involved with you, even if you would have made a good recruit."

"Then why?"

This time, Ignatios stopped and turned around to face him. He looked dead serious. Whatever he said next, Kieran knew he would never forget it.

"Because you're special, Kieran. More than you know."

"What?" Kieran stuttered as he searched for his words. "W-What do you mean?"

"Exactly what I said. Even among mages and sorcerers, you're special." The spy's gaze lingered on him for a while before it shifted to the verdant scenery around them, his expression a mask of aloofness that betrayed nothing of his thoughts and feelings; it was a mask that he must have perfected over the years. "You see," he continued, "human beings cannot manipulate magic until they've had an 'awakening.' It's when your mind 'unlocks' itself and establishes a permanent connection between you and the magic that surrounds us.

"Every mage in existence has experienced it, even the God

Emperors themselves. There are, however, two types of awakening: induced and innate. An induced awakening is when a mage unlocks the mind of someone else and manually establishes that connection for them. Only then can the new mage begin to learn how to control magic."

"And the innate one?" Kieran asked.

"What do you think?"

The lad gazed into the man's gray eyes and shuddered. He remembered. The power rushing through him. The flames erupting from within. The smell of burning flesh.

"So, I had an innate awakening. What about it? Other mages must have had those too."

"No, Kieran, they haven't. None that I know of anyway. Approximately one in three thousand mages have had an awakening like yours—and that's counting those who died. Some of them succumb to their own magic after they first unleash it. Others are killed by the Inquisition or by peons incapable of rational thought. Those who survive are few and far between, and not all of them receive the magical training that would allow them to grow into powerful mages. But to the ones who do…" Ignatios put a hand on Kieran's shoulder and stared into his eyes. "Greatness awaits."

These last two words sent shivers down Kieran's spine, and he felt a weight settle in the pit of his stomach. It had never crossed his mind that his magical talent could be anything other than a burden, and although this realization should have emboldened his spirit, it had the complete opposite effect. Still, his curiosity got the better of him, and he asked, "So, having that kind of awakening does what exactly? Makes me more powerful?"

"No, not at all."

"What then?"

"Depends on who you're asking," Ignatios answered while lowering his hand. "The Seeresses from the Valadorian Expanse would call it being marked by destiny. The priestesses and inquisitors from the Church would label it demonic influence, while scholars from the Ophician Confederation are *still* debating the causes behind the innate awakening and its effects. I think it's much simpler than that." The sorcerer leaned forward and paused for emphasis. "I think those who survive an innate awakening are made stronger by it. I think it's a process of natural selection that culls the weak and elevates the strong. I think you wanted to kill that bully, and that's why you gained the power of life and death over him. Deep down, you're willing to do whatever is necessary to survive. And if there is anything I can do to nurture that kind of raw willpower, I will do so. Because in a world as chaotic as this one, it's people like you that will change it for the better. So, chin up, Kieran. You're going to be a hero."

Ignatios maintained eye contact for several more seconds before he turned away. "That's enough questions for today," he said. "Let's go."

Kieran watched his mentor walk down the dirt road and wondered whether or not he should follow him. He finally had gotten an answer to the question he had asked himself ever since Ignatios had saved him from the Inquisition, and he didn't know what to make of it. The only thing he knew for certain was that Ignatios was his only ally, and that without him, he would die. After all, no one—not even mages—could survive alone in this world.

After a moment of hesitation, he fell into step beside the sorcerer and walked back to town with him.

The first thing Kieran felt was a cold and hard surface against his back. It took him several seconds before he realized that he had already opened his eyes and was sitting in a room plunged in darkness. All he heard were his own breathing and the steady thumping of his heart. Nothing else.

He slowly raised his head and groaned in pain as his neck ached at the sudden movement; he must have been in this position for several hours to feel such soreness. He blinked multiple times in a conscious effort to adapt his vision to the darkness, but nothing changed. Was there really no source of light at all? He brought a hand in front of his eyes to check, only to stop himself when he heard the clinking of chains. Then, he remembered.

The inquisitor and her knight had nearly killed him, but instead of finishing him off, they'd put irons on his wrists and left him to rot in a dungeon so they could bring him back to Holiburg and parade him in front of a crowd hungry for blood. How virtuous of them.

Kieran groped around his arms and found two sets of manacles: one around his wrists and the other higher on his forearms. The first one had chains that were attached to the wall behind him, while the second was a normal pair of handcuffs. He wondered why the inquisitor would bother putting both pairs on him. He tried to draw magic from the aether, failed to even sense it, and then he understood. One pair to annul his magic. Another to bind him to the wall.

After a quick examination of his body, he noticed that his wound in his left shoulder had been healed and that his clothes had been replaced with the garment of a prisoner—a shirt, a pair of trousers, and an ill-fitting pair of shoes. No pockets were sewn into his clothes—a safety precaution against improvised weapons most likely—and when he grazed the fabric with his hand, he recognized the coarse texture of cheap cotton. The edges of his sleeves were also frayed by wear and tear; other men had worn this particular outfit, although he doubted any of them were mages. There weren't many of those left in the Azarian Realms.

Or so he'd previously thought.

He remembered what Breeze had shouted while he choked the inquisitor. She claimed that his pursuer, a woman who had dedicated her life to wiping all sorcerers and witches from this world, was in fact a mage herself—a ridiculous idea, but one that he immediately believed once he heard it. Not only because of his trust in his small companion, but also because of the sheer irony of it. Mages killing mages, while believing they were nothing like them? It was too laughable and ludicrous *not* to be true. It was a wonder Ignatios had never thought of that before. Or maybe he did and never told Kieran about it. Wouldn't be the first time.

Right now, he didn't care about any of that. He was more concerned about Breeze and whether or not she had escaped. Did the inquisitor chase after her? Did she find Breeze like she'd inexplicably found him? And if so, what would she do to the little fairy once she had her cornered? He doubted the inquisitor would hurt her, but she would definitely attempt to turn the fairy against him.

The distant echo of footsteps interrupted his thoughts. People were coming, at least three of them, and he doubted it was for the other prisoners here, if there were any. Kieran tensed up and listened to the footsteps grow closer until they stopped right in front of his cell. He saw the glow of a torch appear in the gap beneath the door and heard the soft jingling of keys. Then the lock turned, and the door opened.

Blinding yellow light flooded into his cell, forcing him to cover his eyes with his hand. Once he got used to it, he peered through his fingers to see his visitors and expressed no surprise when the inquisitor and her knight entered the small room. A lone guard stood in the hallway behind them, his torch burning brightly in the opaque darkness.

The knight turned and extended a hand toward the guard. "Give me the keys," he said. "Then leave us."

The man hesitated for an instant and looked at the inquisitor for confirmation, but she kept her gaze on Kieran.

"*Now,*" the knight insisted.

Flustered, the constable stuttered a response. "M-my apologies, milord." He handed the keys to the knight and prepared to leave but stopped just as he was about to walk past the frame of the door. "Do you need the torch?" he asked.

"No," the priestess immediately answered. "You may go."

"Yes, Inquisitor." The guard hurried out, and darkness returned to the cell, but only for an instant. With seemingly no effort, the inquisitor summoned her white staff and shone its light upon him, allowing him to get his first good look at her.

Now that he wasn't running for his life, he finally noticed the slender figure hiding under that robe of hers, as well as the long, lustrous black hair flowing down her shoulders. The stern expression on her otherwise elegant face reminded him of the inquisitor who'd arrested his mother and handed him to the Lunaris orphanage. Even her sharp green eyes, which gleamed brightly under the white light, looked the same.

He then noticed the absence of blood on her shoulder, and his lips curled into a lopsided grin. "Already worked your magic on that wound of yours, uh?" His remark caused the inquisitor to flinch, almost imperceptibly. "And you even bothered to do the same for me."

"Of course I did," she said with a stony face. "I couldn't leave you to die."

"No, of course not. You'd prefer to kill me in front of a larger crowd."

The priestess didn't bother with a retort. Instead, she switched the Eos from one hand to the other and leaned against it as she continued to stare him down.

Kieran took a gander at her knight, a well-built man with a strange flowery pin on his chest. His expression was even more impassive than that of the woman he served.

"I believe we haven't been formally introduced," the inquisitor said. "My name is Inquisitor Faith Dow, and I've been tasked with your capture."

Tasked, she said? And that surname...

"I've come here to inform you that you are to be transported to Holiburg and that you will be under my supervision until your trial begins."

Kieran stayed silent for a while and pondered what the inquisitor had said. Could it be? No. But her appearance...

"Do not attempt to escape," she continued, "and I promise you fair treatment until we've arrived at our destination. If you behave violently, Sir Hawkon here will be forced to respond in kind, and you will spend the rest of the journey blindfolded. Do you understand?"

Kieran ignored her question and asked one of his own. "What did you say your name was?"

The inquisitor frowned and clutched the staff tighter than before. A stretch of silence followed, until finally she relaxed her grip and said, "Dow. My name is Faith Dow."

It was Kieran's turn to frown. He recognized that last name. How could he not? It belonged to the person who'd killed his mother and ruined his life. And now, twenty years later, an inquisitor with that same name had captured him and thrown him into a cell. Some people would be quick to call it Providence, but him? He would call it a joke. A sick joke played by a bored matron lazing around on her cloud up there in the sky. He couldn't help but let out a derisive chuckle.

"What is it?" the inquisitor asked.

Kieran leaned his head back against the wall and grinned. "You're her daughter, aren't you?"

Faith clenched her jaw and tensed up when he asked that question. She didn't want to talk about her mother. Not with a heretic as reckless and destructive as him. Her first instinct urged her to turn around and leave, but her duty as an inquisitor commanded that she stay to gain more information. Without further hesitation, she raised her chin high and answered him. "Yes, my mother's name is Karolina Dow. You've met her once."

"Hm." He looked down at the manacles around his wrists and started playing with them. "Figures."

"How do you mean?"

He stopped and glanced up at her. "Figures that she'd send her daughter to finish the job."

He went back to examining the shackles, seemingly disinterested in what she had to say, but she didn't buy it. If he were truly apathetic to her presence, he wouldn't have asked her name. Aside from his snide remark and the total dismissal of her warning, he still addressed her in a somewhat civil manner without resorting to insults or curses of any kind. Which indicated to her that he was probing for information, same as her. She had to take advantage of that.

"What job?" she asked.

Fowler turned his attention to the chains attached to the wall and stared at them for a bit. "Killing off my family," he answered.

Resentment—she expected as much. She peeked at Aiden from the corner of her eyes in case he had some advice for her, but when she saw no change in his demeanor, she turned her gaze back to Fowler while thinking carefully about what to say next. "I wasn't sent here to kill you. Only to arrest you and bring you back to Holiburg."

Having finished examining the chains, Fowler sighed and looked at the dark slabs of stone under him. "Where I'll be executed," he said. "It's all the same in the end."

"Not necessarily."

"Really?" He gave her a tired look and waited for her to continue.

"Regardless of the other charges brought against you, you're definitely guilty of assault, attempted murder, arson, witchcraft, heresy, and apostasy. The Inquisitorial Tribunal *will* sentence you to death—unless I intervene."

"You can do that?"

"One recommendation from me, and your sentence will be reduced to imprisonment for life at the Inquisitorial prison of Holiburg. I merely need your cooperation."

"That's not very enticing."

"It's the best I can do after what you did today."

"What *I* did? You mean defending myself?"

Faith pinched her lips together for an instant, and the creases on her forehead deepened as she thought of an appropriate rebuttal. "The fires you started have burned several acres of crops," she said. "Even now, they're still burning."

"And?"

*"And?"* Faith felt a heat spread throughout her chest at the callous response, and she squeezed her staff so hard, her fingers began to hurt. "People depended on the yield of these fields to get them through the next winter, and *you burned them.*"

"The Church will make sure they're fed, won't they?"

"That's beside the point," she said, her jaw clenched.

"If you didn't want me to burn those fields, then you shouldn't have attacked me. I mean, you did know who I was, right? Did you really think that someone nicknamed 'The Pyromancer' wouldn't use fire against you? How stupid are you?"

The words had barely left his mouth before the knight moved next to him and kicked him in the gut. Pain flared up in his stomach and threatened to expel his lunch as the glorified bodyguard chastised him. "Show some respect," the knight said.

Kieran heaved and moaned, unable to reply. The acidic bile in his mouth tasted awful, and he tried to wash it away with his own saliva, with little success. If it weren't for these damn shackles...

"That's enough, Aiden," the inquisitor said. "Do not do that again."

"Yes, ma'am," he answered while moving back to his spot. "My apologies, ma'am."

Faith glared at the prince. She understood his reasons for acting this way, but his zeal might end up hindering her efforts to secure Fowler's cooperation. More importantly, no prisoner deserved to be treated this way. Not even a sorcerer.

"I apologize for my knight's rudeness," she said to Fowler. "He didn't hit you too hard, did he? I can heal you if necessary."

Fowler coughed some more and shook his head.

"Then let us go back to our previous topic of conversation—your cooperation. If you renounce the demon you made a pact with and make amends by helping me, there may be hope for you yet."

"A demon, huh?" Kieran took a deep breath and leaned back against the wall. "Sorry to disappoint you, but there are no pacts of any kind. No demons, no devils, and certainly no promises of ruling in hell. There's only me."

"Stop denying it. The Scriptures are clear—"

"No, they're not. I've read them, so I know. But you don't really care about what I think, do you? So just tell me what you want from me. That'll save us both some time."

It came as no surprise to Faith that he denied the existence of demons. So insidious were the forces of hell that they convinced their own servants they didn't exist. Her teachers had warned her of the considerable time and effort required to bring one of these poor souls back to reason, and she decided to drop the subject for now. She had more pressing matters to attend to first.

"Very well," she said. "I need you to clarify a few things."

"Like what?"

"Like why you were traveling toward Holiburg even though your identity had been exposed."

Kieran shrugged. "I was hoping to find absolution by praying on Alma Azaria's tomb. Isn't that how it works?"

Faith refrained from sighing in frustration by biting the inside of her cheek. "Please don't blaspheme," she said. "It's quite unnecessary."

"So you say."

He clearly didn't want to talk about this, so she decided to broach a more urgent issue. "Have you heard about the Ophician army massing on Faxe's border?" she asked.

"An army?" he said. "Can't say I have, no."

"Are you sure?"

"I told you, no." He narrowed his eyes. "What's that got to do with me?"

"I'm not sure yet. You knew about my inability to annul magic and perform miracles at the same time, which I suspect you may have learned from the Ophicians."

The members of the Inquisition named this weakness the Inquisitor's Blind Spot, but she couldn't tell him this, for obvious reasons.

"Have you ever been in contact with them?" she continued. "Depending on your answer, I might also be able to offer you better accommodations in addition to a reduced sentence."

"Oh? Really? What about some pastries?"

"If that's what you want."

"Wine? Sausage? Fruit?"

"Not wine, but the rest could be arranged for you—*if* your information is good."

"Ah!" Kieran smiled and shook his head. "Can't believe it. You'd really go that far just for some intel on the Ophicians?"

"They're poised to invade the Azarian Realms, Fowler. We need every advantage we can get before they cross the Nanes."

Kieran stopped smiling and frowned at this revelation. "The Azarian Realms, you say? Not just Faxe?"

"Yes. Their army is over one hundred thousand strong. They'll sweep through Faxe and the rest of the Realms if we don't stop them."

"Hmm." Kieran shrugged. "Guess they had to make their move sooner or later. Can't say I care much about what happens to them, so sure, I'll tell you what you want to know."

Faith raised her eyebrows in surprise at this unexpected turn. She had assumed that even if Fowler knew anything about the Ophicians, he would refuse to answer her questions out of pettiness and malice, especially after how poorly Aiden had behaved toward him. And yet here he was, confirming his affiliation to the Ophicians and offering information on them. Could this be a trick? A way to get back at her for his perceived persecution? She had to make sure. Too much depended on what she might learn today. "Then let me start with this: Do you know anything about their invasion?"

"No."

"But you just said—"

"I just said what everybody knew already." Kieran sighed and looked away for an instant. "They were always going to invade the Realms. Doesn't mean I'm one of their agents. They can go to hell for all I care."

"Then what do you know about them?"

"Not much." Annoyed by the dirty look the knight gave him, he shifted his attention back to the inquisitor. "The one who might interest you is the man who took me in after I left the orphanage."

"What?" Faith could barely contain her astonishment. "You mean someone helped you escape the Inquisition?"

"Yeah," Kieran confirmed. "He called himself Ignatios."

"And who was he exactly?"

"A spy for the Ophician Confederation."

The inquisitor's mouth fell open for just a second before she closed it again and regained her composure. She had to press on. "Tell me about him."

"Like I said, I don't know much. He found me in the streets

while the orphanage was burning and hid me in one of his safe houses until the manhunt was over. Then he took me in and taught me everything I know."

"Which was?"

Kieran sighed. "How to read and write in other languages, how to blend into a crowd, who to talk to when you first arrive in a new town, what to do if you're being pursued. Everything a spy would need to know."

"Is he the one who told you about our weakness?"

"He is."

"Did you learn archery from him?"

"Yeah."

"What about your sorcery?"

"That too. But I left before he could complete my training."

"Why?"

Kieran raised his head and locked eyes with the inquisitor. "I don't like slave owners," he enunciated, slowly. "So, ask me your questions. I'll be happy to answer them."

Faith stayed quiet for a while, puzzled by the reason behind Fowler's cooperation. Could it be true? Did he really disapprove of the Confederation's stance on slavery? He was a sorcerer just like the rest of them. It made no sense that he would see eye-to-eye with her on this issue. She had to be missing something. An underlying motive for the dissension between him and the rest of the heretics who walked this earth.

Those questions would have to wait, however. She needed to ask him about this Confederation spy. "Was this man trying to recruit you?"

"No," Kieran answered. "Well, maybe, but I doubt it. I asked him about it once, and it sounded like he had his own agenda. According to regulations, he was never supposed to help me, but that's just what he said."

"What was his objective?"

"I don't know. I left before I got wrapped up in whatever trouble he was training me for."

"When was that?"

"Ten years ago."

"And you haven't seen him since?"

"No."

Faith briefly pondered what this Ignatios could have been planning. If Fowler spoke the truth, then this man had to be a member of one of the political factions within the Confederation, and his scheme at the time had required that he recruit young, impressionable teenagers. But that was over ten years ago, so any knowledge of that plot was long out of date and thus irrelevant. Better to move on to something more immediate. "That's enough about the Ophician spy," she said. "We'll talk more about it tomorrow."

"Tomorrow?"

"Yes. We'll be traveling together inside our carriage, so we'll have plenty of time to discuss the training you underwent. But for now, there's something else we need to talk about."

Kieran stared at her and did his best to keep a straight face; he knew what she was going to say next. Nothing else mattered more to her, not even his ties to the Confederation. But he wouldn't tell her anything, no matter what.

"That little girl," Faith finally said. "Who is she?"

There were only two ways Kieran could answer that question: first, he could pretend that Breeze never existed to begin with and that the inquisitor had imagined everything about her. She'd never believe him, of course, but that didn't matter. As long as he provided no proof of the fairy's existence, the Inquisition might simply choose to dismiss the matter and pretend it never happened. Fairies didn't exist, after all, and it would be far easier to believe that he'd acted alone

However, there were several problems with that story: the

inquisitor's relationship with Karolina Dow, the other three witnesses at The Jolly Stew, and finally, Breeze herself. He doubted that the grand inquisitor would ever doubt the accuracy of her daughter's report—no matter how fantastical it might be—not when there were witnesses who could corroborate these events. As for Breeze, he found it extremely unlikely that someone as naive and buoyant as her would successfully avoid all human contact. Not without his help. Which meant that sooner or later, the Inquisition would pick up her trail again.

All he could do was protect the most valuable secret he had: the location of her village. If the inquisitor learned that they'd met only recently, she would retrace his steps back from Ballybridge to Waterlone, and eventually she'd figure out that he'd spent nearly two days near the king's reserve. He needed to keep the conversation going and trick her into thinking that he and Breeze had been traveling together for quite some time now. Otherwise, the Inquisition would undoubtedly find that village.

"The inquisitor has asked you a question," the knight said.

"So she has," Kieran replied. "I just don't like tattling on my friends."

"You told her to leave you behind," the priestess said. "Why do that?"

"Isn't it obvious? Because you're an inquisitor."

The corner of her eye twitched at the insinuation. "I wish her no harm. In fact, I think you're the one who's exposed her to danger. It's quite obvious that you've been indoctrinating her."

"Oh, really?" Kieran said, raising his voice. "Then what is the Inquisition going to do to her once she tells them that you're all mages?"

Faith pursed her lips and withheld the many insults she wanted to throw back at him; she knew he was only spouting heretical profanity, but the idea that she used magic and not the Kind Mother's divine power made her blood boil. Never before in her life had she heard such blasphemy, and it kindled within her the urge to chide him and dismiss his assertions as groundless delusions—but no. She couldn't do that. She needed to follow Alma Azaria's example and talk to him instead of preaching at him. Otherwise, he would only clam up and dismiss her words.

She glanced at Aiden, but he appeared unfazed by the impious remark. Maybe he'd heard heretics talk like that in his previous missions; her mother did say he had experience dealing with sorcerers and witches. And after seeing him in action today, she believed it.

Faith held her staff closer to her chest and shifted her gaze back to Fowler. "This was obviously an error on the girl's part," she explained. "You're the one who put this idea in her head."

"Right. I took my knee off your throat because she told me something I already knew. Very clever."

The inquisitor bit her lower lip and mulled over the obvious contradiction. "It was a trick," she said. "A lie you came up with to confuse me."

"That's just fucking stupid," he retorted. "Why would I ever risk my life for that?"

"Maybe you're an Ophician agent after all...sent behind enemy lines to sow discord among enemy ranks, and you tricked that girl into helping you."

"By getting myself captured? It doesn't even begin to make sense. And what about Breeze? She *saved* you. It's because of her that you're still here now."

"Then maybe she's the one who lied. Maybe she told you I was a mage to stop you from murdering me because she understood what kind of man you truly are."

"Is that so? Then tell me: How did she heal that kid back at the inn?"

Faith opened her mouth to answer him, but no plausible explanation came to mind. No one but an Azarian priestess should have been able to mend such a serious wound in that short amount of time, not without the Kind Mother's blessing. Unless...

"A miracle," the inquisitor finally said. "She performed a miracle."

Kieran scoffed. "Oh, really."

"This is the only logical explanation. She must be doing God's work, whether she knows it or not."

"Right. And she's been spending weeks with a sorcerer like me because...?"

"I do not know. I would have liked to talk to her about it, but you scared her away before I could. Because of you, she'll now live in fear of God's Word and the—"

Kieran interrupted her with a bitter laugh. "What a pile of horseshit. You've got it all figured out, huh? Fine, then. Forget I said anything. It's not like I'm gonna change your mind. I don't know why I even bothered trying."

Fowler lowered his head and looked at the floor, a despondent expression on his face. He'd closed himself off. She wouldn't be able to reach him anymore. Best that she leave now and resume their discussion tomorrow morning. Maybe then he would be more receptive to her arguments.

"We'll be leaving tomorrow at dawn," she told him. "I'll make sure to grab you something to eat—whatever you want, just like I promised. What would you like?"

The sorcerer didn't respond. Faith waited for a while, but he maintained his silence. Rather than waste more of her time, she turned around and headed for the door.

Just before she crossed the threshold, Fowler spoke again. "Do you think she was lying?" he asked.

Faith stopped and looked over her shoulder. "What?"

"Breeze. Do you really think she was lying?"

She couldn't see his face now that her staff pointed at the

hallway, but she could feel his gaze on her. Aiden stood to her side with his arms crossed, patiently waiting for her to make the next move. Maybe he expected a quick rebuttal from her, one that would shut Fowler up. Her mother certainly would have reacted that way, had she been the one in charge. But Faith said nothing. She only stared at the dark shape slumped on the floor while she pondered the question.

The so-called "fairy" was wrong. It couldn't be otherwise. To even entertain the idea was as blasphemous as taking the Kind Mother's name in vain. And yet...

Faith shook her head and turned away once again. "I must take my leave."

The inquisitor and her knight both stepped out of the cell and closed the door behind them, surrendering the room back to the darkness. Kieran watched the white glow of the Eos gleam from under the door, and once he heard the distinctive *click* of the key turning the lock, he saw the light quickly fade away as the inquisitor and her knight returned from whence they came. Soon, only blackness remained.

Kieran let out a sigh of relief and rested his head against the wall. The inquisitor had been so focused on their argument, she didn't notice his intentional slip that Breeze had been spending the last few weeks in his company. She didn't even think to question him about it—she simply accepted it as truth. He had revealed so much about Ignatios and the education he'd received from him that she didn't catch the one lie he'd slipped into their conversation. If not for that, she would have been a lot more vigilant about what he said. He doubted she'd ever find the location of Breeze's village, not without casting doubt on everything he'd said so far.

Furthermore, while the inquisitor shone her light upon him, he'd also managed to examine his shackles. Just like he'd thought: It would be impossible for him to break out of his chains without magic, and despite it being the first time he had seen manacles like the ones on his forearms, he deduced by the seven-pointed star emblems on them that they were made to restrain sorcerers like him. Despite the severity of his situation, he took comfort in one thing: the certitude that Breeze had escaped the Inquisition and their dogma.

Now, he could dedicate the rest of his time to figuring out how to take his own life. He sure as hell wasn't going to give the Inquisition the satisfaction of taking it from him.

# CHAPTER 19

F AITH CLIMBED THE stairs leading out of the dungeon, mulling over her conversation with Fowler and wondering what she could have said that would have changed his mind. An exercise in futility, probably. Heretics like him seldom repented for their crimes, not without being subjected to more extreme… *arguments*. The kind that inquisitors no longer performed ever since the late Great Mother Aerts had reformed the Inquisition thirty years ago.

When she arrived at the top of the stairs, she moved to open the wooden door that barred her way, but it didn't budge. "Uh, is that you, Inquisitor?" a voice asked from the other side. "Just a moment."

The guard who'd accompanied her and Aiden to Fowler's cell opened the door for them. Although he had previously done his best to remain poised in her presence, now he couldn't help but openly gawk at the Eos in her hand.

"The inquisitor would like to pass," Aiden said from behind her.

"Oh, um…" The guard hastily got out of the way. "Apologies, Inquisitor."

Faith walked past him and stepped into a hallway lined with

torches. "Are you guarding the dungeon alone?" she asked, dismissing the Eos out of existence.

"Uh, yes, Inquisitor," the guard said, transfixed.

"That's not enough. We need at least two men here. Go to your superior and tell him to send someone else with you."

"But, Inquisitor, I can't leave the dungeon unguarded."

"Then we'll wait here until you return. Now, go."

"At once, Inquisitor."

The man hurried down the hallway and disappeared around the corner, leaving her alone with Aiden. The knight closed the door behind them and put the latch back in place. "I must apologize," he said while facing her. "I didn't mean to undermine your authority back there."

Faith was so focused on replaying the previous conversation in her head that she didn't immediately catch what Aiden was referring to. "Oh, that."

The knight waited for her to say something else and visibly twitched when she didn't. For just an instant, his usual composure vanished, replaced by the telltale signs of nervousness—fidgeting and a lack of eye contact. It was almost as if Aiden had reverted to his adolescent self, or how she imagined he would have acted back then. It occurred to her that she'd never asked him his age. How old was he? Twenty-five, twenty-six years old? Maybe even a little older. She'd have to ask him about it later. For now, however...

"It's fine," she replied. "Just make sure not to do it again."

"Thank you," he said, his body relaxing. "I simply thought kicking him might help you establish some kind of trust between you and him, but I see now you'd rather I didn't. I'll refrain from doing so in the future."

Faith raised an eyebrow at the prince, perplexed by his logic. "How did you figure that would help?"

"Oh. It's a technique I learned from my seniors a few years ago. When one of the interrogators acts in a cruel, violent manner, the prisoners are always more likely to talk to the one who's more reasonable."

"Hmm. I see." Faith hadn't considered this possibility before now.

"And also…" Aiden's timid behavior returned. "I… I may have acted more harshly than I usually would have because of the way he was talking to you. I apologize."

Faith looked at Aiden and felt something stir deep within her at his unexpected candor—a desire that she repressed each and every time she met a man who caught her attention. An inappropriate thought crossed her mind, and she sensed a flush spread across her face. For just an instant, she considered reciprocating Aiden's interest in her. Counting the days since her last bleeding, she would have nothing to fear if she invited him to her room for the night. She had often wondered what it would feel like to be held in a man's arms and to delight in the marvel of lovemaking—she had imagined countless scenarios in which she was either the bold temptress leading her lover back to her bed or the meek maiden being thrust onto it, and in many of those fantasies, the man staring into her eyes was a knight solely devoted to her.

The young inquisitor cleared her throat and pushed these thoughts out of her mind. Or at least tried to. "Apology accepted," she said. "It's…nice to hear that you were doing this for me."

By God, what was she saying? This wasn't how a priestess should be acting, not on an important mission like this one. She needed to regain control of herself, and fast.

"I'm glad to hear it," Aiden answered with a hesitant smile. "I'll make sure to run my ideas by you before I do anything like that again."

"Yes. Please do."

An awkward silence settled between the two of them while she continued to imagine what the rest of her night could turn into if she asked Aiden to stay with her. Although he had been the very model of a gentleman these last two days, Faith was fairly certain that he would readily accept her invitation were she to make one. And after the conversation she'd had with Fowler, she sorely needed a distraction to forget the malignant idea he had put into her head.

*She's a mage! She's using magic, just like you!*

Faith closed her eyes and tried to think of something else. She began to mentally recite the Scriptures to herself—they had proven to be a source of comfort in the past—only to remember the fairy desperately holding Fowler's arm instead, begging him not to kill her. Had Breeze not intervened, what would have happened to her? Would she have died? Or would the Kind Mother herself have intervened on her behalf, granting her the power to push him back and defeat him? She didn't know what to think anymore.

*It was an angel, Inquisitor. She's the one who saved my boy.*

No, that couldn't be true either. Angels didn't look like little fairies with butterfly wings. They were grand, majestic entities who remained unseen and revealed themselves only in the most exceptional of cases. They wouldn't waste their time on a common sorcerer like Fowler, nor would they utter blasphemies like the ones the fairy had spouted. There had to be a logical explanation. If she could only speak with her—

"Inquisitor." The guard returned with another man who sported the yellow surcoat of the constabulary. "I'm sorry for making you wait. We'll take it from here."

"It's fine," Faith said, glad of the interruption. "I assume you also informed the captain of the guard of my instructions?"

"Yes, ma'am."

"Good. Thank you. We'll take our leave then. Good night."

"Good night, ma'am."

Faith nodded at the guard and turned around to leave, only

to be stopped at the last second by the other constable, a chest-nut-haired man whose youthful face contrasted heavily with his serious expression.

"Pardon me, Inquisitor." He stepped forward to get her attention, earning himself the suspicion of Aiden, who stared him down and positioned his scabbard at an angle that would allow him to draw his sword in the blink of an eye if necessary. One glance from Faith, however, and he immediately relaxed.

"What is it?" she asked the young man.

"It's about the sorcerer," he said while eyeing the door. "It's just that we heard what he did and...I mean, is it truly safe for us? What if he escapes?"

Faith tilted her head, somewhat confused by his concern. It then dawned on her that a commoner like him wouldn't be aware of the Inquisition's customs and practices. Of course he would worry about the dangerous sorcerer sitting in the dungeon he was guarding. Who in their right mind wouldn't?

"Have no fear," she told him. "We've put handcuffs on him that will prevent him from casting any spell. Sir Aiden?" She motioned for him to show the constables the other pair of man-acles he had been carrying on his belt all day. "With these on, no sorcerer is capable of using their magic, no matter how hard they try. There's no reason to worry. Kieran Fowler can't get out of his cell, not unless I want him to."

"Oh, that's...I mean, wow," the first guard said. "I-I just assumed you inquisitors put them to sleep whenever you weren't around. Or something like that."

"Not unless I need to, no," Faith replied. "Putting someone to sleep isn't as easy as it sounds, but if Fowler becomes too agitated, I may have to. Don't hesitate to warn me if he makes too much noise. Understood?"

"Yes, ma'am."

"Thank you, ma'am," the other said. "Sorry for bothering you."

"Don't worry about it. Oh, and please tell the others about the handcuffs if they get worried too. It's not exactly a secret—"

Faith suddenly froze and glanced at the manacles as Aiden reattached them to his belt. These manacles had been consecrated by powerful Keepers to annul the magic of their wearer, no matter how powerful they were—and they were *always* carried by a knight, not the inquisitor. A tradition that dated back to the sixth century, if she remembered correctly.

"Inquisitor?" Aiden asked. "Is everything all right?"

"Um, yes," she said before shifting her gaze back to the constables. "Sorry. I was thinking of something else. Just make sure to tell the others about the handcuffs if they ask about Fowler."

"Yes, ma'am," the guard answered.

"I have to go now. Good night."

"Good night, Inquisitor."

Faith quickly nodded at the two men and headed down the corridor with Aiden following her two steps behind. She had lost her composure there for an instant, and it was not until Aiden caught up to her and grabbed her by the arm that she realized she was walking faster than usual.

"Faith, wait up."

He stopped her in the middle of an empty hallway that was lit only by a few torches, the closest one shining brightly enough for her to see his look of worry when she turned to face him. His round amber eyes gleamed in the dark, soft and gentle when they looked upon her, and his grip on her forearm immediately loosened when he noticed how intimate he was acting toward her.

"Sorry," he said. "I didn't mean to—I mean, I know I shouldn't have done that, but…" Aiden searched for his words and opened his mouth to say something else, but after a short moment of consideration, he instead dropped his head and let out a long sigh. "Please, forgive me."

The young woman blinked at the knight's sudden change in

behavior. She'd never imagined that she would ever see him act so flustered in her presence, not after he'd presented himself to be a calm, almost aloof protector. Under different circumstances, she might even have teased him about it, but right now, it was the shackles on his belt that preoccupied her. "It's fine, Aiden," she told him. "What is it?"

The knight raised his head and locked eyes with her again. "I think that's my line, isn't it? What happened back there? You froze all of a sudden."

"That was…nothing. Forget about it."

"That's kind of a hard thing to do. Are you sure you don't want to talk about it? I know you didn't choose me as your knight, but we might as well make the most out of it."

"Thank you, really, but I'm fine. I don't—" Faith cut herself off mid-sentence as a new idea—unbridled and untouched by the dogma of the Church—popped into her mind. Something that would cause her mother to throw a fit if she mentioned it to her. To even consider doing such a thing would be treated as foolish at best and sacrilegious at worst. Truly one of the worst ideas she'd ever had in her life. And yet—

"What is it?" Aiden asked.

Faith stayed silent for several more seconds while she debated what to do, until finally, she decided to ask him now and figure out the rest later. Preferably once she was alone. "There is one thing…" she hesitantly said.

"Yes?"

"The handcuffs… Could you lend them to me?"

Aiden flinched back slightly as he attempted to comprehend the reason for that request, but judging by the blank look on his face, none came to mind. "Uh, yes, of course," he answered. "But why? It's the duty of the knight that they carry the manacles for their inquisitor. Are you asking for them because I've displeased you somehow?"

"No, nothing like that. It's just that after what happened today, I think I might sleep easier tonight if I had them with me... So please. Could you lend them to me?"

All traces of worry disappeared from Aiden's face, and he promptly handed the cuffs to her. "Anything to help you have pleasant dreams."

Faith felt a tightness form in her chest as she grabbed the handcuffs and put them into her haversack. She had just lied to a knight of the Purple Order, a man who trusted everything she said and would fall on a sword for her if the situation demanded it.

"Thank you," she said. "I already feel a lot better now."

"Of course. Was there anything else?"

"No. Not that I can think of."

"In that case, may I suggest we rest for the night? Although, now that I think about it, we don't even know where our rooms are..."

Faith took this opportunity to look around the hallway and thus avoid the knight's gaze, which at the moment only reminded her of the sin she'd just committed. "They shouldn't be too far from here," she said. "I asked the steward to put us as close to the dungeon as possible."

"Hmm. He said he'd be in his office until later tonight. Should I go ask him about it?"

"Yes, please do."

"I'll be right back then."

"Actually..."

"Yes?"

Without looking him in the eyes, she glanced over her shoulder and told him, "I feel like taking a walk alone right now. Go ahead and get some sleep, all right? I'll see you tomorrow morning."

Aiden wrinkled his brow in disapproval. "You mean to go outside the castle? Alone?"

"Yes."

"It's too dangerous, Faith. I can't let you do that."

"I'm only going to the church, Aiden. Nothing is going to happen to me."

"We can't be sure of that. That 'fairy' is still out there, and we have no idea what it wants or what it can do."

"I'll be fine. She couldn't do anything during my fight with Fowler."

"But—"

"Aiden." She calmly met his gaze. "Please."

The knight hesitated but finally relented and sighed. "As you wish," he said. "In that case, I'll come get you in half an hour. Will that be long enough for you?"

"Yes. Thank you."

"I'll go see the steward then. Please be careful."

"I will be."

Aiden continued down the hallway and turned around a corner, leaving her alone with her thoughts. She stood there for a minute, contemplating her next move while she put a hand on her haversack and gripped the manacles through the canvas. This wasn't the time to falter. She had come this far and asked Aiden to lend her the handcuffs, so she might as well see it through to the end. And then after that, if she ever met the fairy again, she would have irrefutable proof that priestesses and mages were completely different from one another. Perhaps she could even undo the indoctrination Fowler had inflicted on the fairy.

Bolstered by this idea, Faith nodded to herself and walked down the hallway in the same direction Aiden had taken, but she turned to the left at the next junction, all while doing her best to ignore the possibility that the fairy was right.

Unfazed by the darkness that surrounded him, Kieran wrapped the chain attached to his right wrist around his neck, testing it as a possible substitute for a noose. However, the rings on the wall to which the chains were linked were too far away from him. Was that intentional? Maybe the gaoler had foreseen this possibility and arranged the placement of the rings to forestall this sort of thing.

Wait, no. No one cared enough about their prisoners to have this kind of foresight. Far more likely that someone else *had* successfully hanged themselves and forced the implementation of this preventive measure.

Suddenly feeling very tired, Kieran closed his eyes and let the rhythm of his breathing cradle him to sleep. There was nothing else he could do now except wait for the next morning. Perhaps then he could provoke the knight into killing him. Being stabbed in the heart wouldn't have been his first choice, but it certainly was preferable to being executed by heart attack in front of a crowd.

Then, just as he contemplated how he could prevent the inquisitor from healing him after the knight stabbed him, he heard a voice call out to him from the other side of the door. "Kieran? Are you in there?"

His eyes shot open and he saw the faint glow of a blue light coming from under the door. "Breeze?"

"Kieran? You really are there! Wait a second, I'll open this door for you!"

Kieran stared incredulously at the light gleaming across the surface of the floor and briefly wondered whether or not he was dreaming. This couldn't be real, could it? No way she would risk coming into a dungeon to break him out of there, especially with an inquisitor in the vicinity.

"I think I got it!" the fairy exclaimed.

The sorcerer heard the click of the door being unlocked.

Then, he saw the door opening by itself, as if pushed by an invisible force. On the other side of it was Breeze, hovering in the air, her butterfly wings glowing a soft blue.

"Kieran!"

The fairy lunged forward and zoomed across the room at an amazing speed, and before he could say anything, Kieran felt the girl's arms wrap themselves around his neck and squeeze him as hard they could.

It didn't hurt one bit. Quite the contrary, in fact.

"I'm so glad!" she said. "When I saw them take you away, I thought... I thought..."

A sob escaped her throat and her little shoulders began to shake uncontrollably. Kieran sat there, unsure of how he should react. He thought about hugging her back but stayed his hand, afraid he might accidentally hurt her if he tried to hold her.

"It's all right," he said. "I'm all right."

"But everything is my fault!" she sobbed. "Everything!"

"Don't say that. You didn't put me in here, did you?"

"No, but—"

"Then it's all right. Don't worry about it."

The fairy continued to cry in silence, unwilling to let him go despite his reassurances. If only he could hug her back, he'd feel a lot less awkward right now. He hadn't expected her presence to be so...soothing. The hollowness that'd settled in his chest when he woke up didn't bother him as much anymore. How long had it been since someone other than his mother had hugged him like that? He couldn't remember.

"It's all right," he said again. "Stop crying now. We don't want the guards to find us like this, right?"

She sniffled and shook her head.

"Come on then. Show me your face."

The girl slowly backed away from his neck and rubbed her teary eyes with her hands.

"You feeling better?" he asked.

She nodded and answered with a weak, "Mm-hmm."

"Good. Because as soon as you remove these chains from me, you're gonna have to leave me and get out of here."

"Huh?" She stopped moving and stared at him with wide eyes, and for just an instant, Kieran could have sworn that the blue light emanating from her wings waned ever so slightly. "Wha-what do you mean?" she asked.

"Exactly what I said."

The fairy remained speechless for a while and slowly lowered her hands as she tried to comprehend the reasoning behind his words. "What? Why?"

Her voice choked up, and her eyes blinked as she did her best to hold back her tears. Kieran hated doing this to her, but he had no other choice. It meant the difference between life and death for her brothers and sisters.

"You used telekinesis to open the door, right?" he asked.

"Telekinesis? What's that?"

"That's when you move objects around with your mind."

"Oh, uh…yes, I did. I looked into the hole and moved the small parts until it opened."

Kieran raised his hands and showed her the manacles on his wrists. "Then you won't be able to remove these handcuffs from me. Only the chains."

"Huh? Why?"

"Because they've been consecrated by Azarian Keepers. Although, I guess I should say they've been enchanted by them."

"Enchanted? With magic?" Breeze flew closer to him and examined the shackles fastened on his arms. "Oh! You're right!"

"What? You can tell?" Kieran followed her gaze but saw nothing out of the ordinary. If not for the seven-pointed star enclosed in a circle that was engraved on them, he wouldn't have been able to tell they belonged to the Inquisition. "What do you see?"

"You can't sense it? It's so obvious!"

"No, I really can't."

"Really? That's weird…" The fairy put a finger on her lips and tilted her head to the side. "It's like…there's a pattern written on it—no, *inside* of it, and it traps the magic in a sort of…loop? Yeah, that's it! A loop!"

Kieran narrowed his eyes. "And?"

"And it draws the magic inside of it before pushing it outside in all directions. This is so strange."

"Is that how you knew that the inquisitor was using magic? By sensing it?"

She nodded. "You really can't feel it? Not even a little?"

"No, Breeze, I can't. It doesn't matter, though. Now you know why you have to leave me. You can't unlock these handcuffs. Not with your magic."

"What can open it then?"

"Only the key that was made for it."

Breeze placed her hands on her hips, thrust out her chest, and beamed a wide smile at him. "Then I'll go get it!"

The confidence with which she spoke momentarily stunned him. Was she an idiot? She had to be. She was a cute, honest, and lovable girl, but an idiot nonetheless. No sane person would contemplate such a reckless course of action, not after witnessing the kind of power the inquisitor had displayed, but Breeze didn't appear the slightest bit concerned by it, and that worried him.

"You can't," he said. "It's too dangerous."

"Don't worry. Like I told you, I'm super good at hiding! She won't even notice the key is missing."

"She will. She definitely will."

"You're such a worrywart. I won't even have to touch her! I

can just move the key with my telekomisis and you'll be out of jail in no time at all."

"Breeze, wait—"

"Then we'll go to Firstkin and continue our quest to find Nana. You're really smart, so I'm sure you already have a plan to find her. With your help, no one will be able to stop us!"

"I said—"

"And then, once we finally meet her—"

"I said STOP!"

Breeze flinched at the sudden outburst. He instantly regretted raising his voice and thought about apologizing to her, but he couldn't afford to. Not when the lives of her siblings were at stake.

Kieran lowered his head and gazed at the slabs of stone that shimmered a serene blue between his legs. He then closed his eyes and let out a long sigh. "Just remove my chains and leave me here," he said. "I'll fight my way through the guards."

"But...you won't have your magic," Breeze murmured.

"That's why you can't be with me."

"They'll capture you again!"

*No, they won't*, Kieran thought. Whatever happened today, he wouldn't go back into his cell. But that wasn't something he could tell a girl her age. "Maybe," he said, avoiding her gaze. "But you'll have given me a fighting chance."

"I have magic too!" she persisted. "I can help you!"

"Don't make me repeat myself."

Her tiny hands balled into fists and she hovered closer to him so he could see how serious she was. "I know you don't want to see me hurt, but you're my friend, and friends look after each other."

"We're not friends."

"Yes, we are!"

"No! We're not!" Kieran glared at the little fairy, unable to restrain himself anymore. "You can't become friends with someone you've met only yesterday. You just can't."

"But we did! You helped me so much already! I wouldn't have known where to find you if you hadn't told me about human cities. And I can't find Nana without your help!"

"Then I'll just tell you how to find her. You'll figure out the rest."

"No!" She shook her head emphatically. "We'll do it together!"

"Goddammit, now you're just being childish!"

"I don't care! You're my friend, and you've done nothing wrong. That's why I'll help you get out of here, even if you don't want me to."

Breeze continued to hold his gaze and waited for his next argument, which she would no doubt refute with another misguided declaration of friendship. He should have anticipated this, really. After all, she knew nothing of his past and the years he'd spent wandering the Azarian Realms. How could she? Every time her questions touched on something personal, he either redirected the conversation to another subject or answered her with half truths that somehow managed to satisfy her. Hence her misplaced loyalty.

When Kieran lowered his gaze, Breeze steeled herself for another verbal attack that was sure to surpass the others, but instead, only silence greeted her. She waited for him to speak, until finally she couldn't bear it anymore and talked to him first.

"Kieran? What's wrong?"

He didn't answer her immediately, even though he wanted to. He'd never told his story to anyone before, and he didn't know where to begin, but he had to, or she would never understand who he really was. And then, before he could change his mind, he opened his mouth and told her the truth.

"I killed over forty people."

He kept avoiding her gaze.

"I can't tell you how many exactly because I'm not sure myself, but it's definitely more than forty. It wasn't all in self-defense either: I have shot, stabbed, choked, drowned, burned, and punched people to death ever since I was fifteen years old. Sometimes for money, sometimes because I was angry. So, when you say I've done nothing wrong, I don't know what the fuck you're talking about. If it wasn't for you, I'd already be on my way to Holiburg to find and kill the bitch who executed my mother. Do you understand now?"

He raised his head to look at Breeze again.

"If you do, remove my chains and get the hell out of here. I'll handle the rest."

She stared at him with a dazed expression, seemingly at a loss on what to say in this situation. He couldn't blame her for her indecision; she'd never had to deal with something like this before. Any kid her age would react the same way.

"Hurry up," he said. "The guards might come in at any moment. If they see you here—"

And then, out of the blue, Breeze hugged his neck again. Kieran didn't understand what she was doing until he felt her arms squeeze him as hard as possible.

"Wha-what are you doing?" he asked her.

"Giving you a hug," she said.

"I know *that*. I'm asking why you're doing it. This is not the time for—"

"I know what you're trying to do, Kieran, and it's not going to work. You're my friend, and you're also a nice human. That's why I'm gonna help you escape from here."

"Didn't you listen to a word I said? I've—"

"You've killed people, yeah, but…you looked so sad when you told me about it. Like your heart was gonna break in half. I'm sorry, Kieran. I'm so sorry that you had to go through this."

"Stop it. I'm exactly the kind of person your Nana warned you about. I—"

"No, you're not. I can tell. If you really were a bad human, you would have told me to go find the key and bring it to you even though it's dangerous, but you didn't. So, stop pushing me away, okay? We're gonna get through this—together."

Breeze let go of his neck and moved away from him with a smile on her face and tears in her eyes.

"Are you serious?" he asked.

"Of course I am. Like I said, friends look after each other. So, what do you say? You wanna get out of here?"

Kieran gaped at her like an idiot, and before he knew it, he found himself slowly nodding at her.

"Great!" the glowing blue girl exclaimed. "Then tell me—where do I find the key for these handcuffs?"

Kieran didn't answer immediately; he needed some time to collect himself. He found his thoughts wandering back to the fairy and the tenderness of her hug. Ignatios had trained him how to center himself when thrust into the middle of a battle, but never how to deal with something like this.

Kieran sighed. For better or worse, he'd accepted Breeze's help. It had become evident that he wouldn't be able to persuade her to leave him behind, so he should try to help her as best he could so the inquisitor didn't catch her. Although Breeze was a resourceful girl, her success depended on his guidance. He needed to focus on finding the key.

Where could the inquisitor have gone? Certainly not out of town, not when he was here. It had to be somewhere close and within walking distance. A place where she was allowed to come and go as she pleased, whatever the time of day, and which she might seek after speaking to him. Taking all of these factors into consideration, there were only a few locations that came to mind.

"The church," he finally said. "There should be one near the center of town."

"I saw it on my way here! There's a big star at the top of it, yeah?"

"Yes."

"You think the inquisitor lady is in there?"

"I don't know. Maybe. What time is it right now?"

"Hmm, not too long after the sunset. Why?"

"All right then. If you can't find her at the church, then she's probably resting in her room right about now. Can you tell me where we are?"

"Um, Dallybridge?"

"The name is Ballybridge, and I meant what building, Breeze."

"Oh, that! Yeah, we're in a *huge* building!" She emphasized the size of it by spreading her arms wide. "It's made of stone and there are huge walls around it, but no flowers or plants. It's kind of sad, actually."

"Sounds like we're in the lord's keep, which means the inquisitor should have a room somewhere around here." He paused for an instant to formulate a plan. "Here's what you're gonna do. You're gonna find the inquisitor's room and wait until she falls asleep before you take the key from her. I'm sure the lord of this town has given her a room with a window, so that's how you'll get in. Just go outside and peek inside each room without being seen. Got it?"

"Got it! What about the church, though?"

"I'd be surprised if she was there, but go take a look, just in case. If she is, follow her to her room and wait until she falls asleep, like I told you. Don't take any chances, and be careful around her knight. You saw what he's capable of, right?"

Even in the bright blue glow of her butterfly wings, Kieran saw Breeze turn white at the mention of the knight, and she responded to the warning with a firm nod of her head. "Yes, I did," she said. "Don't worry, I'll be super careful."

"Good. Go then."

"What about your chains? Should I remove them before I leave?"

"No, not yet. Someone might come check on me before you return."

"Ooh! I understand. Okay then. I'll be on my way."

"Good luck."

Breeze turned around to leave but stopped at the door to look back at him, a soft expression on her face. For a second, Kieran thought he might have scared her too much by reminding her of the knight, until the fairy lunged back at him and hugged his neck again. He stiffened and sat there with his mouth agape as he received this unexpected third hug.

"What's wrong?" he asked.

"Nothing," she said. "It's a good luck hug."

"You have those in your village?"

"Now we do."

"Well, okay then… Thank you."

"You're welcome."

She let him go and gave him a bright smile, which to his surprise gave him a fuzzy feeling inside. They had known each other for only two days now, and despite the direness of his situation, he felt comfortable enough to return her smile with one of his own.

"I'll be going now," she said. "I'll be back before you know it."

"Be careful."

"Always!" Breeze left the room and closed the door behind her, shrouding the cell in impenetrable blackness.

"Don't forget to lock the door," Kieran said.

"Oh! Right!" The fairy began to fiddle with the lock using her magic until he heard the *click* of the deadbolt moving back into place, confining him to his cell. The blue light continued to glow through the gap below the door until it moved to the left—the opposite direction the inquisitor had gone—and disappeared down the corridor.

Kieran listened to the oppressive, almost suffocating silence of the dungeon and let out a long sigh as he rested his head against the least bumpy slab of stone in the wall behind him. Breeze couldn't be right about him being a good person, but that didn't matter. Now he had someone to protect, someone who depended on him. And God be damned, he wouldn't let anyone take her away from him.

Least of all an inquisitor like Faith Dow.

# CHAPTER 20

AITH WALKED DOWN the streets of Ballybridge under the gaze of several curious onlookers who had gathered in small groups to discuss the events of the day. Nearly all of them quieted down when the inquisitor passed by them, so captivated by her presence that they momentarily forgot about the fires still burning in their fields. Looking up at the night sky, Faith could see a tinge of red slowly ebb away from the vast ocean of stars that glimmered above her. She estimated that it would take only one more hour before the fire died out—a small comfort for the people of Ballybridge after everything they'd gone through.

She pressed on to the public square, where even more people had gathered. She saw Mother Maeve among them, reassuring those who were still shaken by the manhunt that had taken place within their town. To her surprise, the head priestess excused herself and approached Faith instead.

Everyone's gaze settled on the inquisitor in all but an instant. Those who held lanterns in their hands raised them to get a better look at her, while others murmured in hushed awe at the sight of the woman who'd defeated Kieran Fowler, the Pyromancer of Holiburg. If that wasn't embarrassing enough, she caught the eyes of one of the men—a handsome lad of maybe eighteen years old—wandering down her body and stopping at her waist. He probably didn't mean to because he immediately refocused his attention on her face when Mother Maeve stepped in front of him to greet Faith.

"Inquisitor Dow," she said, smiling warmly. "I'm so glad to see you back at full health. How are you feeling?"

"Uh, I'm fine," Faith replied, her eyes darting around the place. "And you? Is everything all right here?"

"Things could be better, but we've learned to count our blessings. But what about you? Is there something you need?"

"I wouldn't say 'need.' I only wanted to visit the church, but I see now that it is a bad time."

"Oh, not at all, Inquisitor. If you wish to spend some time in the House of our Mother, then I shall do everything in my power to accommodate you. Bianca? Where are— Ah, there you are. Will you please stay here while I accompany the inquisitor to the church? I shouldn't be too long."

The young novitiate—who must have been helping her mentor calm the anxious townspeople gathered here tonight—stepped out of the crowd and bowed low to the matronly priestess.

"Of course, Mother," Bianca answered with reverence. "But before you do, may I say something to the inquisitor first? If she would allow it, of course."

Maeve raised an eyebrow at the unexpected request and turned to Faith for an answer. She didn't seem particularly concerned, so Faith decided to trust the priestess's judgment and listen to what the novitiate had to say. If only there weren't so many people around...

"You may speak," the inquisitor said, hoping to sound somewhat confident in front of such a large audience.

Bianca smiled and nodded, seeming grateful for this opportunity. Faith would have preferred to refuse her request and head immediately inside the church to carry out her plan—or listen to her in a more private setting—but with a hundred farmers and townspeople here, she felt obligated to acquiesce and hear her out.

"I don't want to take too much of your time," the fair-haired novitiate said, "so I will be brief. On behalf of every soul in Ballybridge, I would like to thank you for saving our town from the sorcerer who infiltrated it. Without you, who knows how many lives might have been lost to him and the dark forces he serves. We've been truly blessed by your arrival, and we will pray to the Kind Mother so that she watches over you, just like you watched over us. Thank you."

Bianca then bowed, expressing her gratitude in the most respectful way she knew how. Before Faith could give her an answer, several of the townspeople began to do the same. One by one, they lowered their heads, setting off a reaction that spread through the crowd and caused them to follow suit. Soon, everyone but Mother Maeve was bowing to her, stunning Faith into silence.

She knew she had to say something, but in the face of such devotion and gratitude, her mind went blank and she instead gawked at them, unable to speak. Mother Maeve remained silent, preferring to watch from the sidelines with a grin on her face and a strange twinkle in her eyes, as if this didn't concern her at all.

"I am...touched by your gratitude," Faith said, "but I never would have found the sorcerer without Mother Maeve's assistance. This victory is as much hers as it is mine."

As she tried to think of another compliment she could give the head priestess, she remembered the reason she had come to the church, and Breeze's words echoed in her head once again.

*She's a mage! She's using magic, just like you!*

Faith clenched her teeth and did her best to maintain her composure while Bianca, who thankfully remained unaware of the inquisitor's inner turmoil, raised her head to beam at her mentor. "Really?" she said to Mother Maeve. "But you didn't even mention it!"

"I didn't?" the priestess replied innocently. "It must have slipped my mind."

"Then we should also thank you for—"

Maeve interrupted, "There's no need. The only thing the inquisitor and I have done is fulfill the duty we've taken upon ourselves. But if you really want to do something useful, I have an idea." Her gaze swept through the crowd and stopped on a bulky gray-haired man whose biceps were twice as large as Faith's arms. When their eyes met, he straightened his posture and stood very still as he waited for her to speak. "Elis? I heard you talk earlier about sending any spare farmhand to the families who've lost their crops to help them with their fields. Could you handle that?"

"Yes, Mother," the man said. "But shouldn't we get Lord Harrowmont's permission first? He might not agree with this."

"Don't worry, I'll talk to him about it. I'm sure he's already planning to do the same thing, so why not get a head start? You just focus on finding the farmhands we need."

"Yes, Mother. I will."

"Bianca? Anything else we can do?"

Faith glanced at the priestess, sensing an obvious attempt to let the novitiate take charge and come up with an idea on her own, which she did fairly quickly. "Um, for the next Mass, I was thinking we could ask the congregation to donate food and money to the families affected, so they might make it through the winter. The Church would also contribute, of course."

"Good. You take care of that."

"Me?" Bianca asked, blinking in surprise.

"Yes. I trust you can handle that?"

"Um, yes! Yes, I can, Mother."

"In that case… Inquisitor? I think it's time I opened the doors to the church for you. If you'll follow me, please."

The crowd parted before the priestess and the inquisitor, then clustered around the novitiate to discuss what else they could do for the farmers affected by the blaze. Their chatter rapidly filled the public square.

"Didn't one of Greshen's sons want to become a blacksmith? Maybe we could help pay for his apprenticeship?"

"Oliver, yeah. Wouldn't it be a little much, though? I mean, the fire was big, but they'll definitely recover from it. Right?"

"Are they still out there? Maybe we should check on them."

"You didn't hear? Zane went there with a group to help with the fire. I'm sure they're fine."

"Yeah, the fire seems under control now."

"Did they lose any shed or barn to the fire? They might need new tools…"

"Shit, I didn't think about that."

"Jonah! Language!"

"Ouch! Sorry, dear."

"Everyone! Please!" Bianca raised her hands and interrupted them. "I know you're worried and that you want to help, but it won't do them any good if we make hasty decisions. We're all on edge after what happened here today, so let's wait until tomorrow before we decide anything. Please. A good night's sleep is what we all need right now."

The people nodded and voiced their agreement. Meanwhile, Mother Maeve pulled a set of keys out of her pocket and picked the one that opened the double doors of the church. Faith looked over her shoulder and watched the crowd slowly disperse through the streets while Bianca motioned for Elis and a few other men to stay behind. She probably wanted to discuss their plans for tomorrow.

"Inquisitor? You may enter."

Faith looked back at the priestess, then followed her inside. Mother Maeve grabbed a torch from the sconce next to the door and moved out of the narthex and into the nave. "Let me light a few candles for you," she said. "We usually do it before going to sleep, but it's been a little frantic ever since the sorcerer appeared."

"Please, there's no need to," Faith answered. "I can do it myself, if you'd like."

"Hmm. How about we do it together then?"

"As you wish."

The matronly woman smiled at her and approached the pulpit, on which she had undoubtedly given many sermons in the years she lived here, and stopped at the votive candle stand in front of it. She then picked up a wood stick from a small spill vase and lit it with her torch. "Here," she said, handing it to the inquisitor.

"Thank you," Faith replied. "How many should we light?"

"How about all of them?"

"Really? Isn't that too much?"

"Well, I imagine you would like to be left alone for a while, correct?"

"Yes. I need some time to...center myself."

"I understand. I often come here to do the same thing. I like to light all the candles and gaze at them while I think about whatever is on my mind." Mother Maeve took another stick and helped Faith with the candles, her eyes filled with a melancholic glow. "Whatever is troubling you," the woman continued, "I'm sure you'll eventually find the peace you seek. And if you think that talking to someone else might help, you can always count on me to lend an ear."

"Thank you," Faith said while she peered at one of the new flames she'd ignited. "I appreciate the offer."

"It's the least I can do. Just tell me one thing: Is it something I should worry about? I've noticed you've been a little less confident than usual."

"Is it that obvious?"

"It isn't. I just have a keen eye when it comes to this sort of thing."

"I see... Well, I don't think it's something you need to worry about." *Probably not*, Faith thought. "Besides, you have enough on your plate already."

"Yes, the fire for one, and the families affected by it. Luckily, I have Bianca to help with that."

"I must say, you've taught her well. Other novitiates of her age are rarely so reliable."

"Even in Holiburg?"

"Even in Holiburg."

"My, my, Inquisitor. You're going to make me blush." The corner of Maeve's mouth curled into a slight grin, and she glanced at Faith for a second before turning her attention back to the candles. "Thank you for the compliment, but I've merely encouraged her to develop the qualities she already possessed. She's the one who did most of the work."

The priestess lit the last of the candles on her side and extinguished the wooden stick by gently blowing on it. Once Faith had done the same, she took the half-burnt pieces of wood and placed them in an empty vase.

"I can see she's learned a lot from your example," Faith replied.

"I certainly would like to think so," the woman said. "She surprised me today. After you left to interrogate Kieran Fowler, I went back to the church and saw her talking to the people outside, calming them down. Before you arrived, the only thing they could talk about was how the sorcerer managed to enter town, who should be blamed for it, what he intended to do here, why he was so close to Holiburg. And she addressed all of their concerns, one by one. Truth be told, I don't think I could have done a better job at her age."

"Is that why you put her in charge of looking after the families affected by the fire?"

"Yes. Today proved that it was high time I gave her more responsibilities. I thought this was the perfect opportunity for her to prove that she is ready for her ordination. What do you think?"

"I think you made the right decision. I don't know Bianca very well, but after what I've seen outside..."

"Ah, I hope that wasn't too embarrassing for you."

"No. Just unexpected."

"Quite so." The priestess continued to stare at the rows of flames burning before her while basking in their soft yellow light. Before the silence stretched for too long, she turned to Faith and said, "I apologize for my rambling. I hope I didn't bore you too much."

"No. Not at all."

"I shall return to Bianca and see how she's doing. I'll return to close the church in let's say...one hour? Would that be enough time for you?"

"Plenty. Thank you, Mother Maeve."

"You may call me Maeve when we're alone, Inquisitor."

"In that case, please call me Faith."

"As you wish, Faith." She smiled. "I'll leave you to it, then."

She turned around to leave but abruptly stopped and turned back toward Faith. "There was one thing," she said. "The fairy. When we spoke earlier to Lord Harrowmont about your encounter with Kieran Fowler, you told him that she stopped the sorcerer from killing you, correct?"

"Yes," Faith answered. "Why do you ask?"

"I was simply wondering: Do you think she might be an angel?"

The question took Faith completely by surprise. For several long seconds, she was at a loss for words. "I don't know," Faith said at last. "I mean, would an angel really travel with a sorcerer?"

"And why not? Angels are the eternal adversaries of demons and devils after all. And what is a sorcerer but a man whose heart is shackled to the whims and caprices of evil fiends?"

The inquisitor opened her mouth to say something, only to close it when she found herself unable to come up with a response that wouldn't sound foolish. She felt like a novitiate again, being tested by one of her teachers. Luckily for her, the priestess graciously spared her the embarrassment of having to answer her question. "But I really should go now. I'm sorry for taking more of your time."

"It's no problem," Faith replied.

"You're too kind. Please don't feel like you need to wait for me before you leave. I'll come back later to lock up."

"Thank you."

"No. Thank *you*." Mother Maeve bowed low to her, a gesture that felt strangely inappropriate coming from a woman who was almost twice her age, and then turned around and headed for the exit. Faith watched her go while she tried to ignore the knot forming in the pit of her stomach. When the double door closed behind the priestess, she shifted her gaze to her haversack and slowly opened it.

In it were her copy of the Scriptures, the leather folder that contained all the information available on Kieran Fowler, a very tiny bag she'd found in the sorcerer's haversack (it must have belonged to the fairy), writing implements, a bottle of ink, a few sheets of paper, and finally, the manacles that Aiden had handed to her. It took her a while before she worked up the nerve to pull them out of the bag.

After some hesitation, she approached and sat in the pew nearest to the candle stand. The shackles clanked as she placed them on the seat next to her, and for an instant, she wondered whether or not she really should go through with this. It would be so simple to pretend that she'd never even considered the possibility that the Church had propagated a lie for a millennium. All she had to do was put the handcuffs back into her bag and return to the keep without telling anyone about this.

Instead, she created an Eos and placed it on her right, balancing it against the frame of the pew.

Once she'd made sure the staff wouldn't fall, she took the key out of the inner pocket of her cassock and unlocked the shackles. They opened with ease, just like the ones she'd put on Fowler earlier today. To the best of her knowledge, the only members of the Church who ever wore manacles like these were inquisitors and priestesses who had been possessed by demons, and they never did so by choice.

Her hands trembled while her mind raced at the unspeakable possibility that Breeze was right, that Faith was not a mediator between God and humanity but merely a mage, one who had convinced herself that her power came from a divine being. She had to make sure it wasn't true, that this "fairy" was the one who had been fed lies all of her life. Not her.

Faith picked up the handcuffs and laid them on her lap. She rolled her left sleeve up to her elbow, closed her hand in a tight fist, and slowly lowered her wrist into one of the two open shackles. The sensation of the metal brushing against her skin gave her goose bumps, and she decided to wait until it stopped before she closed the handcuff around her wrist.

The light shining from the Eos decreased in intensity.

It was a subtle, almost unnoticeable change in the staff's radiance, but quite obvious to the person who had created it. Her heart caught in her throat, and with a swift movement of her hand, she closed the handcuff around her left wrist and gasped as she felt the Kind Mother's presence vanish from her mind, along with the Eos before her. Only the flickering light from the candles remained.

Faith stared at the empty space where the staff once rested, her breath stolen by its disappearance. Then, she hastily removed the handcuff from her arm and attempted to create a new Eos to replace the one she'd lost: it reappeared in an instant. With it, the distant and soothing presence she felt every time she communed with the Kind Mother returned, unchanged despite the experiment she had conducted a mere moment ago. She closed the shackle around her wrist again, and it vanished once more, the Eos along with it.

The young woman sprang up from her seat, causing the manacles to fall to the ground in a clatter that resounded in her ears. Her breath quickened at a rapid pace and she staggered away from the small heap of metal, unable to even look at it. The sanctity that previously reigned in the church had been replaced by an overbearing silence. She barely noticed her dull shadow passing over the empty pews of the center aisle, her whole attention now consumed by the lie her mother and teachers had hammered in her head for the last fifteen years.

Faith faltered toward the right pew of the first row and managed to hold herself up long enough to sit down right before her legs gave out from under her. The fairy was right. Every miracle she had performed, every wound and injury she had ever healed, all of it had been made possible only because of magic.

She looked up at the stained-glass windows depicting the life of Alma Azaria, their colorful designs visible even in this obscurity. Were they all lies too? Was Alma Azaria a true prophet, or simply a mage who discovered the power to annul others' magic and heal without having to use blood sorcery?

And what about Elsa? Faith had denounced her childhood friend to the rest of the Inquisition after learning the terrible truth about her. Was that also for nothing? Did she condemn her best friend to a life of misery for a God that might not even exist?

No.

No, it couldn't be.

It couldn't!

What Elsa had done was wrong! Selfish! Heartless! She had to be punished for it! She had to! Otherwise...otherwise...

Oh God.

Faith covered her mouth with her hand and choked back a

sob. Tears welled up in her eyes and rolled down her cheeks and fingers, making a mess of her face. A painful lump formed in her throat; it only got worse when her sobs began to rack her whole body, until finally, she slumped forward and fell down on her knees, her head nearly touching the floor.

Then she wailed like she never had before.

# CHAPTER 21

**B**REEZE LEFT THE keep the same way she got in: through a very small barred window that led into one of the many other empty rooms of the dark place where Kieran was imprisoned. Once she was outside, she decided to check the church first, because she already knew where it was.

To reach the church from here, all she had to do was gain altitude, find the large building in the center of town with the two towers, and then fly over there without getting spotted by the humans on the ground.

Luckily for her, none of the guards thought to look up at the sky. Nor did the large group of humans that had gathered in the open area and who were now returning home for the night. *What could they have been talking about?* she wondered.

Wait, no. That wasn't important at the moment.

The longer she took, the sadder Kieran would get, and she didn't want that for her friend. She needed the key to these magic-stopping bracelets, and the only person who had one was the woman in white. But how was she supposed to enter the church? The double door at the front of it seemed too heavy for her telemikosis, and she doubted anyone would open it anytime soon—which meant that she had to find another way in.

Then she noticed the two open towers, and a smile tugged at her lips. Humans always closed their doors and locked the windows, so they never worried about strangers sneaking in from the roof! How silly of them. But then again, the only people capable of flight, according to Kieran, were these God Emperors, and they apparently died a long time ago. Maybe she shouldn't call them silly.

Breeze shook her head and flew toward the church. She needed to focus on the present, not the past.

When she approached the open area, she spotted five people there, two of whom were women in white. Neither of them wore the red belt she saw on the inquisitor earlier today, but she did recognize the older one. Breeze immediately hid on one of the roofs nearby and poked her head above the ridge to look at them while she eavesdropped on their conversation.

"And what about the sorcerer?" the man in the front asked. "We heard that the inquisitor brought him to the keep."

"That is correct," the older woman said.

"And, uh, he's not getting out, right?"

"Have a little faith, Zane. Inquisitors are trained to deal with situations like this. You know that."

"Yes, Mother. I'm sorry."

"You should go home. Get some rest. You look exhausted."

The three men did look very tired—and dirty. Their faces, hands, and clothes were covered in black smudges, something she had never seen before. What had they been doing?

"We will, Mother," the man said. "Thank you for healing us."

His companions repeated after him and bowed respectfully.

"Please, don't mention it," the woman said. "Go home now, and don't tarry. Especially you, Zane. I'm sure Evelyn is worried sick about you."

"That's what she does best," Zane replied with a chuckle, only to stop when he remembered who he was talking to. "Um, please don't tell her I said that."

"Hmm? I'm not sure what you mean," the woman said with a grin. "Go on, now. I'll see you all tomorrow."

"Will do, Mother. Oh, you don't have a lantern with you. Would you like us to escort you to the presbytery?"

"We'll be fine." The priestess raised a hand and summoned a small ball of white light in it. "See?"

"Oh. Right. I feel stupid now."

"We all do, at some point."

The two other men chuckled, which earned them an annoyed glance from their friend. "Well, I think we'll be going now," he grumbled. "Good night, Mother. And good night to you too, Bianca."

"Good night," the priestesses said.

The three men bowed and turned around to leave, only for the youngest one to stop and look back at the two women in white. More specifically, the one around his age. "Um...good night, Bianca," he said. "See you tomorrow?"

"Yeah," she answered, fidgeting in place. "See you later, Elliot."

The lad nodded and walked away at a brisk pace to catch up to his friends. Once the men were out of earshot, the older priestess moved the ball of light so it would levitate above their heads and looked at her companion with a sly smile. "I didn't know you had your eye on him," she said.

"I didn't. We've just been talking, that's all."

"Mm-hmm. That's usually how it starts."

"Mother Maeve, please. Can we talk about something else?"

The woman ignored the request and instead asked a question Breeze didn't understand. "I trust you remember what I told you about your menses?"

The fair-haired girl looked down at her feet while kneading her hands. "Yes."

"Good. Then that's all I'll say about it. Just make sure to be nice to Elliot. He's a good boy."

The girl answered with a slight nod. "Of course," she said.

The affectionate smile that appeared on the mother's face reminded Breeze of Nana and the many times she would watch over the fairies whenever they played in the forest. It had been so long since Breeze had last seen her…

"Come now," Maeve said as she strolled toward the street adjoining the left side of the church. "It's time we checked on our guests. I'm sure the girls are still awake, waiting for us to come home."

The girl, who appeared very grateful for the change of subject, walked alongside the woman in white, the ball of light floating above them. "I've asked Elsie to look after them," she said, "but I'm sure you're right."

"What about Arthur and his sons? How are they doing?"

"I haven't seen them since they came back from Lord Harrowmont's keep. They should be at the presbytery, but…can I ask what happened? They looked shaken."

"Inquisitor Dow simply explained to Lord Harrowmont how they immediately came to Ballybridge to warn the Church about Kieran Fowler, and how brave it was of them to do so after what he did to them this morning."

"What? But that's—"

"—the right thing to do? I agree."

The older woman gave the young one a strange look, one that reminded Breeze of Nana when she reprimanded one of her siblings. But that wasn't it, exactly. Before she could figure out the hidden meaning behind it, the woman turned away and continued to walk farther down the street, the girl trailing behind her. Their voices barely reached her ears now.

"Right," the girl said. "I'll make sure Elsie hears about it too."

"Good. A lord's gratitude is invaluable, but it's nothing compared to how terrifying their wrath can be. Remember that."

"I will, Mother."

"But that's enough of that. Tell me what you talked about with our congregation. Anything I should know about?"

"Well, there's the matter of the constables."

"What about them?"

"Some people are angry that the sorcerer was able to enter town so easily, even though we were all warned about him. I tried to explain to them that…"

Incapable of making out the end of that sentence despite the silence hanging over Ballybridge, Breeze considered following the women in white for a bit but decided against it. Her priority was to save Kieran, not listen to humans talk about their affairs, no matter how interesting those might be.

She waited until the priestesses had entered a building at the end of the street before she checked her surroundings one last time. Two humans dressed in yellow tunics with spears in their hand appeared at a crossroad not far from her, but they continued forward and disappeared behind the corner of another street, the glow of their torches lingering behind them for a few more seconds before it vanished too.

It was time.

Breeze launched herself into the air and flew to the left tower, the closest one to her. She reached the top in no time and searched for a way down, sparing only a glance at the huge bell hanging from the metal frame above her—although, she did briefly wonder how humans had even brought this up here without magic. Upon finding a wooden trapdoor on the floor, she tried to open it by pulling on the iron ring attached to it but quickly realized the futility of it when it refused to budge.

"Oh, is that how it's going to be?" she asked, her arms crossed and her eyes glaring down at the ring. "Then how about THIS?"

With a flick of her mind, she used her magic to push on the trapdoor from the other side. "Aha! Humans didn't lock you, huh? Lucky me!"

She glided down the stairs and closed the trapdoor behind her without even looking at it, relying on her magical sense instead to determine its position and how to put it back in place without making any noise. Darkness enveloped her, and once she couldn't see past her nose anymore, she stopped and lit up her wings.

"Whooaaaa…" she exclaimed, looking down at the wooden stairs below. "It's so high, I can't even see the bottom. Too bad Bubble isn't here. He'd love to see this."

For an instant, she wondered whether or not her brother had gone to sleep yet, and the smile that had creeped up on her face gradually faded away when she remembered the last time they saw each other. Best not to dwell on that for now.

She let go of the railing and flew down the stairs while thinking of the very real possibility that the inquisitor was also here, doing… whatever inquisitors do after they've caught a mage. Kieran had explained to her what praying was earlier that day, and although it resembled what the fairies did in Dreamland after they killed an animal, it also sounded very different. It was a shame she couldn't ask the inquisitor about it; she might have learned a lot from her.

There were two doors at the base of the tower, both of them closed. Breeze figured that because she'd entered the left tower, the door on the right most likely led to the lobby, so she chose that one. After diminishing the intensity of the light shining from her wings, she pulled on the handle with her telekosimis and opened it just wide enough for her to peek through.

The room was empty.

Then, she heard something strange. It was very faint and difficult to make out, but she could have sworn she heard someone crying. Could it be the inquisitor? She'd seemed like such a strong lady. But if not her, who?

Breeze flew inside the room and just like before, she closed the door behind her without making a sound. Even with the dim light emanating from her wings, she could still discern the frame of the large double door on her right that led outside the church, as well as the shape of another door on the wall opposite her. The sound of heavy sobbing came from the archway on her left.

After some hesitation, she carefully made her way there, peeked around the corner, and gasped at the immensity of the room she saw beyond it. Like trees reaching for the sky, two rows of columns reached for the vaulted ceiling, forming a canopy of stone that *somehow* supported its own weight. Even the thickest of trees in Dreamland couldn't do that.

And the windows! So many beautiful windows! Their colorful designs immediately drew her gaze, and she wished the sun was still up so she could marvel at the intricate scenes they depicted.

Only one word could describe what she was seeing. She'd learned it from Nana a long time ago, but she'd never chanced upon anything that truly deserved it, not until now.

Majestic. This place was majestic.

The sobs reminded Breeze of her task, and with some reluctance, she tore her gaze away from the windows and scanned the room. There were a bunch of candles burning at the end of the aisle on the left, but no human in sight. The echo in this place also made it difficult to pinpoint the source of these cries, but they were definitely coming from somewhere in the front. She needed to get closer.

Breeze dimmed her wings again until darkness enveloped her, and then flew higher in the air to better hide herself. The weeping quieted down, as if the person had cried their heart out. The only time Breeze had ever heard someone cry like that was five years ago, when Nana said goodbye to the other fairies and left Dreamland behind. The weeks that followed had been particularly difficult for her and her siblings, and she wouldn't wish for anyone—not even the inquisitor—to go through something similar.

The same inquisitor who, as she discovered, had been the one crying all along.

Breeze saw her hunched on the floor in front of the benches, her red belt visible even in the dim light of the candles. The inquisitor hadn't noticed her yet. Eventually, she would regain her composure and return to the keep. Breeze only needed to follow her, wait until the inquisitor fell asleep, and then grab the key and scamper away without anyone being the wiser. That would be the easy thing to do.

But that would also require that she do nothing, and that wasn't how the fairies of Dreamland were brought up! So, without giving it a second thought, Breeze brightened her wings once again, flew down to the ground, and landed next to the raven-haired woman.

"Hello? Do you need some help?" she asked.

The woman froze at the sound of her voice and kept completely still for a few seconds while Breeze waited patiently for an answer. Then, very slowly, she raised her head, her eyes full of tears and her cheeks completely red. She didn't utter a word, which inclined Breeze to believe that she really needed some help.

"You look so sad," the fairy said. "What happened? Did someone say mean things to you?"

The inquisitor opened her mouth to say something, but instead she let it hang open as she stared at the blue-haired fairy.

"Hello?" Breeze repeated. "Are you all right? Would you like a hug?"

It seemed that her last question had an effect on the woman in white, because she finally closed her mouth and tried to speak again. "You're Breeze, right?"

"Yup. That's me," the girl answered with a smile. "I'm Breeze the fairy! What's your name?"

"Faith. Faith Dow."

"Wow, you also have a family name. And it's so pretty."

"Wh-what are you doing here?"

"Oh. Well, I guess I was looking for you. Kieran told me I might find you in here, so…"

"Fowler? You spoke to him?"

*Oh, crap,* Breeze realized. Maybe she shouldn't have said that. Quick, she had to think of something!

"Well…he taught me many things this morning," she hastily added while rubbing the back of her head. "About humans, I mean. And now I know a lot more about all of you than I did before! Like how you go to church every Requisday to pray to God and such. Is that what you were doing here? Praying?"

Faith stared at her with a blank look, then lowered her head and slumped on herself like a sad bluebell flower. "You were right," the inquisitor said.

"Huh? About what?" Breeze asked.

"About me being a mage." The woman looked at something lying on the floor on the other side of the center aisle, near the stand where the candles burned. Breeze followed her gaze; after squinting her eyes, she recognized the shape of metal bracelets lying on the ground. The same type that Kieran wore.

"I put them on," Faith explained. "I had to know…"

She hung her head low, and Breeze understood.

"You really didn't know?" she asked. "You didn't even suspect it?"

The inquisitor shook her head. "I didn't."

"What about the other ladies in white?"

"The priestesses? I'm not sure, but…I don't think they know either."

Breeze widened her eyes at this revelation and tried to wrap her head around that weird idea. "So, you're just like Kieran," she said. "You can't feel the magic around you."

"Feel it?" Faith raised her eyebrows and looked at the fairy once again. "I guess I can feel it. I just…never thought it was magic."

"I mean the magic coming from other people. Not from you."

"What? No. No, I can't. Well, not exactly. But you do?"

Breeze nodded emphatically.

"Is that how you knew I was a mage?"

"Mm-hmm! It was very strange at first because I never saw anyone use magic the way you do, but after watching you fight with Kieran, I knew you were one."

"I see." The inquisitor appeared to realize the state she was in and hurriedly wiped her face with her sleeves. "I'm sorry. I must look terrible."

"It's okay," Breeze said. "Are you sure you don't want a hug?"

"No. Well, maybe I do, but—" Before she could even finish her sentence, Breeze was already grabbing on to Faith's neck, holding her in a tight embrace that would be difficult to escape from unless the inquisitor pushed her away.

"There, there. It's all better now."

At first, Faith didn't react, but the longer the hug continued, the more relaxed she became—until finally, she closed her eyes and let out a long, tired sigh.

"Feeling better now?" Breeze asked.

The inquisitor nodded.

"Good." Breeze moved away from Faith and gave her a big smile. "Hugs are the best remedies against sadness! That's what my Nana used to say anyway."

"Your Nana?"

"Oh, that's the fairy who raised me."

"I see." The inquisitor looked down at the ground, but only for a short moment. "Thank you," she said.

"Don't mention it! I was only doing what any other fairy would have done."

"But am I not your enemy?"

"My enemy?" Breeze cocked her head to the side and put an interrogative finger on her lips. "I don't know. Are you going to hurt me?"

"What? Of course not!"

"What about the other fairies? You're not gonna try to force me to talk about them, right?"

"I admit, I'm a little curious to learn more about them, but I won't ask you to tell me anything you don't want to."

"Then we're not enemies!" Breeze happily declared, only for her expression to suddenly change when she thought about another possibility. "Unless..."

"Unless what?" Faith asked.

It was with great difficulty that she finished her sentence. "Unless *you* decide we are."

"Why would I ever do that?"

"Because I'm trying to save Kieran. That's why I'm here. To get the key to the metal bracelets from you." Breeze avoided the inquisitor's gaze, looking down at the floor as she admitted her true intentions. She didn't want Faith to think that she was a liar, but she had omitted the truth when Faith asked her whether or not she had talked to Kieran earlier this evening.

Wait. Had she ruined everything by bringing up the key? Oh no, she must have! In fact, she shouldn't even be talking to the inquisitor right now. Kieran had been very explicit in his instructions, and this wasn't part of it. At all.

Gosh, what had she done?

"Breeze. Look at me."

The fairy raised her head at the surprisingly soft tone the inquisitor used. It reminded her of how Nana would calmly speak to her and to the other fairies after they had done something wrong. And just like with Nana, Faith's voice managed to put her at ease despite the seriousness of her blunder.

"Why do you want to save Kieran?"

"Huh?" The question caught her off guard. "You want to know why?"

"Yes."

"Because he's my friend, of course! Because he's kind, thoughtful, and selfless! Because he's a good human, and he doesn't deserve to die!"

"But has he told you about the bad things he's done?"

Breeze nodded vigorously. "Yes, he did."

"What about the farmers he hurt this morning?"

"The farmers?" Kieran had mentioned something about them earlier today, now that she thought about it. "He said he had to scare some humans away."

"Did he tell you about how he beat them up and broke many of their bones?"

"N-no. He didn't."

"Then you can understand why I don't want to give you the key."

"But I'm sure he had a good reason!" Breeze balled her hands into fists and locked eyes with the inquisitor. "He'd never hurt other people unless he had to!"

"Breeze, I spoke to the farmers myself. He almost killed them."

"But he didn't, right?"

"I—no, he didn't."

"You see? He's not a bad person. What about the other humans? Did they do something bad?"

Faith paused to think about it for a second, and judging by the way her expression changed, Breeze knew she had guessed right.

"They tried to take his bow," Faith revealed, only to hastily add, "but only because he was bivouacking on their land."

"'Bivouacking'? What's that?"

"Uh, it means camping."

"Ooooh. So, they're thieves?"

"I-I suppose they are…"

"Then doesn't that mean he had a good reason to hurt them?"

"No, Breeze. There are no 'good' reasons to hurt people. It's something you do out of necessity, nothing else."

"But you just said they were trying to steal his bow."

"Yes, they were. And maybe they shouldn't have done that, even if he was bivouacking on their land, but that didn't give him the right to hurt them as bad as he did."

"Are they all right?"

Faith took a deep breath and nodded. "Yes, they are." She was about to add something else but winced and hissed in pain instead before she carefully stood up on her feet. "Sorry," she said. "I…I have to stretch my legs a bit."

The inquisitor tried to walk a little but then slumped onto the bench behind her and started to rub her knees.

"Do you need some help?" Breeze asked.

"No, no. I'm fine," Faith answered. "I've been kneeling for too long, that's all."

"Ah, okay…" The fairy didn't know where to take the conversation next. Luckily for her, the inquisitor did.

"The farmers came to Ballybridge to receive healing from the local priestess," Faith explained. "They should be resting at the presbytery right now, waiting for me to write down their testimony."

"'Presbytery'?" Breeze repeated. "'Testimony'?"

"You don't know these words?"

The fairy shook her head. "I'm still learning."

The inquisitor narrowed her eyes for an instant but proceeded with an explanation. "The presbytery is the house where the priestesses of a town usually stay, and a testimony is…how do I say this? It's an official declaration of what you saw happen. We usually put it to paper."

"And why do they need to do that?"

"So the Inquisition can use it as evidence during Kieran's trial."

"Then…you're really going to let him die?"

"What else do you expect me to do, Breeze? Let him go?"

"Yes! I told you, he's a good human."

"No. He's cruel and ruthless. He doesn't help people; he only hurts them. Even back in the field, he—"

"He's helping me!" Breeze interrupted, her fists shaking. "He told me he was going to Holiburg to kill the woman who hurt his mother, but he changed his mind! Instead, he decided to come with me and help me find my Nana, even though he had no reason to. He knew it would be more dangerous for him, but he still came with me!"

Faith's eyes widened at this revelation, but Breeze wasn't done yet.

"He's been doing everything he could to protect me," she said more softly, "even after all the mistakes I've made. So don't say he's cruel, because he's not! He feels bad about the people he's hurt—he just doesn't show it. And if you really can't see that, then you're really bad at helping people! Because Kieran is the one who needs help the most!"

Breeze stared at Faith, a wave of heat flushing throughout her body. She had never talked to anyone like this before, nor had she thought herself capable of it, but now that she had done so, she questioned whether or not she should have. The inquisitor was gaping at her like a fish out of the water, and for a while, neither of them said anything. The silence stretched long enough for Breeze to ponder what she should do next, if anything, only for Faith to make the decision for her.

"He really said that?" she asked. "About killing the woman who hurt his mother?"

Breeze took a deep breath and then nodded. "Yes, he did. But he's not going to anymore."

"Because of you?"

"Because I asked him to help me."

Faith looked down at her hands. Was she reconsidering her decision to imprison Kieran? Maybe she was about to give Breeze the key and tell her to be on her way, giving her permission to free Kieran from his dark cell.

"I'm sorry," Faith said, "but I can't give you the key."

Breeze felt her chest tighten at the response, and although she wanted to voice her disapproval, she found herself incapable of articulating even one word.

"There are two men guarding the door leading to the dungeon," Faith continued. "I can't let Kieran hurt them once he escapes, so I'll be the one to remove his handcuffs."

"Huh?" Breeze blinked at the inquisitor, unsure that she'd heard her right. "Wait, what?"

"I'll remove the handcuffs, Breeze."

"Really?"

"Yes, really."

"For realsies? No taking it back?"

"Yes."

"Pinky swear?"

Faith blinked, then nodded. "Pinky swear."

Breeze rose from the ground with a wide smile on her face and extended a hand toward the inquisitor. "Then it's a promise!"

Faith offered her pinky to the fairy and they shook on it, with Breeze's whole hand wrapped around the woman's finger.

"Thank you," Breeze said. "I wasn't sure you'd agree to it."

"I have to admit," Faith said, "I'm still not comfortable with the idea of letting Kieran go, but…I think I can trust you to keep an eye on him."

"Keep an eye on him? But he's always the one keeping an eye on me."

"Maybe so, but you're the one who saved my life out there,

Breeze. If you hadn't come out when you did, I'm...I'm not sure I would have survived."

"Oh." Now Breeze understood. "You think I can stop him from hurting other people?"

"Yes."

"And that's why you agreed to help me?"

"That, and because he deserves another chance." For an instant, it seemed as if Faith would say something else, only to suddenly change her mind. "We've wasted enough time. We should leave soon."

"Oh, right!" Breeze exclaimed. "So, what do we do next? I've never helped anyone escape from prison before."

Faith lowered her gaze and started thinking really hard. Breeze figured that she was formulating a plan to break Kieran out of jail, so she waited patiently for her to speak again.

"Breeze? It may sound foolish, but there's one last thing I'd like to know."

"Of course! What is it?"

"Are you an angel?"

The blue-haired girl cocked her head to the side and repeated the question in her head. Had Nana ever taught her that word before? It didn't ring any bells, so she mustn't have. Unless it was one of those times when she fell asleep in the middle of the lesson.

"I don't think I ever heard that word," Breeze said. "What is it? Is it something nice? I hope it's something nice."

Before Faith could answer her, Breeze heard the creaking of a door opening, which was then followed by the voice of a man. "Inquisitor? Are you here?"

Faith sprang up to her feet and swiveled her head toward the entrance of the church, then turned back to Breeze and whispered to her, "You have to hide! Quickly!"

Breeze didn't even hesitate. She flew behind the benches on the right side of the room, where the light didn't break through the darkness, and dimmed her wings until the shadows enveloped her. Then, she heard the stranger's voice echo through the main room.

"Inquisitor?"

"I'm here," Faith said.

The fairy stayed behind the bench but risked a glimpse at the man standing near the archway. Even though she couldn't see his face from here, she recognized his silhouette almost instantly: the knight who'd almost killed Kieran.

Breeze shuddered at the memory of his sword cutting into her friend's shoulder and all the blood that flowed down the edge of that blade. She'd thought Kieran had died, leaving her alone in this human world where wielding magic was forbidden for everyone except for those who wore a white robe. She didn't want to imagine where she would be right now if Faith hadn't healed him. Maybe somewhere in the forest, crying herself to sleep.

"Should I come back later?" the knight asked.

"No, no, it's all right," Faith replied. "I was finished here anyway. Just…wait for me outside, will you? I'll be right out."

"Yes, of course." The knight bowed and left. Faith stooped and grabbed the handcuffs off the ground, placing them in the shoulder bag she had brought with her.

Breeze waited for a few more seconds before she came out and joined her. "That was your knight, right?" she whispered.

"Aiden, yes." Faith closed her bag. "We have to leave soon or he's going to wonder what's taking me so long."

"All right. What do I do?"

"You…" The inquisitor took a moment to consider their next course of action. "You follow me back to the keep and wait for me in my room—wait, no, I don't even know where it is. Follow me back to the keep and wait outside until I open my window for you. I'm sure Lord Harrowmont gave me one with a view, especially after what he pulled today—"

"Could I not just hide in your bag?" Breeze asked, her head cocked to the side and her finger on her chin. "I'm super good at hiding! I won't even make a sound."

The suggestion seemed to completely disarm Faith for some reason, and she now stared at Breeze like she had grown dragonfly wings or something. Maybe it was a dumb idea to suggest this in the first place, but how was she supposed to know that? Nana had never taught her what was considered "normal" in the human world. In fact—

"That's, um, a good idea," Faith said.

Breeze broke into a smile at the compliment. "You think so?"

"Yes."

"Phew! I thought I had said something stupid for a second. Like, maybe there's something dangerous in there that everyone except me knows about." Breeze hovered closer to the bag to examine it. "Can you loosen the straps a little? I wouldn't want to run out of air."

"Yes, I can. Are you sure you want to hide in there? I don't know when you might get to come out."

"I'm sure. Nothing will stop me from saving Kieran."

"Very well. Hop in."

Faith opened the bag and Breeze flew inside, retracting her wings so that she would fit in. "Wow, there's so much stuff in here."

"Your wings…" Faith said. "They're gone."

"My wings? Oh yeah, I can grow them back whenever I want. Nice, huh?"

"Uh, yes, it is. Now hold on. I'm closing the bag now."

"Ready and waiting!"

The inquisitor put the cover back in its place and adjusted the straps to leave one hole at each upper end of the bag, which not only allowed Breeze to breathe but also to take a peek at the world outside if she so wished. However, she resisted the urge and instead opted to sit tight and wait until Faith told her to come out.

Too bad she couldn't risk using the light of her wings to take a better look at all the thingamajigs in here. It would have been a fun way to pass the time.

# CHAPTER 22

FAITH FOUND AIDEN standing guard outside the church, his left hand resting on the pommel of his sword and his posture betraying no fatigue or inattention, as befitted a knight of the Purple Order. But when he turned to meet her gaze and the moonlight shone on his face, she saw unmistakable worry in his eyes, and her chest tightened.

"Is everything all right, Inquisitor?" he asked.

No. Everything she believed in was a lie, and she couldn't tell anyone about it. No doubt the other inquisitors would accuse her of being possessed if she so much as alluded to it. And her mother? What would she do if she ever learned of Kieran's intention to kill her and Faith's plan to free him?

"I'm fine," she said. "Also, you called me 'Inquisitor' again."

"I apologize. I figured that since we're out in the open—"

"That's fine. But call me Faith from now on."

"Even in public?"

"Yes." She didn't want to be called "Inquisitor" anymore. Not by him, nor anyone else. "Let's go back to the keep."

She only managed to take two steps forward before Aiden caught her by the arm and stopped her. "Wait. What's wrong, Faith?"

"I told you, I'm fine."

"No, you're not. I can tell you've been crying. I just don't know why." Faith looked at his hand, and he hastily released his grip and took a step back. "I apologize," he said.

An uncomfortable silence hung in the air while Faith pondered what to do. She couldn't very well tell him the truth—that would only add to her problems—but she had to tell him *something*. Otherwise, he would only grow more suspicious of her.

"It's because of what happened in the field," she said. "Before you arrived."

Aiden furrowed his brow and narrowed his eyes. "You mean what that winged creature said about you being a witch?" he asked.

"No, no," she retorted. "Of course not." Faith turned her gaze away and considered her next words very carefully. She hadn't thought that deceiving someone else would prove to be so difficult, and a long moment passed before she spoke again. "I was scared. Scared for my life."

Though her voice was but a whisper, out here in the dead of the night, she knew that Aiden could hear her perfectly. She closed her eyes and turned away from him, cursing herself for her dishonesty before she felt his hand land on her shoulder and squeeze gently.

"I'm sorry, Faith. I-I should have figured it out sooner. It was your first battle against a sorcerer, and I didn't even think about what you were going through."

A tightness formed in her throat, making it harder for her to breathe as she listened to Aiden's attempt to comfort her. She didn't want him to believe her so easily.

"If there's anything I can do to help—"

"I'll be fine," she said, eager to put an end to this. "I just need some time alone."

"Of course." Aiden let go of her shoulder and took a step back. "I didn't want to make you feel uncomfortable."

"You didn't. I'm simply not used to conversations like this. Nevertheless, your concern is…appreciated."

"Of course. Shall we return to the keep? I can walk farther behind you if you'd prefer."

"No, no. Let's just walk like we usually do."

"As you wish."

The inquisitor turned her back to her knight and set off toward the northwestern part of town, where she could see the castle jutting above the roofs. She didn't speak to Aiden, preferring the sound of her own footsteps to whatever awkward conversation they could have made. Her mind kept returning to his words, however, and she felt a knot form in her stomach at the thought of lying to him again.

The man had devoted his life to serving the ideals of the Azarian Church, and when the time had come to put his faith to the test, he did not hesitate to run straight into a raging fire, believing that she would protect him from all threats. And now she was scheming against him.

Why would she go so far for a sorcerer who most likely didn't deserve it?

She wasn't sure herself. Breeze may have thwarted the attempt on her mother's life, and the truth the manacles had revealed had gone a long way to convince her, but these weren't the only reasons. No, it had all started with Elsa Yarwood and the day she'd confessed the terrible sin she had committed.

Breeze might not have been the angel Mother Maeve had speculated her to be, but she was definitely capable of great compassion toward the sinners of this world. The type of compassion that was worth listening to.

It took less than ten minutes for Faith and Aiden to reach the castle, announce their return to the men guarding the portcullis, and enter the empty courtyard. Several torches and braziers had been set up atop the walls and throughout the courtyard, lighting the way for Aiden as he took the lead.

"Where are our rooms?" Faith asked.

"On the upper floor of the keep," he answered. "Please follow me."

The two of them entered the fortified residence and walked through several corridors, the guards standing to attention as they passed, until they reached the living quarters reserved for the lord, his family, and the important guests they sometimes received.

"This is your room," the knight said while pointing at an intricately carved wooden door. "Steward Oakley wanted me to take it on account of my royal station, but I insisted that you have it."

"Thank you. You didn't have to," Faith replied.

"You are one of God's chosen, Faith. It's obvious who this room should go to." When she didn't respond, Aiden opened the door for her. "I asked the handmaidens to bring you some food and to fill your bath with hot water. They've also mended and cleaned your other cassock and placed it on your dresser."

"Oh, um, thank you," she said as she entered the spacious room. "I didn't even think about that."

"It's quite normal. The mind often disregards details like these after a battle. You'll get used to it."

Faith nodded.

"Unless there's anything else," he continued, "I will leave you to rest."

Faith was about to wish him good night when she thought of her plan for tonight. "Wait, there's one thing. Where will you be staying?"

"The room at the end of the hallway." He motioned with

his head to the right. "Don't hesitate to call for me if you need anything."

"I won't. Good night, Aiden."

"Good night, Faith." The knight's gaze lingered on her for just a moment before he closed the door and walked down the hallway to his room. Faith waited for his footsteps to recede before she heaved a sigh and began to inspect her chamber.

It was the most lavish bedroom she had ever seen in her life. A large four-poster bed rested against the wall on her right, its silky cover almost shining under the yellow glow of the candles burning on the nightstands next to it. The rest of the bedroom was shrouded in darkness, but enough moonlight came through the two windows on the wall opposite her that she could discern the outlines of several other pieces of furniture: a large dresser, a desk paired with one plush chair, a couch that faced an unlit hearth, and one large wooden tub, half-hidden by a room divider. She searched for the food Aiden had mentioned and found a plate of fruit, bread, and cold meat sitting on the desk with a pitcher of water next to it.

Faith removed the haversack from her shoulder and sat down on the bed, right next to the nightstand. "I'm going to open the bag now," she whispered. "Try not to make too much noise."

She unfastened the leather straps and unrolled the cover, revealing a tuft of blue hair that shot up from the bag and spun around as Breeze examined her surroundings.

"Whoooaa!" she exclaimed. "That's your bed? It's so much bigger than the one Kieran had back at the inn!"

Despite the fact that she spoke at full volume, she sounded much quieter than she had back at the church. Faith briefly wondered why, and then came to the conclusion that the fairy had been projecting her voice right up until now. Priestesses and inquisitors often used their power to address large crowds, so it only made sense that fairies would do the same to ensure humans could hear them. While Breeze's squeaky voice was charming, Faith needed to pay close attention to understand what she said.

Faith watched as Breeze left the safety of the bag and began to hover in the air to explore her surroundings, but then she noticed that the fairy didn't have her wings out. "How...are you doing that?" she asked, staring.

Breeze, who'd just started to eye the pillow with a great deal of interest, turned and tilted her head at the inquisitor. "Doing what?" she asked.

"Flying," Faith said. "Without wings."

"Oh, that? Magic, of course! My wings can't carry me all by themselves, but they do make flying a lot easier—also, they're pretty!"

The blue-haired girl gleefully landed on the bed and stared down the biggest pillow of the bunch as if it were a foe. Before Faith could say anything, the fairy started running toward it at full speed, like a warhorse charging at enemy lines. The instant her head collided with the pillow, she bounced off of it and tumbled backward, doing a full rotation before she dropped on her belly, her limbs spread out like a stick figure. She then stood up and laughed. "That's a good pillow!" she said.

"Why did you do that?" Faith asked. "Are you all right?"

"Hmm? I was testing the softness of the pillow, silly! This one is much better than the one back at the inn." She stepped forward and started to climb it as she continued talking. "So soft!"

"You don't seem worried at all."

"What? For Kieran, you mean?"

"Yes."

"I don't see why I should be. You said you were going to help him escape." She reached the top of the pillow and sat cross-legged on it. "Right?"

"Right."

"Then there's nothing to worry about! We should talk about

how we're going to do it instead. Like, how are we going to get him out of that basement? I saw only one way out of there, and there are humans all over the castle."

Breeze was right. Faith hadn't factored in these crucial details when she agreed to assist in this prison break. Her face contorted in worry as she racked her brain for a solution. "There are two men guarding the entrance to the dungeon," she whispered. "We will need to pull them away from there before we can free Kieran."

"Great! How do we do that?"

"I'll talk to them. Tell them to go take a break while I go check on Kieran."

"Ooh. And they're gonna listen to you?"

"They will." Although she couldn't guarantee they wouldn't find this suspicious.

"Sounds good! Then we can leave all sneaky-like by jumping off the wall."

"Jumping off the—wait, what?"

"Yeah! That's how Kieran and I snuck past the guards: we jumped off the wall and slowed our descent with magic."

So that's how they did it. She had wondered why no one else had seen them pass through the gates, and although she'd speculated that Kieran had used a rope to climb down the wall, she and the constables hadn't found any on his person or around the town.

"Should we go?" Breeze asked

"Hmm?" Faith refocused her attention on the fairy. "Go where?"

"The basement, of course. You called it a 'dungeon'?"

"Right, the dungeon. No, we're not going immediately. We'll wait for Aiden to fall asleep first."

"Then how about we take a bath while we wait? That man said he had hot water brought here just for you. It'd be a shame to waste it."

The fairy stood up from the pillow and grew butterfly wings

on her back, which began to glow a bright blue as she flew to the wooden tub. "Ooh! There's a lot of steam coming off of it."

Breeze returned to the bed with a wide smile on her face, and Faith watched her as she retracted her wings into her back—a fascinating phenomenon to behold. She swiftly averted her gaze, however, when the girl also began to undress.

"Here. We. GO! Go away, shirt!"

Faith risked a glance and noticed that Breeze felt no shame at showing her body. The novitiates of the inquisitorial abbey had a communal bath that they all shared, so it wasn't the first time Faith had seen a woman naked. But a fairy? Furtively, she examined Breeze from head to toe, searching for any obvious oddities, but to her surprise, she found none. No scales, no variance in skin color, no scars near the shoulder blades. Her anatomy matched that of a normal human woman in every way—except for her impossible size and bright blue hair.

And also, maybe her beauty. Breeze not only possessed the youthful allure of a young woman, but also a figure that was more lovely than Faith's own. This contrasted heavily with the innocence she'd displayed previously, making it impossible for Faith to see her as anything more than a child who'd matured very quickly.

"You're not very shy, are you?" the inquisitor asked in a whisper.

Breeze finished laying her clothes on the bed before she turned around to face Faith again. "Shy?" she repeated. "Why would I be shy?"

"Because you're naked?"

"Huh?" Breeze looked at herself and searched her body for the reason behind this question. "Is there something on me?"

"No, that's not—I mean, there's nothing wrong with you. It's just that humans are usually shy when they strip in front of each other."

"They are? That's so weird. Does that mean you're not going to take a bath?"

"No," Faith said, standing up. "I've taken baths with other people before. It's nothing new."

"Oh, good. See you in the tub then!"

And just like that, the blue-haired girl flew in an arc, hugged her knees close to the chest, and let gravity do the rest. "Woo-hoo!"

*Plop.*

Faith grinned at this sight and began to untie her cincture as she listened to the fairy splash in the water. And for a moment, just a moment, she forgot all about the worries and concerns that had plagued her since she put the manacles on.

She summoned an orb of white light over the tub, and for the next fifteen minutes she relaxed in the water while she watched Breeze swim around and play with the sponge—which she promptly claimed as her own personal boat. It didn't take long before the fairy started talking about her brethren and the many adventures they went on together, such as the time she and her brother Cosmo convinced a wild rabbit to let them ride it for a whole afternoon, or how she and her sister Dewdrop organized a hide-and-seek contest that spanned their whole village. The girl grew more animated as she told her stories from atop the sponge, eager to share them with the inquisitor.

"So we shrunk our wings and climbed aboard the basket," she said, "and before he could change his mind, I made us fly really fast all around the forest! Bubble was so scared, he screamed every time we took a turn! Hahaha!"

"Didn't he get angry with you?" Faith asked.

"He pretended to be for a while, but I knew he didn't mean it. He's not the type to stay angry for long anyway."

No sooner were the words out of her mouth than Breeze's expression fell, and she turned away from the inquisitor. Faith stayed silent for a moment, pondering the reason for the sudden shift in mood, until she remembered her own exchanges with her mother and how they usually ended. "You must love your brother very much," she said.

The fairy nodded. "He's my best friend."

"I'm sure he misses you a lot."

"You think so?"

"I'm certain of it."

Breeze sat down on the sponge while she considered the possibility. "We had a fight," she said, "and we haven't spoken to each other since. I wish we could make up like we usually did, but…" She shook her head. "I don't know. He was very angry."

Faith chose her next words carefully. "I'm not sure I'm the best qualified to give you advice, but trust me—if there is love, there is hope. A little something one of my teachers used to tell me."

Breeze raised her head, her eyes wide. "You fought with your family too?"

"Yes. Most families do."

"And did you always make up?"

The inquisitor often wondered the same thing. Best keep it concise for now. "We've had our disagreements, but yes. I think we did."

The fairy smiled. "In that case, I'll make sure to bring him back a gift! Something he'll like a lot."

Faith chuckled. "Like what?"

"Hmm, I don't know. There's so much to choose from. But if I bring him something, I'll also need to find something for my other brothers and sisters. They deserve one too."

"Sounds like you have a lot of them."

"Oh, yes! Two hundred and ninety-nine of them!"

"Two hund—*you're joking*."

"Never! Not about my family."

"And you all have the same mother and father?"

"We don't have parents like you humans do. We were sleeping in magic until Nana, the oldest of all fairies, woke us up! That's why I'm not back home with the others. I want to find her and ask her why she left us without telling us about you and the Inquisition. Then maybe we can learn how to better defend ourselves!"

"And this Nana, she's out here, near human cities?"

"I don't know. Kieran said he had an idea on how to find her, but I didn't want him to tell me before we rescued him from the dungeon. I know which direction she went, though, and that she's trying to wake up other fairies."

Faith gawked at the blue-haired girl who, oblivious to the ramifications of her revelation, began listing ideas of gifts she could bring back to her siblings. Just when Faith had begun to come to terms with the truth about the source of her power, she now learned that Breeze had embarked on a quest to find her mother figure, one who was powerful enough to "awaken" three hundred fairies. Was this normal? Who was the real neophyte here?

"—you think?"

"Um, sorry, what?"

"Food or knickknacks?" Breeze asked. "What should I give them?"

"Uh, both?"

"Oh, right! Why didn't I think of that? They can also share the gifts if they want to. I just need to come up with something for Bubble!" Happy with her decision, the girl stood up from her sponge and dove into the water, only to return to the surface right next to Faith. "So! How much longer do we need to wait? Kieran must be getting worried."

Faith thought about it for a second, troubled at the prospect of tricking the constables into leaving their post. She briefly considered delaying it for a while longer but decided against it. Not only had she made a promise to the fairy, she also knew she'd regret it forever if she handed Kieran over to the Inquisition. They had to break him out. "Let's get dressed," she said, "and then we'll have something to eat. We'll go right after that."

"Great! Do you have any towels? I left mine in my bag and it's gone now."

"Oh, right."

The inquisitor climbed out of the tub and quickly dried herself with a towel she took from the dresser. She then went to the bed and rifled through her haversack until she found the tiny bag she'd taken from Kieran's own belongings and handed it to the blue-haired girl. "Here. This is it, right?"

Breeze beamed and leaped in the air, grabbing it. "Yes, it is!" she exclaimed as she opened it. "It was in your bag the whole time? I didn't even see it."

"It was probably under the rest of my things. Nothing is damaged, right?"

"Nope! Everything is there, thank you. Oh, here it is." Breeze placed her bag on the dresser and dried herself off with her small towel, starting with her head and finishing with the tip of her toes. She then put her clothes back on while Faith did the same with her cassock, and after a few minutes, they were ready to sit down and eat.

Well, almost ready. Breeze had conjured a tiny flame at the tip of her index finger and raised it near her head, biting her lower lip as she moved it closer.

"You can conjure fire?" Faith asked with wide eyes.

"Yeah, but I'm no good at it."

"Did Kieran show you how?"

"No, Nana did."

"And, uh, what are you planning to do with it?"

Before Breeze could answer her, the flame began to flicker wildly. Faith waited for the fairy to regain control over the fire, only to see her snuff it out of existence before it could hurt her.

Breeze then let out a long sigh and slumped on the dresser. "I'm still nowhere near Bubble's level."

"A-Are you all right?"

"Yeah. I just thought I'd try it once, but I still have a long way to go before I can control it."

"What were you trying to do exactly?"

"Dry my hair. Some of my brothers and sisters can keep the fire in place and pull the heat toward them, but that's harder to do than it looks. I wish Dewdrop was here. She's the one who usually does it for me."

Faith blinked in confusion. "You use magic...to dry your hair?"

"Yeah, it's a lot faster this way. It also feels really nice! I would totally have done it for you if I could. You would love it!"

The inquisitor stared blankly at her, too preoccupied by the idea that magic could be used for such a mundane activity as drying one's hair to even consider what it would feel like to be on the receiving end of it. Breeze proceeded to fly to the other end of the room, where she used the light of her wings to find the plate of food the handmaidens had placed on the desk.

"Woo, grapes!" She plucked one of them from the vine and examined it from multiple angles before biting into it, her lips slowly curling into a smile. "Isch sho good! Faid! Cawn haf shum!"

"Oh. Right," Faith replied. Now wasn't the time to think about magic theory. Better focus on the task ahead and get it over with as soon as possible. Her hands were already trembling at the idea of lying to the men guarding the dungeon, and she wished she knew how to make it stop.

Breeze seemed to have noticed it too because she stopped eating and cocked her head to the side. "Are you okay?" she asked.

"Yes, I'm fine," Faith said, unconvinced by her own words. "Just a little nervous."

"What about?"

"Breaking Kieran out of jail. Don't worry. Once we're there, I'll be as cool as a cucumber. Somehow."

"Oh, I like cucumbers. They're nice as an appetizer, but I don't see any here. Want a grape instead?" She presented the one she was holding in her hands to Faith.

"Yes, please." After eating the fruit, Faith brought the plate with her to the bed, and they ate together in the dim light of the candles while Breeze continued to share stories about her siblings. Listening to her talk managed to put Faith's heart at ease, and she surprised herself by wishing it wouldn't end. It had been so long since she'd engaged in such idle talk that her heart ached at the prospect of saying goodbye to Breeze soon—but considering the Church and the Inquisition's views on all things magical, this was probably the safest choice for the fairy. She'd hate to see this little bundle of joy get hurt.

"It's time we went," Faith declared.

"It is? Okay, let me get my bag first. I gotta make sure I have everything with me, and…there! I'm ready to go! Do I hide in your bag again?"

"Yes."

"Okay then—oh, wait." Breeze flew back to the plate of food on the desk, took one last bite out of one of the untouched grapes, and then returned to Faith's side. "Ham weady!" she said, her mouth full like a squirrel's.

The priestess chuckled at the fairy's silliness and opened the cover of her haversack for her. Once Breeze had tucked herself inside, Faith released her mental grip on the orb of light floating above the tub, dispelling it in the blink of an eye. She then left the room and slowly closed the door behind her, careful not to make any noise and alert Aiden, before she walked down the hallway and toward the stairs.

It was time.

Faith couldn't stop thinking about what she would tell the constables once she arrived at the dungeon, and her mind pictured the worst outcomes possible. Nevertheless, as she came closer to her destination, she became a lot calmer—a result of years of training under the strict guidance of battle-hardened inquisitors who knew how to instill the correct amount of confidence and readiness in their students. If not for that, she would never have been able to face Kieran out there in the field.

By the time she'd reached the door to the dungeon, her hands had stopped shaking.

"Inquisitor." The oldest constable straightened his posture and saluted her. "What can we do for you?"

His comrade did his best to imitate him, but his stiff movements and furtive glances betrayed his anxious state. They hadn't expected to see her again so soon.

"I couldn't sleep, so I've come to check on the prisoner," she answered. "Anything to report?"

To her surprise, they did.

"Um, yes, ma'am. Maybe. We know that you wanted us to warn you if the sorcerer made any noise, but we weren't sure it was worth waking you up for this."

Faith frowned. "What happened?"

The constable licked his lips and looked at his colleague, but the young man remained silent as a statue. "He yelled," the man finally said. "Not sure what, but it wasn't long after you left. We thought about telling you about it, but he hasn't made a peep since then, so…we figured it might be better to wait until morning before we said anything."

"Hmm." Normally, Faith might have chided them over this, but this worked in her favor. "I'll go check on the prisoner," she said. "Go take a break. I'll find you at the barracks once I'm done."

The two men exchanged a glance as they considered the inquisitor's command, but they merely nodded at each other once they'd made their decision. "Yes, ma'am. Here are the keys. We'll make sure to tell the others not to bother you."

And thus, the constables left without another word. She watched them round the corner of the hallway while she pondered what exactly they thought she had planned for Kieran. Torture? She knew inquisitors had a certain reputation when it came to their treatment of prisoners, but they hadn't been allowed such free rein for the last thirty years. Not that she cared about rectifying misconceptions about the Inquisition. Time would naturally take care of it.

Faith looked back at the door and took a deep breath. With the constables out of the way, it should be fairly easy to free Kieran and sneak him out of here now. No one would think to come check on her here—except perhaps Aiden. She hoped he was asleep.

She unlatched the door and opened it wide, revealing a stairway that descended into darkness. Then, she called upon her power—its presence as familiar as it always had been—and summoned an Eos to light her way forward.

There was no turning back now.

# CHAPTER 23

KIERAN WOKE TO the noise of footsteps echoing in the hallway. He didn't know how long it'd been since he fell asleep, but judging by how groggy he felt, it couldn't have been more than a couple of hours. He sluggishly lifted himself off the ground and tried to clear his head before the door opened, but the white light that flooded inside the room roused him better than any slap on the face could have.

He shielded his eyes with his right hand and waited for the inquisitor to walk in. Doubt seized him when he heard the distinct sound of straps being unfastened. Was it morning already? Had the inquisitor come to take him to Holiburg? And if so, what had happened to Breeze? He'd told her to be very careful when approaching the inquisitor, so she couldn't have been captured, not when their plan required her to stay at a safe distance and—

"Kieran!"

Oh no.

Kieran lowered his hand despite the blinding light and glowered at the inquisitor, expecting to see her holding the fairy in her hand, a hostage to be used against him. Instead, he saw Breeze hovering in the air in front of him with her hands on her hips and a smile on her face, unharmed and unbound.

"Breeze? Are you all right?"

"Yeah! I'm peachy! I'm sorry for making you wait, but everything is gonna be fine now! I brought some help."

"Help?" Kieran looked back at the inquisitor, who was still standing at the door's threshold, her long white staff in her right hand. "What do you mean, *help*?"

"Faith!" Breeze cheerfully said, as if that explained everything. "She's going to help us."

He must have misunderstood something because what she said didn't make any goddamn sense. The inquisitor must have realized that too, but instead of clearing up the confusion for him, she only added to it. "I've agreed to let you go," she said.

Such a simple statement, but one he couldn't parse. He blinked back and forth between the fairy and the woman, unable to respond. Breeze noticed his confusion and launched into an explanation, gesticulating wildly as she spoke.

"She knows that her power comes from magic! She put on her pair of bracelets while she was in the church, and now she's willing to help you escape. Isn't it awesome? She's a good human after all, just like you!" Breeze let out a laugh and flew over to pat him on the head, relieved at the outcome they had reached.

Kieran couldn't say he shared her optimism. He glared at the inquisitor, ready to shield Breeze with his own body if need be. He half expected Faith to trap the fairy in an Aegis and threaten to hurt her unless he answered her questions, but instead she stared back at him, her lips pinched together and her fingers clenched tightly around her staff. Thinking. Hesitating. For what reason, he couldn't tell.

The inquisitor stepped into the cell.

"So, Faith, can you free him?" Breeze asked. "We shouldn't be staying here for too long, right?"

"In a minute, Breeze," the inquisitor answered. "There's one last thing I'd like to ask before I do."

Kieran narrowed his eyes and balled his hands into fists. It was all he could do in this situation.

"You were traveling to Holiburg to kill my mother," Faith said. "Why? Why now? Why wait until your cover was blown before you tried to assassinate her?"

Kieran froze, rendered speechless by her question. He'd been so careful about what he told other people, there was no way in hell she could have learned about—

Suddenly, his gaze shifted to Breeze. The blue-haired girl looked back and forth between him and Faith, her eyebrows raised in an expression of confusion so innocent, he couldn't get mad at her.

Of course. That's how Faith had learned about his plan to kill the grand inquisitor. Why else would she bother to visit him again? She already had Breeze.

Depending on his answer, what would she do? Kill him? Torture him? No, he doubted she had the temperament for that. Regardless of her connection to the Inquisition, she didn't appear to be the sadistic type who enjoyed inflicting pain on others. Which perplexed him even more.

She clearly didn't approve of him, but she wasn't angry at him either. Something weighed on her mind, something he didn't understand. Usually, he'd retort with a scathing remark, but he had Breeze to think about, and he wasn't about to risk her safety just to get back at the inquisitor.

The fairy depended on him.

Both Faith and Breeze waited as Kieran struggled to find the right words, until finally he simply shrugged it off. "I guess I wanted to go down fighting," he said, "and not get killed in front of a bunch of rabid dogs like my mother was."

Faith pondered his response for several seconds before she asked, "That's not all, is it? There's something else you're not telling me."

He wanted to say no at first and tell her he'd been truthful with her, but he felt it wouldn't be totally accurate. He wasn't sure what to say. Until Breeze approached him and put a hand on his cheek.

Comforting him.

No one but his mother had ever done that for him, and for the first time in twenty years, he felt something give way inside of him. Tears threatened to spill out of his eyes, and it was with the utmost effort that he held them back. But now he knew. Now he understood why he had left Waterlone without killing Henry, the only man who knew about his real identity; why he'd embarked on a journey to Holiburg, the last place where any sorcerer should go; and why he'd been so hell-bent to battle Faith and her knight, despite his nonexistent chances of victory. He knew, but he still had to say it.

Both Faith and Breeze waited as he lowered his head and averted their gaze. He couldn't bear to look at them when faced with the prospect of telling them the truth. He wanted to close his eyes and disappear, but that wouldn't solve anything. Breeze's safety rested in his hands, and he owed it to her to do everything in his power to protect her from the Church and the Inquisition. And so, disregarding what little remained of his pride, he opened his mouth and answered the inquisitor's question.

"I…I just wanted everything to end."

No one said anything for a while. Breeze stayed at his side, rubbing his cheek as if it'd make the pain go away, but she stopped when Faith stepped forward and kneeled down before him. Kieran didn't want to look at her and kept staring at the floor instead—until she showed him the key resting in the palm of her hand. She then spoke to him with a soft and gentle tone, one he'd never heard from her before.

"If I am to let you go, you have to promise me one thing."

He raised his head and looked at her green eyes. Gone was

the contempt she'd previously expressed for him, now replaced by something he couldn't quite identify. Something warm and sincere but also hesitant. He'd never expected an inquisitor to look at him this way, and it disarmed him better than any sermon could have.

"Don't kill anyone on your way out," she said. "No matter what."

"You're...you're serious? You're really going to let me go?"

"Only if you promise not to hurt anyone. Can you do that?"

Kieran looked back and forth between the inquisitor and the key in her hand, only now realizing that she wasn't bluffing. She genuinely wanted to let him go. Which didn't make any fucking sense. "Why?" he asked. "Why the hell would you do that?"

"Because Breeze convinced me to. Because she told me that despite everything you've done that you were a good man. And also..." This time, she was the one to avert her gaze. "Because I'm a sinner too. And I have to atone for the mistakes I've made, just like you do."

Kieran watched her for several long seconds as he mulled over her answer. He might have expected as much from an Azarian like her, even one who'd just learned the truth about the source of her power. At this moment, however, he was more concerned with the safety of his companion than the reasoning behind Faith's actions. "What about Breeze?" he asked. "What are you planning to do with her?"

Faith raised her eyebrows in surprise and turned to look at the small fairy who hadn't dared to speak ever since Kieran told them the truth. "I'm not planning to do anything," she said. "She's free to go wherever she wishes."

"Really? Just like that?"

She shifted his gaze back to him. "Yes. She's innocent in all of this. There's no reason for me to involve her."

"In that case, you have my word: I won't kill anyone on my way out."

Satisfied by his response, Faith nodded and unlocked his handcuffs. She then took out a keyring and was about to remove the chains that attached him to the wall when Breeze interrupted her.

"Wait! Let me handle that. I wanna help too."

The blue-haired girl lit up her wings and came to take a better look at the shackles. The inquisitor handed the keyring to her, but Breeze shook her head and said, "I'll do it with magic. This will be good practice!"

"You can unlock the chains by yourself?" Faith asked.

"Sure, I can," Breeze confirmed with a nod. "I can also unlock doors like that one over there, but—"

"—but not the handcuffs?"

"Oh, is that what you call them? Yeah, my magic doesn't work on them."

"I see. Then I'll keep watch while you work on that. But don't take too long."

"Got it!"

Faith stood up and left through the door, taking the white light of her Eos with her. Breeze didn't waste any time and began to examine one of the keyholes of the remaining manacles, prodding the mechanisms inside with her telekinetic magic.

"Thank you, Breeze," Kieran said.

"Huh? But I'm not finished yet," the fairy replied.

"I'm not talking about the chains. I'm talking about her." He motioned at the door with his chin. "I don't know how you convinced her to help, but it couldn't have been easy."

"So...you're not angry?"

"Angry? Why would I be angry?"

Breeze looked down at her feet and began fiddling with her fingers. "Because I didn't do what you told me to..."

"Mhm. Yeah, it was probably careless of you to show yourself and talk to her, but...maybe you knew better than I did." He shrugged so as not to draw attention to the fact that he'd just complimented her. "It wouldn't be the first time someone proved me wrong."

"You think so?"

"I mean, she's here now, isn't she? Come on now, you gotta hurry. We can't stay here too long."

Breeze stared at him just long enough for him to start feeling uncomfortable, until finally, she smiled and nodded at him. "On it!"

A minute later, they were out of the cell and standing next to Faith, basking in the glow of her Eos. Kieran rubbed his wrists while he looked down at the hallway and saw a set of stairs leading up at the end of it. A quick peek behind him confirmed that it was indeed the only way out of here. "So how do we do this?" he asked.

"You wait until I give you the signal to follow me," Faith said. "There shouldn't be anyone waiting for us outside, but we can't take any chances. Actually, I could use your help, Breeze."

"Sure thing! What do you want me to do?"

"I'd like you to stay close to the ceiling and peek around the corners for me. If someone comes, I'll need you to tell me before they arrive."

"Oh, then let's use my family's signals!"

"Signals? What kind of signals?"

"She can flash her wings," Kieran explained. "One blink means 'stop.' Two, 'hide.' Three, 'follow,' and four, 'go.'"

"Really? You can project light from your wings?"

"Yup!" Breeze proudly exclaimed, her hands on her hips. "There are many other signals, but Kieran thinks we can stick to these four. That's how I helped him get out of town."

"Do you need to hear them again?" he asked.

"No, I think I got it," Faith answered, her brow furrowed. "But it might not be a good idea to flash your wings in the middle of the night. The guards might see you."

"Oh, don't worry. I can make it so the light isn't too bright. Lookie here." She showed them her back and proceeded to do just as she said. "See? Not a problem!"

"Hmm. It should be fine then."

"So where do we go?" Kieran asked.

"Breeze told me you jumped off the wall to escape the city. Can you do it again?"

"Yes, I think we can do it again…but what about the patrols?"

"Fortunately for us, Lord Harrowmont—the idiot—has been pretty lax with security ever since we captured you." She shook her head. "The keep is connected to the curtain wall, so it should be a short walk from here. Just stay close to me."

"Any chance I can get my stuff back?" Kieran asked.

Faith shot him a look that clearly conveyed her thoughts on the matter.

"Fine," he said. "It's just that I had some money hidden in my clothes."

"I know. We found it after a quick search. It's Aiden who has it now. Your bow and arrows too."

"I'll make do without them."

"You'll have to. Let's go."

The inquisitor locked the door of the cell and then walked toward the stairs, staff in hand. No guards were waiting for them outside the dungeon. By this point, Kieran trusted her enough to follow her commands, and so he hung back while she and Breeze scouted the way forward, using the signals the fairy had taught them. The place was quiet—very quiet—and they didn't come across anyone as they sneaked through the corridors and climbed a spiral staircase that led to the second level. Faith had dispelled her staff by now and relied on the light from the torches to show the way forward.

The wait was excruciating. Kieran could feel his heart skip a beat each and every time Breeze's wings flashed in the dark, and when she was out of his sight, it was Faith's hand signals that gave him palpitations. The hour he'd spent hiding throughout Holiburg after he set the orphanage aflame had been far worse than this moment, but it was still nerve-racking.

Then finally, they reached the outside.

They'd arrived at the top of the fortifications that surrounded the keep and overlooked the rest of town. The section of the wall they stood on connected the keep to the great hall, and there were no torches or braziers here. The nearest sources of light came from the courtyard, where a few men stood around, looking terribly bored. However, Kieran spotted two other men standing on different sections of the wall, their backs turned to him.

They needed to hurry.

"Here," Faith whispered, looking down a crenel. "This should be safe to climb down."

Breeze landed on the merlon next to her and did the same. "Yeah, I don't see anyone down in the streets," she whispered before facing Kieran. "We just need to do the same thing we did earlier today. Are you ready?"

"Yeah, I am," he answered.

"Great. What about you, Faith? Do you wanna come with us?"

Both the sorcerer and the inquisitor gaped at the fairy when she asked that. "Wha-what?" Faith replied.

"Do you wanna come with us?" Breeze repeated. "You don't seem to have telekimosis powers, but I'm sure me and Kieran can carry you down if you want to."

"I...no, I can't."

"You can't fly down the wall?"

"No, that's not... I mean, I can't come with you."

"Why not?"

"My place is here. With the Inquisition."

"But you're not an inquisitor anymore—you're a mage. And you're helping Kieran escape." Breeze joined her hands together in a supplicating manner, her brow wrinkled in worry. "What if someone learns about it? Won't they hurt you?"

*Of course she'd ask Faith to join us,* Kieran thought. Why wouldn't she? He felt stupid for not even considering the possibility. He only wished that she had done so *before* they had left the dungeon, back when it was safe to talk. The men on the other sections of the wall hadn't moved from their spot—not yet anyway—and although Kieran was hiding behind the parapet, the white cassock of the inquisitor should still be visible even in the darkness.

"This isn't the time," he said. "We need to leave. Now."

"But Faith has to come with us!" Breeze retorted.

"If you're gonna keep talking, at least hide behind the wall. Both of you."

Thankfully they both did as he asked and moved behind the parapet. "He's right," Faith said. "You can't stay here."

"But what about you?" Breeze asked.

"I'll be fine. Nobody will know that I've helped you. They won't even think it's a possibility. But you need to get as far away from here as possible. They'll be chasing after you, and I'm not sure I'll be able to stop them. Understand?"

"Yes," Breeze nodded, her head low. "I understand."

"Good. Now go."

The fairy hesitated for a second, glancing back and forth between Faith and Kieran, until finally, she landed on the sorcerer's shoulder and held on to his earlobe to keep herself balanced. "I'm ready," she said.

Kieran leaned over the parapet and looked down at the ground. He couldn't say the same about himself. "Uh, yeah. I am too."

He was about to climb over the wall when Faith grabbed him by the arm and stopped him. She stared at him fiercely, and it took her a while before she said anything. But when she did, it was with a tone that told him she wouldn't tolerate dishonesty. "Remember. You promised."

Kieran held her gaze and forced himself not to flinch away at her touch. He had always loathed physical contact with people, and in the case of the inquisitor, it was even worse. Still, she had risked much to save him, earning herself his begrudging respect if not his gratitude.

"I'll keep my word," he answered. "You should worry more about yourself."

She let go of his arm and stepped back. "I am. That's why I freed you."

This response disarmed Kieran. When he realized he couldn't think of an appropriate retort, he turned back to the parapet and looked down at the ground, focusing his mind on the ambient magic. "Say goodbye, Breeze."

"Goodbye, Faith!" The fairy waved at the inquisitor with her free hand. "Thank you for everything!"

"Goodbye, Breeze," Faith said with a smile. "Take care now."

"You too!"

"Breeze? You ready?" Kieran asked.

"Oh, uh, yeah! I'm ready. Jump whenever you want, I'll catch you."

"Right." Kieran bit his lower lip while he worked up the courage to let go of the merlons and let himself fall. It was only when he thought of what Faith might say to him if he hesitated any longer that he went through with it and jumped off the wall.

"Easy does it," Breeze said as they began their descent to the ground. "We're almost halfway there."

It took them a little less than fifteen seconds before they landed on the pavement of the street. Once the magic that had carried him dissipated, Kieran let out a sigh of relief and looked back at the crenel Faith stood behind, her eyes fixed on them.

Breeze waved goodbye at her again, and he set off for the nearest alleyway, intent on leaving the town immediately.

He did his best to ignore the drumming in his chest and the sensation of elation that threatened to make him shout in victory. He wasn't out of the woods yet, not by a long shot, and even though the inquisitor had helped him escape from the dungeon, she still would have to chase after him next morning. His only hope of survival was to get as far away from Ballybridge as possible before someone noticed he was gone.

Breeze, however, had other things on her mind.

"It's too bad she couldn't come with us," she whispered. "I would have liked her to travel with us."

Kieran refrained from commenting on that; he himself didn't know what to make of the inquisitor and what she'd done for him. All he knew for certain was that time was short and the distance separating them from safety was quite long. "I'll need you to check the streets ahead for me," he said.

"On it," Breeze answered. She grew her wings, flew into the air, and slipped into the shadows.

Faith watched as Kieran and Breeze disappeared into the alleyway. She was too preoccupied by the possibility that they might get spotted and captured by a patrol to even consider returning to her room—but after a minute of standing there, gazing at the sleeping town, she reminded herself that Kieran had escaped the full vigilance of the local constabulary once already and should be able to do so again. In fact, it should even be easier to accomplish now that the patrols had been relaxed.

The inquisitor closed her eyes and slowed down her breathing. If anyone was at risk of making a mistake, it was her. She'd have to convincingly pretend to be shocked and angered by Kieran's escape and then mount a full-scale manhunt that would end in failure. Luckily for her, Kieran had quite the head start.

Somewhat reassured by this idea, Faith left the wall and went back inside the keep. It took her only a few minutes to find the barracks and return the set of keys to the constables, who hurriedly went back to their post after she explained she was done talking to Kieran. She even took the opportunity to admonish them for drinking what smelled like wine. She knew they had done so only to calm their nerves, but she still needed to keep up the facade of the strict inquisitor.

Once she had returned to her room, she locked the door behind her and slowly removed her cassock. Too tired to bother folding it into a neat pile, she threw it on top of the dresser instead. Then, she slipped under the covers of the bed and nestled her head in the pillow Breeze had smashed into not an hour ago. She found herself wishing that she could speak with her again.

Instead, Faith could only stare at the canopy of her bed while trying to ignore the knot in her stomach. So much had happened today, and now that the fairy was gone, she was no longer sure she had made the right decision. What would her mother say once she'd learned that Kieran had escaped? Would she blame Faith for it? Or would she simply assume that the mysterious fairy was the sole reason behind this failure? She had no idea.

Faith closed her eyes and shut out these thoughts as best as she could. There was nothing she could do except dwell on it, and that wouldn't be very constructive. Already she could feel her consciousness ebb away into a shrinking puddle of disorganized thoughts, and she briefly considered turning on her right side, her preferred sleeping position. The soft sensation of the covers on her skin, combined with the lulling rhythm of her own breathing, caused her to forget about it, and soon, she began to dream of hide-and-seek contests, rabbit riding, and butterfly wings.

# CHAPTER 24

FAITH AWOKE TO the frantic sound of someone pounding on her door, calling her name. "Faith! Wake up, Faith!"

The inquisitor sat straight up in bed, and her eyes darted around the room before settling on the door, whose upper half shone in the first rays of sunlight beaming through the windows.

The pounding continued. "Faith! It's me, Aiden!"

Her drowsiness evaporated almost instantly and she got up to open the door. She needed to pretend she didn't know the reason for his presence, or else she'd end up imprisoned herself.

"Faith? Are you—"

She opened the door just before Aiden knocked again, and she gave him the sternest look she could muster. "What happened?"

Aiden's mouth fell open when he saw her wearing only her white undergarments, but he promptly brushed off the matter and walked into the room. Faith closed the door behind him and waited for him to explain the situation.

"It's Fowler," he said. "He escaped."

"*What?*"

"He's not in his cell anymore. I went to check on him and

ask him what he wanted to eat before we left for Holiburg, but he was gone. Just...*gone!*"

"Was anyone hurt?"

"No."

"And the handcuffs?"

"Still in his cell, unlocked."

Faith hurried to the dresser and started to put on her cassock, heedless of the man present in her room. "You'll need to go get them," she said. "We're going to need them."

"Understood."

"What about Lord Harrowmont? Has he been warned?"

"I don't think so. Not yet. I ran here as fast as I could. Except for the guards, you're probably the first to learn about it."

"Did anyone see Kieran leave?"

"I've only talked to the two guarding the dungeon, but they haven't seen anyone."

"Anything else?"

"Not that I can think of."

Good. He must have spoken with the constables from the late-night shift and not the ones she saw yesterday. Otherwise, he most likely would have mentioned her visit to the dungeon. She doubted he'd start to suspect her if she brought it up, but she'd rather play it safe and avoid the discussion altogether. Better go with the motions and hope that Kieran and Breeze had put enough distance between them and the town by the time the manhunt began.

Having finished buttoning up her cassock, she sat on the bed and put on her shoes. "We'll need to talk to the guards first," she said. "Figure out what they know. One of them could be working with Kieran."

"A spy? I find it unlikely."

"As do I. But we have to consider all possibilities."

"In that case, I can think of only one person who could have helped him escape: that 'fairy.' We don't know where she went after your fight with Fowler, and—"

Aiden suddenly fell silent. Faith tied her second shoe while she waited for him to continue, but when he didn't, she turned to look at him. "What is it?"

He swiveled his head back at her, looking away from the desk, where his gaze had wandered off to, and said, "I was just thinking about what we would do if the fairy is able to unlock consecrated handcuffs."

"I'm not sure yet." She got up from the bed and picked up her haversack from the dresser. "We'll have to cross that bridge when we get to it."

"Yes, ma'am."

"It's Faith."

"Yes, sorry. Where to first?"

"To the steward's. I'm sure the guards will warn him before the lord, so let's go meet him."

They exited the room and encountered Lloyd Oakley in the middle of the hallway. He must have woken up quite some time ago because he was already dressed and groomed for the day, which didn't exactly surprise Faith since he was the one responsible for the management of this household and town. He said, "Inquisitor Dow. I take it you've heard the news?"

"Yes. I assume we can count on Lord Harrowmont's support in this matter?"

"Of course. I've already ordered the constabulary to seal off the town and patrol every street and alley we have. If the sorcerer is still here, we'll find him."

Although he spoke with a placid and dignified tone, the slight shaking of his hands and the twitching in his eyelids left no doubt as to how the steward really felt about this incident. Despite these circumstances, he still put on a brave front.

"Thank you, but we'll also have to consider the possibility that Fowler has left town already," Faith said.

"Then we'll put our best horses at your disposal—and our hunting dogs. We have several of them in our kennels. They'll just need something that belongs to the sorcerer to pick up his scent."

"I have his belongings in my room," Aiden said. "I'll go get them."

The knight walked past them and headed down the corridor and around the corner.

"I must inform Lord Harrowmont immediately," Oakley said. "Where should we meet?"

"Down in the courtyard—but first I must talk to the guards who were posted at the dungeon."

"Then I'll see you there, Inquisitor." The steward bowed to her and continued down the hallway. Once he was out of sight, Faith leaned against the wall and used the opportunity to reorganize her thoughts and figure out her next move.

Hunting dogs.

She had never worked with any before, but from what she knew of their tracking ability, they would most likely pick up Kieran's trail and find him again.

She heaved herself off the wall and started walking toward Aiden's room. She couldn't think of any way to stall the manhunt without raising suspicion, except by talking to the constables first. Maybe if she asked for Mother Maeve's help? Her clairvoyance appeared limited in scope and probably wouldn't be able to pick up Kieran and Breeze's when they were kilometers away from town already. But what if Maeve suggested that she come with them? Her power combined with the dogs' sense of smell might prove deadly for Kieran, and Breeze too.

By the time Faith arrived at her knight's room, she had made the decision not to ask for Maeve's assistance, not unless Aiden brought up the idea.

She knocked on the door and waited for the prince to open it, only for several seconds to pass before he even spoke to her. "The door is unlocked."

She entered the room, wondering why the pause, but she understood at once when she saw him putting his armor on. He'd been in such a hurry to wake her up, he hadn't even brought his sword with him; it leaned against the wall, next to the desk, on top of which lay Kieran's broken bow, his quiver, and the canvas bag holding the rest of his belongings.

"Need any help?" she asked as she closed the door behind her.

"No, thank you. I'm almost done."

Neither of them said anything while the knight finished fastening his armor, keeping his back to her. The silence between them became increasingly uncomfortable, until it proved too much for Faith and she pondered the best way to break it without drawing attention to herself. But it was Aiden who spoke first. "What do you think happened?" he asked.

The inquisitor watched the prince put on his belt while she considered how best to answer that question. "It's just like you said. The fairy must have found a way to unlock the handcuffs."

"Can we really call it a fairy?"

She raised an eyebrow. "What do you mean?"

"That 'girl' you saw with Fowler. Can we really call it a fairy, or is it something else entirely?"

Faith paused to ponder the possibility. At first, she had speculated about Breeze's true nature and whether or not she was a demon in disguise sent to tempt and corrupt humans on this earth, but after speaking and interacting with the little girl, she doubted she was capable of deceiving anyone, let alone manipulating them into committing sinful acts that would send them straight to hell.

That wasn't something she could tell Aiden, however.

"I don't know," she said. "I thought she might be a demon, but it doesn't feel right."

"Hmm." Aiden hung his scabbard on his belt and turned to face her. "So we're off to interrogate the guards?"

"Yes. And get the handcuffs from the cell."

"Then what?"

"Then we get on our horses and hope the dogs can pick up Kieran's scent." Faith almost grimaced when she unintentionally used Kieran's first name. She was almost certain she never had before. Best that she limit herself to his last name from now on.

"I'm sure they will," Aiden said as he grabbed his sword, then the canvas bag. "And I can assure you that Lord Harrowmont will do everything in his power to help us recapture Fowler."

"Why is that?"

"Because Fowler escaped from his dungeon. So until he's back in our custody, the Kantnerian nobility will hold Lord Harrowmont responsible for this blunder."

"This will work in our favor then. Let's go."

Faith exited the bedroom. As she headed for the stairs, she thought about what she had done: liberating a sorcerer from his bindings on the promise that he wouldn't hurt anyone during his escape, which now forced her to lie to everyone else about it. All because a fairy had convinced her it was the right thing to do. God, just what had she gotten herself into? If anybody learned about it, she'd not only be stripped of her rank but also branded an apostate. Maybe she should have accepted Breeze's offer to follow them when she had the chance. Living as a fugitive would be impossibly hard, but at the very least she wouldn't have to feel the shame that came from deceiving those who believed in her.

But it was too late for that. She could only move forward and hope that Breeze and Kieran were far enough away to lose their pursuers. Or else she'd have to take more drastic measures to ensure their freedom, and she didn't want that.

Nobody would.

Kieran ran through the woods as fast as he could, weaving through the trees like a fox dodging lightning bolts. He hadn't stopped jogging ever since he left Ballybridge, relying on the glow from Breeze's wings to light the way forward, but when the sun peeked above the horizon and colored the sky orange, he broke into a run. The City Watch would soon realize he had escaped, if they hadn't already.

Only when his lungs were about to give out did he slow down and lean against a tree to catch his breath. Breeze continued for several paces ahead of him before she noticed he had stopped. She swiftly came back to his side. "Kieran? Are you okay?"

He shook his head, short of breath. "I can't...run... anymore..."

"Can I help? What do you want me to do?"

"Go...above the trees." He pointed at the canopy. "Look... for pursuers."

"On it!" The small girl fluttered up in the air and vanished behind the leaves. Once he was sure that she couldn't see him anymore, Kieran collapsed against the tree and landed on his rear, drained of all of his strength. His mouth tasted like old socks, his legs burned like they were on fire, and a thirst gripped his throat so fiercely that he felt sick to the core. And yet he had to keep running.

He looked up at the canopy for Breeze but failed to spot her. She was taking longer than expected, although that didn't necessarily mean anything. They had been running through the forest for a while now, and it wouldn't surprise him if she was wondering how exactly she was supposed to look out for pursuers with trees in the way.

If only he had a horse. He'd briefly considered taking one

from the stables when sneaking through town, but it would have been impossible to leave through the gates without raising the alarm. At least by running through the wilds, they'd have to follow him on foot.

God, he was so thirsty.

"Kieran!" Breeze came down from the sky and landed on the ground in front of him. "I couldn't hear anything but the birds and the wind, so I don't think anyone is following us. We're safe."

"No, we're not," he said, breathing almost normally. "They'll send their dogs after us."

"Dogs?" she repeated, her head cocked to the side.

"It's an animal. Not sure how to describe them—"

"Oh, I know what a dog is. Nana told us about them once—even drew a few pictures for us too. But why would the humans send dogs after us? Aren't they their pets?"

"They are, and sometimes they also help humans hunt animals and people down. Guessing your Nana didn't tell you about that part."

"N-no. I mean, I knew they were great smellers, but not about the hunting part."

"That's why we have to keep running."

"And Faith really can't stop them?"

"I wouldn't count on it." With some difficulty, he rose to his feet and started walking again. "Let's go. We can't stay here."

"But you need to rest!"

"I just did. You see anything else up there? Landmarks? Villages?"

Breeze was about to protest but resigned herself when she saw the urgency with which he was walking. "No, nothing," she said. "Just more hills and trees."

He sighed. "Well, at least there aren't any roads they can use to catch up to us. Come on, you're lagging behind."

And thus, they made their way deeper into the woods.

"...and then there's the forest north of here," Lieutenant Adam Kidd said. "This is where I'd say we're most likely to find him. There are leagues of untamed land up there, especially northeast." The lieutenant, a middle-aged man with a graying beard and scarred skin, pointed at the area of the map that corresponded to the region he had just described.

"But," he continued, "there's a path further east of here that cuts through the forest and goes north—right here. Our loggers use it to carry the lumber back to Craigsburrow's sawmill. Assuming the sorcerer's trail leads to the forest, I'd suggest we skip the pursuit through the woods and immediately head there to cut off his escape. And if he's already crossed the road, then chase after him."

"Why are you so certain that he'll be there?" the steward asked.

"It wouldn't make sense for him to go anywhere else. When he came into town, it was from the south, so he should know that most of that land is already settled and full of roads. Even the king's reserve, that forest over there, is surrounded on all sides by them. The west and the east are also out of the question since there are only plains and fields in both directions for two leagues out—which leaves only the north. And since Holiburg is northwest of here, I can't imagine he'd risk going there."

"Which means northeast," Faith murmured.

"Exactly."

"We can't be sure of that," Aiden said. "He might have picked another direction regardless of those factors. It wouldn't be the first time a sorcerer made that kind of mistake."

Kidd said, "I disagree. Kieran Fowler is a shrewd man, and it would be stupid of him to pick any other direction—too many roads, not enough cover. But the forest might give him a chance."

Aiden frowned. "You call him 'shrewd'?"

Adam Kidd pursed his lips and lowered his gaze. "I'm the one who let him into town. I suspected he might have been the sorcerer we'd heard about, so I tried to trick him into revealing his identity, but he didn't take the bait. I figured I was just being paranoid. Biggest mistake of my life."

"Don't blame yourself," Faith said. "He was trained for this. You weren't."

"Thank you, Inquisitor. That…that means a lot, coming from you."

Faith immediately regretted speaking up and did her best not to let it show. She didn't deserve his gratitude, not when she was the one who'd unleashed Kieran upon the world. She could already imagine him shooting arrows at the constables and their dogs, shouting at them like madmen do when they've been backed into a corner.

She had to remember to tell the constables not to bring any arrows with them before they set off on this hunt.

"What about the river?" Lloyd Oakley asked. "Couldn't he have taken a boat and headed downstream?"

"Someone would have noticed if he did," the older constable said, having regained his composure. "We have men patrolling the bridge and the docks at night to prevent that sort of thing, but just in case, I asked that they check that every boat was accounted for. They should be back soon to confirm it."

"Good," Aiden said. "How much time before the dogs pick up Fowler's trail? They've been gone a while."

"Depends on what path Fowler took to get out of town, but they should be back any minute now. We also have a carriage ready to transport the dogs once it's time to leave. It's waiting for us in front of the church."

"Hmm. Anything else?" Faith asked.

"No, ma'am."

She nodded and turned to face the steward. "What about you, Mr. Oakley?"

"I have nothing to add, but I would like to know what you learned from the men who were on duty last night."

There was the question she'd feared.

"Nothing conclusive, I'm afraid," she said. "They swear that they were awake all night and that I was the last one to exit the dungeon."

"And do you believe them?"

"Until I have a reason to think otherwise, yes, I do."

"Then the one responsible must be this 'fairy' you mentioned, correct?"

"Possibly. We don't know enough yet."

"If I may," Aiden interrupted, "shouldn't Lord Harrowmont be here to hear all of this?"

The steward stiffened at the insinuation regarding his master and answered the question matter-of-factly. "In a period of crisis such as this one, Lord Harrowmont needs to make himself presentable before he can appear before the people. I can assure you that he will be here shortly and that in the meantime, I speak with his authority."

"Very well."

"If that's all, let's wait in the courtyard," Faith said. "Aiden? Take the map with you."

The knight nodded and began to roll the parchment while she headed for the door and tried to think of a way to lead the men away from Breeze and Kieran without revealing her treachery. Before she could curse herself again for her lack of forethought, Lieutenant Kidd stopped her just as she was about to step outside. "Ma'am? One last thing."

The prince and the steward both turned to look at him, obviously curious as to what he wanted to talk about. She wasn't interested in prolonging this conversation any longer than needed, and so she responded with a tone blunter than she would otherwise use. "What is it?"

The lieutenant visibly faltered at her reaction, but that wasn't enough to discourage him. He instead pushed his shoulders back and raised his chin high, determined to go through with this. "What do we do once we've found the sorcerer?"

"We capture him. That should be quite obvious."

"Yes, but how can our men help with that? From what I've heard, Fowler can throw fire at will and shoot arrows without a bow. And there's this fairy people keep talking about…"

It was true that Kieran's magic posed a problem. Although he had sworn not to hurt anyone during his escape, she couldn't ignore the possibility that he would break that promise. At the very least, she had to prepare the men for that eventuality.

As for Breeze…she didn't want anyone to hurt her.

"Don't engage either of them if you can avoid it," she said. "Call for me and Sir Hawkon instead. We'll be right there by your side, so there's no need for you to risk your lives. Cutting off Fowler's escape will be enough."

"As you say, ma'am."

"Oh, and make sure that your men don't bring any arrows with them. No reason to give Fowler ammunition that he could use against us."

"I will do so immediately."

"Was there anything else?"

"No. Thank you, Inquisitor."

Faith turned around and left through the door, her mind already on other things. It was becoming increasingly clear that she should have planned this more carefully. Freeing Kieran could have waited until she and Aiden were on the road and far away from Ballybridge. It would have made the following turmoil so much easier to manage.

The dozen men who had gathered in the castle's courtyard

were muttering among themselves, worried about the mission they were about to embark on. Some of them occupied themselves by checking the saddle of their horses for a second or third time, while others munched on some jerky or bread in an effort to calm themselves.

When they saw that the inquisitor had stepped outside of the gatehouse, everyone stopped. No more talking, no more chewing. Only an expectant silence that was occasionally broken by the neighing of a horse.

Luckily for her, the lieutenant was there to call his men to attention. "All right, listen up! We've received our orders, so gather 'round! And put that food away!"

He walked to the middle of the courtyard and waited until they had formed a semicircle around him before he started briefing them on the mission and their role in it. As she watched, Aiden shuffled next to her with his left hand still resting on the pommel of his sword, and he told her, "The men said that you went to speak to Fowler alone yesterday."

She had been waiting for him to ask her about that. "Yes, I did," she said, measuring her words carefully. "They told me he screamed once or twice after we left, so I went to check on him."

"Did he say anything?"

"Nothing useful, no. I tried talking to him, but he kept deflecting and mocking me."

"How exactly?"

Faith didn't let it show on her face, but she was mentally fumbling for an answer that would sound plausible. Thankfully for her, one of the men who'd been sent to follow Kieran's trail came back right at that moment.

The steward approached him as soon as he ran through the portcullis, his face red with exertion. He was a young lad, eighteen years old at most. "Steward Oakley!" he panted. "We found his trail!"

"You did? Where, boy!"

"North of here, toward the forest! He circled around town to try to confuse the dogs, but we double-checked, and we're sure that's where he went!"

Adam Kidd exchanged a knowing glance with Faith and waited for her to give the order.

In that instant, she knew there was no other way around it. Unless she gave the order to head for the path that crossed the forest, everyone here would begin to suspect her. Maybe not of treachery, but certainly of incompetence and arrogance, and it would be only a matter of time before Aiden and her mother discovered what she had done.

God preserve her, she had no other choice.

"Everyone, saddle up. We're cutting him off on the road to Craigsburrow."

The constables mounted their horses at once. At the same time, the lieutenant grabbed the reins of two—a white mare and a chestnut stallion—and led them to Faith and Aiden.

"These are the finest horses we have," he told them. "They'll carry you through the fires of hell itself if you command them to."

Faith marveled at the spotless white coat of the mare as well as the strong musculature that flexed underneath it. Although she had been trained to ride horses and knew her way around them, she wasn't an expert on them, but even she could tell that this one was exceptional. She carefully approached the tall animal and placed a gentle hand on its face, stroking it between the eyes as she continued to admire its strength. "What's her name?" she asked.

"Shae."

"Shae," she repeated, caressing its neck. The animal didn't even twitch under her touch. Aiden's stallion was just as disciplined, and it didn't protest when the sinewy knight climbed onto its back. These truly were the best horses they could have asked for.

Faith climbed onto the mare and repositioned her haversack on her hip so it wouldn't get in the way once they rode off. She then turned to Lieutenant Kidd, who'd just mounted his horse, and told him, "You take the lead for now. You know these streets better than us."

The man gave her a stern nod before he spun to face the rest of the constables. "You heard the inquisitor! We ride for Craigsburrow!"

He spurred his steed and left the courtyard through the portcullis, closely followed by Faith and Aiden, and then by the dozen men armed with batons and swords. It was at this moment, galloping through the streets of Ballybridge and under the gaze of curious onlookers going to work, that Faith began to hope that Breeze really was an angel.

Maybe she could perform a miracle that would save them all.

The sun was well above the horizon now and shining its warm summer light through the trees. If Kieran's jailers hadn't noticed his disappearance already, then Faith's knight certainly would.

Despite his best efforts, Kieran could barely run. His thighs and calves were burning to the point of pain, and his mouth was so dry that his tongue felt like a hardened piece of meat. It was only when he saw the trees suddenly give way to an open space that he stopped.

"Kieran? What is it?" the fairy asked.

Kieran stared at what he had just stumbled upon: a dirt path that stretched from left to right, cutting straight through the forest and toward the horizon. He knew instantly what it meant. "Shit," he muttered under his breath. "Fuck my life."

"What is it?" Breeze asked again.

The sorcerer searched for the nearest branch with plenty of

leaves on it and snapped it from the tree. He then crossed the road while removing every trace of his passage here.

"Kieran, I don't understand." The poor girl was staring at him with her hands clasped together, her brow furrowed in worry.

"The people coming after me might use this path," he explained. "I have to wipe my footprints in case they do."

"Didn't you say they had dogs?"

"Yeah, they do, but that's no reason to make it easy for them."

As soon as he was finished, he entered the woods on the other side of the path and threw the branch under a tree of the same species. Then he resumed his run through the forest with Breeze in tow.

What he hadn't told her was that his pursuers might forego following his trail and head here immediately instead. He had hoped that no such road existed, and if there was, that the constables wouldn't think to cut off his escape here. He needed to come up with another plan. He stopped and leaned against a tree to rest.

"Kieran?" Breeze appeared immediately at his side. "Are you all right? Can I help?"

"I'm fine," he said, a taste of bile climbing up his throat. "But I need you to do something for me."

"Anything!"

"Go above the trees again and tell me what you can see. Buildings, ruins, cliffs. Anything other than trees."

"On it!" The fairy spread her wings wide and flew toward the sky faster than any butterfly could. How remarkable. If only he'd learned how to fly like that years ago, maybe he would have escaped his pursuers already. It seemed a lot less tiring than running through the forest at full speed, that's for sure. But then again, exerting his magic for that long might bring more migraines than he could handle. Which raised the question: How did Breeze avoid this problem altogether?

The answer to this mystery would have to wait. Breeze

had returned from her reconnaissance. "There's a big lake over there"—she pointed northeast—"bigger than any I've ever seen! But it's also pretty far away."

"A lake? Are you sure?"

"I think so—the sunlight was shimmering on it. Why? Do you think we can use it?"

"I don't know. Was there anything else?"

Breeze shook her head. "No, there wasn't. Nothing but that road and the forest."

"Then I guess we've got no other choice." Kieran stood a little straighter and took the first step in the direction Breeze had pointed to. God, he was so thirsty. Finding water might be a stroke of luck for him.

"Kieran?" Breeze landed on his right shoulder and grabbed on to his earlobe. "Are you sure you're not pushing yourself too hard?"

"Oh, I am. But I have to."

"But no one is chasing us! We're safe now."

"No, Breeze, we're not. Trust me on that."

His little companion fell silent and let him press onward. She was powerless to stop him, and she knew it.

He would have liked to reassure her and say that it was almost over, that pushing to that lake would solve all of their problems and give them a moment of reprieve, but he couldn't. For some reason, he felt that this lie would be one too many. Instead, he gritted his teeth and kept walking, forcing himself to hurry.

The pursuers rode through the countryside at full speed, drawing the attention of the farmers laboring in the fields. Although the sight of a dozen or so armed men was already enough of a cause for concern, it was the woman leading them who would undoubtedly cause the rumor mill to spin.

Faith had switched places with Lieutenant Kidd after they got out of town, even though she would have preferred to let him take the lead. As an inquisitor, however, she understood that everyone expected her to take charge and that refusing this role would only draw their suspicion.

It didn't change the fact that she was out of her depth. One mistake could cost her the rank of inquisitor, if not her freedom. She hoped that Kieran and Breeze were too far away by now for the group to catch up to them, but she also knew that she had to plan for the likelihood that they weren't. Otherwise...

Otherwise, this could end in a massacre.

Faith noticed the thatched roofs of a village in the distance before Lieutenant Kidd overtook Aiden and rode up next to her. "That's Craigsburrow!" he shouted, his voice almost drowned out by the sound of the horses' hooves against the road. "We have to ride through it and take a left at the third fork after the village!"

"Third fork!" she repeated, confirming to him that she understood.

The lieutenant nodded and went farther back in the line, right behind Aiden. They had ridden for only an hour and had already covered a great distance, even with the carriage slowing them down. She realized now that there was no way Kieran could escape these men on foot, no matter how dense the forest was. It was only a matter of time before they'd catch up to him.

The inhabitants of Craigsburrow rapidly cleared the main road when they saw the group approach, and some of them hid in their homes while others grabbed the nearest tool that could be used as a weapon. However, the yellow surcoats of the constables and the white cassock of the inquisitor soon made it clear that they weren't here to attack the village. Far from it.

Men, women, and children stood with their mouths agape

at the sight of this woman of God riding a mare as white as her outfit. She merely glanced at them and saw in their eyes the admiration and deference they had for her, a woman whom they'd never met before. She pinched her lips and held the reins tighter than before, unable to look at the people any longer.

It only took her a minute to cross the village and come out the other side. She could see the forest beyond the fields on her left and started counting the forks after she'd passed the first one. When the third one got closer, she signaled the riders behind her to slow down while she loosened her reins and relaxed her posture, telling the mare to canter while they turned left. Then, she spurred the horse once again.

It wouldn't be long now. Unless Kieran had taken another path, they would soon find his trail and set the dogs after him. He could never hope to outrun his pursuers when he already had been running for the better part of the night.

She knew she needed a plan, but no matter how hard she thought about it, nothing came to mind. How stupid of her to let him go while he was in Lord Harrowmont's custody. Stupid and reckless.

"Faith! Slow down a little! The men are trailing behind!"

The head of Aiden's steed appeared at the edge of her vision and she looked behind to see that her knight was the only other rider present at the moment: the others were almost twenty meters behind, while the carriage was still at the fork, having just finished turning left. She reined in her horse and slowed down to a trot, allowing the rest of them to catch up with her. And as she waited, the solution she had been looking for finally presented itself to her.

The horses. Hers and Aiden's. The lieutenant had told them that these were the finest mounts they had, and she'd inadvertently confirmed it. If she could somehow get Kieran to steal one of them and flee on it, maybe—just maybe—she could avoid any bloodshed today. The hard part would be to find Kieran before the constables and to inform him of this plan. Maybe Breeze could help with that?

She doubted that the constables would take the horses into the woods. In all likelihood, she'd have to leave them somewhere on the road with a handful of men while the rest went into the forest on foot. Kieran would only have to double back and steal either her horse or Aiden's to make his escape.

This plan was full of holes, but it was better than what she'd had before.

She was in the middle of thinking of a way to contact Breeze without informing the rest of the group when the fields finally gave way to a forest of broadleaf trees. From here on out, it was up to the dogs to signal to their masters when they'd pick up Kieran's scent. With a bag of his belongings at their disposal, it shouldn't be too long now before they started barking to warn them.

And so they did, ten minutes later.

The group came to a halt in the middle of the dirt path that, judging by the absence of tracks on the ground, appeared to have not seen a lot of traffic lately. Immediately, the dogs jumped down from the carriage with their masters in tow while the riders waited for confirmation that the sorcerer really had passed through here. It only took them a minute for them to find a trail heading east.

"Here!" one man who had ventured into the forest exclaimed. "Footprints!"

Faith took a deep breath and dismounted her horse. Only then did Aiden and the other constables do the same, as if they had been waiting for her permission to do so, and Lieutenant Kidd quickly sprang into action and began barking orders at his men.

"Bailey, Owen! You two take the horses and tie them up to the trees! Kendrick and Bryn, you stay here with them and watch the perimeter! Do not let anyone pass through here, you understand?"

"Yes, sir!"

The four of them spread out in all directions while the other men readjusted the weapons on their belts and grabbed whatever supplies they needed from their saddlebags. Aiden was already at her side, a determined look on his face and the silver pin of his order shining on his chest—the very embodiment of a knight. If only he knew the truth.

"How do we proceed?" Aiden asked.

Faith hadn't received much training on how to lead a manhunt into a forest, but she knew the basics of it. She eyed the three dogs and their masters for a moment while she considered her best course of action. Whatever she did, she had to stay close to the dogs to make sure she was one of the first people to come into contact with Kieran. She had no idea how she would tell him about her plan without arousing the suspicion of the constables, but finding a solution to that problem would have to wait until later. For now, only the search mattered.

"Are we sure these are Fowler's footprints?" she asked the three dog masters who had gathered at the edge of the forest.

"Yes, ma'am," the older of them said. "I'd recognize these footprints anywhere—they were made by the shoes that we give to the prisoners."

Faith brushed a stray lock of her hair behind her ear and raised her eyebrows in surprise. "You know what shoes the prisoners wear?"

"It's Lieutenant Kidd, ma'am. He's the one who decided that."

The inquisitor turned to the man in question and waited for an explanation.

"I'm the one who bought these shoes," he said. "They make tracking prisoners a lot easier in case one of them ever escapes."

"Um. Clever." Very clever, she thought. That kind of forward thinking was not only unexpected but also very dangerous for her in this situation. She'd have to keep an eye on him in the future. "Anything else about his clothes I should know about?"

"No. We wanted to give the prisoners uniforms, but we're still waiting on the steward for that. He doesn't want prisoners to wear new clothing, so we give them old trousers and tunics instead."

"But he agreed to the shoes?" Aiden asked.

"No, he didn't." Lieutenant Kidd shifted around uncomfortably, as did several of the other constables gathered here. Faith understood: he'd asked Lloyd Oakley for easily recognizable uniforms to give to the prisoners but was met with refusal and thus decided to take matters into his own hands. It wouldn't surprise her if Lord Harrowmont was ultimately the one responsible for this issue. This disregard for the safety of his subjects sounded very much like him.

"This doesn't matter right now," she said. "Let's focus on the task at hand. Lieutenant Kidd, divide your men and the dogs into three groups. Sir Hawkon and I will accompany the one in the center while you take one of the others. We'll move in tandem and never stay more than fifty meters apart from each other. Understood?"

"Yes, ma'am!" Without delay, the lieutenant turned to his men and began assigning them to their respective groups. "Breen, you take Gale and Patel with you and go left. I'll be with Powell and Graham on the right, while Cole and Rowland stay with the inquisitor and her knight. Keep your eyes peeled, and for the love of God, don't stray away from the group. We don't need heroics here, especially not against a sorcerer like the one we're chasing. If you see him, you warn the others. Got it?"

"Sir, yes, sir!" they responded in unison.

The men entered the forest and spread out as their superior had commanded. The lieutenant was about to join them when he looked one last time at Faith and nodded at her, causing her to feel a pang of guilt at what she had done. She had assigned him to one of the other groups not because she thought his leadership might help them stay alive, but because his presence would limit her options if she were to meet Kieran and Breeze first. She needed him gone, especially with Aiden at her side.

"Lead the way," she told the two constables assigned to her.

"Yes, ma'am."

The one named Rowland pulled a piece of clothing out of a small satchel and presented it to his dog, a black retriever. The animal sniffed it for a few seconds before it whirled around and headed east, pulling on its master's leash to guide him to the target.

"This way!"

Faith briefly glanced at Aiden before she followed suit, wondering just how she could keep him and Kieran from killing each other—and started doubting it was even possible.

Breeze held on to Kieran's ear as he ran through the woods and toward the lake she had pointed him to earlier. His pace was much slower than before, and she doubted he could keep this up for much longer either. He needed to rest, and soon.

But how? Kieran said that the bad humans were chasing them, even though she hadn't heard or seen any over the last few hours. At first, she doubted they would bother going after her and Kieran when they had covered such a great distance already, but she changed her mind when Kieran explained to her what a dog could do. With such powerful noses, anything seemed possible.

Besides, Kieran was more experienced with human customs than she was. If he said humans were still chasing them, that's because they were.

Which was why for the last half hour, she had tried to come up with a plan to save them both from their pursuers. She wasn't as smart as Bubble, as foresighted as Dewdrop, or as strong as Cosmo, but if she put her mind to it, she'd find a solution! She knew she would! Because if she didn't, her friend would pay the price for her mistakes, and she couldn't accept that. However, she couldn't be naive about it. One false move and the humans might capture the both of them. Whatever she did, she'd have to be very careful about it.

"Breeze," Kieran said while slowing down. "How much farther till the lake?"

"I'll go check!" she replied.

A few seconds later, she was flying above the canopy, her eyes fixed on their goal. It took her only an instant to calculate the distance left between them and their destination. Then, just as she was about to return to Kieran's side, she heard something strange coming from far behind her. Something new.

She listened attentively to this sound and attempted to identify its origin. It was an animal of some sort, one she had never encountered before, and it was yapping. Wait, no—*they* were yapping. There were at least two of them, maybe three, and if her estimation was correct, they were coming this way.

There was no time to lose. Breeze dashed back to her friend's side, hoping he'd have an idea on how to lose them. "Kieran! They're almost here!"

His reaction was instantaneous: his eyes narrowed into a menacing expression that would have petrified her had they only just met, while the muscles in his whole body tensed up under the threat looming over him. "Are you sure?" he asked her in a calm voice.

"Yes! I heard animals yapping from over there, and they're coming this way! It has to be the dogs that you were talking about, right?"

"Give me a minute. I'll try listening for them."

Kieran turned his ear in the direction she had pointed to and closed his eyes. She was certain it would take him only a moment to confirm their presence. She bit her lower lip and clutched her tunic when the near silence of the forest continued for longer than she had anticipated. Maybe the chirping of the birds and the rustling of the leaves were distracting him?

"I can't hear them," he said.

"What? But I heard them, I swear!"

"You probably just have better hearing than me. How much farther until the lake?"

"Oh, um, from where we were before, we have a quarter of the distance left to walk. Maybe a third."

Kieran clicked his tongue and set his gaze to the east again.

"Do you have an idea?" she asked him.

"Maybe," he said. "I'm just not sure it will work."

"What is it?"

"To burn down the forest."

Breeze widened her eyes and stared agape at Kieran while he examined the trees, already calculating his plan's chances of success. At first, she wasn't sure she'd heard him correctly. Burning down a forest seemed like a ludicrous idea, even for a mage like him, but the more she thought about it, the more plausible it became. She remembered the lessons Nana had taught her and her siblings about the dangers of using fire and how to extinguish one if necessary. A single spark could set ablaze a whole forest, she told them, and in Kieran's case, he could conjure up a lot more than that.

He was the one who'd burned down all those fields outside of Ballybridge, after all, and the only reason the fire hadn't consumed all of them was because the humans worked hard to smother it. If she did nothing to stop him, he'd do the same thing to these woods.

"If I can cut them off, they won't be able to follow us," he said. "The smoke will prevent the dogs from picking up my trail again. We just need to go to that lake and—"

"You can't do that!" she exclaimed.

Kieran turned away from the trees and looked at her. He didn't say anything for a while as he carefully considered her words, until finally, he closed his eyes and shook his head. "I have to do *something*, Breeze. I promised not to kill anyone, but if I can just slow them down, then we'll be safe."

"But you'll hurt the animals living here! That's where their homes are!"

Kieran blinked and stared at her in confusion, as if he hadn't considered that perspective until now.

How could he not?

"You wouldn't want anyone to burn down *your* home, right?" she asked in an almost pleading tone.

Kieran averted his gaze. He stayed quiet for several long seconds, and Breeze secretly hoped that he would change his mind and abandon this plan of his. It was only when he met her gaze again, an expression of unease on his face, that she realized she had been holding her breath.

"Fine," he said. "I won't burn down the forest."

The corners of Breeze's mouth slowly curled into a smile; it was as if a weight had been lifted off her chest. Kieran had once again proven that he really was a good human.

"You mean it?" she asked. "For real?"

"I wouldn't lie to you about something like that."

"Thank you, Kieran. I'm really glad to hear that." A few tears began to well up in her eyes, and she wiped them away with her hand. "I'm sure the animals would say the same if they could."

Kieran grunted and turned away, ready to start running again. "Come on now, we have to keep moving," he said.

"You're right." She landed on his shoulder and grabbed his ear once more. "I'm ready!"

The mage hummed in the affirmative and resumed their retreat east, toward the lake. It was still quite a distance away, but she had a good feeling that once they reached that place, a solution would present itself. Until then, she had to watch his back for any dog or human that might attack him. No doubt she could use herself as a distraction to slow them down if they got too close to him.

Anything to help him keep his promise to Faith.

Kieran hadn't lied to Breeze. He did not intend to set the forest on fire anymore; she had dissuaded him from it. In truth, he hadn't given so much as a second thought to the animals living here until Breeze mentioned them. But they weren't the reason why he'd agreed to her request—she was.

He knew that starting a fire was the smart thing to do in this situation. Perhaps the only sure way to escape his pursuers. But after remembering the blaze he'd caused at the Lunaris orphanage, he couldn't bring himself to repeat that incident. Not even to save his own life. Not if it meant that Breeze would have to witness the death of the animals so dear to her heart.

Kieran kept running east, hoping that by the time he'd reached the lake, he would have a new plan to present to his companion. One that didn't end with his death.

Faith and the rest of the hunting party made good progress through the forest. The constables stopped from time to time to examine Kieran's trail and make sure he was still in front of them, and by the fifth time they had done so, the one named Rowland suddenly announced, "He's two leagues away at most."

The inquisitor felt her pulse quicken. She had hoped to get Breeze's attention before catching up to Kieran, but how was she supposed to do that with the constables here? She still hadn't figured out how to split up the group without arousing suspicion, and even if she did, Aiden would insist that he stay with her. There was no escaping his sense of duty. "Let's keep going," she said.

The dog barked and continued tugging on its leash, leading the men forward...possibly toward their doom.

After a whole night pushing his body to the limit, Kieran wasn't able to run anymore. Only to walk at a fast pace. He'd probably collapse on the ground right now if he stopped, and Breeze wasn't sure he would get back up. She could hear the dogs steadily gaining on them with each moment, and they sounded even more dangerous than what Nana had told the fairies about them.

Without saying a word to Kieran, she flew high into the air and dashed toward the canopy once more. It took her only a second to estimate the distance left between them and the lake before she returned to her friend's side to relay the information. "We're almost there, Kieran! Just a couple more minutes and we'll be at the lake!"

He was breathing too heavily to reply and responded with a nod instead.

The constables weren't stopping to check Kieran's trail anymore. Even Faith could tell by the depth of his footprints and the space between them that he had passed here recently and that he couldn't run anymore. It was humanly impossible for him to escape them.

Faith bit the inside of her cheek and hurried forward, fearful of the very real possibility that Kieran might go back on his word and try to kill them. Maybe he was lying somewhere in ambush, waiting for the right moment to strike the men with his fire magic and burn them to a crisp. The idea alone was enough to send shivers down her spine.

What could she possibly do to prevent that?

The first thing Kieran saw of the lake was the glimmer of the sun on its calm surface, shining through the trees like the eye of a god winking at him.

Kieran leaned against the trunk of a small oak and shook his head; his mind was playing tricks on him. He was so tired that he could feel his ability to reason slipping away, and he wondered what would be left of it by the end of the day. He couldn't afford to stop and rest, no matter how much he needed it. His pursuers were not far behind him.

"You're almost there!" Breeze said. "Come on, just a little more!"

The fairy hovered right next to him with her brow wrinkled in worry. Even now, all she could think about was his safety, having no concern for her own. It was sweet, really, but also incredibly naive. And naivety could be deadly in this sort of situation.

Kieran used the tree to push himself forward and wobbled toward his destination. Before he knew it, he was standing at the top of a cliff, looking down at a lake.

It was bigger than he'd imagined it would be. Much bigger. Judging by its size, it would take many hours, if not the whole day, to walk a complete circle around it. It also surprised him that no one had settled here, considering how fertile this land appeared to be. Maybe they had in the past but had left for one reason or another. In any case, he couldn't just stand there and admire the view. He needed a plan, and fast.

He searched for a landmark of some sort that he could use

to his advantage, like the ruins of an old village or a natural formation projecting out of the earth. Anything that could help him. But all he found was more water and trees, no matter where he turned. Just as he'd expected.

Kieran let out a weary sigh and shuffled to the edge of the cliff. The clear water down below gently splashed against the rocky face, almost caressing it, and one glance was enough to tell that it was also quite deep. The cliff continued on his left for a few hundred meters before it dropped to water level, while on his right, it curved downward after thirty meters or so from his position. He had nowhere to hide.

Kieran lowered his head and cursed internally. "Guess this is it," he said. "One last stand."

He faced the forest and opened his mind to the magic that flowed all around him. The power came to him more easily than he had expected despite his exhaustion, but he nevertheless felt a resistance when he tugged at it. No matter. He'd still be able to mount a decent defense with his telekinesis alone.

"Kieran? What are you doing?"

Breeze must have sensed his manipulation of the aether, judging by the agitation he heard in her voice. He did not even glance at her when he answered, concentrating his energy on his spell instead. "I'm preparing to fight," he told her.

"But you promised not to hurt anyone!"

"I promised not to *kill* anyone. If I'm lucky and Faith doesn't get in my way, I might just be able to scare them off."

"But the knight won't leave!"

Kieran clenched his jaw and tightened his hands into fists. She was right. That man would never back down from a fight, not even if Kieran threw fire directly at him, and since Kieran had made a promise to Breeze not to set the forest ablaze, he couldn't even use that against the knight. He had to limit himself to his telekinetic magic, which he wasn't very proficient at beyond moving light objects like rocks and arrows, and there weren't a lot of those around here.

He debated over the feasibility of taking the weapons away from the constables and using them at a distance when Breeze suddenly called out to him. "Kieran! Wait!"

He glanced at her, wondering what she was on about, and saw her staring down at the lake below. "What?" he asked curtly.

"I think I have an idea. Let me go check first."

"Wait, where are you—"

But before she could explain herself, the fairy had already spread her wings and flown down the cliffside, where she began to search for something. Kieran looked back and forth between her and the woods, cursing the so-called Kind Mother for putting him in this situation, until finally, his companion came back, her brow furrowed in determination.

"I've found one!" she said.

"Found what?"

"A place where you can hide!"

# CHAPTER 25

THE DOGS GREW more agitated the closer they got to their prey, and after gradually coming together, the rest of the hunting party were now in sight of each other. It wouldn't be long now before they'd catch up to Kieran, and once that happened, Faith didn't know what she would do. Create a diversion and help Kieran escape? Or maybe join with him and make a run for the horses? She had no idea. Every option she could think of encountered the same problem: Aiden and the constables. If she didn't remove them from the equation, then no matter what she chose, they'd always stop Kieran and Breeze from escaping. Then they'd arrest Faith too.

The group suddenly slowed down when they approached the edge of the forest, and only now did Faith notice the lake beyond it. Not a small one either but a vast body of water that would take many hours to circle around if they continued this way—which they would most likely have to, depending on how far ahead of them Kieran was.

And then, they arrived at the top of a cliff.

"Where is he?" Aiden asked, slightly out of breath.

Lieutenant Kidd turned to his men and waited expectantly for an answer, but one look at his eyes was enough to tell what he was thinking—what everyone was thinking.

"I-I think he jumped, Sir," Rowland said, his face turning pale despite the warm sun on his back. "Right here."

The dogs sniffed and growled near the edge of the cliff, but except for the tracks he had left in the grass, there were no other signs that Kieran had been here. This didn't reassure the men, not one bit, and several of them glanced around as if they anticipated an ambush from the woods. Recognizing the opportunity to regain control of the situation, Faith stepped forward and headed for the part of the cliff where Kieran must have stood not too long ago. The constables parted before her with reverence in their eyes.

She did her best to ignore them as she walked up to the precipice and looked down from it, but she saw only water and a rocky cliffside. The bottom of the lake wasn't visible from here either, and although the cliff was at least fifteen meters high, she surmised that with his magic, Kieran could have survived a fall from this height before heading to the shore.

The men behind her must have reached the same conclusion. On edge, they waited for her to speak. Truth be told, she had only one course of action available to her: to split the group in two and continue the chase on both sides of the lake. Chances were that Kieran had jumped into the water with this exact goal in mind, and now she had to decide where to assign the men and who to follow. What if she was sending them to their deaths?

And then she saw it. That unmistakable shade of blue, sticking out of the cliffside like a marmot looking out for predators.

She was so tiny from this distance that Faith almost didn't see her, and she might have missed her altogether if they hadn't made eye contact. When they did, the fairy retracted her wings and hid behind a rocky protrusion, only to stick her head out a few seconds later when she realized who it was that stood at the top of the cliff. Faith did her best to stay calm and not move a muscle when she figured out where Kieran was hiding. If only she could manage to talk to Breeze like she had planned! Then perhaps Kieran could escape without anyone being the wiser.

"Lieutenant Kidd," she called.

"Yes, Inquisitor."

"Split your men into two groups and send them to scout ahead. Sir Hawkon and I will wait for you here while you search for Fowler's trail. Once one of you has found it, give us a signal, and we will all regroup at that location. Understood?"

"Yes, ma'am!"

"Then go." Faith stayed on the cliff and continued watching the lake while the lieutenant gave his orders. Of the three dogs available to them, he assigned two to the group on the left and one to the group on the right. He then joined the latter, choosing the shore that was much closer to the cliff. If Kieran had truly jumped and then headed for the shore, he most likely would have picked that direction. It was good thinking on the lieutenant's part, but also pointless in this case. If only she could have thought of a reason to send Aiden along with them...

"Move out!" Lieutenant Kidd said.

The constables departed in their respective direction with a newfound albeit shaky resolve. She watched them shrink in the distance while she racked her brain for a reason to send Aiden away from here, but she came up short of anything useful. Aiden was her knight, sworn to defend her from all threats to her life. She couldn't just order him to leave her alone, not with a sorcerer on the loose nearby; it would be perceived as both careless and foolish on her part.

Maybe she should just incapacitate him and flee with both Kieran and Breeze? This would be the easiest way to avoid a potential bloodbath, if a little risky. However, as far as she knew, only her healing would work on him. Just like the handcuffs she had put on Kieran, Aiden's sword and armor had been consecrated by powerful Keepers to nullify magic, and any attempt to forcibly put him to sleep might inadvertently turn against her.

Nonetheless, she believed she had a good chance to knock him out with her Eos if she took him by surprise.

And yet, when thinking about the consequences of such an action, of what she would lose if she committed to it, she hesitated. She could feel her insides quiver at the simple thought of it, made worse by the rising sunlight warming her skin. Nausea gripped her throat so tightly that it became hard to breathe, and for just an instant, she wished she had never learned the truth about her power. Everything would have been so much easier if Breeze had never told Kieran about her magic.

But then again, had the fairy not stopped him by telling him the truth, Faith would be dead now.

Faith closed her eyes and focused her attention on the breeze blowing on her face. *Think*, she told herself. *Think of what Alma Azaria would do in this situation.* She would not have run away from this predicament; she would have faced it head on, regardless of the cost she would bring on herself by making the right choice. That was the kind of woman she had been. The kind of woman Faith had always aspired to be. She knew what she had to do. She knew it was the only way to save Kieran and Breeze from their pursuers, and yet she still hesitated.

"Faith?" Aiden said. "There's something I'd like to ask you."

Her eyes flew open at the sound of his voice, and she did her best to calm herself before she turned around to look at him. When she did, she saw a strange expression on his face, one she wasn't sure how to describe. Reluctance? Worry? She couldn't tell. Whatever it was, it most certainly concerned Kieran and the fairy accompanying him.

She felt a chill run down her spine, and her legs shook slightly. She opened her mouth to speak, only to find herself unable to get a word out. She had to clear her throat once before she managed to say something, and even then, she didn't sound as confident as she had hoped.

"What is it?" she asked.

Kieran leaned forward in the crevice as he tried to listen to the conversation between Faith and her knight. Being careful not to poke his head out also made it difficult to hear them. He'd understood most of what Faith had told the men since she had spoken in a loud voice, but now that it was only her and the knight, he could barely make out any of their words.

That wouldn't be a problem for Breeze, though. She had left the crevice not too long after their pursuers arrived, confident she wouldn't be spotted by any of them. He didn't share her confidence and had tried to keep her here with him, but he barely managed to get a word out before she flew out of the crevice and up the cliffside. Because of course she did. Breeze wouldn't be Breeze if she didn't act recklessly. But then again, what did he really know about her? Maybe she had a good reason to believe they wouldn't spot her. He'd certainly never imagined that she had the ability to heal or to sense other people's magic. For all he knew, she could turn invisible once every full moon. In her case, it seemed improbable enough to be true.

Did Faith know he was hiding right under her feet? Maybe Breeze had given her a signal that prompted her to send the men away. In that case, should he wait for her next move, or was she waiting for him to do something? This crevice wasn't very deep, and there was nowhere else to go but in the water. He doubted she wanted him to come out now when her knight was right beside her. Better to wait for Breeze to come back and tell him what she'd seen.

How he wished he could eavesdrop on the inquisitor's conversation with her knight. Judging by the grim tone of their voices, it sounded serious. Maybe he should risk coming out of the crevice for a little bit, just so he could make out what they were saying and maybe learn of a way to escape this predicament.

Breeze waited until the humans and their dogs had spread out on both sides of the lake before she climbed up the cliff, almost reaching the edge. She needed to speak with Faith and ask her to help them escape, but she didn't know how to do that with her knight here. Although she couldn't see him, she could sense something from right behind Faith: a void that warped the magic around it, just like the metal bracelets Kieran had been forced to wear.

"What is it?" Faith asked.

Breeze hurriedly leaned against the cliffside and pricked up her ears.

"It's about Fowler's escape from the dungeon," the knight continued.

She couldn't explain why exactly, but all her senses screamed at her that something was amiss. But what could she do about it? Coming out now would only make the situation worse. No, she had no other choice but to stay put and listen. Before she tried anything, she first had to understand what was happening. That's what Kieran and Bubble would tell her to do.

And so she waited.

"What about it?" Faith asked.

She gazed at Aiden with what she hoped looked like slight disinterest while at the same time she closed her hands into fists to keep them from trembling.

*Don't breathe too fast,* she told herself. *Don't breathe too fast, or he'll learn what you did.*

Despite her best efforts to keep herself under control, she couldn't help but think that something must have appeared off to Aiden. The way he stared at her—observed her—was more than a little unnerving. He couldn't possibly have figured out how Kieran had escaped. How could he? They had found no evidence of her involvement whatsoever. No clues, no hints, nothing. Then why? Why look at her like that?

She waited with bated breath for him to say something that would lighten the mood, only to be met with crushing disappointment.

"How do you think he managed to take the handcuffs off?" he asked.

"With the fairy's help, of course," she replied. "You said so yourself."

"That I did." Aiden shifted his posture and rested his left hand on the hilt of his sword, something he had done plenty of times before, but never when talking to her. Faith's whole body tensed up. For just an instant, she felt the sudden urge to turn around and flee—but she couldn't, not with the edge of the cliff behind her.

Her heart was beating so fast, she could hear her blood thumping in her temples, like a mad drummer playing to the beat of an even crazier conductor. The only way out of here was through Aiden, and she could tell by the glint in his eyes that he would never let her pass, not before he got the answers he wanted. She was trapped here with him, with no chance of escape.

"I had one last question," he continued.

Faith didn't say anything—the lump in her throat hurt too much for that. She feared that if she opened her mouth, only a pitiful croak would come out. When Aiden spoke again, his words were enough to rattle her to the core.

"Why was the fairy in your room last night?"

Faith blinked in confusion for the next few seconds, unsure

as to whether or not she'd heard him correctly. This couldn't be right. She must have misunderstood him somehow. "W-what?" she replied. "What are you talking about?"

"The fairy. She was in your room last night."

"No, that's…that's ridiculous. There's no way she could have—"

"I *saw* the grapes on the desk in your room, Faith. Something small, very small, bit into one of them. What else could it have been but that 'fairy'?"

Aiden now glared at her, having fully abandoned the pretense of serving as her bodyguard. So that explained why he'd suddenly stopped talking this morning after he entered her room; his gaze had fallen upon the plate of food. And yet he'd acted as if he didn't see anything, carrying on his duties with seemingly the same dedication she had come to know him for. Why? Why go through this charade and wait until now before confronting her about it? Was it because of Harrowmont's men? Did he fear she would pit them against him? No, that was impossible. She would never do that to him. Not even to save her own life.

"Won't you say *anything*?" he demanded.

Faith realized she had stopped breathing. She slowly started to inhale again, her mind racing through the many ways she could refute Aiden's accusation. But when she opened her mouth to speak, it was the truth that came out.

"I met with Breeze last night, yes."

Aiden's eyes narrowed at the mention of the name, and he tightened his grip on the hilt of his sword. "Breeze?" he repeated.

"That's what she calls herself. Breeze, just like the wind."

"And why did you speak with her?"

"Because she needed my help." Aiden's expression turned into one of doubt. This was where she should be taking this conversation, she realized. She had to talk with Aiden and make him see reason. Together, maybe they could find a solution to this problem. "We were wrong about everything, Aiden," she continued. "Magic isn't what we were taught it was."

"What the *hell* do you mean by that?"

"I'm a witch, Aiden. Me, the other inquisitors, the priestesses—we all are."

"*What?!*"

"We don't perform miracles; we cast spells. Just…different types of spells than the ones you're used to."

"Are you *insane*? How could you even entertain the idea that—"

"I have proof!"

Aiden stared at her in disbelief.

She continued: "That's why I asked you for the handcuffs yesterday. So I could see for myself."

"What are you talking about?"

"Did you never wonder why it's always the knights and never the inquisitors who carry the handcuffs?"

"It's tradition. Knights have always protected their charge from the heretics and criminals who may pose a threat to them. Inquisitors shouldn't be the ones to put shackles on these people—we are."

"No, Aiden. It's because we lose our power when we get too close to them."

"What nonsense has this little she-devil put in your mind? Have you gone daft?"

"It's the truth! And like I said, I can prove it."

"What, by putting the handcuffs on? Is that it?"

"Yes."

"You're insane." Aiden turned away from her and started pacing back and forth along the edge of the cliff without taking his eyes off of her. "Is that what she told you to do? Put on the handcuffs and you'll see the 'truth'?"

"No," she answered firmly. "I did that before she showed up."

The knight stopped in front of her and openly gaped at her brazenness. "You did what?"

"I tested the handcuffs. She didn't have anything to do with my decision."

"W-what? *Why?*"

"Because she's not a liar, Aiden. Because right when Kieran was about to kill me, she stopped him by telling him that we were both mages. She's the reason I'm alive today."

"That was obviously a trick, and you fell for it. You should know better!" The prince's upper lip curled into a grimace of revulsion, which stung her more than she would have liked to admit. It wasn't so long ago that he'd looked at her with devotion and desire, a mix of emotions she had never witnessed before, and maybe would never see again. "Tell me you're not the one who freed Fowler from his cell," he said. "By God, at least tell me that."

The long and heavy silence that followed was the best answer she could muster. She saw his face fall as he grasped the severity of what she had done, the crime she had committed, and his expression slowly hardened into one bereft of compassion and mercy. That hurt her more than anything he'd said up until now.

"Please," she said. "Let me prove it to you."

"Prove what?" he asked curtly.

"That the handcuffs really take away my power."

"You've already gone against everything the Church and the Inquisition stand for, what Alma Azaria stood for. You have no power. God took it away from you."

In retort, she summoned her Eos into her left hand, which immediately shut Aiden up and prompted him to reach for his sword. He didn't draw his weapon, however, opting to examine the staff of light instead, searching for flaws that would reveal its demonic nature to him—he didn't find any.

"This is a trick. An illusion," he said.

"It's not. I can still do everything I could do before I met Breeze."

"It's not possible."

"*It is!* I can still shield people with my Aegis and heal them if they're injured! My powers aren't gone at all. They haven't even diminished."

"No." Aiden shook his head. "No, that can't be."

"Give me the handcuffs, and I'll show it to you. I can even cut myself and heal my own wound if you want me to."

"Blood magic can do the same!"

"Yes, but I would need someone else's blood to fuel the spell. We're alone here. You're the only one I could draw blood from, and you have your armor to protect you."

For a brief moment, Aiden appeared to consider her proposition.

"Please," she said. "Either way is fine. Just…trust me on this."

She extended her right hand to him, hoping that he would listen and give her one of the two pairs of handcuffs attached to his belt. Then he would see reason and accept that inquisitors and mages weren't so different from each other. That she was still the same woman he'd met in Holiburg.

*Please, God, let him see reason.*

"Do you really still possess God's power?" he asked.

"Yes," she answered.

"Do you swear it?"

"What?"

*"Do you swear it?"*

Faith only had to think about it for a second before she nodded and said, "I swear to God, and to you, that it's the same power you've seen me use before."

Aiden stood still for a long while as he continued to peer at her from under his wrinkled brow, until finally, he let go of his sword and reached for the handcuffs on his belt. Faith held her breath as he approached her one step at a time, wary of any sudden movement she might make. She didn't move a muscle and waited until he had placed the shackles in her hand before she wrapped her fingers around the chain and took them. Aiden then quickly retreated to his previous position, seemingly unaware that the light from the staff had already diminished in intensity.

"Now watch," she told him.

She let go of the Eos and held it within the crook of her elbow while she reached for the key in her cassock and unlocked the handcuffs. Once they were open, she locked eyes with Aiden and made sure that she had his full attention. And then, she cuffed her own wrist.

Aiden was on her before she understood what he was doing.

"Wait, no! What are you doing?"

He grabbed both of her arms and held them up so tightly that they began to hurt. Faith struggled against him and tried to free herself from his grasp, but he was too strong for her.

"Aiden! Stop it!"

"I'm sorry, Faith, but there's only one way I can make sure that God hasn't forsaken you." He lowered her arms and held them together in a lock while he took the key from her hand and cuffed her other wrist. "May the Kind Mother watch over you."

"Aiden! What are you—"

But before she could finish her question, the ground disappeared from under her feet and she felt her body fall backward toward the lake below. She reached for something to grab on to, but it was already too late.

The man she'd once called her knight was watching her with a grim expression on his face, his arm still outstretched after pushing her over the edge of the cliff, and for just an instant, she thought that this was the end. That she'd crack her skull on the ground and become a bloody mush of meat and bones for the vultures to peck on. She was so certain of it that she closed her eyes and prayed that her death would be quick and painless.

It wasn't going to be. She hit the water so hard that it almost knocked the air out of her lungs. She didn't know that falling into water could be so painful, and as she sank deeper into the lake, she realized what Aiden was aiming to achieve.

The Trial of Faith.

*Oh, God. Not like this.* She couldn't die like this. She began to flail around with her arms and legs as the sky slipped farther away from her, but she only sank deeper. Feeling her chest beginning to hurt because of the lack of air, she started tugging at the manacles instead, hoping that Aiden hadn't secured them properly. She had to take these off somehow! She had to!

Breeze pointed at Faith down in the water and projected her will toward her, just like she had done so many times before when she needed to lift something with magic. This time, it didn't work. Unsure as to why, she tried again, only to feel the magic slide off Faith like beads of rain on a leaf.

The metal bracelets. They were repelling her magic.

She dashed back to the crevice where Kieran was hiding and found him staring at the spot where Faith had vanished. He was standing only a few leaps away from her. Why hadn't he dived in already? "Kieran! It's Faith! The knight is trying to hurt her!"

"Yes, I heard," he whispered.

"My magic doesn't work on her!"

"Yes," he answered, his eyes still fixed forward.

Kieran half expected the inquisitor to resurface any second now, even though he knew she should have already. But she hadn't, and he could only surmise that she didn't know how to swim or that she was unable to. Best to stay back and wait until she either drowned or saved herself from this fate. Depending on the outcome, he might be able to slip away unnoticed. If he used his telekinetic magic to create a current in the water, he could push away Faith's body toward the shore where—

"KIERAN! HELP HER!"

Breeze's voice startled him so much that Kieran flinched away from the blue fairy and almost knocked his head against the wall of rock beside him. When he turned to look at her, he saw her shaking like a leaf, her eyes welling up with tears. She wanted him to do what she couldn't: to go out there and risk his life to save someone else.

He shifted his gaze back to the water and hesitated. To plunge after Faith was nothing short of suicidal, and he couldn't think of any good reason to do it. And yet, before he could change his mind, he opened his mouth and said to Breeze: "You need to distract the knight."

He dove into the water.

Breeze let out a sigh of relief and, without any hesitation, flew up the cliff to confront the man who'd dared to push her friend into the lake.

When she arrived there, she saw him with his weapon already drawn, a very long knife that Kieran had called a sword, and although she'd only just appeared in front of him, he was already raising it toward her. He'd heard her shouting at Kieran down there.

"The little she-devil," the knight growled. "I should have known you were here."

"Hey! What's the big deal?" she retorted. "You can't do that to your friends! Only mean people do that!"

"Silence! You defile the earth by your very presence. I shall banish you from this world forever and send you back to where you belong."

"I was born into this world, you big idiot!"

He swung at her faster than she had anticipated, but she managed to avoid his attack and get behind him in an instant.

"Missed me! I'm right here!"

Aiden snarled like an angry raccoon, spun expertly on his feet to face her again, and then struck once more at her tiny body. She evaded the attack and then tapped him on the back of his head for good measure.

"Missed me, missed me, now you gotta kiss me!"

"Begone!"

She could sense that direct magic wouldn't work on him, nor on his sword, and so she opted for hit-and-run tactics, as her brother would call them. "*You* be gone!" she shouted back. "I'm here to protect my friends, you oversized brute!"

He didn't bother to answer and lunged at her instead, his face now contorted into a scowl of fury. She didn't know how long she could keep him busy like that but resolved to do her very best. Kieran and Faith were counting on her to keep them safe, and she wouldn't let them down, no matter what!

"I've met squirrels who were faster than you!"

Aiden doubled down on his attacks and attempted to close the distance between the two of them while she toyed with him. *A few more minutes*, she told herself. A few more minutes of this and Faith would be saved.

Faith stopped pulling on the handcuffs when she realized how futile her attempt to remove them was. Aiden wouldn't make such a sloppy mistake as leaving one of them open. Instead, she started kicking her legs toward the surface as fast as she could.

She barely moved at all. In fact, it only worsened her situation. Her head felt like it was about to explode and the pain in her chest became unbearable. For an instant, she wished she could take back every mistake she had ever made. Like not following that nice boy during the Spring Festival. Or denouncing Elsa when she learned about that terrible sin her friend had committed. But most of all, she wished she had followed Breeze and Kieran when given the chance.

And then, just as the spasms were about to force her mouth open, she felt a hand grip her arm and pull her to the surface.

Fresh air filled her lungs and relieved her of the pain that had been pressing down on her. But then the water engulfed her once more, and the person who'd grabbed her arm now seized her by the collar and pulled her up.

"Put your arms around my head!" Kieran exclaimed. "No, not like that! You're going to—choke me!"

Faith held on tight while she coughed out the water that had threatened to fill her lungs. He was swimming toward the shore, she realized. It would take a while before they'd reach it, but nevertheless a wave of relief washed over her at the thought of standing on land again. She opened her mouth to thank him, but another coughing fit shook her whole body and she promptly abandoned the idea.

He'd saved her despite the obvious risk it presented to himself. Her, the daughter of the woman who'd executed his mother. This act of courage didn't match with the impression she had of Kieran, and she started to wonder what his motives could be. Then she remembered that Breeze was with him and everything fell into place.

She owed her life to both of them.

Faith looked around for the fairy. When it became obvious that she wasn't here, she asked, "Where's Breeze?"

"Distracting your knight!" he said, trying to keep his head above water.

Her stomach sank at these words and she instantly turned her gaze to the top of the cliff, where she'd stood only a few minutes ago. She couldn't see anything from this angle, and so she spurred Kieran like she would a horse. "He's going to kill her!" she exclaimed. "Hurry! We have to help her!"

"*Stop wriggling!* I'm going as fast as I can already!"

Kieran wished he could knock some sense into the inquisitor right about now, but Breeze needed their help and he didn't have time to argue with Faith about it. He pressed on, trying not to think about all the different ways the knight could have hurt her. He'd made a promise to her, and he'd be damned if he was going to let that knight make a liar out of him!

Breeze continued to taunt the knight and whirl around him, determined to annoy him long enough for Kieran and Faith to return to the shore without him noticing. She'd seen them swimming right after she avoided a particularly fast chain of attacks that almost sliced one of her wings, and she retaliated by shouting the most vicious and vile insults she could think of.

"You're slower than a caterpillar on his off day! You couldn't catch one even if I stopped and handed one to you!"

"Demon filth!"

"You're calling *me* trash? Takes one to know one!" She stuck her tongue out at him. "Nah nah nah nah nah! Catch me if you can! You're a big garbage man!"

"SILENCE!"

Aiden charged again in another futile attempt to cut her in half. He didn't appear tired at all. He must have been in great shape if he could maintain that kind of assault without even breaking a sweat—but she was a fairy of Dreamland, and not even eagles or falcons could rival her speed when she went all out!

"You might be better off fighting with a pillow!" she said. "At least you'd have a better chance of catching it!"

Aiden feigned an attack from the left and swung from a lower angle instead, only to miss her again. His intent had been so obvious! Breeze used the opportunity to fly by his head and flick the tip of his nose with the palm of her hand.

"ARRRGH!"

Breeze looked down at him with her hands on her hips and a smile on her face. Her diversion was working perfectly, and it was only a matter of time before Kieran got Faith out of the water. Until then—

Wait, the knight had stopped moving. His gaze shifted from her to the lake down below, and in that instant, Breeze knew what he'd seen. He glared at Breeze for a split second before he turned his back on her and headed down the cliffside.

He was going to intercept them before they could step onto dry land!

"Hey! You haven't beaten me yet!"

He ignored her challenge and broke into a run down the slope that led to the small rocky beach—but that didn't mean she was going to give up and let him hurt her only human friends! The fairies of Dreamland were a lot more tenacious than that!

"Hey! Big face!" Breeze flew after him and overtook him in a matter of seconds. If he wasn't going to fight her anymore, then she would have to be more forceful about it! She stopped a few leaps away in front of him and waited until the right moment before she raised her finger and drew on the magic that surrounded her.

"I WON'T LET YOU HURT THEM!"

Just as he was about to run past her, fire erupted from the tip of her finger and surged at his face. She'd only intended to conjure enough flames to stop him in his tracks, but she surprised herself when a wide ray of fire came out instead. To her tiny ears, it bellowed like an unnatural monster hungry for fresh meat, and the knight barely had time to raise his sword to try to protect himself before the flames reached him.

But the fire itself wasn't magical, only the method by which it had been summoned out of thin air.

The man screamed louder than Breeze thought possible for a human. She immediately ended the spell, but it was already too late; Aiden's whole head had been set aflame. He dropped his sword and desperately tried to put out the flames, to no avail, and began running to the edge of the cliff. Breeze could only watch in horror as he flailed around and inevitably fell into the lake, his screams resonating in her ears until they were abruptly cut off by a loud splash that shook her to the core.

It all happened in the span of a few seconds, and only after she found herself alone did Breeze understand what she had done. The magnitude of her action pressed down on her, heavy and suffocating, and she almost let it get the best of her before she remembered that Kieran and Faith would soon reach the shore.

They needed her help. She was their only friend here, and whatever else she may be feeling at the moment didn't matter as much as finding them. She should be focusing on them and not the human who threw himself off the cliff.

Then it hit her.

The other humans might have heard Aiden's screams. No—they most definitely had. They had tracked Kieran so easily before, they would surely do it again if they found out what had happened to Aiden! She had to warn them!

"We have to go back for him!" Faith said.

"You go back for him!" Kieran retorted. "I'll wait for you on the beach!"

Faith couldn't do that, of course; she would most certainly drown if she went into deep water again. She could only watch the spot where Aiden had fallen with his head on fire and pray that he would resurface on his own.

He didn't.

Kieran hoped that would remain the case and continued toward the shore, his mind now fully preoccupied by Breeze's safety. What had happened up there? He hadn't seen anything. They'd heard the knight grunt and yell at the fairy, right up until she shouted at him and did something that caused him to fall. Was it another unknown power of hers? What could possibly defeat a knight of the Purple Order fully clad in an armor created to repel magic?

Whatever it was, he first had to go check on Breeze and make sure she was safe. Nothing else mattered at the moment.

Finally, they got close enough to land that Faith could now move on her own without fear of drowning. She let go of Kieran and got out of the water just in time to see Breeze fly toward them, her blue wings a welcome sight after her brush with death. "Breeze!" Faith exclaimed. "Are you all right?"

Even with her cassock completely soaked and slowing her down, she hurried to the girl's side, her chest tightening at the mere idea that Aiden could have hurt her. Luckily for her, the fairy appeared unharmed, if a little shaken. She would have liked to make sure of that by using her power to sense for any possible injury, but the shackles restraining her would not allow it.

"You're shaking," Faith noted. "What happened?"

Kieran, having noticed the same, slid next to the inquisitor without saying a word. His small companion was on the verge of tears, and the way her lips quivered and her gaze shifted reminded him of that day twelve years ago when he ran out of the Lunaris orphanage and met Ignatios. He knew that she had done something she would regret for the rest of her life.

"I-I was trying to help," Breeze said. "I wanted to scare him off with fire, but...but..."

"You lost control," Kieran finished.

Breeze nodded as tears began to run down her cheeks, and Faith immediately stepped forward to comfort her. She knew that whatever had happened, Breeze hadn't meant to do it. She raised her hand and placed it behind the fairy, gently guiding the poor girl closer to her.

"Come here," Faith said.

Breeze understood what the inquisitor was trying to do, and she almost leaped at her neck when given the chance to hug someone. Intentionally or not, she gradually retracted her wings into her back and once they were gone, Faith carefully rubbed her back with the tip of her fingers.

"I'm sorry," Breeze sobbed. "I'm sorry…I didn't mean to. I swear, I didn't mean to!"

"Shh. It's all right, Breeze. It's all right."

"I didn't mean to!"

Breeze cried her eyes out and held on to Faith's neck as tightly as she could, never wanting to let her go. Her chest ached so much it became hard to breathe, and it reminded her of the old times when she'd hurt herself playing with her siblings and then went to Nana for comfort. The old fairy would always embrace her and pat her on the back to make her forget the pain, and as Faith did the same, for just a moment, it felt like she was back in Dreamland with the rest of her family.

Nana had warned her to use magic only in the defense of herself and others, but she had never mentioned how painful it could be to hurt other people like that—like a bear was trying to crush her little heart under its paw. She couldn't imagine that pain ever going away.

"Breeze?"

The fairy opened her eyes, surprised by the soft tone of Kieran's voice. Remembering where they were, she let go of Faith's neck and wiped away her tears. She needed to regain her composure and prepare to fly away from here. It wouldn't be long now before the other humans returned. "I'm sorry," she said. "I know we need to leave. I'll stop crying, I promise."

"Breeze—"

"I know I've only been a bother to you, but...I'll be better, okay? So please, don't send me away."

"Breeze, it wasn't your fault."

The fairy became still and stared at her friend with wide eyes. "It wasn't your fault," he repeated, more softly this time.

Tears threatened to spill out once more, but Breeze did her best to hold them back. It wouldn't do any good to cry more now, not when they were so short on time. And yet, despite the danger closing in on them, she couldn't help but sob a little at the thought that Kieran and Faith could be so kind toward her. She really didn't deserve it.

She wiped away the last of her tears and responded with a small nod. "Thank you," she sniffled.

Kieran looked away and glanced at Faith. He had no idea what she was thinking, and it embarrassed him that she'd seen all of that, but the inquisitor simply nodded at him, a sign of approval he hadn't expected.

"You should go," Faith said. "You don't have long before Lord Harrowmont's men come back here, and I won't be able to protect you from all of them."

"What? You're not coming with us?" Breeze exclaimed.

"That's crazy," Kieran said, surprising himself by agreeing with the fairy. "They'll put you in a cell and throw away the key, no matter who your mother is."

"I know, but...I just can't leave Aiden like that. Not without making sure he's still alive."

"I-I can go check on him," Breeze said. "It'll take just a moment—"

"No. You both need to get out of here. Aiden is my

responsibility, and it's my fault that he fell into the lake. If I had explained things better—"

"He would have killed you," Kieran finished for her. "Don't be an idiot. Come with us. It's the only way you can survive this."

"My life doesn't matter as much as—"

The sound of rocks grinding under boots interrupted the three of them, and they turned around to see who it could be.

It was Aiden. He was soaking wet, just like Kieran and Faith, and it seemed he had walked alongside the cliff to get here instead of swimming directly to the beach. His face, however, bore no resemblance to the man they once knew: the fire had burned the first layer of skin off, as well as his eyebrows and some of his well-kempt hair. Only a grimace of pain and fury remained, directed at the people responsible for this.

Faith gasped and stared at him, dismayed by the severity of the burns he had suffered. She wanted to heal him but remembered that the handcuffs on her wrists wouldn't allow that.

She watched as he pulled a long knife from his boot, his gaze fixed on them.

The instant he started walking toward them, Kieran summoned a fireball out of thin air and hurled it at Aiden, but it fizzled out and died like a cheap firework before it could even reach its target. Kieran was too exhausted to maintain an advanced spell like this one.

"Kieran! Don't!" Faith shouted.

Kieran ignored her and searched for something else to use, then set his gaze on the small rocks on the beach. He chose one the size of an apple and exerted his magic on it, but just as it began to rise in the air, Aiden threw his knife. In a fraction of a second, the blade flashed in the sunlight, flying directly at Kieran's chest. But then, a rush of telekinetic energy pressed on his back and pushed him to the ground.

Instead of his chest, the knife buried itself deep into his right bicep. Kieran cried out in pain and fell among the rocks on the beach, having lost his grasp on the ambient magic. It would take a while before he'd be able to draw on it again.

"Kieran!" Faith hurried to his side to examine his wound, but she stopped herself when she saw Aiden coming for her next. "Aiden, stop this! We're not—"

"Liar!" the prince shouted, his hands balled into fists, ready to strike.

Breeze aimed her magic at him, thinking about how exactly she could defeat him. She'd somehow managed to save Kieran by pushing him to the ground, but she knew by observing the knight's aura that such magic would undoubtedly fail against him. Only indirect attacks would work.

"Don't touch them!" she yelled, her previous anguish now replaced by fearful resolve. She lifted a rock twice her size from the ground and hurled it at Aiden, who swiftly dodged it while keeping his attention on the inquisitor.

Before the rock Breeze had thrown even touched the surface of the lake, Aiden picked one for himself and threw it at Faith's face. Breeze hastily knocked it aside with a bit of telenekosis, but that gave him the time he needed to close the remaining distance between him and his target. Faith, still reeling from the surprise attack, attempted to run away from the burned man, to no avail.

A few seconds later, he had his arm wrapped around Faith's neck, using her as a shield to protect himself from any other rocks while swiveling around to cover all possible angles of attack. But the only rock that remained aloft in the air was one Breeze held at her side. Aiden stopped turning and faced her instead. "Why hesitate?" he asked. "Afraid to hit her?"

Faith tried to reason with him. "Aiden—"

"You shut up!" he growled, tightening his grip around her neck. "You don't get to speak, you filthy apostate."

"Leave her alone!" Breeze shouted.

"Or what? You'll burn both of us alive? Try it! I'm at peace with God, so I'm not afraid to die here. I can't say the same for this heretic."

Faith struggled against him once more, but he was too strong. He choked her a little and she stopped, incapable of defending herself.

He continued talking as if nothing had happened. "So why hesitate?" he asked. "Do you need her alive?"

"She's my friend!" Breeze retorted. "I don't want you to hurt her!"

"Friend? Demons and fiends don't have friends. No, it's something else, and I'm going to find out what."

"I'm not a demon! I'm a fairy!"

"A lie wrapped in pretty words. I know all of your tricks. You can't deceive me."

The fairy ground her teeth at the human's stubbornness, but before she could counter with an argument of her own, Kieran interrupted them both. "Don't waste your breath on him, Breeze. He's not going to listen."

She looked back at her friend and saw that although he was clutching his wounded arm, he had managed to get up on his knees. There was blood everywhere. Even the multiple hunts she had been on with the rest of her siblings could not have prepared her for the gruesome sight of her friend bleeding. She almost lunged at him to heal him, but Kieran raised his free hand to stop her.

"Don't!" he told her, his gaze fixed on the scowling knight. "Keep your eyes on him. We don't know what he could do."

*Yes, he's right*, she thought. She had to stay calm and focus on the immediate danger for now. Aiden could easily hurt Faith if he wanted to. They had to save her! But how? One wrong move, and he'd break her neck in an instant. They had to find a solution, or else something awful was going to happen to her. She could feel it in her bones.

Faith stared at both the fairy and the sorcerer with tears in her eyes. She wasn't struggling anymore, nor did she appear hopeful of their attempt to save her. No, she had resigned herself to her fate, Breeze realized, and nothing they could say would change that. After all, Aiden had them exactly where he wanted them.

"This has gone long enough," he snarled, his expression made even uglier by the fresh burns on his face. "We all know you won't try anything, not if you want this heretic here to live. So here's what you're going to do: you're going to stand up and get the hell out of here."

Kieran let out one short chuckle before he winced in pain again. "Oh really? Then what? You'll gather your men and come after us?"

"No, we won't. I don't want these men anywhere close to you two."

Kieran stared at the knight in disbelief, unable to comprehend the logic behind that statement. They had chased him for the sole purpose of imprisoning him again, but now that he was injured and too weak to fight them off, the zealot wanted to call off the manhunt?

"You're letting us go?" Breeze asked in equal shock.

The man glared at her as if offended by her choice of words, but after a moment of consideration, he relaxed his grip on Faith's neck—almost imperceptibly—and spat his response back at her.

"*Yes*. We need an inquisitor to capture the two of you, and this tramp isn't one." He glanced at Faith as one would look at a piece of trash and then returned his attention back to the fugitive and the would-be fairy. "Leave. Now."

"Not without Faith!"

Aiden held the girl's gaze and began to squeeze Faith's neck. She gasped for air.

"Stop it!"

"Then you know what you have to do."

Breeze stood still and hesitated, her hands clenched into tiny, trembling fists. He had no right to hold Faith hostage like that. No right! She'd only tried to do what she believed was right, and this human now treated her as if she was a bad person—but she wasn't! In fact, if someone was in the wrong here, it was him! Not her!

She thought about flinging her floating rock at the man's head and knocking him out before he could do anything, but the risk was too great. She might end up hitting Faith if she attacked him from the front, and Aiden might just kill her if he sensed an attack coming from the back. Was there really nothing they could do?

Then Faith did something unexpected: she slowly nodded at her and Kieran, telling them to do as Aiden demanded. Breeze briefly considered the possibility that she was merely struggling to breathe, but the look on her face told them everything.

"Fine. We're leaving."

Breeze did a double take at Kieran when she heard him say that, and she saw him stand up to his feet, ready to turn around and leave.

"Kieran? Where are you going?"

"Away from here. There's nothing we can do, Breeze. He'll snap her neck if we even try to approach him. It's over."

"No, it's not! We can try to save her! We *have* to!"

Kieran pulled the knife out of his arm and dropped it to the ground, cursing under his breath as he placed his bloody hand on the wound. "Fuck saving her! You think I'm going to risk my life for someone like her? An inquisitor?"

"She did it for you!"

He slowly approached the blue-haired girl, looked right into her eyes, and spoke to her in a steady, lower-pitched voice. "Well, she shouldn't have. Look at where that got her." He glared at the former inquisitor, who could barely breathe because of the knight's grip on her. "She can't even save herself now."

Breeze was about to retort when suddenly she felt a filament of magic reach out of Kieran and drift to her right. It wasn't moving toward Faith and Aiden, however; it descended to the ground. The moment she realized where it was going, it wrapped itself along the whole length of the knife Kieran had dropped earlier and seized it as firmly as any hand could.

Kieran then met her gaze again and winked at her, his expression of exasperation masking his true intentions. She widened her eyes when she understood why he'd been so mean to her and almost gasped in relief, but she restrained herself and did her best to keep a straight face.

"Drop that rock and let's go," he said, his voice now dull and weary.

Then everything happened all at once.

The knife lunged forward at an unnatural speed, flying through the air faster than any arrow. She barely had time to register the blast of magic that Kieran had unleashed when she heard a short gasp as the knife hit its target. When she turned to look at where it had lodged, the whole world stopped making sense.

Blood stained the front of Faith's robe. The knife had buried itself deep into her stomach, right up to its hilt, and both Faith and Aiden were now staring at it, unable to react. Faith's legs gave out from under her and she crumpled to the ground, falling on her right side. Aiden didn't even try to hold her up as he realized how meaningless that would be. For just an instant, he seemed to forget about Breeze and Kieran, too stunned by what he had just witnessed.

"Breeze, now!"

The sound of Kieran's voice brought her back to her senses, and she turned her gaze to the knight who had threatened to kill her friend. A friend who was now lying still on the ground, bleeding to death. Shouldn't she be focusing on Faith instead? She needed healing and quick, before—

Then realization hit her, and she shifted her attention back to the man who wanted to harm them. Only a few seconds had passed since Kieran had shouted at her, but it had been enough for Aiden to recover and prepare himself for the battle ahead.

That didn't matter. She wasn't going to let him hurt her friends ever again. No matter what.

She'd always had good control over her own magic, at least when it came to talakonesis, and the rock at her side still hovered in the air despite the direness of their situation. Remembering the many lessons Nana had taught her and the rest of her siblings about magic manipulation, she carefully aimed the rock at Aiden's chest and shot it with full force.

The knight narrowly dodged it with a sidestep and pounced forward like a wolf, his expression warped into a murderous scowl. Breeze grabbed another rock with her magic and aimed it at him again, but he was almost on her already.

Kieran stepped between the two of them and slammed into the knight with his left shoulder.

"Out of my way!" Aiden took a fighting stance and hit the wound on Kieran's right arm, eliciting a cry of pain. Undeterred, Kieran threw a punch at the knight's head. Aiden deflected with ease and retaliated with a jab to Kieran's belly, followed by a right hook to his temple. Kieran doubled over and collapsed on the beach, well and truly beaten.

When Aiden turned to look at Breeze again, he saw ten more rocks levitating in the air behind her, all lined up to hit him at her command. Breeze furrowed her brow, pressed her lips together, and then shot all of her projectiles one by one. The first hit him right in the chest. The second in the belly. The third on his left shoulder. The fourth on his right forearm.

The rocks flew so fast, he had no chance to escape any of them and could only shield himself with his arms as Breeze continued to bombard him. The fifth rock hit him in his chest again while the sixth brought him down to his knees. The seventh broke his left hand and the eighth knocked him right in the gut. With the ninth rock, she curved its trajectory at the last moment and hit him right in the face, avoiding the arms that protected him. The knight stumbled and fell backward, landing on his back with a thud while his body went limp. The tenth rock hovered at her side, ready to shoot forward at the slightest movement he made.

He didn't. He was still breathing, she was sure of that, but that last attack appeared to have knocked him out. She let some more time pass just to be sure, until finally, she let go of her last projectile and dashed to Kieran, who still lay on the ground.

The sorcerer strained to sit up while he massaged his bruised cheek.

"Kieran? Are you all right?"

"Yeah, I'm fine," he said, groaning in pain.

Reassured by his answer, Breeze flew to Faith's side while preparing a healing spell. When she landed next to the priestess and examined the extent of her injury, her face blanched and she lost her breath. It was a whole lot worse than she had hoped it would be.

Blood had started to form a pool under Faith, staining her white robe more than it already had, and it continued to spread between the rocks and pebbles like rivers overflowing their banks. Breeze began to tremble as she stared at the blood, unsure of where to even start, until Faith looked at her and gave her a pained smile.

"You're all right," she croaked. "I-I was worried…"

"Don't talk too much!" Breeze replied. "I'm going to heal you."

"Heal me?"

Kieran shuffled closer to the two of them, his brow wrinkled in both worry and pain. He ignored his own injury and focused on Faith's instead.

"How bad is it?" he asked as he kneeled down next to her.

"It's bad. I need to check her wound."

Breeze closed her eyes and extended her hands over Faith's body as she gathered magic to unlock her other sight, the one that could see through people and objects. This time, however, it did not work.

"The bracelets!" she exclaimed. "We have to take the bracelets off!"

"We need the key," Kieran said.

"Aiden…" Faith murmured. "Aiden has it…"

The priestess shakily pointed at her former knight who lay unconscious on the ground. Kieran didn't waste any time and walked up to him, ready to kick him in the face if he tried anything, while he searched his pockets. It took him but a few seconds to find the key, which he then brought back to Faith and used on the manacles to allow the fairy to resume her work. Once Kieran had thrown the shackles as far away from them as he could, Breeze raised her hands again and focused on the wound. The gruesome mental image she obtained from her examination horrified her, but it wasn't worse than what the little boy had endured yesterday.

"You're bleeding inside and your organs are damaged," Breeze said, "but I should be able to take care of that. Kieran? Can you remove the knife when I tell you to?"

With no hesitation whatsoever, the sorcerer grabbed the hilt of the knife and waited for her command. "Ready when you are," he said.

"Okay." Breeze released a wave of magic intended to numb the pain, and the effects were immediately visible as the muscles in Faith's face relaxed and her breathing returned to normal.

"How…how did you learn to do that?" she asked.

"My Nana taught me," Breeze said, opening her eyes. "Now, don't move. It'll be over soon. Kieran? Pull it out now."

Her friend did as she instructed, and Faith gasped as the blade left her belly and blood started to spill everywhere.

While maintaining both the anesthetic and her second sight, Breeze cast a third spell and began to mend the gash itself. First, she stopped the bleeding and drained all of the blood from places it shouldn't be, making sure not to leave any inside. Then, she closed the wound and accelerated the natural healing process of the body until not even a scar was left behind as proof of today's events. Then came the hardest part: the restoration of the inner organs themselves.

Just like she did with the skin, she needed to maintain control over multiple spells at once—the anesthetic, the second sight, and the acceleration. However, the energy required to speed up the healing would be much greater, and she feared she didn't have the mental strength to pull this off.

Kieran watched the fairy mend the wound in silence while he avoided Faith's gaze, wary of what he might find there. She probably hated his guts right now for putting her in this state, but no other solution had come to mind. Had he aimed for Hawkon instead, the knight would have used her as a shield and she might have suffered a worse fate, one that Breeze couldn't have remedied. It was only because of what he'd witnessed back at the inn that he had been relatively confident that Faith would survive his attack.

He looked back at the unconscious knight, prepared to throw another rock at him if he so much as twitched a muscle. In Kieran's current condition, he could only manage a single telekinesis spell, but it should be enough to knock Hawkon unconscious if he threatened them again. He almost wished Hawkon would.

Then, he felt something warm on the back of his right hand. When he turned to look at it, he saw that it was Faith's hand.

"Thank you," she said as she looked up to him, a shaky smile on her face.

Kieran blinked at the unexpected gesture, uncertain on how to respond. No one had touched him like that before except for his mother, and she'd been dead twenty years now. The hell was he supposed to say? *"You're welcome"?* She was showing him gratitude when she should be cursing him instead. At least that he would understand.

"Pretty sure I almost killed you," he retorted.

"But you didn't."

Kieran shifted around uncomfortably and looked away for an instant. "Let's just call us even then."

Faith simply nodded. She understood that men like him preferred tacit understanding to frank discussions like the ones she'd had with Elsa and Inquisitor Harlow.

She slowly turned her head toward the blue-haired girl and watched her work her magic. It was the second time someone had healed her like that—the first time being after she'd broken her wrist during one of the exercises at the abbey—but this was different. This time, she understood the true nature of the power that mended her flesh. Magic was simply another instrument through which God manifested herself. Kieran had proven it when he dove into the water and saved her.

As all traces of pain slowly receded from her belly, she looked up at the blue sky and smiled, thankful to be alive.

"It's done," Breeze finally said, beads of sweat on her forehead.

"Can she move?" Kieran asked.

"I think so. Faith?"

The priestess carefully rose into a sitting position and held on to Kieran's shoulder to support herself. She half expected a pang of pain to shoot through her as she moved, but it quickly became evident that Breeze was a very skilled healer, if not Faith's equal. Once she was certain that her injury was truly gone, she stood up with Kieran's help and examined the bottom of her cassock; it was stained red everywhere.

"You're a little pale," Breeze remarked.

"It's because of all the blood I've lost," Faith said. "Don't worry. I think I'll be fine."

"I can replace the blood you've lost, if you want. Just give me a few minutes and I'll—" But before she could finish her sentence, she heard the distant barking of dogs. The three of them spun toward the lake and looked at the two sides of the shore, but they saw none of the men nearby. They still had time before they arrived.

"I hope you can run, because we gotta go," Kieran said. "We have ten, maybe fifteen minutes before they get back here."

"But what about you?" Breeze asked. "You're still injured!"

"I'll manage. With a bit of luck, they'll be too busy with Mr. Knight here to bother coming after us anyway. We just need to double back toward the road and—wait, where are you going?"

Faith had let go of Kieran's arm and was now walking confidently toward Aiden, seemingly unconcerned by the immediate danger.

"What are you doing? We gotta go, now!"

The priestess ignored him and kneeled next to the prince, her eyes drawn to the burns on his face. It wasn't as severe as she'd feared it would be, but he was bound to get an infection if left untreated for too long, and Mother Maeve was many kilometers away from here. No one else could treat his wounds.

Faith closed her eyes, took a deep breath, and then raised her hands above Aiden's face.

"Almazar, you gotta be kidding me." Kieran rolled his eyes and shook his head, turning away to go grab the knife on the beach instead.

Breeze, however, watched with bated breath as Faith slowly undid the damage she had inflicted upon the mean human. Thank the stars he wasn't going to bear these scars for the rest of his life. It was already hard to accept that she had hurt him, but to live with the knowledge that she had also disfigured him would have been unbearable. Not even he deserved that.

Breeze came closer to her priestess friend and looked over her shoulder to get a better view of his face. His skin was returning to its previous state before her very eyes, and it wouldn't take long before he completely healed. The barking also gradually became louder, and she wondered if she should not help Faith with the healing process. That might save them some time.

After some hesitation, she opted to stay silent and trust that Faith knew what she was doing.

"Are we done now?" Kieran asked, surveying their surroundings while gripping his injured arm with his left hand and holding the knife in the other.

The skin on Aiden's head finished healing as he spoke, and although there were a few patches of hair missing, his appearance had been restored thanks to Faith's magic. Breeze landed on the priestess's shoulder and grabbed her ear to support herself while she looked down at Aiden to examine his face. "Is he going to be fine?" she asked.

"Yes, he will be," Faith answered.

Breeze released all the tension in her body and breathed a sigh of relief. "Thank you," she told her friend. "I...I really didn't want to hurt him, but...he just wouldn't stop."

"Shh. It's all right, Breeze. You only wanted to protect us, didn't you?"

The fairy held back a sob and nodded.

"Then as long as you're sorry for what you did, God will forgive you."

"I'm not sure that God likes fairies."

"Well, if she doesn't, I'll be the one to forgive you."

Faith offered her a warm smile and Breeze immediately felt a little better. Only then did she realize how much she'd needed to hear these words.

"Sorry to cut this short, but can we get a move on?" Kieran asked, his eyes darting left and right. "We're really cutting it close here."

"Yes, you're right," Faith said, getting to her feet. "Let me take a look at your arm and I'll—"

"No time. Let's go." Kieran had already turned around and begun to walk away before any of his companions could utter an objection. Leaving them with no choice but to follow him, the two women exchanged a brief glance and fell into step behind him, but as soon as they started walking toward the forest, a strained voice called out after them.

"You can't run away forever."

Kieran spun around and prepared to shoot another spell at the knight, but he held off when he saw that the knight was still lying on the beach, unable to stand up on his own.

Breeze hid behind Faith's head and peeked around it to keep an eye on him. She'd had enough of fighting humans, even one as mean as him. Better to let Kieran and Faith handle this; they had much better control over their magic than she did.

"No matter where you go, the Inquisition will find you," Aiden continued, struggling to hold himself up. "*I* will find you."

The prince glared at the former inquisitor, his healed face twisted into a scowl. Faith stared right back at him, pondering how she could respond to such a blatant threat. She couldn't simply brush off or ignore the man who, only yesterday, had risked his life to protect her own. She had to say something back to him. She *had* to.

"We have to go," Kieran urged her, urgency in his voice. The barking of the dogs had grown even louder, and Faith estimated that if they kept this pace, they would arrive in less than five minutes.

Kieran was right. They really needed to get a move on.

Faith stood still for a few more seconds, debating over whether or not she should ask Aiden to pass along a message to her mother, only to decide against it. Whatever she needed to say to her should be done in person, and not through someone who had already judged and condemned her.

Faith raised a hand toward Aiden and gathered a wave of magic in front of it. "May the Kind Mother watch over you," she told him, releasing the energy in his direction.

The prince attempted to resist the effect of her spell by blinking and shaking his head, but it was futile. His eyelids closed and his body slumped back down to the ground as fatigue overwhelmed him. Once she was certain that Aiden had fallen asleep, Faith interrupted the spell and turned back to Kieran and Breeze. "Let's go."

She walked off toward the forest without sparing a glance at Aiden, resolute in the decision she had just made. Kieran followed her two steps behind, eager to finally get the hell out of here. Breeze lingered on the beach to look one last time at the slumbering knight.

Would he really come after them again? Would they have to fight him one more time? She shivered at the mere thought of it. She didn't want any of this to happen, but what else could she do? Some humans were too dangerous to reason with, she realized, and Aiden was one of them.

The fairy continued to gaze at the knight, her mind a jumbled mess of conflicting thoughts, when Kieran called out after her. "Breeze! Come on!"

"Coming!" she shouted.

She fluttered her wings to spin around and join her two friends, who were waiting at the tree line for her. She was beginning to understand why humans did so many terrible things to each other, and she hoped with all her heart that she would never have to hurt anyone else ever again to protect the people that she loved.

Because if she did, she wasn't sure she would like the person that she would become.

Nana opened her eyes and smiled, impressed by all the progress Breeze had made in the last two days. She had turned these two mages from bitter enemies to hesitant allies and brought them to her side, and—assuming this "Pyromancer" really knew how to find her—they were now on their way to meet her.

With her arms crossed and her head held high, she watched the young fairies finish building the platform upon which they stood. They were now proficient enough with their telekinesis to carry the wooden planks and nails to the top of the tree by themselves while also maintaining the spell that allowed them to levitate in the air. To think that only three years ago, they were barely able to survive on their own. Now, they didn't even need her help with the design and construction of the village's buildings. It was only a matter of time before she'd need to move on and leave these fairies on their own.

"Nana! Nana! Look at what I found!" A dark-haired boy with yellow butterfly wings flew to the tree branch she stood on and presented her with a tiny rock he held in his arms—a gold nugget.

"Hello, Raven," she said with a smile. "What's that you got here?"

"I don't know!" he happily exclaimed. "I found it while fishing at the Teary River. Have you ever seen anything like it before? It's so shiny!"

"It's called gold, Raven. A rare mineral that you usually find deep underground, but sometimes in rivers too."

"Ooh! What can we do with it?"

"Except use it as decoration, not much. We'd need to find a lot more nuggets to make anything useful out of it—although, maybe we could make a new fishing lure out of this one…"

"Because fishes like shiny stuff too?"

"That they do."

"Then I'll find some more!"

"Don't look too hard for it, Raven, or you'll be losing precious time for something that isn't very valuable. You don't want to be like those fishes who don't know any better, do you?"

"Hmm. No, I don't. I'll go back to fishing then!"

Nana smiled at him and gave him a small hug before sending him back to his chores. "Good. Be careful now."

"Always!" The boy waved goodbye at her and flew back to the ground, unaware of the importance of the lesson she had taught him.

Nana turned her gaze back to the unfinished platform and watched the fairies nail another plank of wood while she reminisced about the last day she'd spent in Dreamland. The fairies cried so much when the time had come to say goodbye, Breeze even more so. When she approached the girl to give her a hug, Breeze refused to let her go despite Bubble's and Dewdrop's best efforts to comfort her. To think that this same tearful girl had now embarked on a perilous journey to find her…she couldn't help but smile at how much Breeze had grown.

Nana closed her eyes again and reached for the girl's location with her mind once more. She had sworn to never assist her in her quest, no matter what, but that didn't mean she couldn't keep an eye on her. If anything happened, it would fall to these two mages to defend and protect her, and with the dangers that were sure to befall them soon, she wasn't sure that would be enough.

"Good luck, Breeze," she whispered.

# CHAPTER 26

*ONE DAY LATER*

INQUISITOR EDITH HARLOW walked down the hallway that led to the Mazet chapel, in the northern wing of the Apostolic Palace. The sound of her hurried footsteps echoed off the finely structured walls and vaulted ceiling of the hallway, announcing the urgency of the task that had brought her here.

Two young inquisitors who had just turned around a corner stopped and moved out of the way when they recognized the person who was moving with such haste. Inquisitor Harlow didn't even spare them a glance as she continued to her destination, her right hand clutching a roll of parchment that bore the broken seal of the Hawkon family. It didn't take long before she finally reached the two large doors of the chapel and pushed them open, interrupting the grand inquisitor's moment of prayer.

Karolina immediately arose from the kneeler in the front row and turned to see who had interrupted her. She raised her eyebrows in surprise when she recognized the older inquisitor. Realizing that something very serious must have happened, she abandoned her prayer and went to meet her sister in the center aisle, her brow now furrowed in worry.

"Edith? What has happened?"

The inquisitor didn't say a word and swiftly handed the letter to her. Karolina's first thought went to the Ophicians and their assault on the Azarian Realms, and she surmised that they must have launched a surprise attack on one of the other kingdoms. But then she saw the emblem of Kantner's royal family on the parchment—a hawk flanked by two wolves—and her heart sank.

She snatched the parchment out of Edith's hand and unrolled it as fast as she could, her eyes darting back and forth over the contents of the page. Inquisitor Harlow, a grim look on her face, waited patiently for her superior to finish reading it. She knew what this news would do to the grand inquisitor and had come prepared for it. She was merely waiting for her to give the order.

"Who else knows about this?" Karolina asked, her voice seething with anger.

"No one else but us and Sir Hawkon," Edith answered.

"What about Lord Harrowmont's men? Do they really believe she's merely been kidnapped?"

"This happened only yesterday, ma'am, so I can't say for sure, but I do believe that Sir Hawkon wouldn't spread this around, especially not to Lord Harrowmont."

"Good. Then prepare the carriage. We're leaving at once."

"It's already waiting for you, ma'am."

The grand inquisitor handed the letter back to her subordinate and marched toward the double doors with fire in her eyes. Nothing mattered more in this moment than saving her daughter from the sorcerer and demon who had duped her, and if she had to move heaven and earth to do it, then so be it.

May the Kind Mother have mercy on anyone who dared get in her way.

Kieran examined the small clearing he and his two companions had stumbled upon and decided that it would make for a suitable campsite, at least for tonight. There was enough grass for the horses to graze upon, plenty of wood they could use to make a fire, and a source of water not too far back the way they'd come. All they were missing was some booze and everything would be perfect. "We'll stop here for tonight," he said, dismounting from his horse.

"Are you sure?" Faith asked. "We still have a couple of hours of sunlight left. We can keep going."

"You saw the marker back on the road. We're out of... what's-his-name?"

"Lord Harrowmont?"

"Yeah, him. We're out of Harrowmont's territory, so he can't send his men after us without pissing off the local lord or whatever. We'll be safe here, at least for tonight."

"'Pissing off'?" Breeze repeated, sticking her head out of Faith's hood. "What does that mean?"

"Uh..." *Shit*, Kieran thought. Now he had to explain crude language to her. "It's another way of saying that you annoy someone," he answered hesitantly.

"Oh, okay."

"Maybe don't use those words yourself," Faith added as she dismounted from her white mare. "They wouldn't suit a nice girl like you."

"You think so? Then I'll make sure to only use good words from now on!" The fairy smiled, deployed her blue butterfly wings, and flew up in the air to examine the clearing Kieran had selected as their campsite. "Ooh! This is nice. You really made the right choice stopping here for tonight. Can we light a fire this time? Last night was so gloomy because we couldn't."

"Sure," Kieran said. "The road is far enough away that we can risk it."

"Awesome! I'm gonna go gather some wood!" The fairy zipped through the air without waiting for approval and was already on the other side of the clearing when Kieran called out to her.

"Don't go too far!" he shouted.

"Okay!" She then disappeared behind the trees, eager to get to work.

Kieran grabbed the reins of his stallion and led it to a leafy tree with low branches he could hitch the horse to. Faith removed the gray cloak she had been wearing since yesterday to hide her identity and followed him farther down the tree line with the reins of her mare in hand. She had discarded her bloody white robe and changed into the one that Lord Harrowmont's servants had washed; it still had a pink stain around the left side of her chest, where Kieran had shot her two days ago.

It made her far too recognizable.

"Do you think it's wise?" Faith asked. Kieran turned to look at her over his shoulder. "Sending Breeze out there all alone, I mean," she added.

"You're worried about her?"

"It's hard *not* to. She's like a child."

"She'll be fine," Kieran said, waving his hand in dismissal before attaching his reins to the lowest bough of a large oak tree. "I'm more worried about your clothes. We need to find you something else to wear, and soon, or we'll have new inquisitors coming after us."

Faith didn't respond and instead walked up to his left to secure her reins to another bough. *This must be a sore subject for her*, Kieran thought, and he decided to avoid bringing it up again. At least for now. Best to focus on more pressing matters, like their food situation.

The sorcerer opened one of the satchels on the saddle of his horse, took a small bag out of it, and began rummaging through it, trying to figure out how long their provisions would last.

"You'll need a change of clothes too," Faith said.

"Hmm? These are fine for now," he replied. "I just look like any other peasant."

"Not really, but it's your shoes you should change. They were made to track you down more easily."

"What?" Kieran closed the bag and looked at the sole of his shoes: they had cleats placed in a pattern that would leave a distinctive footprint each time he took a step. "Fucking hell."

"The lieutenant who was with us told me about it. Said he was the one who came up with the idea."

"Taking a page out of the Ophicians' book, huh? I shouldn't be surprised." The sorcerer clicked his tongue and surveyed the clearing for a spot where they could rest for the night, then walked farther down the tree line as he picked out the place where Breeze had disappeared into the forest.

"What do you mean?" Faith asked, following close behind him.

"About what?" he said.

"The Ophicians. What do they have to do with this?"

"It's just something I heard once. That all their slaves wear shoes like these in case they ever try to escape."

"Do they really?"

"Never saw it for myself, but that's what I heard."

"From this 'Ignatios' you spoke of?"

"Yeah. Him."

Faith contemplated the disturbing parallel Kieran had made between the Ophician sorcerers and her own people, only to realize that she wasn't an inquisitor anymore. In fact, she wasn't sure she even qualified as Azarian either. No doubt her mother and the rest of the Inquisition would soon disavow her, seeing as how she had freed Kieran and opposed Aiden. It wasn't her place to pass judgment on her people anymore; she would have to leave that responsibility to the priestesses and inquisitors who hadn't abandoned their duties.

Kieran plopped down to the ground, leaned back against the trunk of a tree, and sighed as he released all the tension in his body. Faith wordlessly spread her cloak on the ground and sat opposite him, her mind still focused on the life she had left behind and the people she would never meet again. Neither of them said anything for a long while, feeling more comfortable listening to the chirping of the birds and the rustling of the leaves than striking up a conversation with each other.

Finally, Faith gathered enough courage to look into Kieran's eyes and say, "I'm sorry. For not looking immediately at your wound after Breeze healed me."

The apology took Kieran by surprise, and he blinked at her as he attempted to understand the reason for it. "Um…don't worry about it," he said. "It wasn't very serious anyway."

"Yes, it was. You might have lost your arm if I hadn't looked at it."

He didn't respond.

"I would have drowned without you," Faith continued, "and the first thing I did after you healed me was to go check on Aiden. I'm sorry. I should have looked at you first."

Kieran found it hard to maintain eye contact with the priestess. He shifted his gaze back to the calluses on his hands instead. "You don't owe me a thing," he said. "Much less an apology."

"But you saved my life."

"Yes, and then I stabbed you in the stomach."

"To save me from Aiden," she continued, now frowning at him. "Why are you making this so difficult?"

He briefly glanced at her and fiddled with his hands as he pondered the question. "I told you: we're even."

"You're not used to people apologizing to you, are you?"

Kieran winced and turned his face away from her. He couldn't have been more obvious about it if he tried.

"Well, I'm still sorry for what I did," she said. "For that, and for throwing you into prison. I hope you'll find it in your heart to forgive me."

The silence between the two of them returned, and Faith turned her attention to the flowers that peeked out of the grass, hoping that they might distract her from the awkwardness of the situation. She was about to stand up and excuse herself when, out of the blue, the sorcerer spoke.

"I'm sorry for almost killing you."

Faith froze, shocked to hear him give an apology of his own, and she hurriedly responded lest he decide to take it back. "I told you, it's fine. I understand it was the surest way to save me from Aiden. If you had tried to aim at him instead of me, he would have—"

"No. I meant back at the field, outside Ballybridge. I'm sorry for almost killing you there." Kieran avoided Faith's gaze while he preoccupied himself with a small rock on the ground between his feet. He couldn't quite believe he had said that, and for an instant he wished he had just shut his mouth and pretended everything was fine.

"I forgive you."

Her response came so quickly, Kieran gave her an incredulous look when he heard it. He couldn't remember anyone saying these words to him—ever—and when he saw the faint smile on Faith's face, he knew they were genuine.

"I'm back!" It was Breeze, flying through the trees with a small pile of twigs and branches floating behind her. Oblivious to what had just occurred, she put down the kindling between the two mages and puffed out her chest as she presented the results of her efforts to them. "Look! There are all sorts of trees in this forest! Oak trees, leafy beeches, and even red ashes! I also brought the bark of a fallen tree. That should help with the fire, right?"

"Thank you, Breeze," Faith said. "You're right. That should burn nicely once we get a fire going."

"Now we're only missing a few logs, and we're set! But I've never been really good at cutting wood with my magic. My brothers and sisters usually took care of that. So, what were you two talking about? Kieran has a weird look on his face."

The man in question twitched at the sudden accusation and did his very best to keep a straight face. "Nothing important," he said. "Just making small talk."

"Hmmmm?" The fairy placed a finger on her lips and peered into his face. "Are you sure? I think you might be blushing."

"It's true. We were just having a friendly chat," Faith said, her mouth still curved into a smile.

"Oh, that's good then! You should have more of those! I'll go gather some more wood so we have enough for the whole night. Don't start supper without me, okay?"

"We wouldn't dream of it."

The fairy waved at them and then flew deeper into the forest. Kieran let out an imperceptible sigh of relief once she had left, and he began rummaging through the sack of provisions for a second time, certain that Faith could see right through him. Thankfully, the priestess didn't say anything and simply admired the flowers in the clearing while he finished counting the provisions. This provided him the perfect excuse to escape and go for a stroll alone in the forest.

"We need more food," he said, standing up. "I'll go hunt while we still have sunlight."

"Hunt? How are you going to hunt?" Faith asked.

Kieran raised an arm and mentally tugged at the dagger he had taken from Aiden, which was strapped to one of the saddlebags of his horse. The blade flew across the clearing and landed in his hand, completely clean after he'd washed it in a brook yesterday afternoon. It wasn't the kind of weapon he would usually use, but it would suit his immediate need to provide for the two women he now traveled with.

"I'll be back before sunset," he said, following the same path Breeze had taken. But before he could disappear into the forest, Faith called out to him.

"Kieran?"

The sorcerer stopped at once and looked back at the priestess, hoping that she wouldn't tease him, while at the same time, not really minding if she did. One peek at her serious expression, however, reminded him of the few occasions his mother would take him aside and have a serious talk with him. "Yes?" he said, waiting for her to continue.

"Thank you," she replied.

Kieran stood there in silence while his heart skipped a beat. His first thought was to turn around and flee, but he knew it would only make their future interactions all the more awkward if he did. Instead, he nodded and waited until she'd responded with a nod of her own before he turned away and walked deeper into the woods.

Once the sorcerer was out of her sight, Faith stood up from her spot and headed toward the horses. She thought she might as well tend to them while she waited for her companions to return. She didn't mind that Kieran was so reserved when talking about his feelings—not after he'd made the effort to apologize to her. It was a lot more than she had expected from him, to be honest, and she knew that if she gave him enough time, then he might open up more about himself one day.

Until then, she could rest easy knowing that she had made the right decision saving him. And hopefully, he felt the same about her.

Kieran returned to camp just as the sun was setting over the horizon and the hues in the sky shifted from bright purple and red to a uniform blue. The first thing he noticed as he approached the clearing was the shining glow of a fire burning where Breeze had placed the kindling, followed by the distinct sound of two people laughing. No doubt that it was Breeze and her cheerful attitude that were responsible for that the joyous chatter. He wondered what story she could have told that would provoke such genuine laughter from Faith.

"—and then, we all had to go wash ourselves because of how sticky we were! That was the messiest we've ever been!"

"I can't believe you managed to win that. You're so slim and tiny, I can't imagine you with apple pie all over your face."

"Oh, I did feel sick for a whole day after that. *That* wasn't really fun. But then Bubble watched over me and made sure I didn't eat anything too heavy for my stomach, so it's still one of my favorite days ever."

"Bubble—that's your closest brother, right?"

"Yeah. We live together—uh, lived together—ever since we first built our houses. He's the best."

"I wish I could have met him."

"Yeah, me too…. I'm sure he would have—oh, hey Kieran! You're back!"

Kieran emerged from the tree line and stepped into the light of the campfire. The two women were sitting on a cloak Faith had laid down on the ground earlier, right next to a small circle of rocks that prevented the flames from spreading to the forest. Breeze had also gathered a decently large pile of wood, Kieran noticed, one that would most certainly last them through the night if they kept someone on watch.

"Oh! You've found some rabbits!" Breeze exclaimed.

The fairy stood up from her crossed-legged position and ran up to him with childlike wonderment in her eyes. Evidently, the sight of blood didn't affect her as much when it originated from an animal and not a human—an understandable consequence of living in the woods for so long, he surmised. What he didn't expect from her was to greet him with such a genuine smile, not when he was holding two dead rabbits in his right hand and a dagger in his left one. Maybe he'd underestimated how resilient she could be in the face of death. She'd been willing to fight Aiden head on, after all.

"Are you all right?" she asked him. "You've been gone for so long."

"Yeah, I'm fine," he answered. "It just took me a long time to find these rabbits."

"Were they hiding very well?"

"Hunting's never been my strong suit, that's all."

"Oh, I can teach you if you want. My brother Cosmo taught me a bunch of nice little tricks for tracking animals in the forest. I'm sure he wouldn't mind if I shared them with you."

"Uh, thanks. I could use the help."

"No problem! Now, put the rabbits on the ground. Not too close to the fire, though, or it will burn their fur."

"Sure, but why?"

"So we can pay our respects, of course."

Kieran raised an eyebrow at that but did as she asked. Breeze thanked him with a nod and joined her hands together, placing her right hand on top of her left while she lowered her head. But before she could begin, Faith leaned forward and asked her, "Breeze? Is there something we can do?"

"Huh?" The girl raised her head and looked at the priestess. "We just pay our respects, that's all."

"But is there something we should say?"

"No, not really. Wait, don't you guys pay respects to the animals you kill?"

"No," Kieran replied.

"I can't say I've ever heard of this custom before either," Faith confirmed.

"Whaaaaat?" Breeze looked back and forth between her two friends, her mouth agape. "Not even a little 'sorry'?"

"Um, no," Kieran said as he sat down, now feeling a little uncomfortable. "Why? Is it that important to you and your siblings?"

"Of course it is! The poor rabbits...they had a life and a family, and it was taken away from them. The least we can do is tell them how sorry we are and assure them that their deaths will not be in vain. Otherwise, we're just meanies!"

Tears welled up in the corners of her eyes as she talked, and Kieran suddenly regretted opening his mouth. She could be very sensitive about the weirdest of things.

"We do something similar," Faith suddenly said, having moved into a kneeling position on her cloak. "But it's usually done right after the meal has been served."

"Huh? Really? Why not before?" the fairy asked.

"Because not everyone hunts for their food, Breeze. They have to give their thanks to someone else, so they give it to God instead."

"Ooh! Now I see. And you do it often?"

"At every meal. I'm sure Kieran has also done it before, right?"

"Back when I was younger, yeah," he said. "Can't say I remember how the prayer goes."

"I can recite it once the meal is ready. For now, please continue what you were doing. I'm sorry for interrupting you."

"No, that's all right!" Breeze said. "I'm always glad to learn more about the customs you guys have."

Breeze exchanged a smile with the priestess before she faced the dead animals once more. Faith followed suit by joining her hands together and lowering her head, assuming a position that Kieran, having lived in an Azarian orphanage, was very familiar with. He didn't want to give Breeze the wrong idea by pretending that he cared about this tradition, but he nevertheless bowed his head and stayed silent so as to not disrespect her feelings on the matter.

For the next minute or so, the only sounds they could hear were the crackling of the flames and the chirping of the crickets, which made for a soothing ambient noise that Kieran rarely had the chance to experience. It was so calm and serene out here that it was difficult to believe that only two days ago, he was sitting in a dark cell searching for a way to kill himself. How did he get here? It felt so surreal.

Fairies were supposed to be creatures of folklore, whimsical entities that sometimes appeared in tales to play tricks on people or assist them in their quest. They weren't supposed to be real. And yet, here she was, standing right in front of him. Evidently, his assumptions about magic and every mystery connected to it were wrong.

Just like he had been wrong about Faith. And Faith had been wrong about him.

"There!" Breeze exclaimed, clapping her hands together. "Now we can skin the rabbits and prepare them for our meal. Do you know how to do that?"

"Just the basics. Most of what I know about hunting I figured out on my own."

"Okay then. If you need any help, don't hesitate to ask!"

"Thanks."

"And what about you, Faith?" Breeze asked. "Do you know how to skin an animal?"

"Um, no," she answered, clearly caught off guard. "I've never had to do it before."

"Never? Never ever? Not even once in your life?"

"No. Very few people in the city do—except for the butchers, of course."

"Oh, right. Kieran told me about them. That's fine, you can learn about it now! Don't worry, it's very simple. And you get used to the sight of blood, I swear."

"Very well then. I'll watch while you work on that."

For the next half hour or so, Kieran skinned both rabbits while Breeze watched over him, pointing out what he was doing wrong and teaching him more efficient ways to remove the skin and cut the meat. Although Faith looked a little sick once she saw the skinless bodies of the dead animals, she didn't avert her gaze and listened attentively to everything Breeze had to say. By the time they were ready to cook the rabbits, the twilight sky had been replaced by a tapestry of stars that gleamed more beautifully than Kieran remembered them ever being. A side effect of his recent brush with death, surely.

Since they didn't have the tools or the time to tan the hides, Breeze suggested they bury them at the base of a tree alongside the innards and the bones, so nothing would go to waste. Kieran volunteered for this task and chose a spot at the opposite side of the clearing while Faith and Breeze prepared the meat and cooked it above the fire. When he came back to the campfire, supper was ready.

"Here!" Breeze said, using telekinesis to hand him a stick with his portion on it. "Don't burn your mouth."

"Thanks," he replied.

"Faith is the one who cooked it."

"Oh, uh… Thank you, Faith."

"You're welcome," she said with a shy smile.

"Now it's eating time! Oh no, wait. You also have to give thanks for the meal, right?"

"This is usually when I would do it, yes."

"All right then. We'll wait until you're finished."

Kieran was about to take his first bite when Breeze said that. Feeling a little embarrassed, he stopped himself and opted to wait before he started eating. No doubt Breeze would admonish him if he didn't.

The priestess planted her stick of meat into the ground and joined her hands together once more. To his surprise, Breeze was eager to participate in this blessing and did the same thing. She'd probably recite the words too if she knew the prayer.

"O Kind Mother," Faith said, "bless this meal which we are about to receive so that we may gain the strength to carry on thy will. And for this day, for our friends, and for this food, we thank thee. *Itafiat.*"

Faith then opened her eyes and with a nod of her head confirmed to Breeze that the prayer was over. With a wide grin on her face, the fairy called upon her magic to remove the single piece of meat from her stick. Once it was within reach, she grabbed it with her tiny hands and threw the stick into the fire, where it burned quite nicely. Then, as if she had been waiting for the chance to say this, she took a deep breath and exclaimed, "Eat earthy!"

At first, Kieran thought they would be eating in silence, but he had greatly underestimated Breeze's capability to hold a conversation between the ravenous bites she took. Not that he minded it; in fact, he quite enjoyed listening to her talk about the herbs and spices her siblings would use with their meals, and she expressed her regret of not searching for some while he was hunting the rabbits—it would have added more flavor to the meat.

She nevertheless happily nibbled on her meal like it was the greatest thing she'd had all year while conversing with Faith about her favorite recipes for outdoor eating. "That reminds me," she said, "we'll need to smoke the rest of that meat before going to sleep." She looked at the untouched flesh of the other rabbit.

"Smoke it?" Kieran repeated. "Don't we need to build some sort of tent for that?"

"Usually, yeah, but we can also do it by digging a hole in the ground!"

"Really?" Faith asked. "Is it something your Nana taught you?"

"Yes! She's really smart! I can't wait for you two to meet her."

"Meet her?" Faith gave Kieran a questioning look, to which he responded with a shrug.

"I told you Kieran was helping me find her, remember?" Breeze continued. "You'll come with us too, right?"

Faith hesitated for a second. "Should I?" she asked. "Accompanying you might not be a good idea."

"Why not? You're my friend now, and friends stick together!"

"But the Inquisition—"

"—is already looking for me," Kieran finished. "Besides, it's not like you have somewhere else to go, do you?"

"No," the former inquisitor admitted.

"Then it's decided!" Breeze said, happy to have a new companion along on the journey. "And don't worry, we'll protect you from the Inquisition if they send baddies after you. Right, Kieran?"

Kieran stopped chewing on his food while he tried to think of an appropriate answer. He'd never been asked to protect someone else before, not without the promise of gold at the end of it. "I'm pretty sure she can protect herself just fine," he said. "But sure. It's best that we stick together."

"Well, in that case…" Faith said, a smile forming on her face. "Yes, I'll join you."

"Great!" the fairy exclaimed.

"There's just one thing I'd like to know more about," Faith asked.

Both Kieran and Breeze turned to look at her.

"It's about this Nana you mentioned. You told me she's the one who raised you, correct?"

"Yup, that's her."

"And you've left your village to find her?"

"Yes. She told us she was going somewhere east to wake up more fairies, but I don't know where exactly. Kieran said he had an idea on how to find her, though."

"I'm not sure I understand. She *chose* to leave your village?"

"Yeah. Why, is that weird?"

"No, I was just under the impression that you were trying to rescue her."

"Oh no, she doesn't need rescuing! At least, I hope she doesn't."

"Then why are you trying to find her?"

Breeze fell silent as she pondered the best way to answer that question. Kieran knew it wasn't as simple as wanting to see her again. It was a lot more complicated than that.

"Because she lied to me and the rest of my family," Breeze finally said, her brow furrowed. "She knew all about the human world and the people living there, but she never told us anything about it. If she really wanted to protect us from the bad humans, then she should have prepared us by teaching us more about them—who they were and how to defend ourselves from them. But she didn't, and I want to know why."

"Is she the one who taught you how to use magic?"

"Yeah, she is. She didn't teach us everything she knew, though."

"Why not?"

"She told us we should learn the rest by ourselves."

"And what about my magic? My…'spells'? Can you do any of them, other than healing?"

Breeze shook her head. "I don't know how to create that shield or that glowy staff you have. I didn't even know it was possible to stop magic from being used until Kieran told me about it."

"I see." Faith lowered her stick and turned her gaze to the fire burning before her, her forehead wrinkled in doubt.

"What about your knight's armor?" Kieran asked. "Why didn't it stop you from healing him?"

Breeze widened her eyes at that observation and swiveled her head toward the priestess. "That's right!" she said. "We couldn't use our magic directly on him, but you did! How?"

Unperturbed, Faith continued to stare at the flames while she calmly answered their question. "Inquisitors have always been able to heal the injuries of their knights," she explained. "If I had to take a guess as to why, I'd say it's because the armor they wear has been 'consecrated' to allow it."

"Sleeping spells, too?"

"Yes. People can usually resist that one, but Aiden was far too weak. We use it to put the wounded to sleep."

Kieran nodded and took another bite from his stick; he had deduced as much when he saw her mend the knight's injuries. But the answer seemed to affect Breeze more than he'd expected, as she was now staring at the minuscule piece of meat in her hands instead of eating it.

"What's wrong?" he asked her.

"I don't know," she said. "It's just…I thought me and my brothers and sisters were the ones who didn't know anything, but it's even worse for you."

"How so?" Faith asked.

Breeze lifted her head to meet their gaze. "You thought your magic was something the other didn't have, and that was enough for you to try to kill each other. Even now, you can't sense other people's magic, can you? Not even my own. Why? Did someone lie to you like my Nana did to us?"

Kieran exchanged a glance with Faith as they both considered this new possibility. It was true that Ignatios had kept many secrets from him, and one of them could very well have been about the true nature of the Church and the members of its clergy. But as for Faith…

"No, I don't think so," she said. "I think… I think all of the priestesses and the inquisitors really believe they're the only ones who are blessed with God's power."

"Hmph. You still believe that God exists?" Kieran remarked.

"Maybe not like I did before, but yes, I do."

Kieran finished his meal and threw his stick into the dwindling fire, a little annoyed by Faith's unwavering conviction. He wasn't interested in starting an argument with her about it, however, and chose to answer Breeze's question instead. "I don't know if the man who trained me was aware of the Church's delusion," he said, "but I wouldn't be surprised if he was. It sounds just like the sort of thing he would keep a secret from me."

"Why would he do that?" Breeze asked.

"Dunno. Maybe it was another one of his tests to see if I could figure out the truth on my own. The sly bastard."

"Maybe *that's* why Nana told us to never leave our village."

Kieran and Faith both looked at each other, confused as to what she meant by that.

"Can you elaborate?" Faith asked.

The fairy started nibbling on her meat once again, an innocent look on her face. "Hmm? Ya don'd ge' id?"

They both shook their heads.

"I thing"—she swallowed the rest of her food— "I think she may have been testing us."

"Testing you?" Faith repeated. "Why?"

"I'm not sure why, but it's the only thing that makes sense! Nana was very smart, so she should have known that one of us would leave Dreamland one day."

"Do you think she wanted you to find her?"

"Maybe. She only said that she was going east, so I don't know where to look for her—but Kieran does! Right, Kieran?"

The fairy turned to look at him, certain that he had the answer to her problem. He couldn't say that he shared her confidence in this matter, but he did have a pretty good idea of where to begin their search. He only hoped that he wouldn't disappoint her in the end. "I won't say that I'm absolutely sure of my guess, but yeah—I think I know how to find her."

The two women waited with anticipation for him to continue.

"First, we'll have to go to Firstkin, where the royal archives are. The place is going to be very well guarded, so we'll need help to get in—"

"Wait," Faith said. "The *royal* archives? Are you serious?"

"Yes. That's where we'll find the information we need. Lucky for us, I know a few people in the city who owe me a favor or two. They can help us get inside the building. Once we have the information we need, we get out without raising any alarm, and hopefully no one will ever notice we were there."

"What are we looking for?" Breeze asked.

"Records of every royal reserve that exists in Kantner. *That's* where I think your Nana has gone to."

The fairy blinked at him, not fully grasping the significance of this revelation. "What's a royal reserve?" she asked.

"It's a forest no one is allowed to touch, not without the king's permission," Faith answered, somewhat stunned. "So that's where you've been living?"

"Um, I don't know. Kieran?"

"I heard it from the farmers who tried to rob me a few days ago just outside your forest. Breeze's village is on a royal reserve."

"A few days ago?" Faith said. "Then that means…"

"Yes. Her village is only a few leagues out of Ballybridge."

Faith gawked at him like he had grown two horns or something; it seemed she'd just realized how he had tricked her into believing Breeze's village was much farther away than it actually was. She'd never even considered the possibility that it could be so close.

"So, I've been living in a royal reserve?" Breeze asked.

Kieran nodded. "That's why you haven't seen any other human before me. Entering a reserve is forbidden under pain of death."

"Then...if we find another reserve east of here, we'll also find Nana?"

"Hopefully, yes."

"That's great!"

"Wait, no," Faith interrupted. "Why do we have to go into the royal archives to find where the reserves are? Couldn't we just travel east and ask people about them?"

"We can't risk that," Kieran said, shaking his head. "We're fugitives now, Faith. The Inquisition and the highborn in Kantner will be looking for us, and if they learn that we've been asking where the royal reserves are, they'll start looking into them."

"And then they'd find Breeze's family."

"Exactly."

"We can't let that happen!" Breeze exclaimed.

"No, we can't," Kieran agreed. "That's why we're breaking into the royal archives. That's where we'll find the information we need."

The fairy nodded. "That's a good plan. I like that plan."

"Easier said than done," Faith retorted. "We still need to break into one of the most well-guarded places in all of Kantner."

"Huh?" said Breeze. "Why is it so well protected?"

"Because the archives are located inside the royal palace," Kieran explained. "That's where the king lives. Remember what I told you about the kings?"

"Oh, right! They're the leaders of the human kingdoms. They're loud and scary and they all wear a big crown!"

"That's right."

"Please, Kieran," Faith said. "Don't give her any wrong ideas."

"About what? The kings?"

"Yes."

"You're saying they're none of those things?"

"I'm only saying that you haven't met any of them."

"Neither have you. Until then, they're big, beardy men with egos the size of their castles. Right, Breeze?"

"Right!"

The two of them laughed, and Faith couldn't help but smile along with them. It was crazy, but after everything they'd been through these last few days, this certainly was a nice change of pace. She would have liked the moment to last longer, but she needed to address a few concerns first—not for her own sake but for Breeze's. "Are we sure this is the only way?" she asked Kieran.

"Without tipping off the Inquisition about our goal? Yes. I'm sure. But if you have a better idea…"

"No. I don't."

"Then it's settled!" Breeze said, standing while putting her fists on her hips. "Tomorrow morning, we're going to Fistkane to find out where Nana has gone to—"

"Firstkin," Kieran corrected.

"—and if she's really at one of those royal thingamajigs, then she won't be able to stay hidden for long! We'll meet her, have a nice long talk with her, and then celebrate our reunion with a big picnic! Easy peasy!"

Breeze punctuated her declaration with a radiant smile, one so bright that both Kieran and Faith momentarily forgot about their uncertainties and fears.

For Kieran, it was the apprehension of once again meeting the crooks and thugs he once called "mates." For Faith, it was the anxiety brought about by the monumental task they had to accomplish, one that might very well end their lives. But right now, these concerns didn't seem as important as the fairy standing in front of them. It seemed her very presence would be enough to tilt the odds back in their favor.

The blue-haired girl looked at both of them, a twinkle of confidence in her lovely green eyes, and with the most cheerful voice ever, she asked them, "So who wants to learn how to fly?"

# EPILOGUE

*TWO DAYS LATER*

ADONIS WALKED DOWN the street that led back to his home, a lantern in his hand. The rain that'd started to fall when he left Lord Harrowmont's keep was now swelling into a heavy downpour, and he knew that by the time he got home, he would be completely drenched. Nevertheless, he quickened his pace, hoping he could at least save his underwear.

A patrol of two constables, resigned to their fate, walked toward him from the other end of the street, spears in hand. The one on the left, Jacob, raised his lantern when he noticed the lone man approaching them. When he recognized Adonis, a grin appeared on his blemished face and he hollered a greeting: "Lieutenant! What are you doing out here at this hour? Going for a walk, maybe? You know you're going to catch a cold if you stay out here for too long, right?"

"Fuck you too, Jacob," Adonis said, not bothering to slow down for them.

"Aww. We love you too, Lieutenant!"

His partner, Harry, laughed and urged him to keep moving. "Ignore him, Lieutenant. You have a good night now."

"You too."

Adonis left the duo behind and headed farther down the street. Since most of the townspeople had already gone to sleep, the only source of light came from his lantern, which made shadows dance on the houses around him. That and the sound of the rain pouring down on the cobblestone street made Adonis feel like he was walking through an abandoned city.

Finally, he reached the threshold of his house—a small two-story building with closed shutters that were long overdue for a new coat of paint. Adonis wasted no time unlocking the door, already thinking about the bliss he would feel once he'd be out of these clothes and armor.

The lieutenant entered the house and closed the door behind him. Because he lived alone, his only welcomers were the sounds of the rain falling on the roof and the water dripping from his clothes. Adonis placed the lantern on the shelf fixed next to the door and began taking off his clothes. He'd always hated wearing that yellow surcoat, even though he had gotten used to it over the years. It was a constant reminder of the life he had left behind.

Adonis grabbed a towel from the coat rail and dried himself with it. He then picked his change of clothes from the shelf—he always kept one there just in case—and savored the moment when the soft fabric touched his skin. That was the best part of his day. Everything else had been pretty shitty in comparison.

After he put on the pair of indoor shoes he kept beside the front door, he grabbed the lantern again and headed for the kitchen in the back, leaving his wet clothes to dry on the coat rail. He needed to eat something before he went to bed. But the instant he put his hand on the handle of the pantry door, a voice called out to him from the dark corner of the room. "Hello, Adonis."

Adonis immediately jumped away from the intruder and almost knocked down the lantern he'd placed on the counter. He grabbed a knife, his heart pounding in his chest as he faced the man—no, the woman—who was standing only six podes away from him. She didn't move a muscle and seemingly kept staring at him, even though her eyes were covered by the hood of her gray cloak. It was then that Adonis realized she had used his real name.

"Are you expecting anyone else tonight?" she asked in an almost mellow tone.

Adonis gazed at the hooded intruder, uncertain of her identity. He had never met her before, of that he was certain, but he knew that to meet him here like this, she had to be a high-ranking member of the organization.

"Please lower the knife," she said. "You won't be needing it."

Adonis hesitated for a couple of seconds before he asked a question of his own. "Who's the king of Kantner?"

"A deluded madman who believes in a heartless mother," she answered, matter-of-factly. "Now, are you expecting anyone else tonight?"

Now certain that this woman was indeed an ally, Adonis lowered his knife and put it back on the counter, next to the lantern. "No," he said, a little calmer than before. "Not unless there's an emergency at the keep."

"Is your cover intact?"

"Yes. No one suspects anything."

The woman walked to the window located above the kitchen counter to look into the small back alley that ran parallel to the street—except that she couldn't see anything, Adonis noticed. Her eyes were covered with a black blindfold that should have hindered her movements, and yet she knew exactly when to stop and where to put her hand so it would rest on the counter.

Without sparing him a glance—if she could even do that— she conjured a tiny ball of white light right in front of her, then made it flicker in and out of existence in a standardized sequence of two different signal durations. It was a code he couldn't decipher, but the meaning behind it was clear.

Adonis turned his gaze to the small door that led to the back alley and waited. He knew who the woman was now. There was only one person in the whole organization who wore a blindfold like hers. He wasn't supposed to know that, however, and he made a mental note to never reveal anything to her about it. No doubt she would eliminate him if he did.

But what really made his heart race was the knowledge that in a few seconds, *that* man would step into this room. He was the only person who could be traveling with the blind woman.

The door opened with a creak that made Adonis's stomach churn, and he repressed the urge to wipe his sweaty hands on his pants. He couldn't afford to look weak.

The door closed with a quiet thud, and a middle-aged man stood before him, unremarkable in his appearance. Just like his aide, he wore a long gray cloak that concealed the weapons he was surely carrying underneath it. Unlike her, he chose to pull back his hood and reveal his face to Adonis.

"Greetings, Adam Kidd," the man said with a disarming smile. "That is your name in this town, correct?"

"It is, sir."

"Good. Mind if we switch back to your real name?" The man surprised Adonis by removing his wet cloak, which he placed on the kitchen counter as if he'd just come back from a hard day at work. He wore simple traveler's garb, which consisted of a pair of gray trousers, a dark blue jacket worn over a white tunic, and leather boots weathered by many weeks spent on the road. A small satchel and a long dagger—sheathed in a used scabbard—also hung on his belt.

"Of course not, sir," Adonis answered.

The smile receded from the man's face, but not completely.

A trace of mirth remained behind as he looked over Adonis. "Do you know who I am, Adonis?"

"Sir?"

"I know you, Adonis. I know how smart and how prudent you are. So just tell me the truth—do you know who I am?"

The man kept staring at him, his expression unchanged. His graying hair made him look fifty years old, but his stance and the lean musculature underneath his clothes belonged to a man twenty years his junior. He could easily break Adonis if he wanted to.

"Yes, sir," Adonis finally answered, his mouth dry like cotton. "I know who you are."

"Then what is my name?"

Adonis hesitated for a second, wondering if he should say it out loud. But he thought about the woman standing behind him, and this gave him all the motivation he needed to answer the question. "Your name is Ignatios Arvanitaki."

"Good. What about my right hand? Do you also know her name?"

Adonis glanced back at her and swallowed. She was still gazing at him with her blindfold on. "Elsa Yarwood. Former novitiate of the Church. You recruited her five years ago."

"You are as well informed as I was led to believe." Ignatios now smiled at him. "Which, quite frankly, isn't usually well regarded when it comes to operatives like you. Were you captured, you might end up endangering the whole organization with this knowledge. Wouldn't you agree?"

The former Azarian priestess moved almost imperceptibly, but Adonis knew that she had taken a fighting stance and placed a hand on the blade that was surely hidden under her cloak. One signal from her superior was all that she needed to end Adonis's life.

Unmistakable, bitter, and painful fear gripped his throat and twisted his insides. It had been a long time since he'd felt this way, but years of training had prepared him for such situations. He looked back at Ignatios and stood his ground, ready to accept whatever fate this man had in store for him. It wouldn't be death. Had that been the case, they would have already killed him, or worse. No, this was a test, and Adonis quickly understood the purpose behind it.

"I won't tell a soul," he said. "I swear it on the Great Serpent itself."

Ignatios studied him in silence but soon nodded approvingly. It was the signal Elsa Yarwood had been waiting for, and she relaxed her stance. Adonis almost let out an audible sigh of relief.

"You don't scare easily," Ignatios said. "That's good. We'll need more of that if we are to win the war."

Adonis immediately redirected his attention back to the man in front of him. "The war, sir?"

"Oh yes." Ignatios passed by him as he walked to the pantry to look inside. "The Ophician Confederation has launched an invasion of the Southern Realms, starting with Faxe. Our forces should have crossed the Afrodis River already." The man grabbed a sausage and a loaf of bread, which he took to the counter and then cut with the knife that Adonis had left there.

"So, it has begun," Adonis said, scarcely believing what he had just heard.

"Yes, it has. But the war isn't what brought me here."

"Yes, sir. I figured as much."

"Tell me then: What was your first impression of Kieran Fowler?"

Adonis narrowed his eyes when he heard that name. This was who he wanted to discuss first? Not the fairy, not the inquisitor, but the escaped fugitive? Why? What could be the reason?

"Well?"

The spy set aside his other questions for now and concentrated on the one his superior had asked of him. It was not wise to make a man of Ignatios's stature wait. "He's smart, sir," he replied. "Smart enough to know a few tricks of the trade. I called him another name than the one he gave me, one that sounded similar, and he didn't even flinch. He also wore an Azarian star on his neck, which I used as an excuse to let him inside the town to see if he could be recruited, but then the incident happened and—"

"One thing at a time, agent." Ignatios turned around and tossed a piece of sausage at Elsa, followed by a slice of bread. She snatched them both from the air and took a big bite into the meat. "Do you have any wine?"

"In here, sir."

"Go pour us a few cups, and then bring that block of cheese."

"Yes, sir."

"Elsa? The lantern please."

Adonis set off to work. A few minutes later, they were all sitting around the small table, eating while the rain continued to pour outside. "What do you think happened to the inquisitor?" Ignatios asked.

"Sir?"

"Your report said that Aiden Hawkon claimed that she had been kidnapped, but we all know how ludicrous that idea is. So, I ask you: What do you think happened to the inquisitor?"

The agent had considered many possibilities, but the one that seemed the most likely was also the craziest by far. It went against everything he knew about the Azarian mind-set, and for an instant, he wondered if he should keep quiet about it. But then he remembered who he was talking to. "I believe she defected, sir."

Elsa Yarwood stopped eating and raised her head to "look" at him...however she managed to do that. "That's impossible," she stated calmly. "Faith Dow would never do that."

"I agree, it is an absurd idea, but it's the only possibility that makes sense to me."

"Why is that?" Ignatios asked.

"Because she went to meet Fowler the night before he escaped and sent the guards away. It was the only time he could have slipped by them."

"No, it's the fairy," Elsa retorted. "It must have done something to help him escape."

"I don't see how. Magic-suppressing handcuffs cannot be removed with any spell that I know of."

"Anything else?" Ignatios asked.

"There's also the fact that after Fowler fled from the lake, he reappeared alone at the road and took the two best horses, even though he had no way of knowing which ones they were. He didn't ask the men any questions, only threatened them, and then he left without hurting any of them."

The former priestess let that new information sink in before she murmured, "She told Fowler which ones to take?"

"I believe so, yes."

Silence creeped back into their conversation, and only Ignatios continued to eat and drink; he didn't appear in the least surprised by this theory. "Tell me about the fairy," he said.

Adonis hesitated for a second. "There's not a lot I can say about her, sir. I never saw or spoke to her. The only ones who did are Kieran Fowler, Faith Dow, Aiden Hawkon, Finlay Pyresky—their driver—and the Marsh family. More specifically, Mathilda and Malcom Marsh. The father wasn't there when the girl appeared."

"The Marshes. What were their impressions of the fairy?"

"Malcom was injured and didn't get a good look at her. The boy was curious and asked if he could meet her again."

"What about the mother? Was she as well disposed toward the fairy as her son was?"

"She believes that the fairy was an angel, sent down from heaven to save her son."

Elsa Yarwood scoffed and drank from her cup of wine.

Clearly, she didn't share the same opinion, which wasn't surprising considering what the Inquisition had done to her. Adonis made a mental note never to ask her about her former vocation, lest he incur her wrath.

"We heard that Grand Inquisitor Dow was here yesterday," Ignatios continued. "What can you tell us about her?"

"Not much, sir. Officially, she came to investigate the kidnapping of her daughter and to reprimand Lord Harrowmont for obstructing the manhunt she had initiated. I don't know if he'll face any punishment for that."

"Who did she talk to?"

"Lord Harrowmont and his steward, Lloyd Oakley. Mother Maeve and her pupils. The prince, Aiden Hawkon. The driver, Finlay Pyresky. The Marsh family. The men of the Whitewood family—they're the farmers who first encountered Fowler near Toring's Hold—and every constable who saw or spoke to Faith Dow and Kieran Fowler. The grand inquisitor stayed here for a full day and left early this morning. She was followed by the prince, another inquisitor named Harlow, and a retinue of twelve holy guards. They left through the eastern gate."

"Then east we will go," Ignatios said. "Pack your bags. We're leaving at first light."

Adonis widened his eyes when he realized what that meant. "Sir? I-I don't understand…"

"A man of your talent is wasted here, Adonis. It's time you were put to good use."

"But, the invasion, sir—I'm supposed to be the man on the inside when our forces arrive here."

"We can replace you with someone else here before that happens. They won't be as deeply embedded as you are now, but we'll have someone on the inside. Besides, what really matters now is that we catch up to Fowler and see this fairy for ourselves. This trumps any contribution you could make here."

Adonis bit his tongue and nodded to his superior. There was simply no refusing this man. Ignatios, however, saw right through him and stopped eating to look directly into his eyes. "Are you dissatisfied?"

"No, sir. Absolutely not."

"Yes, you are. You spent years infiltrating Ballybridge's constabulary, dedicating your life to the service of our country. It is only natural that you are reluctant to abandon this task with nothing to show for it—which is why a reward is in order."

"Sir?"

"How old is your son, Adonis? Nearly ten, correct?"

Adonis nodded somberly. "Yes, sir."

"Then he's almost of the right age to join the Magus Academy. I know that you've had him take an aptitude test to see if he could become a mage one day, but there's still the problem of finding him a master who will agree to take him in once his basic training is complete. What if I took care of that for you? I know Kyrios Kapodistrias is searching for new apprentices, and he owes me a favor or two. Would you be agreeable to that?"

All of Adonis's doubts and concerns were instantly washed away by the unexpected offer, and he found himself nodding eagerly to his superior. This was the opportunity of a lifetime. He'd be a fool to refuse it. "Yes, sir," he answered. "I would be eternally grateful if you did."

"Then it is done. Your son will join the academy next year, and once this mission is over, you will be given a six-month leave to visit your family."

"That's...more than I ever hoped for. Thank you, sir."

"Now that that's taken care of, you must go meet Steward Oakley and inform him that you'll be leaving at first light for Amerster, where your mother is waiting for you. She doesn't have long to live and asked the both of us"—he motioned at Elsa—"to inform you of her condition. We are travelers who happened to be heading for Ballybridge and who took pity on this old woman. She wants to see her son one last time before her spirit joins those of her ancestors in heaven."

"I understand, sir. I will go there immediately." Adonis stood up and prepared to leave the room, only to stop at the last second when he remembered something. "One last thing, sir. When the grand inquisitor was here yesterday, she examined Fowler's belongings before she ordered them to be burned, but I still have them. Should I bring them to you?"

Ignatios raised an eyebrow and then put his cup of wine back on the table. "How did you manage that?"

"I was the one ordered to burn the effects. Instead, I hid them here in case we might find a use for them."

"Bring them to me."

"At once, sir." Adonis went into the hallway, opened the door of a small closet located under the stairs, and brought back a broken bow, a quiver empty of arrows, and a canvas bag that contained the rest of Fowler's effects.

"On the table," Ignatios said. "Now, go inform the steward. We have a long journey ahead of us."

"Yes, sir. Ma'am." The agent nodded at the both of them and turned around and left. Only when the front door closed did Ignatios allow himself to grab the two broken parts of the bow and examine them in the glow of the candlelight. He didn't say anything for a long while.

"Is it the same one?" Elsa asked between two bites.

"He replaced the bowstring and the quiver is different, but yes, this is the one." His hand ran the length of the upper limb of the bow and found new indentations in the wood that hadn't been there before; Kieran had clearly made good use of it since Ignatios gave it to him twelve years ago.

"What does that tell you?" Elsa asked.

"That Kieran knows how to take care of his weapons. And that he might not hate my guts if he's kept this bow for so long."

"Hmm." The former priestess sipped her wine while she considered his words. "Do you think you can bring him to our side?"

"Possibly. Maybe the last decade wandering the Realms taught him something." Ignatios placed the bow back on the table and looked at the young woman. "What about you? Do you think you can bring Faith Dow to our side?"

Elsa stopped chewing her food and pursed her lips in that particular way she did whenever she scowled. He'd learned to read her facial expressions over the years despite the blindfold that covered the upper part of her face, and also not to bring up Faith Dow's name unless the situation absolutely required it—which it now did.

"I can try," the former priestess answered bluntly.

"Thank you. This is all I ask."

"What about Fowler? What will you do if you can't convince him to hand over his 'fairy' to us?"

Ignatios leaned back in his chair, pondering the likelihood of that happening. The rain beat harder on the kitchen window, isolating them further from the outside world. Finally, Ignatios turned to look at his right hand and—with a smile—told her exactly what he planned to do.

"I will give him the same choice the Confederation gave me when they captured me."

# AFTERWORD

Thank you for reading *The Blue Fairy and the Pyromancer*.

There are so many great books available on the market today, and so little time to read them all, so it means everything to me that you gave this one a chance. If I may ask for a little more of your time, please consider leaving an honest review of this novel. Self-published authors like myself depend heavily on them, and if enough people do it, it would allow me to dedicate all of my time to writing Breeze's next adventure: *The Blue Fairy and the Apostate*.

I'm sure you can guess who the apostate is by now.

Thank you again for coming on this journey with me, and I hope to see you on the next one.

Zeiss Schreiber

# NEWSLETTER

If you would like to be notified of my future book releases,
I invite you to sign up to my newsletter.

https://zeissschreiber.com/newsletter

www.ingramcontent.com/pod-product-compliance
Lightning Source LLC
Chambersburg PA
CBHW050845210726
48290CB00004B/1091

* 9 7 8 1 7 3 8 9 4 2 9 0 9 *